C000230245

THE VILLAGE

Sarah Shears

BANTAM BOOKS
TORONTO · NEW YORK · LONDON · SYDNEY · AUCKLAND

THE VILLAGE
A BANTAM BOOK 0 553 40261 7

Originally published in Great Britain by
Judy Piatkus (Publishers) Ltd.

PRINTING HISTORY
Judy Piatkus (Publishers) Ltd edition published 1984
Bantam edition published 1991

Bantam Books are published by Transworld Publishers Ltd.,
61–63 Uxbridge Road, Ealing, London W5 5SA, in Australia
by Transworld Publishers (Australia) Pty. Ltd., 15–23 Helles
Avenue, Moorebank, NSW 2170, and in New Zealand by
Transworld Publishers (N.Z.) Ltd., Cnr. Moselle and
Waipareira Avenues, Henderson, Auckland.

Printed and bound in Great Britain by
BPCC Hazell Books
Aylesbury, Bucks, England
Member of BPCC Ltd.

THE VILLAGE

MARSTON PARK

Sir Neville and Lady Franklin
Beatrice
Cynthia
Sylvia
Penelope

RUSSETS FARM

Bert and Lucy Blunt
Harry
Tom
Albert

RICHMOND ROW

Tom and Ruby Simmons
Albert
Freddie
Jack
Carrie

DOCTOR'S HOUSE

Dr Ernest and Dulcie Saunders
Lesley
Roger
Dennis

PARSONAGE

The Reverend Archibald and Eleanor Wellington
Irene
Marion
Cecily

VILLAGE SCHOOL

Andrew Robinson
Martha Carter
Betty Mason

WHEELWRIGHT'S

Sam Carter
(and daughter Martha)

PART I

Chapter One

The muffled bells rang all that day in a melancholy, unchanging dirge, as inescapable as the message they conveyed – THE QUEEN IS DEAD.

The bellringers had been summoned by Parson Wellington who had received the sad tidings by direct communication from Sir Neville Franklin of Marston Park, to whom he was indebted for the living of All Saints in the village of Fairfields. After he had requested his eldest daughter, Cecily, to proceed post-haste in the governess-trap to the several places of employment in which the bellringers could be located, Parson hurried to the church to pray for the soul of the late Queen, in whose long and illustrious reign the nation had prospered exceedingly. 'Land of Hope and Glory' was almost a national anthem.

The Union Jack dropped at half-mast on the Norman tower, he noted with satisfaction at the lych-gate. Removing his hat, he bowed his grey head in revered memory. It was a flat pork-pie hat, shabby with age, and his tall spare figure was wrapped in a cloak on this memorable day of January, 1901. The cloak had a greenish tinge, but had once been black. His shirt cuffs were frayed, and his boots but recently sold to him by the indispensable Peg-leg, a one time batman to Colonel Spencer-Smythe.

3

On retirement, the Colonel had allocated Peg-leg to the Parsonage as general factotum, and the entire household wondered how they had ever managed without him. The two elderly servants, Cook and Annie, the house-parlourmaid, made a great fuss of him, for he enlivened the dull monotony of their lives with tales of heroic deeds and gruesome skirmishes on the North West Frontier.

'Where be it then, Peg, that North West Frontier?' Annie had asked, innocently, for she was not very bright, and had little schooling. Cook had snorted indignantly and pretended a superior knowledge of geography, but she waited for Peg to confirm it was India, for she couldn't abide being made to look a fool. Cook plied him with second helpings of pudding, and Annie did his washing and darned his socks. They had soon recovered from the shock of seeing the wooden leg propped against the settle in the chimney corner when the day's work was done.

In return for their kindness, Peg-leg would bring back a pint of stout for their consumption on Saturday night. There were four pubs in the village, but he always patronised The Three Nuns.

The Verger, who had climbed the steep spiral stairs to the Norman tower with the Union Jack, was waiting in the porch to greet Parson, wearing a drab cassock and an expression of intense gloom, as befitted the occasion. He could always be relied upon for the appropriate expression for christenings, weddings and funerals were his speciality. Only the gentry and the middle-class recognised his services in a practical way, and a florin was a florin in that day and age. A lad could work all week on a farm for a shilling, and a working-class man would spend a shilling a week on his beer and baccy.

The three distinct classes – gentry, middle class and working class – were separated by a tangible,

4

indisputable barrier, but the Parson and the Verger, with their unique familiarity with all classes, had allocated the pews according to status. Front pews for the gentry, centre pews for the middle class, back pews for the working class. This arrangement was seldom disputed. The back pews were rarely filled to capacity at the Sunday morning service, for it was customary for servants to attend the evening service. The tradesmen, with their wives and families, all went to Chapel where no distinction was made, and the service had a heartiness completely lacking at All Saints. The children of the Church Sunday School, escorted by their teachers, tip-toed quietly through the West Door and down the side aisle into pews facing the ornate tomb of the Franklin ancestors of Marston Park. The effigies had afforded a welcome diversion to several generations of village children, and smothered giggles had been promptly repressed by each succeeding generation of parsons' daughters.

Of Parson Wellington's three daughters only Cecily was available, however, in this year of grace. Irene, the second daughter, was too delicate to do anything more strenuous than embroidery or the knitting of interminable garments for the heathen in Darkest Africa. These all took the shape of a long vest, intended to cover the 'private parts', but Irene had little imagination, or she would have realised a garment of this nature would be totally unsuitable and unnecessary to the happy piccaninnies of the Mission School.

It was assumed that Irene was consumptive.

The youngest daughter, Marion, was living at Marston Park as governess to the two elder girls, the younger girls being still in the nursery. Four daughters and no heir to that big estate. It was a cruel blow to Sir Neville.

'What have we done, you and I, my dear fellow, to be so afflicted?' he whispered confidentially at the private baptism of his fourth daughter.

'God moves in a mysterious way, Sir,' was the uncompromising answer.

To which his irritated patron retorted, 'Well, it's damn ridiculous!'

Parson often wished Sir Neville would control his language, but he was a hot-tempered man, accustomed to speak his mind and give full vent to his feelings.

'One does not bite the hand that feeds one,' Parson's sensible wife, Eleanor, would remind him.

At the village school where limited space did not allow for segregation, boys and girls had been lined up in orderly fashion to be decorated, according to sex, with a black armband or a length of black tape to tie back untidy hair. Some of the mothers had already provided black ribbon for this purpose, since the aged Queen had been lingering on the brink of Eternity for some days. These same mothers, recognised by grateful teachers as 'clean mothers', also took the precaution of plaiting the girls' hair in order to escape the head lice the 'dirty mothers' overlooked. This was not the only indication that certain children were obviously brought up with higher standards of cleanliness, for the girls of clean mothers wore starched white pinafores, and their button boots were polished daily. Their brothers were distinguished by neat Norfolk suits, handed down by the sons of the gentry, or hand-knitted jerseys, worn with short knickers and long stockings.

It was a solemn occasion, but the children found any diversion from the normal routine most agreeable. One by one they paraded before the portrait of the Queen in a gilt frame that had been hanging in an honoured place above the schoolmaster's desk for sixty years. The parents of the children could remember when it was unveiled by the late Lady Franklin. The girls bobbed a curtsey, the boys bowed. Even the Infants were included in this formal ceremony, though most reluctant to leave the warmth of the coke stove in their stuffy classroom, and the slates and sand-trays on their tiny desks. The sombre mood was reflected in the grave, bearded face of the schoolmaster, and the sad demeanour of the three women teachers. Then the children filed into the playground to form a large double circle around the tall flagpole, on which the Union Jack fluttered at half-mast. Shivering in the icy wind and flurry of snowflakes, their shrill voices echoed across the fields. 'Land of Hope and Glory' was a fitting epitaph to a long and glorious reign.

When the schoolmaster was satisfied that his patriotic duty had been properly accomplished, he dismissed the children and bade them walk home quietly. They were so surprised to be sent home after one hour's attendance – and their irate mothers even more surprised – they ran all the way, giggling and pushing each other in gleeful appreciation of the holiday, but dare not raise their voices for fear of punishment on the morrow. Only the tolling of the muffled bells disturbed the sad and silent village, and only little Carrie Simmons, peering from a window of The Three Nuns smiled and waved as they ran past.

The Grocer, the Baker and the Butcher, Miss Bates in her Haberdashery and Widow Price in her tiny shop selling sweets and tobacco had been busily removing all their goods from the windows, and portraits of the Queen, draped in black crêpe, had been placed in strategic positions in the empty windows. Miss Bates had already sold her entire stock of black ribbon, tape and crêpe to early customers. The post office, situated for convenience in a front room of a cottage in the High

7

Street, had a laurel wreath fastened to the letter-box. The attached black-edged card bore the inscription: IN REVERED MEMORY OF OUR BELOVED QUEEN FROM HER DUTIFUL AND DEVOTED SERVANTS. WILLIAM WHITE. POSTMASTER. THOMAS ASH. POSTMAN. HENRY SPOONER. POSTMAN. JOHN BOLES. POSTMAN.

All the employees of the post office were wearing black ties and black armbands. Outside the baker's shop the horse, wearing a black rosette in its studded collar, had been harnessed to the delivery cart. The butcher's boy was reverently decorating a sheep's head with artificial roses of black crêpe paper. Behind the closed doors of The Three Nuns the publican's wife was draping the portraits in the saloon and public bars, wiping tears on her apron, for she was a very sentimental woman. Little Carrie Simmons, still hugging her ragdoll, had a bow of black ribbon in the curls that framed her pink cheeks. Carrie was 3, and a great favourite at The Three Nuns. Her mother was the daily charwoman, who came from an alley called Richmond Row. The child was the youngest of a family of four children, but three had died in infancy. Being the only surviving girl, her three brothers – Albert, aged 14, Freddie, 13, and Jack 12 – all working, made a pet of her. Carrie was surrounded by love, but nothing or nobody could protect her from the curses of the drunken neighbours, the stench of the earth closets in the yards, or the rats that scavenged in the muck heap in the O'Brien's back garden. There was no escape, and she accepted the curses, the stench and the rats as she accepted the damp crowded cottage that was home.

Father Dominic, the Catholic priest, was praying for the soul of the late Queen. A tall, wax candle was burning side by side with the small tallow candle lit by Mrs O'Brien at the early Mass. Father Dominic was not

8

swayed by emotion, nor influenced by any member of the privileged society, and he saw no reason why Mrs O'Brien's candle, for which she had paid a halfpenny, should not glow beside the other for which Miss Letitia Langtry had paid a guinea. His allegiance to the Holy Father in Rome was profoundly loyal, and it was the Pope's portrait, not the Queen's, that hung in the Sacristy. Only a small minority of the prominent families in the surrounding countryside worshipped at his beautiful little church, tucked away at the back of the High Street, and sheltered from the wind on this bleak January day by a tall hedge, on which the snowflakes had already fallen. It is true these particular parishioners occupied reserved pews, for which they paid a generous subscription, but otherwise they were not favoured in any way, and their regular attendance at Sunday Mass, on Saints' Days, and weekly Confession was obligatory. It was the poor members of his flock, such as the O'Briens in Richmond Row, to whom Father Dominic was attached, probably because of his own lowly birth in Limerick, some sixty years ago. Poverty was something he understood, and he was no stranger to the gnawing pangs of hunger. So his concern for the poor and the under privileged was genuine, his smile for them was warm and friendly. He was their spiritual Father and they were his children. Like little Carrie Simmons, who lived next door to the noisy, quarrelsome O'Briens, Father Dominic accepted them without questioning their right to be there. He had their confidence and trust, and they consulted him on every aspect of family life. He was closer to his parishioners than Parson would ever be. Even the bullying, blasphemous Michael O'Brien, who had fathered ten children out of which five had survived, respected the Father and was as frightened by the

9

penalty of purgatory as his long-suffering wife. It was indeed a kind of obsession, this terrible threat of punishment after death, and his weak mentality struggled to control his violent temper. At each fall from Grace he confessed his sin, and wept copious tears in the Confessional.

There was no portrait of the Queen to decorate with black crêpe at No. 4 Richmond Row, for patriotism was not encouraged. They lived in such squalor, even Mrs Martin at No. 3, who had a nasty habit of throwing her slops from the bedroom window, was disgusted.

The six small cottages, being railway property, housed the families of the gangers, and Richmond Row was regarded as a slum in the village. The rough pathway that led to the cottages was pitted with holes that filled with water on wet days, and were frozen solid for several weeks in the bleak mid Winter. On these frozen puddles the boys would spin their halfpenny peg-tops, while the girls would be watching enviously, clutching swaddled infants in their skinny arms. The school playground was the only place to whip a top or skip with a length of clothes line. Peg-tops were the boys prerogative, and so were the frozen puddles. The girls were often kept home from school to mind younger brothers and sisters while mothers were charring. 'Book learning' was considered a waste of time for girls, who would be packed off to service at the age of 12 or 13, and their brief childhood over.

The years had taken their toll of the children of Richmond Row, for several had died in infancy, while older children had succumbed to the dreaded diphtheria. With no less than three religious denominations in the Row, Parson Wellington, Father Dominic and Minister Larkin of the Methodist Chapel all had funerals to arrange for their respective families and donations to contrive from their meagre funds. The

10

poorer the family, the more elaborate the trimmings, and the funeral tea was a feast to which all the neighbours contributed with surprising generosity, ignoring the fact the children would be back to bread and margarine on the morrow, and the hard-working men and boys would be back on their bread and fat bacon.

Of the six families in the Row, only Tom and Ruby Simmons strived to rise above their environment, but their efforts were not only discouraged by their neighbours, but openly abused. Tom was a quiet, unassuming man, who actually handed over his weekly wage to his wife and received his shilling for beer and baccy as regularly as Ruby received a kiss from her devoted spouse on his return from work. Ruby had been married at 16, already big with child after a romp in the hay-field one warm Sunday evening in June. Tom had been 18 at the time, and old enough to know better, according to his shocked parents, but it was Ruby with her impudent smile and her cuddlesome curves who had enticed Tom into the hay.

When the last of the children had passed The Three Nuns, Carrie slid off the wide window seat and went in search of her mother. She was a friendly child, and she liked company. She found her, as usual, on her hands and knees, scrubbing. With a sacking apron tied about her comely figure, and her sleeves rolled over her plump arms, she pushed away the tendrils of hair that clung to her damp forehead and smiled at her daughter. The child was a replica of the mother – blonde hair, pink cheeks, wide blue eyes. They glowed with health and happiness in an atmosphere that would have stifled lesser mortals. Smoke from the customers' clay pipes still lingered in the public bar, for it was too cold to open a window. The stale smell of beer and unwashed bodies was so familiar, neither the woman nor the child complained.

11

Drying her roughened hands on the apron, the mother cuddled the child and asked, 'You all right then, love?'

'Why was they comin' 'ome from school, Mum, all them children?'

'Summat to do with the old Queen, I reckon.'

'What to do?'

'She's dead, luv.'

'Won't she never wear 'er crown no more?'

'No, luv.'

They both stared at the portrait of her late Majesty, draped in black crêpe.

'Is that why she 'as that stuff round 'er picher then, 'cause she's dead?'

'That's right.'

'Why?'

'It's out of respect.'

'Like Dad, when 'e touches 'is cap to Parson?'

'That's right.'

'Them bells is funny. Why don't they ring proper?'

'They're muffled, luv.'

'Out of respect?'

'That's right.'

'When is it dinner time?'

'Not for some time yet.'

'Can I 'ave a pepmint?'

'That's the last one, luv.'

It was sticky, and it had gathered a bit of dust in the pocket of the sacking apron, but it still tasted of peppermint. The publican's wife always kept a supply of peppermints because she suffered with acute dyspepsia. A gaunt woman, with sharp features, she was more than a little jealous of her buxom char-woman. But she was fond of the child, and didn't begrudge the peppermints. She was a good little soul, and no trouble to anyone. With a pair of blunt scissors

12

and out-of-date copies of magazines, she would amuse herself for hours, cutting out pictures for a scrapbook her brother Freddie was making. Wherever she went she carried the ragdoll. No, you couldn't honestly say the child was a nuisance. It was just that she was alive, and still running around on her sturdy legs while her own little girl, the only child of her bosom, was lying in the churchyard.

Woollen mittens covered her hands, and the unsightly chilblains. It was bad circulation, the doctor had told her, testily, and advised a certain brand of ointment she could have purchased without bothering him. She was one of those women who consulted the doctor on every opportunity. She paid her bills, however, and that was more than could be said of fifty per cent of his patients. The worst offenders lived in Richmond Row, in such unhealthy conditions the children contracted all the infectious diseases that had to be reported – scarlet fever, diphtheria, measles, whooping cough – they went down like ninepins, the poor little devils. There was seldom any money for doctor's bills.

The Simmons were the only exception, a decent, honest couple who somehow contrived to keep out of debt and lift their heads above the squalor of the slum in which they were obliged to live.

Doctor's wife, Dulcie, still lamented the fact her husband had no ambition. Straight from Medical School into his father's practice in this isolated village in the Weald of Kent. Twenty years later they were still here, and likely to remain here for the rest of their days. With three handsome sons enjoying all the privileges of the upper class and graduating from prep school to Winchester and Cambridge, it was *her* money that was paying for all these privileges. Of course she spoiled them, but they adored her. At least, the eldest and the

13

youngest adored her, but she was not quite sure of Dennis, for his behaviour often lacked that courtesy and respect to which a fond mother was entitled.

Dulcie Saunders was inordinately proud of her sons, and her cleverness in producing them when Her Ladyship at Marston Park had only produced four daughters! No wonder Sir Neville Franklin was casting a baleful eye on that attractive wife of a well-known actor. His horse had been seen tethered to a tree in the drive of The Laurels on several occasions quite recently. Doctor insisted it was mere coincidence that the husband happened to be on tour in America. It could be quite an innocent liaison, but Sir Neville was disappointed that he had no heir, and made no secret of the fact he found his lady wife a little tedious. Dulcie could never condone infidelity, whatever the circumstances. She held very strong views on the subject. Marriage vows were sacred. Even if Ernest bored her to tears with his everlasting dedication and devotion to his tiresome patients, she would remain faithful.

There would be three separate services of memorial to the late Queen. It was unthinkable that all three denominations should combine, for they were as far removed from one another as the three classes of society. Parson could claim the biggest flock, and his church was normally filled to capacity every Sunday morning, and bursting at the seams on Easter Sunday and Christmas Day, when the gentry and the middle-class parishioners all had visitors.

Father Dominic, in comparison, had only a small minority, but he served several parishes, so some of his children walked four or five miles to attend Sunday Mass. He knew every man, woman and child, and greeted them by name with a smile and a shake of the hand. That was more than could be said for Parson,

14

who relied on his churchwardens to escort the gentry to their pews, and the sidesmen to escort the middle-class families to their respective seats. The working class found their way into the side aisles or the back pews quietly and unobtrusively, very conscious of their humble status. Their shabby, old-fashioned clothes contrasted strongly with the well-dressed congregation in the centre aisles.

As for the Methodist Chapel, and its dedicated Minister – Matthew Larkin – the friendly invitation to participate in the hearty services was so genuine, so emphatic, it left no shadow of doubt in the minds of all who gathered there that here was the House of the Lord, and here alone was 'The Word made Manifest and Dwelt Among Us'. It was universally agreed that all the trimmings, the pomp and ceremony of the Church of England and the Roman Catholic Church were verging on idolatry, and far removed from the teaching of Our Lord. The white-washed walls were bare, but for the portrait of the Queen, and there were no hassocks in the pews. Simplicity was the key-word. They worshipped with a heartiness and enthusiasm that was really enjoyed. So the memorial service to Her Late Majesty would be no solemn affair. They would rejoice in Victoria's long and glorious reign, and raise their voices in such firm favourites as 'Fight the Good Fight', 'Rock of Ages', 'O God our help in Ages Past' and 'Abide with me'. A garland of Christmas roses would adorn the Queen's portrait, but there would be no black crêpe. The tradesmen, all intensely patriotic, would be wearing the black suits they normally wore on Sunday, and carrying bowler hats. Their wives would be wearing the black hats and gloves they kept for the funerals of relatives and friends. The boys had already been issued with black armbands and the girls with black hair ribbons.

Matthew Larkin and his wife, Lena, were a devoted couple – devoted to each other, and to their 'brothers and sisters'. Since they had no children of their own, the Sunday School was a source of pleasure and interest throughout the year. Matthew combined the duties of superintendent with that of minister. Lucy taught a class of girls and played the harmonium. The Good Friday tea party had a special appeal to the children who lived with the gnawing pangs of hunger. They stuffed themselves with buttered hot-cross buns, currant and plain cake, washed down with hot sweet tea, filled their pockets, gabbled a Grace, then clattered up the gallery stairs. Their renderings of 'There is a Green Hill Far Away' was loud and boisterous, with empty stomachs filled to capacity. The holiness of Good Friday was not marked by mournful references to the Crucifixion, but the emphasis was on SALVATION. The children would be reminded once again, in a short address from the super-intendent – while the butter melted in the hot-cross buns – that all were saved and could look forward to the ever-lasting home in the Kingdom of Heaven.

'What's everlasting?' some small girl would enquire in nervous apprehension.

'Everan never,' came the prompt reply.

The well-fed children of the local tradesmen helped themselves delicately to the food provided, the hungry children grabbed with both hands, the older children urging young brothers and sisters to 'eat up quick'.

Scuffling their feet in the gallery while they waited to be released from the sermon, the Martins from Richmond Row would empty their pockets to compare their pickings with their neighbours. They never went hungry to bed on Good Friday, Sunday School Treat Day, Chapel Anniversary, and Boxing Day. These were red-letter days on the calendar. Signing the

16

pledge at the Band of Hope was a solemn occasion, particularly for those who regarded drunkenness as a normal feature of Saturday night.

Young Jack Simmons – Carrie's youngest brother – owed his job as grocer's boy to the fact that his Uncle Albert was a second cousin of Grocer's wife. Such vague family connections and their influence were not uncommon in the village. Jack had completed his formal education by his 12th birthday, but had much to learn about trade in a grocer's shop which was also the village general store. An earnest, conscientious disciple, he had quickly endeared himself to Grocer's wife by his willingness to run errands on domestic or social matters not connected with the business. Grocer's mild protests carried no weight, for everyone knew who 'wore the trousers' so to speak, in that household. Their three daughters had attended a Dame's school in Fairfields, and considered themselves superior to Butcher's daughters and Baker's daughters whose parents had more sense. The village school provided a general standard of education that was sadly lacking at the 'Dame's'. The two spinster ladies had no proper qualifications for teaching, but none were required or demanded. Their genteel manner disguised their own elementary knowledge.

Unfortunately for Grocer, not one of the girls could be relied upon to add up a column of figures or make out a customer's bill. To serve behind the counter was considered an undignified occupation by an ambitious mother determined to see her daughters married into middle-class society. Few trades people aspired or wished to aspire in that direction. In a sense they had their own close community and their own establishments held a certain prestige for they employed apprentices and a domestic servant. Yet all were as

17

dependent on the patronage of their well-to-do customers as the labourers and servants on the whims of their masters and mistresses.

'We are servants of the public and don't you forget it,' was the first principle instilled in every apprentice to the trade. Prompt attention and courtesy were expected by even the poorest customer living on credit. No middle-class lady set foot in the shop, but waited in her trap on the forecourt for a young assistant to run and hold the mare's reins. Then she gave her order to Grocer and Butcher in person. Whatever the weather they would stand there, patiently and politely, taking down the order in the appropriate book, while giving advice on the quality and flavour of bacon and cheese, sirloin or English lamb. Baker was spared this ordeal, for his regular deliveries six days a week were as reliable as night following day.

As for the gentry, they employed housekeepers to deal with such mundane matters. Tradesmen called at the entrance clearly indicated by the sign TRADESMEN, and were usually invited into the housekeeper's sitting-room. It was quite a social occasion, with cups of tea and biscuits served by a third housemaid with a glass of sherry and a mincepie when the Christmas order was under discussion.

It was customary for apprentices to live in, and to pay a premium for board and lodging and the privilege of being taught a trade. But for young Jack Simmons, with his feet firmly planted on the bottom rung of a tradesman's ladder, it took only five minutes to walk to the shop from Richmond Row. His working day started at 7 in the morning, and finished at 7 in the evening, but his meagre wage of half-a-crown a week was supplemented by 'elevenses', dinner and tea. This was a great advantage to a lad from a poor family, and his mother could be congratulated on her foresight, for all three boys had been placed in situations where meals were provided in the kitchens of their employers. Albert was working at Monks Farm, in the valley, a distance of some four miles. So he lived in all the week and trudged home on Saturday evening to spend Sunday with the family. Freddie, the middle one, at the age of 13, had been recommended to the local solicitor as a bright lad, and was currently employed as office boy, but aspired to a clerkship at a later date. It would take all of seven years to save enough to pay the premium, but Freddie would study. Books could be borrowed. Ambition was a spur to an intelligent boy, encouraged by sensible parents. All three boys were thin and wiry, with their father's sharp features and dark eyes. All three were dedicated workers, and had left their childhood behind the day they left school.

Only little Carrie had inherited her mother's plump prettiness and sunny nature. Mother and child together contributed the gaiety and charm in a household predominantly male and quietly serious. Their quarrelsome neighbours could neither understand nor emulate the happy relationships of the Simmons family, and the O'Briens openly resented it.

The muffled bells could be heard as far away as the branch railway line running through the valley, and the group of gangers working on the line found it dreary and disturbing. With every pause in the clatter of pickaxe and shovel the sound reached them, faintly but persistently, throughout the day.

'The poor old bugger's gawn at last then,' Mike O'Brien commented.

'Seems like it,' his mate agreed, beating his arms across his chest to put a little warmth in his thin body.

They were repairing a section of the line that connected a number of villages in the Weald. Crops of apples and cherries for Covent Garden, dried hops for the breweries, as well as coal and timber for the industrial Midlands, was carried on the freight trains that passed at infrequent intervals on the adjoining track. It made a welcome diversion when the foreman blew his whistle and they moved away to the embankment to watch the trains pass.

'Lucky buggers,' O'Brien would growl, enviously, for the driver and the fireman were warm and snug in their cab, while the gangers were miserably cold and wretched. There were no apples and cherries and no dried hops aboard the trains at this season of the year, but no lack of coal and timber. The sparks from the fire flew upwards in the belching smoke from the funnel, and the engine driver, as cocksure as a Roman overlord in his chariot, raised a hand in greeting and blew a loud blast on the hooter. It was enough to arouse O'Brien's Irish temper, for it didn't take much, and he spat in the direction of the cab and shook his fist as the engine rattled past. His mates would cheer, but whether they were cheering the engine driver or the irate O'Brien was never quite clear. It was always advisable to keep on the right side of that tempestuous character anyway, for he was a nasty customer, and a swing of that hefty fist to a man's jaw could send him sprawling and senseless.

A stolid figure, with broad shoulders and strong, sinewy arms, his powerful sweep of the pickaxe had no equal. A heavy drinker, and a bullying husband and father – that was O'Brien. Those who were lacking proficiency with the pickaxe did most of the shovelling, and their spades were sharp as razors. A tool is a valuable instrument to a manual worker, and the

20

gangers were no exception. Each man carved his initials on the handle, so ownership of the tools was not in doubt – only the long hours and the low wages were disputed. Once a ganger, always a ganger it seemed, if you lived in railway property and had no other skills and no ambition. Hard work, grinding poverty and large families. That was the pattern of their lives. At least one member of a family must work for the railway, or the cottage would be confiscated. A father could bring along his son when he left school to pick up stones and brew cocoa in the hut where they ate their dinner and sheltered from the snow blizzards that swept across the Weald in mid Winter. The lad would be paid a shilling a week. But it was not a job to be recommended by a parent at all interested in or concerned about his son's welfare.

Village boys hadn't a very wide choice, but still the prospects were more promising as a farm labourer, a gardener's boy, or a tradesman's delivery boy. The important factor was to earn a shilling or two to help pay for your keep if you lived at home. Few of the gangers lived to be old. Ill-health and accidents claimed a heavy toll. Old age was no sweet reward for hard labour in the working class, but a dreaded future as an inmate of the Workhouse. Sometimes a married daughter with an obliging husband could make room for one parent in their overcrowded cottage, but if both survived and a tied cottage had to be handed over, there was no alternative for the old couple but the Workhouse, with its cruel segregation of the sexes just when a couple most needed to comfort and sustain each other. The Poor Law Institutions were governed by heartless and antiquated regulations that dealt with human lives as statistics to be numbered and catalogued. The Workhouse was also the penalty for a

21

servant girl who had 'got into trouble' if her shamed parents refused to shelter her and the unborn child. Unmarried mothers, the homeless, the destitute, the aged poor, all were entitled to a roof over their heads, a meal and a bed in a crowded dormitory. The 'Workus' was a last resort. It offered no comfort or sympathy. It was a sentence as widely opposed and feared as prison.

On a clear day, Ruby Simmons could see the tall Elizabethan chimneys of Russets from the attic window of The Three Nuns. Her twin sister, Lucy, had done very well for herself, and their circumstances seemed so far removed from the childhood they had shared, it was surprising they had not only kept in touch, but still enjoyed the close relationship of twins. Both had married at 16 when both were expecting their first babies. Both had three boys, all working, but Lucy had not yet been blessed with a girl. There was still time, since her 30th birthday was only a week away, on that eventful day of January, 1901, and she was strong and healthy. Bert was five years her senior, and had fallen in love one hop-picking season. Lucy was 12 and 'ripe as a little peach' he had told himself, completely captivated by the golden curls, the wide blue eyes, and the budding breasts under the tight bodice of her childish frock. Why it was Lucy and not Ruby that took his fancy it was never explained. But they were not identical twins, and Lucy had always been the dominant twin.

The family had been picking hops at Russets since the twin babies were pushed in an iron-wheeled pram-cart, but Bert had seen them with boyish indifference as just another of the families toiling all day in his father's hop-gardens, for six long weeks in late Summer. At 17 he was ready for marriage, but an only son was reminded he had a duty to his parents when a hundred acres of hops and fruit, a herd of Friesians, and a flock of sheep were concerned. The Blunts had been tenant farmers for several generations on the vast estate at Marston Park. It was passed from father to son – a goodly heritage for those who were willing to work seven days a week at all seasons of the year, for the work on a farm is never finished. Farmer's daughters were two a penny, so to speak, but Bert was just not interested in girls till he discovered Lucy, that hot September day, perched on the edge of a bin, picking hops with lazy indifference. His attendance at the village school had been nothing more than an interlude in his boyhood, for he was a poor scholar, and the farm was his whole life. The hop-picking season was the busiest time of the year for a Weald farmer, and it had the added excitement of driving the waggon to the railway station to pick up the Cockneys disembarking from the 'Hoppers' Special'. Swarms of cheeky, mischievous children plucked at the hazel nuts and blackberries with greedy fingers, and crept around the orchards, lying low in the long grass. Nothing was safe from their darting fingers. They went in fear of no man, but a single cow, unexpectedly encountered behind a hedge, could send them screeching in terror for the nearest shelter.

Fate, however, had intervened with Bert's plans, and the sudden death of his father the following year from a heart attack put the pretty little Lucy out of his orbit for almost three years. When she left school at the age of 13, she was immediately engaged as a housemaid in the doctor's household, so there was no more hop-picking at Russets. Bert became a man of responsibility almost overnight, and the burden lay heavy on his young shoulders. Fate can play some happy tricks as well as cruel ones. Who would have supposed the door of the doctor's surgery would be opened by a pretty house-maid in answer to Bert's urgent rat-tat on the shining brass knocker that September afternoon? He had brought an injured child and his distraught mother straight from the hop-garden in the wagonette to save time, for he could tell at a glance it was a serious injury that would need hospital treatment, possibly an operation. To see a venturesome small boy suddenly struck down by the heavy hoof of a Shire horse was a shock, and he was still trembling when the door opened. She hadn't changed, only grown plumper and prettier. She smiled as though she had been expecting him for some time.

'Hello, Bert,' she said, and he was the one to blush and stammer with embarrassment.

'Hello, Lucy. How – how are you?'

'Fine, thanks. Couldn't be better.'

'That's good,' he said.

Then Doctor came, and she hurried away to attend to her other duties with a swish of the long, starched apron.

For the next two hours or more his time was fully occupied with getting the child to hospital and taking the mother back to the farm, but his mind was not wholly engaged with the emergency. Like a ray of sunshine after a heavy shower, that captivating smile shone across his vision – and this time there was no forgetting her, no tragedy to separate them. He wanted her – for his wife.

Chapter Two

The School Governors made an impressive list – Sir Neville Franklin, The Reverend Archibald Wellington, Colonel Lionel John, Richard Spencer, Miss Letitia Langtry. Between them they conducted every aspect of the church school, and Robinson had little authority, though he made a brave show in public, and ruled his little world with disciplined exactitude. Boys and girls alike were caned, but not unjustly. Corporal punishment was expected, and only the boys received more than one stroke of the cane.

A 40-year-old bachelor, 'Old Robbie' was a lonely soul, who had nothing in common with his staff or his pupils. A brilliant scholar, he was probably wasted in a village school, but his appointment had been providential under the circumstances. His mother's death had left him completely devastated. She had supported and inspired him, and he had adored her with the singular devotion of an only son. His safe little world was shattered, but life went on. An elderly housekeeper was engaged for the School House, and the surrounding countryside would provide the solace and solitude for his peace of mind. Under the disciplined armour that he habitually wore, dwelt a man of nervous apprehension. Without her moral support, Andrew Robinson had to lecture himself very severely before he could summon the courage to face a new day. It is a cruel experience when a man of 40 is severed from the umbilical cord. Possessive maternal love can strangle as well as stimulate.

In the privacy of his small study, surrounded by books, he could relax. Weak tears could wet his beard when his loneliness became intolerable. The housekeeper was too concerned about her own comfort to worry about her employer. The meals she served were poor and scanty, but the housekeeping allowance had also to provide her daily pint of stout and fish for her cat. Mr Robinson would be served with a couple of herrings, but Pussy would only touch a cod cutlet. It was a comfortable post for an elderly widow. She kept her counsel and did not gossip about her employer.

On that first Sunday morning following his appointment, the new schoolmaster found his way to All Saints for the morning service, and was shown to a pew directly behind the one reserved for The Parsonage. It was in the side aisle facing the vestry, and only a few yards from the pulpit. The choir had proceeded in slow and solemn procession from the vestry to the choir stalls, followed by Parson with a shining, uplifted face. This was his big moment of the week, and he enjoyed it tremendously, as a leading actor will enjoy his role. His wife and two daughters felt only an amused affection as he passed by, for they knew him too well and he was no saint.

Andrew Robinson noted with interest that the younger daughter remained seated throughout the service, and remembered one of the teachers had told him Miss Irene was delicate. Miss Cecily, on the contrary, seemed quite a formidable young woman, and when they were formally introduced after the service, he found her manner brusque and unfriendly. Miss Irene had smiled quite sweetly. She was a pale, intense little creature, with haunting dark eyes – and they had haunted Andrew Robinson for six months. He remembered the clasp of her small gloved hand, and her frailty appealed to his ascetic taste. He wondered about her at the end of the day, in the privacy of his study, while the fire burned low in the grate.

Throughout the long and tedious sermon his eyes rested tenderly on the narrow shoulders, and the clustering dark curls under the velvet bonnet. When the service was over he walked back alone to the School House to his dinner of cold mutton, boiled potatoes and pickles, followed by Bakewell tart. He always knew exactly what his housekeeper would provide seven days a week. The hours stretched ahead in endless procession. He longed for company, but was too shy to make the first overture. His mother had encouraged a brisk walk for health's sake, and habit was still strong in him, so he dutifully donned an overcoat, wound a woollen muffler about his neck, and pulled on the 'deerstalker' hat. He was much attached to the deerstalker, and it distinguished him from his fellows.

Striding through the silent village on this bleak Sunday in January, he noted with satisfaction that all the shop windows had been cleared of their produce to display the portrait of Her Late Majesty, draped in black crêpe. It was the end of a wonderful era. A pity it had to pass. The new Edwardian era would sweep away all the old stuffiness, they said. The new monarch was gay, and his Queen would be a leader of fashion. No more crinolines and poke bonnets. No more demure maidens, they said. He sighed. He was prejudiced. Even to remove the portrait of Her Late

27

Majesty and hang the new portrait that would be presented in due course by Sir Neville Franklin would depress him beyond measure. But it would be compulsory, as everything was compulsory in this new appointment with the School Governors. He was a fool. A private tutor for twenty years, now this.

Much troubled about Miss Irene, he felt protective towards her. She ought not to be allowed to attend the Sunday morning service in the bleak mid Winter, but perhaps she insisted? The spirit could be strong when the flesh is weak. It was comfortably warm in church. There would be a coke furnace in the crypt to heat the pipes. No money would be spared from the church funds for that particular purpose, since the gentry and the middle-class parishioners were accustomed to warmth and comfort in their own homes, and would not tolerate discomfort in their place of worship. The ladies and the children were conveyed in carriages and traps, the gentlemen rode horseback. The Sunday morning scene was lively and picturesque, with snow draping the mellowed roofs and gravestones. Grooms and coachmen attending the families would bide their time in the bar of The Three Nuns. With horse blankets covering their charges, and bags of oats to keep them quiet, the horses could safely be left. A cursory glance from the window from time to time was sufficient. It was a social occasion for the grooms and coachmen, but nurses and governesses were still on duty with their charges. They envied the men their freedom and independence. Outdoor servants hadn't to endure the confinement and supervision of the indoor servants.

The Parsonage trap was inconspicuous in this Sunday morning gathering, and the mare was tethered to a tree facing the West door. It was driven by Miss Cecily. When the service was over, they did not wait for

Parson, but hurried Miss Irene down the path and into the trap. Wrapped in a rug, with a shawl about her shoulders, she looked very small and frail. Andrew Robinson was almost moved to tears as he watched from the dark shadows of the yew trees, then went on his lonely way, filled with dismay at his own temerity.

As Sunday followed Sunday and the pattern was unchanged, he could do no more than bow his head at the ladies as they left the family pew, and receive the sweet benediction of her smile. It was not enough, but he sought in vain for an answer to the problem. They were worlds apart, separated by the careful attendance that surrounded her, and his own acute shyness. Nothing in the past could help him now. His mother had claimed all his love and devotion. Desperately seeking a substitute for that irreplaceable loss, his feet crunching on the frozen snow, he stared at the magical beauty of the fields, trees and hedges with unseeing eyes on his afternoon walk. The silence was broken only by the sound of his own footsteps.

When first he walked these lanes in late Summer, he had seen cows and sheep in the fields. Now the sheep were huddled behind distant hurdles, awaiting the early lambs, and the cows in the sheds till May Day, when they were driven out to green pastures – so they said. Intellectually brilliant, he had quickly realised his appalling ignorance on country matters, but he was gradually gleaning a little knowledge from two of the teachers who had been born and bred in the village. The third, Miss Mason, was a 'foreigner' like himself. She was living in lodgings and being secretly courted by the doctor's second son, Dennis, so they said.

When first he walked these lanes on Sunday afternoons, Cockney children scrambled through gaps in the hedges and swung on the branches of trees, their

29

shrill voices echoing across the fields. The lanes meandered pleasantly past orchards where apples were ripening, and hop-gardens, where rows of bins awaited the pickers on the morrow. At 7 o'clock the whistle would blow, and the pickers start work – so they said! It was all so strange, and he was not yet sure that he could bear the solitude of the School House and these lonely walks on Sunday afternoons. In one of the nature books that his predecessor had left behind in the study, he found the names of the wild flowers still blooming in late Summer. There was a trailing plant on the hedges called Old Man's Beard and honeysuckle. Golden Rod in the ditches. Hips and haws had been ripening in the hedges. Hazel nuts and blackberries would help to fill the stomachs of hungry children when they started back to school. Country-bred children would know exactly when the kernels of beechnuts and chestnuts were hard and ready for eating. When the hops had been picked and the Cockney families returned to London, the new term would start for the local children, and he was dreading his initiation. Such had been his thoughts in late Summer, but the first term had passed without the trouble he had anticipated, and another was passing. Everything passes, he reminded himself.

Living in the city, he had hardly noticed the changing seasons, and his daily exercise had been taken in the company of nurses pushing prams, and maids with their mistresses' dogs, on the tidy paths of a well-kept park. Another world, so far removed from this. Would he always be regarded with suspicion as a foreigner in this bleak isolation?

To see Teacher picking hops was so unexpected, the children in the home-pickers' set at Monks Farm gaped and mumbled uncomfortably that first day. It was bad enough to have to put up with teachers at school, but to have one intruding on the holiday was downright mean. Not that picking hops was exactly a holiday, but it made a nice change being outdoors all day, and they could run wild in the woods in the dinner hour, stuffing themselves with nuts and blackberries. They need not have worried, for Betty Mason ignored them completely. Seated on the edge of a half-bin she had been allocated, dressed in a clean but faded cotton skirt and blouse, and a pink sunbonnet, they could see she was a novice.

'Teacher don't 'arf pick slow, don't she, Mum?' was disrespectful, said Mum, and promptly boxed the offender's ears. But when they were out of earshot in the dinner hour, he persisted, 'Ain't Teacher got nuffink better to do in the 'olidays, then?' He was one of the cowman's six children, and an older sister explained, 'She ain't got no 'ome, see. She lives in lodgings. Mum knows Mrs Davis what's Teacher's landlady, see, an' she says Teacher's a norphan.'

In the momentary silence that followed, the children felt sorry for their orphaned teacher, but she was soon forgotten as they climbed over the gate and swarmed into the wood.

In the meantime, the young woman who had caused such a controversy, was drinking tea from a thermos flask. Watching her, as surprised as the children to see her in such an unfamiliar setting, was the doctor's son, Dennis, home from university for the Summer vacation. Already bored with tennis parties and picnics, he was looking for some fresh diversion, and the young woman on the sunny bank was dashed attractive. They had met but briefly on one previous occasion at a pianoforte recital in the drawing-room at The Grove. The Misses Langtry were both devotees of

31

the arts, and liked to encourage young musicians and artists. Invitations had been issued to many, including the schoolmaster, who was not musical, and had passed on the ticket to Miss Mason. The doctor and his wife had also been invited, but Doctor was too busy to bother with recitals during an outbreak of scarlet fever, and his wife excused herself politely. Of their three sons, only Dennis was musical, and his mother considered his performance on the pianoforte quite brilliant when he felt in the mood. The trouble with Dennis, however, was his unreliability. He was unpredictable. You knew exactly what to expect from Roger, who had passed all his examinations with credit, settled down as a junior partner in a firm of solicitors, and married the daughter of one of the masters at Winchester College. Lesley, the youngest, had chosen the Army as a career. Now he was a cadet at Sandhurst. They had known exactly what they wanted, and set about achieving it. But not Dennis.

It was disappointing to have a son so irrational, and his mother could not bear to contemplate the possibility that Dennis may have inherited a weakness of character from her side of the family. Her youngest brother had disgraced himself with excessive drinking and gambling, and finally had been despatched to the tea plantation in Ceylon. She had paid her son's debts at university, and excused his behaviour because she hoped he was just 'sowing his wild oats'. Time would prove. One black sheep in the family was one too many.

Seated next to a young woman so obviously enraptured by the Chopin recital, Dennis Saunders found himself more interested in his companion than the performance. She had taken off her hat, and her chestnut hair, drawn back into a tight bun, had a lovely

32

sheen in the lamplight. An oval face, intelligent grey eyes, a slim figure, and a tiny waist. All this he had noted when they were formally introduced, and he liked what he saw. But when he suggested they walk home together, after refreshments had been served by the parlour maid, she declined politely, and said she had a bicycle. That was during the Easter vacation six months ago, and since then Dennis had also acquired a bicycle. It was an indispensable means of transport in a university city.

It was leaning on the gate beside him, and he left it there and climbed over the gate with an easy grace. When his sulky mouth dissolved into a smile, and his blue eyes flirted disarmingly he could be very charming and persuasive. But he met no response from Betty Mason. She was not looking for a handsome beau, and this self-confident young man was wasting his time. Deceived and seduced by just such another before her 17th birthday, she was not making the same mistake again. Practically all her meagre salary as a teacher went to the support of her child, a little girl aged 2, living with foster parents at Tonbridge. She herself had been fostered and, luckier than most orphaned children, she had been encouraged to sit for a place at the High School, and had passed the entrance examination. From there she had graduated to Fairfields Church School as a pupil-teacher. So she tilted her chin, and her grey eyes met his beguiling blue ones unflinchingly.

'So, we meet again, Miss Mason!' said he. 'How charming you look in that pink sunbonnet.'

'What are you doing here?' she demanded, coldly.

'I could ask you the same question, could I not?' he answered – and flung himself down on the bank in a single movement of his lissom body. Dirty, barefoot

33

gypsy children were chasing each other down the long aisles. Their shrill voices stopped suddenly as they came upon the couple on the bank, and they stood there, framed in the green archway, their sloe-eyed beauty enhanced by their ragged garments. Betty Mason smiled and offered them sweets, but they hung back suspiciously, then darted away like nervous little animals.

'Filthy little beggars,' her companion remarked blandly. 'What are they doing here?'

'Picking hops. This happens to be the dinner hour.'

'I thought gypsies only sold pegs and lucky white heather?'

'They would starve if they depended on that. The farmers employ them for seasonal work. They've been working in the potato fields, now it's six weeks' hop-picking, then apple picking. You don't know much about your own country environment if you don't know that.'

'I loathe my country environment, as you are pleased to call it. Do you come into close contact with those dirty little ragamuffins when you are picking the hops?'

'No. The gypsies pick in their own set of bins. The Cockneys pick in their own sets with their own people. So do the home-pickers. You *are* ignorant, aren't you?'

'Frightfully,' he agreed. 'Three classes of society in the hop-garden?'

'Exactly. It seems to work surprisingly well, though I've not had time to judge. This is my first day. I have been allocated a half-bin in one of the home-pickers' sets.'

'Are you enjoying it?'

She nodded. 'But I think I shall wear a pair of cotton gloves tomorrow. It's a nasty stain. I am told it's the sulphur they spray on the hops.' She was looking at her hands and wondering if pumice stone would remove the stain at the end of the day. 'I suppose I'm too fastidious. The other women in my set are not wearing gloves. Most of them have been picking hops since they were children, I understand. I'm just an amateur, but I should be quite professional, shouldn't I, at the end of the six weeks?'

When she smiled she was really lovely, he thought. She was too serious. He wanted to see her smile more often. He wanted to know her better – much better!

'Six weeks is a hell of a long time. Will you stick it out, do you suppose?'

'I shall.'

'Must you?'

'I need the money.'

'I see.'

'No, you don't see. Money is something you ask for when you are broke and it's there for the asking. Isn't that so?'

He had the grace to blush. 'Your shrewd observations do you credit, Miss Mason! I see you have a poor opinion of me. Supposing I told you I was willing to work for an honest penny?'

'I wouldn't believe you.'

'Then I shall take you up on that. I can't resist a challenge. To whom should I apply for a job in the hop-garden?'

'The farmer or his overseer.'

'The other half of your bin – has it been allocated?'

'I don't know – but – are you serious?'

'Never more so, my dear Miss Mason.'

'You won't stick it for more than a week. I'll bet you sixpence.'

'Make it a florin.'

'All right.'

35

He leapt to his feet, shiny-eyed with enthusiasm. It would be a fine old lark. His mother would say he was lowering his dignity, but he had no dignity. His father would shrug indifferently.

'Where's the farm?' he demanded.

'You passed it on the way down. Don't be ridiculous. If it's fun you are looking for, you won't find it here. Nobody picks hops for fun. It's slogging and tedious. Ten hours a day with an hour's break for dinner, five days a week, and from 7 till 12 on Saturday.'

'What you can do, I can do.'

She shook her head. 'I'm a working-class girl. You're middle class.'

'What has class got to do with it?'

'Everything.'

'Not for me. I rejected such ethics years ago at Winchester.'

'Are you a rebel?'

He grinned. 'What is your definition of a rebel, Miss Mason? Come on, you're a school teacher.'

'Someone who refuses to accept the discipline and obligations of a normal society.'

'Right! You've hit the nail on the head.'

'But why? Surely you're lucky to be born into a privileged society?'

'If you mean material advantages, yes, but otherwise I doubt whether the scales are actually balanced in our favour. At least the working class *know* their children. With nurses from infancy, then governesses and prep school, followed by public school and university, most parents are strangers to their children.'

'But you did have a sense of belonging, and that was something I have never known.'

'You mean you're an orphan?'

'Yes.'

36

'I'm sorry.'

She shrugged. 'I'm used to it. I can stand on my own two feet.'

'Obviously! Then you don't object to sharing the bin with me?'

'Not if you're determined to make a martyr of yourself. I've warned you, Mr Saunders!'

'I never listen to warnings, Miss Mason!'

'We start work at 7 o'clock, remember. You won't be awake, let alone here in the hop-garden.'

'I shall get the maid to call me!'

'I still think you're mad.'

'I know, but I told you, I can't resist a challenge. I'm off to the farm. See you later!'

In his suede shoes and grey flannel suit, he looked completely out of his element, loping across the clods. But he vaulted the high gate with the easy grace of an athlete, and was off on his bicycle without a backward glance.

The overseer was blowing his whistle and yelling 'ALL TO WORK'. With a sense of rather pleasant anticipation Betty Mason hurried back down the green archways. He was gone for nearly two hours, and she had decided he had changed his mind. It didn't surprise her, for he just wasn't the type to work on such a tedious job to earn a few pounds. Why should he if he was paid for being idle and having fun? Even so, she was disappointed that he hadn't taken up the challenge for he seemed so eager. Then, suddenly, he was there, pushing his bicycle over the clods, grinning boyishly, and obviously enjoying his debut.

'Afternoon, Mr Dennis.'

'Good-day to you, Sir,' the home-pickers chorused.

Of course they all knew the doctor's son. Betty Mason was disconcerted by the publicity, and the

37

whisperings amongst the women in the set. She had wanted only to remain inconspicuous, and for that reason had ignored the children and merely passed the time of day with her near neighbours. Now she could foresee the tongues wagging over her innocent head, as though she had deliberately arranged this meeting.

Propping his bicycle against the bin, he explained gaily, 'The farmer was having his dinner in the kitchen, and he invited me in. His wife fed me with home-baked bread, cheese and butter from the dairy, washed down with a draught of their own cider. I do declare it was the best meal I've ever tasted!' His gay young voice carried along the set, smiles were exchanged and heads nodded. 'Tomorrow I shall bring sandwiches and a flask of coffee. It's going to be tremendous fun!'

His silent companion went on stripping the hops from the bine she had slung across her side of the bin, and he watched her nimble fingers.

'Where do I start? Do I have to pull down one of these vines?'

'*B*ines,' she corrected primly, and the listening women and children tittered with amusement.

'I'll do that, Sir. It's my job to pull them bines for the 'ome-pickers.' An elderly man had appeared with a hook on a long pole. 'I'll pull 'alf-a-dozen while I'm about it, then you can share them with the young woman,' he decided.

'Thank you very much.'

The doctor's son had nice manners, they were saying. But wasn't it forward of Teacher to invite him to share her bin?

'She's a dark horse, that one. Reckon they've knowed each other for some time,' Shepherd's wife whispered to her neighbour. The other woman agreed the quiet ones weren't to be trusted.

38

'Well, it won't do 'er no good if she's 'anging up 'er 'at to Mr Dennis. Class is class, and 'is Ma won't stand for it,' Shepherd's wife continued sagely. 'A young gentleman 'as to sow 'is wild oats, don't 'e? 'Tis only natural. Last year it were that ginger-'aired barmaid at the Adam and Eve – a saucy bit o' goods, so they say. A gentleman can pick an' choose. A pretty face an' a shapely ankle an' 'e's like a bee to a flower, my old chap reckons. You wouldn't think, to look at 'im, that Sam were a bit of a poet, would you? You'd be surprised what 'e comes out with, after a pint of beer. It don't take much to 'ave 'im waxing all poetical. Looks is deceiving, I always maintain, and Sam's no beauty, but then you wouldn't call me 'andsome, would you now? Looks don't count for much on a farm, leastways, the only thing that counts is whether you're strong and healthy, and willing to work all the 'ours God made. We got to keep at it, my girl, you an' me, if we wants to keep a roof over our 'eads, my Sam was saying only yes'day. Makes yer laugh, don't it, 'im calling me a girl when I got six youngsters an' another on the way,' she chortled happily.

'You'd better sit down on the edge of the bin, or you'll be tired out by 5 o'clock. It's 2 o'clock already,' Betty Mason was saying.

'Now you are being sarcastic, Miss Mason,' he reproved her. But he did as she suggested, and tucked his long legs in the folds of the hessian. 'It's just a knack, and I shall soon master it,' he insisted, confidently.

'Not if you snatch off the leaves with the hops. Take it slowly.'

'Yes, Teacher,' he teased, and again the titter of amusement ran along the set.

By mid-afternoon most of the children were tiring and looking for some diversion.

39

'Can I 'ave a bite o' bread and marge, Mum?'

'Mum, I'm hungry.'

It was as catching as measles, and spread along the set to the far end where the doctor's son was beginning to wonder if he hadn't been a bit of a fool. Miss Mason was picking hops as though her life depended on filling the bushel basket that was on the way. He could hear the measurer's voice intoning 'five-six-seven' in the set that had moved into a fresh position nearby.

'How many bushels in your bin – any idea?' He peered into the other half and studied his companion's face. She was looking tired, but of course she had been picking since 7 o'clock, with only an hour's break for dinner.

'Not more than four or five,' she sighed, and let her busy hands fall idle in her lap. 'I only measured out three bushels this morning, so I haven't earned more than two shillings in my first day's picking.'

'Look here, why don't we remove this string that divides the bin into two separate halves, then I can pick for you?' he suggested artfully. It hadn't taken him long to realise how tedious and boring such a job would prove to be, hour after hour, day after day, for six interminable weeks. If they shared the bin, he could come and go freely, and there would be no obligation. Besides, he didn't have to slog away like this to earn a few pounds. Mother was pretty generous.

'You can't do that. It's not allowed,' Betty Mason protested, but he was already untying the string. 'Wait! Please! I don't want your hops mixed with mine, not until I have picked out all your leaves.' And she tucked up her skirts, climbed into the bin, and tossed out handfuls of leaves.

'I'll help,' he insisted. His long arms reached down among the hops and he found her hand and held it till she pushed it away. He could see the blush deepening on her pale cheeks, under the brim of her sunbonnet, and he enjoyed watching her discomfort.

'Unless you can pick clean, you're going to be more of a hindrance than a help,' she scolded.

'I'll pick clean, Teacher,' he promised, glibly.

When she was satisfied that most of the leaves had been removed, he helped her out of the bin, took hold of the corner, and tipped the few hops he had picked with those she had picked.

'There, it's quite a nice little pile, isn't it? Aren't you pleased?' He was like a child that had to be praised for getting a sum right or making a neat page in his copy book. His boyishness was very appealing, and her prim mouth relaxed into a smile.

'Thank you, it has made a difference,' she conceded.

'I'm 'ungry, Teacher,' he mimicked, and she looked in her bag for the square of ginger-bread she had been saving for mid afternoon and there was a little tea left in the flask. She gave him half the ginger-bread, poured the tea in the small cup, and handed it to him.

'After you,' he said, so she drank her share, and he put the cup to his lips and drank after her, tasting her wet lips on the rim of the cup. 'Nectar,' he teased, for the tea was stewed and tepid.

Now she laughed, because she could not help herself, and the ripple of girlish laughter surprised the children. Teacher was not one to laugh or smile. Dead serious was Teacher as a rule.

Several of the children were scrunching apples.

'I say, where did you get those rosy-red apples?' Mr Dennis called out, in his rich, gentleman's voice.

'Back door of farm, Sir. Penny a pound,' the Carter's eldest boy piped up.

'Run along to the farm, there's a good lad and ask for

six pounds – with your mother's permission, of course,' he added, diplomatically.

The buxom figure in the print apron and sunbonnet nodded agreement. 'Take young Albert along to 'elp carry. Six pounds is a lot of apples, Sir?' she queried.

'Not if we share them.'

She beamed at such lavish generosity. A proper gentleman was Mister Dennis.

'Take my bag, Frank,' said Teacher, addressing one of her pupils for the first time that day. The sixpence and the bag changed hands, and the boys ran off, delighted with this unexpected turn of events. Mum wouldn't refuse to oblige Mr Dennis. Tomorrow they might be sent to the farm to buy more apples. Who knows, he might even buy them sweets from the little cart old Mother Farley drove around the hop-gardens in September? Friday was the day for Monks Farm, so they said. To get away from the bin on any pretext whatsoever was an absolute necessity, especially for the boys, who could not contain their energy and high spirits for as long as the girls, and were not expected to. Even with a bite of bread and marge, or a hunk of bread pudding to relieve the monotony, the afternoon hours would seem to be never-ending. Frank remembered from last year how Mum's heavy hand would box his ears if he strayed too far from the bin for a pee. For a 'big job' the children crawled through a gap in the hedge and squatted under a bush in the wood. They were quite clever at pretending a belly ache! 'Artful as a cartload of monkeys!' the mothers would grumble.

This was the first day, and this year would be different with Teacher and Mr Dennis in the home-set picking hops. When the farmer reached their bin with his bushel basket, he greeted Dennis Saunders with the

42

respect and courtesy to which he was accustomed. A doctor's family held a privileged status in the village, and his father was a dedicated and much-loved physician. The farmer's youngest son was acting as 'tally-man' and entering the number of bushels in the books.

'I won't need a book. Thanks all the same. I have decided to share the bin with Miss Mason,' Dennis explained with his charming smile.

'That's up to you, Sir. I daresay Miss Mason won't find no fault with that arrangement. A little help is worth a lot of pity, they say.' He measured out four bushels into the sack a labourer was holding.

'What a lot of hops it takes to fill that basket of yours. I declare I haven't wasted a second, and I doubt whether I have added more than half a bushel to Miss Mason's share.' The young man seemed surprised and disappointed, but the farmer was reassuring.

'Considering you never started to pick till after dinner, and it's barely 3 o'clock now, that's not bad for a novice. It takes a lot of practice to pick quick and clean. All these folks have been at it since they was knee high to a grasshopper, you must remember.'

'Knee high to a grasshopper!' Dennis exploded with laughter. He had taken off his jacket and tie. They hung on the crossbar of the bin. He looked very handsome in his white shirt, with his fair skin tanned a golden brown. The first two weeks of the Summer vacation had been spent almost entirely outdoors. His companion was still pale, but she hadn't enjoyed his advantages, or the tennis parties and picnics.

When the farmer had moved on to the next bin, she started immediately on one of the bines waiting to be stripped, but he could see the boys racing back down the long green avenue, and he wanted to share out the apples among the children, keeping two for himself and two for Betty Mason. The mothers were not too pleased to see their offspring wasting more time. You can't eat apples and pick hops.

'You be spoiling our youngsters, Mr Dennis,' Shepherd's wife objected, mildly. 'They come out 'ere to work, not to mess about,' she added carefully, not wishing to offend.

'But they are so *young* to work,' he protested. 'If I had my way, they would all be running wild in the woods.'

The children tittered, the mothers shook their heads. 'They 'as plenty o' time in the dinner hour, Sir, for running wild. We 'ad to pick all day when *we* was youngsters. They 'as to learn to like work, else they won't be no use to nobody when they leave school,' Mrs Carter insisted.

'Teacher don't 'old with larking about, do you, Miss?'

'There is a time for everything under the sun. A time for work, a time for play, a time to laugh, and a time to cry,' she quoted, but she hadn't memorised the quotation correctly.

'A time to embrance, and a time to refrain from embracing,' her companion added with a mischievous gleam in his blue eyes. She blushed. She was pretty when she blushed, he thought.

'Eat your apples, they're delicious,' he said persuasively.

And she let the bine fall in her lap, took a bite from the apple she had slipped into her pocket, and met the intimate glance of his laughing eyes with a sense of falling headlong into a situation she had sworn to avoid. It couldn't happen again, could it? It *mustn't* happen again! For nearly three years she had avoided

44

the company of the opposite sex. Yet she had not forgotten that brief meeting with Dennis Saunders at the recital, during the Easter vacation. She was not, by nature, suited to the kind of life that satisfied the other two teachers at the village school. Both had been born in the village, and after three years of higher education, had returned to teach at the school in which they had been pupils. They were typical spinsters, and the schoolmaster was a typical bachelor. They all would be profoundly shocked if they ever discovered she had a child born out of wedlock. There was no reason why anyone in Fairfields should connect her with a little girl in Hawkhurst, for Mason was a common name. Now her real self was disguised behind this veneer of severity, her pretty mouth was prim, and her frigid manner did not invite a relationship. She was afraid to make a friend of her own sex, for sooner or later questions would be asked, and she would have to tell falsehoods – and falsehoods could lead to embarrassing disclosures with a slip of the tongue.

Last year she had spent the whole of the six weeks the village school was closed for hop-picking working as a waitress in a hotel at Hastings, and her salary, together with the tips, had been spent on clothes for the child, who had grown out of all her baby clothes. The Easter weekend had been spent with her own foster-parents, and she spent Christmas with her little girl. Her landlady had been duly informed that this year she would not be visiting relatives, but picking hops. These mythical relatives had been around since early childhood, since she refused to accept the fact that she was an orphan. Betty Mason was not the only child at the Orphanage with an inventive imagination. It coloured the drabness of their lives, and uniforms, the austerity and the piety. A deliberate lie would be severely punished, but who could prevent an imaginative child from having a family of mythical relations?

The young pupil-teacher had not come directly from the High School for Girls, as it was assumed, and schoolmaster had not enquired too closely into Miss Mason's background and credentials. The baby had been conceived in an orchard conveniently situated between school and home. A frolic in the long grass was fun, and kisses still held the freshness of childhood on lips not yet acquainted with passion. Curiosity was the motive, and newly awakened senses a little frightening, but curiosity had been satisfied. Sex was no longer a dirty word but an actual experience more exciting than anything they had ever known. Unfortunately, the boy had to boast of his manly conquest, and that was the first and the last time they were allowed to meet. The boy escaped with a warning, the girl with a child to carry for nine long months of shame and disgrace. It was a bitter pill to swallow – one law for the male, another for the female. It was not fair! But she could count herself lucky in her kind foster-parents, and she was spared the awful degradation of the Workhouse. Her child was born in the privacy and comfort of her own little bedroom, with a midwife in attendance. Her lost youth, and the dire necessity to earn a living as soon as possible after the birth, had not broken her spirit, but intensified her fierce determination to walk alone in the unknown future. In that cruel year of adolescence she had matured, and she had endured the agony of childbirth. The whole pattern of her life was changed irrevocably by that one act of sexual intercourse.

Now, on this hot day of August, in the most unlikely place, she found herself face to face with the one

46

person she had been trying to forget for the past six months. Only the width of the bin separated her from that lounging figure with the mocking eyes. The clasp of his hand among the hops had sent a shiver of sensuality through her sun-warmed body, and he knew it! His reputation in the village was no secret. Mr Dennis was sowing his wild oats. It was a gentleman's privilege. If a girl got caught with a baby, she had only herself to blame. The general opinion had only been modified in the case of little Maud Channing, who had been molested by a gypsy and died in childbirth at the age of 14. Every outraged father of the working-class community would have strangled the scoundrel with his bare hands, but he had vanished, as gypsies do. That was a long time ago, but country folk have long memories. A gypsy and a gentleman were worlds apart, however. The one was persecuted, the other privileged. Betty Mason was as fully aware of this distinction as all the other young women of her own class. No blame would be attached to this charming individual if she succumbed to his charm. He was already a favourite with the home pickers this first day, and if he found her an attractive alternative to the pretty, befrilled young ladies in his own class of society, she had no escape – unless she gave up the hop-picking and offered her services at the same hotel as a seasonal waitress.

'I know what you are thinking, Miss Mason. I can read your thoughts like a book,' he said, his voice lowered discreetly. 'But you are mistaken. My intentions are strictly honourable.'

As the blush swept over her face, she dropped her eyes, picked up the bine, and began to strip off the hops with trembling fingers.

'You flatter yourself, Mr Saunders. I have much

47

more important matters on my mind, I do assure you!' she retorted.

But he knew better. Variety was the spice of life, and he was a little tired of the blandishments of the blonde barmaid. So he contented himself with anticipation. The chase was the most exciting part of a new affair, not the conquest.

Parson's youngest daughter, Marion, had been constantly reminded of her good fortune in obtaining the post of governess at Marston Park, but it was a doubtful privilege for a young woman of a rebellious nature. Although she had escaped from the small confined world of The Parsonage, into the wider, privileged world of the gentry, she was not a participant, and her life was still restricted and bounded by the conventions of Victorian society. A governess had no status, she had discovered, and was as far removed from the drawing-room as the servants hall. To be friendly with the servants was undignified, to be familiar with any member of the family other than her pupils would be presumptious. So Marion Wellington had escaped from one restrictive environment to another, and she sometimes feared she was doomed to spend the rest of her working life in the schoolroom.

In this eventful year, at the end of the Victorian era, two of the children were still in the nursery, and the elderly nurse ruled her little domain with the assistance of a nursemaid. She had the advantage of being a long-serving and respected servant, for her first charges at Marston Park had been the young Sir Neville and his brothers and sisters. The nurses and the governess had nothing in common; indeed, there was a kind of enmity between them that amused the other staff. Loyal and faithful servants reaped their reward in old age, when they were retired to small cottages on the estate. So Nurse had no qualms about the future. Married gardeners and the grooms had their own cottages, and the coachman lived over the stables. The indoor staff, comprising Butler, two footmen, Housekeeper, four housemaids, parlourmaid, Cook, kitchen-maid and scullery-maid, were allocated accommodation according to status and protocol. The butler and the housekeeper enjoyed the privacy of a bed-sitting-room. Cook had a cosy little cubby-hole adjoining the kitchen, the footmen shared a room in the basement, and the kitchen-maid shared an attic bedroom with the fourth housemaid. All the maids were accommodated in the attics that were stifling hot in Summer, and so freezing cold in Winter, they had to break the ice in their jugs for early morning ablutions. As for the poor despised little scullery-maid, she curled up on a straw pallet in a corner of the boiler room, but nobody enquired where she slept. In the servants' hierarchy, a scullery-maid was less than the dust, and she ate her meals in the kitchen. But the servants were well-fed, and the housemaids enjoyed a healthy familiarity with the footmen and the groom. A romp in the coach-house or the basement bedroom went undetected in mid afternoon, when the butler and the housekeeper were enjoying their 'forty winks'.

The governess touched only briefly on this enviable freemasonry among the lower orders. She was young and she was lonely, always attired in grey – it was unseemly for a governess to wear bright colours, and the servants' outdoor uniforms were black. Her figure was too thin for beauty, and her dark eyes the only redeeming feature in a pallid face. There was a similarity between the young teacher at the village

49

school and the governess at Marston Park, since both seemed destined to a life sentence of teaching – an occupation for which they were neither suited nor dedicated. Only marriage could save them, but it was extremely unlikely that any man would wish to marry a young woman with an illegitimate child, and a governess had no opportunity to meet the opposite sex. Their pupils, fortunately, were not too demanding. The daughters of Sir Neville were not expected to be brilliant scholars. Prettily engaged in such ladylike pursuits as playing the pianoforte, singing sweet Victorian ballads, and doing their embroidery, their lessons in deportment had one objective – to attract elegible young gentlemen as future husbands.

As for Betty Mason, the majority of her pupils would leave school with only a slight acquaintance with the three Rs, the Atlas, the Kings and Queens of England, and the familiar poems of William Blake. The small majority of 'bright children' would make their own way in the world, no matter how humble their environment.

Such a one was young Freddie Simmons from Richmond Row. From office boy to solicitor's clerk, and finally to the private sanctum of his own office, this was a goal almost too ambitious to contemplate.

'We be working class, son, and working class we was intended to be. It don't seem right to set yourself above your betters,' Ruby reminded the ambitious Freddie.

One mellow October day, in that same eventful year, Marion Wellington set out for a brisk two-mile walk to the parsonage, soon after breakfast. Permitted a free Sunday once a month, and anxious not to waste a moment, she hastened down the drive and turned sharp left on to a bridle-path that led to one of the estate farms. Russets was a short cut to the village, and she hoped to reach the Parsonage in time to accompany her mother and sisters to Matins.

The buxom farmer's wife was leaning on the sill of a bedroom window, and she smiled and called 'Good morning, Miss. Lovely day!'

The governess lifted a hand in greeting and went on her way. How she envied that woman! Lucy Blunt, on that mellow October day, seemed to be enjoying all the advantages she, Parson's daughter was lacking. She was pretty. She had married the only son at Russets at the tender age of 16. She was the mother of three boys. She had security for life. No wonder her cheeks were so blooming, her golden hair so lustrous. They said she had a twin sister whose fortune had been poor in comparison, married to a ganger on the railway, with four children, living in the slum at Richmond Row. She worked as a charwoman at The Three Nuns.

It was Cecily who knew the history of the majority of her father's poor parishioners, for it was one of her duties to visit them when they were sick, to take offerings of beef tea and calves'-foot jelly. It was Cecily who would summon her father to the bedside of a dying parishioner of the working class, and Cecily who collected the discarded clothing from the upper class.

Poor, delicate Irene was so cherished and cosseted, she would have wilted like a hot-house flower if exposed to the rigours of visiting.

Marion found Cecily's saintly charity a little irritating at times, but they were a close-knit family, and the harmonious atmosphere at The Parsonage on her free Sundays was seldom disturbed by her thoughtless tongue.

Bonfires were still smouldering in the hop-gardens, and the acrid smoke from the piles of wilted bines drifted across the hedges. Hips and haws and trailing

Old Man's Beard were further proof that Autumn had arrived. It was a lovely season, and today they would be celebrating Harvest Festival, her favourite festival of the Church calendar. Neither the Easter lilies nor the Christmas holly could compare with that rich bounty of harvest laid out in colourful profusion on every ledge and sill, on pulpit and choir stalls. Tall Michaelmas daisies would be massed in the font, and shaggy chrysanthemums in the Grecian urns. The smell would linger in the church for some days when all had been removed. Cecily needed helpers to distribute all the fruit, vegetables and flowers. The huge harvest loaf was delivered to the Workhouse together with hampers of vegetables that would have been wasted on the villagers, who had their own gardens and allotments.

The hop-gardens and orchards had been stripped. The fields had been ploughed. There was beauty in the straight furrows, and the circling gulls. 'How did they know when the fields were ready for ploughing?' Marion Wellington wondered. They were miles from the coast, yet the gulls flew inland in droves at this season of the year. A few late swallows were gathering on the telephone wires, and that too was a mystery, the amazing journeys of migrating birds. How she wished she had wings and could follow the swallows to some warm clime before another hard Winter! Compulsory walks with her young pupils for health's sake did nothing for their tempers. She suffered from chilblains, and the walks were a form of torture on those bleak Winter afternoons. But she would not think of Winter today. She would enjoy the beauty and bounty of Autumn. Shedding the veneer of demure refinement in which a governess was habitually clad, she picked up her skirts and ran through the copse that bordered the broad acres of Russets with a sense of happy anticipation.

Peg-leg was filling baskets with logs for the drawing-room and dining-room fires, and he greeted her cheerfully as she pushed open the wicket gate. She was fond of the Colonel's ex-batman, as they all were. He had created a new, exciting world for the two elderly servants, and his capacity for work was not hindered by the handicap of a wooden leg. She stopped to chat with him for a few minutes before greeting Cook and Annie in the kitchen. She always used the back entrance because the servants liked to see her as soon as she arrived. They were part of the familiar pattern she had known since childhood. Only Peg-leg was a recent addition to the household.

They were busy with the preparations for Sunday lunch, and Annie, whose bedroom chores were restricted to making beds and emptying slops on Sunday mornings, was peeling apples for pies. The latest litter of kittens was curled in a basket in the inglenook where Peg-leg would be relaxing later in the day. It was a homely scene, so far removed from the grandeur of Marston Park.

'How many to lunch today, Cook?' The usual question, for it was customary for Parson to invite visiting clergy and the curate.

Cook counted on her fingers. 'Seven in the dining-room, Miss Marion. There's a young gentleman missionary on leave from Africa, so Miss Cecily told us.'

'The object of 'is visit, Miss, being to thank Miss Irene for making all them garments for the little 'eathen children,' Annie explained.

'Good heavens! I hope we shan't be treated to a long discourse on the mission field over lunch. Missionaries are tiresome people as a rule,' Marion asserted. 'Has he arrived, Annie?'

'Yes, Miss.'

'How did he get here?'

'Miss Cecily took the trap and met him at the station.'

'That means we shall have his company for Matins,' she sighed. 'Well, he will be obliged to walk to church with Father, for there will be no room in the trap.'

'Yes, Miss. He seems quite a pleasant young gentleman, Miss. When I took in the coffee Miss Irene was laughing.'

'*Was* she, indeed? Then he must be exceptionally entertaining, for my sweet sister is not given to laughter, as we all know.'

'I think 'e were teasing 'er, Miss, 'bout them woolly vests. She were flushed.'

Marion chuckled. 'I'm beginning to feel curious about this young man. And how are the varicose veins, Cook?'

'A bit easier, thank you, Miss, with them new elastic stockings Miss Cecily got for me.'

'Good.' Her smile was warmly affectionate as she bid them goodbye and promised to look in again in the evening before she left for Marston Park.

The lively conversation in the drawing-room ceased abruptly as she opened the door. Her father and the young man seated beside the sofa on which Irene reclined, sprang to their feet. Her mother and sisters smiled a greeting. Her father was the first to speak.

'Good morning, my dear.' She went to him first, instinctively because she loved him best, and he alone had understood her reluctance to accept the post of governess at Marston Park. They all were dependent on the patronage of Sir Neville Franklin. The fact could not be denied. Father and daughter were closely involved, but the rest of the family could not escape the sensitive nature of the living at All Saints.

'Good morning, Father.' She took his outstretched

54

hands and kissed his cheek. Later, when they were alone in the study after lunch, she would give him a hug, but not yet, not in front of the rest of the family, and a strange young man who was watching her closely as she kissed her mother and sisters. It was Irene who introduced them. His name was Malcolm McKenzie – a lean Scot with sandy hair that badly needed a trim, and a tweed suit that had seen better days. But the clasp of his hand was firm and strong, and his dark eyes appraised her.

'How do you do, Miss Marion?'

'How do you do, Mr McKenzie?'

Was it imagination? Could a spark be kindled in that first moment of meeting – a spark that would light the flame of love in the hearts of two kindred souls? Was it mere chance that Malcolm McKenzie should choose this particular Sunday to visit The Parsonage at Fairfields, the very Sunday that Marion Wellington came home to visit her family? They would not think so, and when they were better acquainted, they would insist it was God's divine purpose that had brought them together.

When Annie appeared in the doorway with the customary cup of coffee for the visiting daughter, Malcolm McKenzie stepped forward to take it, then motioned Marion into the chair he had vacated. Annie gathered up the coffee cups scattered about the room, and went back to the kitchen to report to Cook that the young gentleman had nice manners, and now it was Miss Marion who was flushed. Nothing escaped the notice of these old-established servants. They were part of the family, and had their place in the affections of the family. No offer, however attractive, would have dislodged Cook and Annie from The Parsonage.

'It's time we were getting ready, my dear,' Parson

reminded his wife, as the chimes of the grandfather clock echoed across the hall.

'We have been enjoying Mr McKenzie's stories of his little piccaninnies,' Irene was saying. 'I must confess I was sadly mistaken in the nature of their garments. In future, I shall confine my activities to something more suitable!' And she joined in the ripple of laughter that followed such an honest assessment.

'You and I have to walk to church, my dear fellow. The ladies have the use of the trap. It's only a short distance,' Parson explained, as he ushered his guest into the hall.

When Marion had finished her coffee, she awaited her mother and sisters who had gone upstairs for coats and hats. From the door of the drawing-room, she could see Mr McKenzie assisting her father into the voluminous cape. The younger man had no coat or hat, and he turned to lift a hand in salute as they went out. She returned the salute and smiled at the retreating back. Then Peg-leg brought the trap to the front door, and held the mare while the four ladies seated themselves, when he handed over the reins to Miss Cecily. They ambled down the mossy drive, bordered by overgrown shrubs. Their shabbiness reflected on their status in the middle-class society to which they belonged. A parson's family was not expected to follow the fashionable trends, or to indulge in gay colours. They were under-privileged, but respected. Over the top of the hedge as they turned into the road, they could see the two figures striding purposefully across the field towards the West gate of the churchyard. They were ill-matched in appearance – the tall, ungainly figure in the flapping cape and pork-pie hat, and the young Scot, with his hands thrust in his pockets. They reached the gate and passed through, without a backward glance, deep in conversation, and oblivious of the approaching trap.

'Mr McKenzie seems to have made a hit with Father,' Irene observed.

When Cecily had secured the mare and left her with the bag of oats to which she was accustomed, they filed into church. Malcolm McKenzie was waiting, and he followed them down the aisle to the family pew. Since Marion always stood back to allow her mother and sisters to precede her, it was natural that she found herself seated next to the young missionary. Irene turned to smile over her shoulder at the man who was seated immediately behind. Andrew Robinson inclined his head with a gracious little bow. Cecily's glance travelled across the nave to the side aisle where the Sunday School children were seated. One Sunday in the month when her sister Marion came home for the day, she handed over her responsibility to Miss White.

'I canna remember when I last attended Harvest Festival,' Malcolm McKenzie whispered in his rich Scottish brogue, under cover of the organ voluntary. The choir had assembled in the aisle for the traditional processional hymn – boys and men in clean surplices that crackled with starch as they went by – 'Come ye thankful people, come; Raise the song of harvest home.' The congregation joined in the splendid volume of voices. The deep baritone in The Parsonage pew accompanied the combined charms of the four ladies. Marion sang like a choirboy, the clear high notes effortless and pure. She sang with a fervour that matched her companion's, her face flushed, her eyes starry. It was one of her favourite hymns. She knew every word, and did not need to glance at the book she held out between them, in a gloved hand. She could see the blunt thumb holding down the opposite page, and

57

feel the vibrations that travelled between them. Their voices blended harmoniously, and they were linked together by the small hymnal, familiar since early childhood. Emotionally disturbed by his nearness, she could not look at him, but she had no need to look to know that he was experiencing a similar reaction. In the crowded church, no two people could have been more aware of each other, more certain they had discovered something infinitely precious and unique.

The schoolmaster's contact with the delicate Irene had a nebulous quality, lacking substantial reality to sustain it. But it suited them, this dreamlike attachment, fostered only by a smile, and the gentle pressure of a hand on Sunday morning. Not for them the swift decisive knowledge of a fundamental compatibility, or the natural curiosity of a man and a woman so suddenly aware of one another.

With her gloved hands folded demurely in her lap, and her eyes fastened on the tall, grey-haired figure in the pulpit, Marion Wellington was not listening. Never before in her whole life had she felt so disturbed by the close proximity of the opposite sex, and her virginal heart was beating so strongly she wondered if he could hear it.

He was very still and attentive. The pattern of the service was probably unfamiliar, but he had followed it in the book of Common Prayer, and they had shared the book for two more hymns – 'We plough the fields and scatter, the good seed on the land, But it is fed and watered by God's Almighty hand,' another old favourite, and 'Praise my soul, the King of Heaven'. Kneeling side by side on the stiff hassocks for the closing prayers, the general thanksgiving for a rich harvest had a poignant and personal significance for these two young people on this Harvest Festival, 1901.

The young missionary followed the rustle of petticoats down the aisle, and wondered how soon he could open his heart to this wonderful girl. His native caution had deserted him. She was the answer to prayer, and he had found her without consciously seeking in the House of God! For the rest of his days the smell of apples would evoke a memory of a village church in the Weald of Kent, celebrating its Harvest Festival.

When he had helped the ladies into the trap, he stepped back raised a hand in salute, and walked away to await Parson. He could see him standing in the porch, shaking hands with his upper-class parishioners. Carriages and traps had been assembled beyond the churchyard wall. Grooms and coachmen were back on duty, fortified by the beer at The Three Nuns. It was a lively, colourful scene, new to the young missionary, whose birthplace had no such class distinction; all were equal in the eyes of God and the kirk. They travelled by wagonette or Shanks's pony to their Sunday worship, and no public house would open its doors on the Sabbath. There was a Spartan hardiness in such an early environment that he carried to the ends of the earth with follow Scots, together with a sack of oatmeal. He had practically lived on porridge and oatcakes during his training at the Theological College in Edinburgh, but it was no hardship when other students kept him company. Their sturdy independence was both admired and ridiculed by their contemporaries.

But it hadn't taken Malcolm McKenzie long to notice the faded shabbiness at The Parsonage. The overgrown drive was another indication of genteel poverty. Probably the manservant with the wooden leg, who had carried in the basket of logs, had also to tend the garden. Yet the air of refinement and good breeding was evident in their speech and their manners. They were friendly and courteous to the servants as members of a family. He felt no awkwardness in their company, only a quiet sense of belonging that was most satisfactory under the circumstances.

Yet this prearranged visit had in no way prepared him for such an astonishing development. It was intended as a duty visit, out of gratitude for Miss Irene's devoted hours of knitting for his little flock. There were many such visits to be made during the next few weeks, after he had attended the conference at the headquarters of the Missionary Society to which he was affiliated.

The parcels from The Parsonage had always contained a letter, and the Christmas parcel also contained a plum pudding, a cake, a tin of home-made toffee, a calendar for the coming year, and a pair of hand-knitted socks, totally unsuited for the climate. He had contrived to preserve them, however, for his home leave, and Miss Irene had been most gratified to see him wearing a pair; he had also been rather sweet about the woolly vests. So many of the gifts received were unsuitable, and so many hours wasted, and money spent on useless oddities. Perhaps he could persuade the ladies of the Guilds to contribute the money instead.

Three months' home leave and one month already slipped away. Dear God! There was so much to do, so much to decide. His whole future was at stake – unless – unless . . .

The curate also accompanied them to The Parsonage for Sunday lunch – not a very impressive figure in his shiny black suit and unpolished boots, but he seemed to have quite a good opinion of himself, and obviously had designs on Cecily, who was perfectly happy and content in her role of Parson's dutiful eldest daughter.

No three sisters could have presented a greater contrast to their father's guests. They were different in appearance and character, and only Marion reached out to a wider world not encompassed by the restrictive domination of the Squire of Marston Park. Their genteel poverty was a permanent reminder of this benevolence. Generations of children had grown up at The Parsonage under this archaic system. Nobody could foresee a time when it would collapse in the revolutionary changes of the twentieth century.

But the main topic of conversation at the lunch table that eventful day of October, 1901, was not the African Mission, or the Harvest Festival, but the strange disappearance of Betty Mason from her lodgings, and the urgent necessity to engage another teacher for Standards One and Two.

Chapter Three

Police Constable Brown had organised a search party at the request of Parson and the schoolmaster, both extremely puzzled by Miss Mason's disappearance. She had not been seen since the Sunday following the end of hop-picking, and her landlady reported she had left her lodgings after lunch that day and had not returned by nightfall. When she failed to report for duty on the first day of term, it was assumed she was ill, and Miss White was asked to call on the landlady later in the day. In the meantime, the children she normally taught were herded into an adjoining classroom, and their own classroom was still unoccupied two weeks later. It was a mystery, and her pupils were enjoying their importance in upsetting the schoolmaster's curriculum.

'He be proper vexed,' was the general opinion, and he was certainly very much disturbed. Another reshuffle among the teaching staff was not a simple matter of advertising for a replacement, but a gathering of the School Governors to interview prospective candidates. The strict authority he maintained depended on a regular, uninterrupted system, and now it was disorganised by the discourtesy of a young woman deliberately ignoring the terms of her contract.

One month's notice, in writing, was required on either side.

Only when Miss Mason was missing did the schoolmaster realise that her two contemporaries, Miss White and Miss Carter, were as ignorant of her private life as he himself. He had naturally assumed they had formed a friendly attachment, and met for recreational purposes after school, and at weekends. It was not so. He felt a little guilty that he hadn't enquired, then excused himself on the grounds it was not his business. Both teachers reported that Miss Mason had been invited to their respective homes for Sunday tea because they felt sorry for a young woman in lodgings at the weekend, but she had politely refused the invitations. What did she do with herself at weekends? The question was raised, and the schoolmaster called in person on the landlady.

'It's not my business to enquire, Sir, what the young person is about, once she's out of my house,' came the prompt reply.

'Quite so,' he agreed, and bid her 'Good-day'. But it had to be somebody's business, or the mystery of her disappearance would never be solved. Nothing was missing from her bed-sitting-room. Everything was neat and tidy. She had been wearing her best grey costume and her best felt hat. That much her landlady had noticed, but since it was the custom among working-class people in that day and age to keep certain garments for Sunday best, this information was not particularly helpful.

The constable had since inspected the room, and stated in his report that nothing *appeared* to be missing – the word 'appeared' was significant. No letters were found, but then the young woman in question did not receive any, the irate landlady explained.

63

'No letters – not even a Christmas card?' the constable persisted.

'Not to my knowledge.' And the door was closed.

'She don't seem to 'ave taken much account of the young woman, do she, Sir?' the constable reflected when questioned further by his superior officer in Maidstone.

'Maybe she thought she did her duty to her lodger by providing board and lodging? It seems a bit unnatural, but the young woman may have preferred it.'

Constable Brown agreed, for he seldom disagreed with his superiors.

By the time the search party was officially under way, all the working-class population of the village had been informed of the absent teacher. Children and neighbours were adding a little spice to the event in the telling. It was not often that an adult person went missing. It was little children who got lost. Speculation on the young woman's whereabouts had become an interesting topic of controversy over mugs of beer and cups of tea.

Servant girls going home on their free Sunday afternoons had carried the news back to kitchens and servants halls of the upper-class establishments where they were employed. Gardeners' boys and errand boys, ex-pupils of Miss Mason's, were enjoying a sudden notoriety when questioned by their elders. 'What was she like?' This question evoked a variety of answers too contradictory to be taken seriously: 'She were terrible strict'; 'She 'elped you when you was flummoxed'; 'She never 'ad no favourites, not Miss Mason'; 'I dunno, I wasn't one of 'er favourites'.

'They found that young woman!' Mike O'Brien announced importantly, a week or so later, in the public bar of The Three Nuns.

'Where were she then?' his companion demanded.

'Marston Park – 'idden in the bushes nearby the lake.'

'Dead?'

'She were dead all right – strangled.'

'The poor little bugger.' A hush had fallen over the bar.

'Ain't nobody claimed the body then?' someone enquired at length.

'Seemingly not. They do say she were a norphan.'

'That's bad.'

A murmur of sympathy and a sad shaking of heads among the customers.

'What were she doing up in the Park then? That be private property,' old Josiah Higgins observed; 'and why were she left in the bushes when the lake were nearby?'

'Dunno.' Mike O'Brien, having reported the discovery, had nothing more to add, for he was not a very intelligent fellow, even in his most sober moments. They all agreed old Josh had a point. A shrewd old fellow was Josh.

'It don't make no sense, do it, not with that lake so 'andy for a dead body?' he persisted, morbidly.

'With the body in the lake, nobody would 'ave knowed that poor woman was murdered, and when she didn't show up at the school no more, then folks would take it for granted she were gone for good,' the landlord reflected from behind the bar.

'Constable won't 'arf be flummoxed, for 'e ain't used to dealing with a case of murder. A few brawls in 'opping time with them pestering gypsies, and a few drunks on Sat'day nights, and that's about all.'

Josh took up the story again. 'Do you reckon it were a gypsy then what strangled that poor young woman?'

65

The landlord nodded. 'Could well be. I wouldn't trust one of them diddicoes farther than I could see 'im. Cunning as foxes they be, the 'ole buggering lot.'

'But if it were a gypsy what done 'er in, then 'e wouldn't 'ave left 'er lying around in them bushes, 'e would 'ave dumped 'er in the lake,' the wheelwright asserted.

'I mind the time that little maid were insulted, some years back, and they never laid eyes on that gyppo, and never will.' A murmur of agreement followed that statement.

'You know what 'appens now. Every man Jack of us is going to be questioned.' The landlord was an authority on such matters.

'What for? We ain't 'ad nothing to do with it.' A surly voice complained from the chimney corner.

'Well, *somebody* did it, and a lot of time 'as been wasted. An Inspector from Scotland Yard will 'andle the case proper like. Doctor will be the first person to be questioned, as to 'ow long the young woman 'ad been lying there dead. If it be a matter of weeks, then it could well be one of them pestering gyppos, for they was 'anging around on the farms for some days after the picking were finished. That I do know, for they was up 'ere for their beer, and I never took them tables and benches away from the front till I were sure they was gone.'

The customers drained their mugs. It was thirsty work trying to unravel the mystery of the murdered teacher, as respectable a young woman as anyone would wish, by all accounts. She wasn't courting, and she minded her own business. That was more than could be said of the other teachers, with tongues as long as rulers.

'My missus reckoned right from the start that poor

66

soul were dead. She 'as an uncanny way of knowing such things, 'as my missus. Don't ask me 'ow 'er mind works, for I couldn't tell 'e, and I been married to the good woman for nigh on twelve years.'

The landlord liked an audience, and this new train of thought injected into the mystery was welcomed by the customers. Empty mugs were refilled, and they settled down to further discussion, for it was seldom they had such an absorbing topic in the public bar of The Three Nuns.

'I 'ad a cousin what knowed 'er son 'ad been killed in the Crimea weeks afore she got the news from the proper quarter,' Josh reflected. ''Tis second sight,' he added, knowledgeably.

'And more often than not my missus sees it 'appening in a dream, then I be feared, for t'ain't natural.' The landlord shivered involuntarily.

Josh wiped the back of his hand across his wet whiskers. 'Women is strange contrary critturs, and you won't never get upsides 'em, not if you lives to be a n'undred,' he concluded.

'What a shocking affair to be sure, this business of poor Miss Mason. I declare I can't get the poor creature off my mind,' Victoria Langtry reflected. Her sister, Letitia was arranging a bowl of shaggy chrysanthemums in the ante-room they called the flower room. The parlourmaid, having opened the door to the postman that morning, had imparted the tragic tale to the two ladies when they came down to breakfast.

'Yes, it is indeed a sorry affair, Vickie, and so inconvenient since it necessitates another meeting of the School Governors and all the tedious business of interviewing prospective candidates for the vacancy. I doubt whether we shall see it settled before Christmas. Silly girl! Why did she have to go wandering about on private property? It's asking for trouble, and such a nuisance for dear Sir Neville, with all his male servants being questioned by the police, and everyone under suspicion.'

'Do you have any theories concerning the murderer, Lettie?'

'Not yet. There is not enough evidence to work on.'

'A tramp, perhaps, on his way to the Workhouse – though I don't know what he would be doing in Marston Park.'

'There's no motive. Why should a tramp kill a young woman so obviously of the working class? She wouldn't be carrying more than a shilling or two on her person.'

'A shilling or two to a penniless tramp would seem like a fortune. There could have been another reason, Vickie. Had you thought of that?'

'You mean – a man with a maid?'

'Exactly.'

The subject was too delicate to pursue, but Letitia would speculate on the young woman's attacker and the nature of the assault while she arranged the flowers. Her vivid imagination would invest the scene with all the horror of a Victorian melodrama. *The Murder in the Red Barn* was particularly vivid in her memory.

Travelling theatrical companies visited the village twice a year. It was undignified to sit on a bench in a marquee erected in Sutton's field, and a lady should not expose herself to gossip, but Letitia Langtry could not bear to miss a single performance. Victoria's tastes were more refined – a pianoforte recital, chamber music or poetry readings by Irene Wellington in The Parsonage drawing-room. For the sake of propriety, all these boring functions had to be attended and endured with good grace. It would be unseemly *not* to attend, particularly when the invitation came from Marston Park. It was almost a royal command. It was much too dangerous to venture into the marquee without a companion, however, so Lizzie, the elderly parlour-maid, would accompany her mistress and share the agony of suspense in the exciting melodrama. The female members of the audience would moan and whimper. The atmosphere would be dense with the smoke of pipes, and the smell of sweating bodies mingled with the tang of oranges. Servant girls would be wearing cheap scent to entice their sweethearts to furtive fumbling in the semi-darkness.

Now a real-life drama had been enacted in their midst, and its repercussions reached out to all classes of society. Letitia Langtry was not the only person to speculate on a sexual motive for the murder. Doctor Saunders had already suggested it to the Chief Constable from Maidstone before the arrival of the Detective Inspector from Scotland Yard. The evidence was there, in the disturbed nature of the petticoats, and a missing garment that had not yet been found. The victim's hat was discovered near the body. It was soaked with rain. Her clothes were saturated, and clung to her slender body. Her hair was plastered to her head. She was indeed a sorry sight, and could not have been wetter had they fished her out of the lake. All these sordid details came to light gradually, through the medium of the postmen, the servants, the gamekeepers, and the school children. 'Teacher' had become a legend at the village school in the weeks that followed the discovery of her body. Ex-pupils speculated on her innocence and purity, and vulgar suggestions, passed from hand to hand on slips of grubby paper, were intercepted en route. Boys were caned. Girls giggled under cover of their pinafores.

'If Teacher 'ad a bloke, she were terrible sly. Nobody never see'd 'er courting,' Hetty O'Brien whispered to her bosom friend one Saturday morning, as she awaited her turn in the confessional.

'Just imagine, it might have been our Wellie!' Marion Wellington's eldest pupil at Marston Park speculated, shivering excitedly at such an appalling possibility. Servants had no right to gossip in front of the children, and the governess was annoyed. Her annoyance was tempered with the uncertainty of her own position regarding Mr McKenzie. They had taken a walk together on that memorable Sunday afternoon, and he had driven her back to Marston Park in the evening, after supper. The romantic nature of the journey back had been enhanced by the moon, and the nearness of her companion. She had only to stretch out a hand to touch him, yet she kept her hands folded demurely in her lap, waiting for a sign, a gesture, a word. His silence unnerved her. Why had they seemed so close earlier in the day, to be separated now by this barrier of silence? What had happened to curb his tongue, and set his lips so firmly? Had she been immodest? Had she allowed her emotions to override her discretion with this man, this stranger? For he was a stranger; no matter that her heart contradicted such logic.

On the afternoon walk, she had discovered that he had been visiting his widowed mother and married brothers and sisters he had not seen for five years. She also discovered that he was utterly and completely dedicated to missionary work, and would spend the rest of his life in Africa, if God so willed, with home leave once every five years. She could not conceive such a way of life, or such a long separation from all that was dear and familiar. Yet, with the natural contrariness of

70

her sex, she was disappointed that he hadn't included her in this hazardous future. And when they reached the end of the journey in the stable yard, he handed her out of the trap, held her hand for a long moment in a warm, firm clasp between his own two hands, then let it drop. The blunt features that confronted her in the pale light of the moon would be carved on her memory for all time. The searching dark eyes regarded her with unblinking intensity. She wanted to weep on his shoulder. She wanted only that he would kiss her. She could not bear to let him go, but convention was too strong at this critical moment of parting. Three generations of parsons and their solid, respectable wives did not breed radical daughters, and her rebellious moods were shortlived.

'Goodbye, Miss Wellington.'

'Goodbye, Mr McKenzie.'

He climbed into the trap and took up the reins.

'Will you write?' she asked, with pathetic eagerness.

'Aye,' he replied gruffly, and she was choked with mortification at her own unladylike suggestion. Then he was gone.

She stood there, trembling with misery, choked with tears, till the clip-clop of the mare's hooves died away.

Malcolm McKenzie had conquered the strong desire to open his heart to Marion Wellington with the stubborn deliberation he had shown at every step of the way since he first set forth on his Christian pilgrimage. He saw all too clearly that it would be cruel to take her away, and to rob the parson of his favourite daughter. It was a very close relationship, and their devotion was apparent throughout the hours he had spent in their company. His own need of affection and the companionship of a loving wife was not so desperate that he must make a fool of himself with a very interesting

71

young woman whose acquaintance he had made for the first time that day, he reminded himself. His natural caution had reasserted itself. The afternoon walk and the evening drive had provided ample opportunity to open his heart, but he had not spoken, and now it was too late. The Harvest Festival had moved him profoundly. It was such an emotional and joyous occasion, shared by a kindred spirit. Such an occasion might not come his way again for a very long time, when they were separated by thousands of miles.

He could not, he *must* not take an irrevocable step on impulse, on a single day's acquaintance. Yet he could not bear to leave her with nothing more tangible than a promise to write. That she had been expecting him to speak, and was disappointed at his silence, was apparent in every glance of those candid eyes. The excited flush on her cheeks had died away, leaving a deathly pallor. In the light of the moon, her slight figure seemed to droop with sadness as the mansion took shape at a curve in the drive. He knew, even at this last moment, he had only to reach out his hand and touch her to see a transformation. Her vivid little face would shine with an inner radiance again. He had witnessed such a transformation in church only this morning, when the splendid volume of voices rose in thanksgiving and they shared a hymn-book.

But he kept his free hand clenched in his pocket and held the reins with the other. There was still time in the stable yard to take her in his arms and kiss away the sadness of parting. A lesser man may have been tempted, but not the young Scot with his strong principles and Spartan determination.

So he left her standing there, and the clip-clop of the mare's hooves held the poignant ring of a tolling bell.

'There's a letter for you, Miss.' The third housemaid

who waited on the schoolroom was laying breakfast. A fire blazed in the grate, and a heavy scuttle of coal had been carried up three flights of stairs. On this grey morning of late Autumn the schoolroom was a cheerful place with Toby jugs on the mantelpiece, and the still-life pictures Marion had painted. It was her one creative talent, for her musical ability was elementary. Fortunately, her young pupils were not expected to play anything more than the simplest compositions when they performed in the drawing-room. Neither showed an aptitude for the pianoforte or anything else for that matter. They were good, obedient girls, but rather dull.

'You should 'ave seen 'er face when she picked up that letter. I never knowed she could blush!' the young housemaid reported later, in the servants' hall.

'Did she read it, Glad?' the second housemaid enquired eagerly.

'Not she. Slipped it down 'er bodice quick as lightning afore the young ladies come in for their breakfast.'

'She's a sly one. Never let on she 'ad a beau, and so prim and proper, you'd think butter wouldn't melt in 'er mouth.'

'It's the sly ones what snare a man into the marriage bed, my girl, and don't you forget it!' the second footman observed, quietly.

The second housemaid had been tilting her cap at the good-looking young footman for some time past. Had she been too brazen? She had often been reprimanded by her superiors for cheekiness and a quick temper. Well, if George didn't fall for her some other chap would. Opportunity was a fine thing. Visiting guests brought their servants. Valets and grooms as well as ladies' maids had their meals in the servants' hall. She listened avidly to their gossip, especially the London contingent, for London was the Mecca of her day-dreams, and they all knew she was only waiting for a housemaid in Sir Neville's town house to get married to step into her shoes. Grosvenor Square would be much more to her liking. Marston Park was too isolated. All those acres of parkland, and the splendid trees so often admired from their attic bedrooms by visiting servants, would be gladly exchanged for a glimpse of Bond Street. But she joined in the general speculation on the nature of the letter the governess had tucked in her bosom.

'Likely as not it's the curate,' the parlourmaid suggested.

'That soppy 'apporth!' the cheeky housemaid retorted, shovelling sugar into her tea.

'You want to watch yourself, my girl, with that sugar bowl. Look at your figure,' the head groom cautioned.

'What's wrong with me figure?'

'Nothing, not as far as I'm concerned, duckie. A nice fat bum to smack. Just my cup of tea!'

They all yelled with laughter, knowing the groom's wife was as skinny as a beanpole, and nagged the life out of the poor man.

The speculation about the murder seemed to have dried up since the police investigation had not produced any fresh evidence, but the whole sordid episode would be revised at Christmas, for the benefit of visiting servants from Grosvenor Square. It was not often the country establishment could compete with the town house in matters of importance, but the murder had actually been committed on the estate, and all the male employees, indoors and outdoors, had been questioned by the Detective Inspector. Sir Neville had been much offended by all the publicity in the daily press, but the crime had not been solved, and the villagers were still being questioned.

74

The second footman was glancing sulkily at his superior, already pushing back his chair – the silly bastard. Ten minutes was allowed for elevenses, not nine-and-a-half. The butler was the boss, and had the last word on everything. The housekeeper's authority was limited to the female staff. The butler was subservient to Sir Neville, and the housekeeper to her Ladyship, so protocol was established. It was a small world, governed by the principles, politics and privileges of tradition. Generations of Franklins had inherited this undisputed kingdom. The Victorian era had slipped away, and the Edwardian would bring changes, but not at Marston Park. The old regime would continue for another thirteen years, when a devastating world war would topple the edifice of the landed gentry.

The letter was disappointingly brief and formal. It contained nothing that could be considered even mildly personal, and was signed, 'Yours Truly, Malcolm McKenzie'. Even so, it was read three times before it was locked away in the small drawer of the bureau. But she had an address – a hostel in Tottenham Court Road – to which she could reply. It was a difficult letter to pen, because she had to conceal her real feelings, and because the days had passed slowly and uneventfully since the Harvest Festival, and there was little of interest to relate. After three attempts, she was reasonably satisfied, and the torn fragments of the early attempts were tossed into the fire. Housemaids invariably sorted out the contents of the waste paper baskets. The tone of the letter matched the one she had received with one small exception. It was signed, 'Your sincere Friend'.

After she had dropped it in the letter box at the lodge gates on the afternoon walk with her pupils, the governess began to count the days; she could expect to receive a reply for she had enclosed a donation of half a sovereign towards the funds of the Missionary Society – a sum she could ill afford on her meagre salary. A governess's board and lodging were taken into consideration, so it was quite a pittance. This particular Missionary Society was one of several charities the church supported, and for which her sister Irene and the ladies of the working party laboured so conscientiously on such impractical garments. The young missionary had made discreet suggestions, however, on that eventful Sunday, and now the ladies were busily stitching gaily coloured frocks for the girls of the mission school.

It had been a last-minute decision to enclose a donation, and Marion was congratulating herself on her cleverness. Now he *must* write again, if only to acknowledge the gift.

A week or so later, the second letter was duly reported in the servants' hall.

'And it ain't the curate. It were a London postmark.' The young housemaid was proud of her deductions.

'London? Then I'll bet you a tanner it's that valet of Lord Percy Edwards who was down here for that last house party. I saw him in the stable yard on more than one occasion talking to the young ladies when I was saddling up their ponies, and she was there,' the head groom recalled with much satisfaction.

'That don't prove nothing,' argued the parlourmaid.

'Ah, but you didn't see the way he looked at her.'

'What sort of look?'

'A come-hither look.'

'She wouldn't take no notice, not her.'

'That's what *you* think. With those eyes, I reckon she could be quite a gal if she let herself go.'

'What's so special about her eyes?' the cheeky housemaid demanded.

'You take a good look at her sometime. You'll be surprised.'

'Well, if it's the valet, we can ask 'im straight out if 'e's fallen for'er. Every man Jack of 'em will be down 'ere again for the Christmas and New Year 'ouse party.' The groom shook his head. 'Why not?'

'Because it's not polite, and likely as not he would tell us to mind our own business.'

'I'll let yer know when she 'as another letter – if she do 'ave another letter.' The schoolroom housemaid had the last word.

But no further letters arrived, and the correspondence appeared to have ceased after that second letter. The governess could not hide her disappointment, and her furtive glances at the breakfast table did not escape the maid's watchful eyes.

'She's looking proper poorly, if you arsk me,' she reported.

'Nobody's asking you, my girl,' the head groom answered with surly disinterest. His wife was making life a hell, and there was no escape from her nagging tongue.

The long walk home on her free Sunday in the November mist only added to Marion's dejection. The curate would probably be the only guest for Sunday lunch at The Parsonage. November was a dull month, unless you happened to be a middle-class housewife, or a cook in one of the vast basement kitchens of the gentry's establishments, when you would be busy with Christmas puddings and cakes. By Christmas Malcolm would be on his way back to his African mission. She liked to think of him now as Malcolm. To remember him as Mr McKenzie was so formal; the name did not

77

match the sweet recollection of his nearness during that memorable hour at the Harvest Festival. She had not been mistaken, she told herself convincingly, as she trudged along the winding country lanes. They had shared a spiritual experience, a communion of souls, as uplifting as the soaring volume of the harvest hymns. In every sensitive nerve, every racing pulse, she had felt the exaltation of a shared intimacy. She had *not* been mistaken. How many times had she repeated this assurance since that moment when she found herself alone in the stable yard, with nothing more than a promise to write, and the clip-clop of the mare's hooves on the cobbles? He had kept his promise.

She had actually smiled at the maid as she tucked the second letter into her bodice. For the second time, in the privacy of her room, she searched in vain for some mention of that wonderful experience they had shared, but it was not there. His enthusiasm for the two new recruits he was taking out to the mission was genuine enough. Teacher-missionaries from the same Theological College, they would make his job less arduous. All three were taking a compulsory course in the treatment and cure of tropical diseases. In the five years that Malcolm McKenzie had been abroad, hospital laboratories had been working on new techniques. All three were dedicated Christians, and Marion was no stranger to such dedication. Yet, being a woman, the ethics were not enough. Her emotions and her sensibilities were involved.

She had wept with disappointment over that second letter. Reading between the lines she had found nothing but blank spaces, not the slightest indication that he remembered her as she remembered him, with a deep and lasting affection. She knew his strong character had been formed in the Spartan environment of a working-class family, that his stubborn Scots pride was something formidable. She had caught a glimpse of it in the pony trap, that Sunday evening, when they drove in silence into Marston Park. She could not speak first. It was wholly and completely improper. But if he did not open his heart before he returned to Africa, how could she bear to go on living? She would sooner die.

'You have hardly touched your meat, dear; such a waste,' the parson's wife reproved her daughter, as the plates were cleared away.

'I'm sorry, Mother. I'm not hungry.'

'That long walk from Marston Park should have given you an appetite, Miss Marion,' the curate simpered.

She found his presence even more irritating than usual today. Why should a bachelor curate expect to be entertained to lunch every Sunday at The Parsonage? He was such an insufferable bore. Cook's apple pie was delicious, and the pastry usually melted in the mouth, but not today.

'A little more cream, dear?' Her mother passed the jug across the table. It was easier to accept than to refuse. Dear Mother! Her recipe for a broken heart would be found in the kitchen.

With an effort at self-control, Marion forced herself to finish the generous helping of pie on her plate. It was the delicate sister, Irene, who had always been served with small helpings. Cecily and Marion were expected to have good appetites. Irene's delicacy had been resented in the nursery, when her healthy sisters had been compelled to eat up their cabbage, and were purged with a weekly dose of senna, while Irene was served with a little dish of buttered spinach – and only a mild laxative on Saturday night.

79

But Parson's sympathetic glance had not missed the lassitude, or the dark circles that shadowed his daughter's eyes. In the past month she had lost weight, and when he embraced her affectionately on arrival, her slight form seemed almost as frail as Irene's. This would never do. Consumption in his own family had killed his two sisters in their early twenties, and Irene was already doomed. He had no fear of Cecily, who was every inch her mother's daughter. It was Marion, with her highly-strung temperament and sensitivity, who might succumb to this fatal malady, unless her present environment could be changed. That she was unhappy in her post was all too evident, and the curb she kept on her natural feelings at Marston Park was taking its toll. She wept more easily, and her temper was short. Only in her own home, and the privacy of her bedroom at Marston Park could she allow herself the emotional indulgence that most young women of her class enjoyed. His heart ached for her on their Sunday afternoon walk, when the grip on his arm tightened at the question, 'What's troubling you, my child?'

'Nothing, Father,' she lied bravely.

'Come now, we have no secrets from each other, you and I,' he coaxed gently.

The familiar landscape that he loved so well was as beautiful in late Autumn as in the early Spring. When the sun broke through the mist, the valley was bathed in a mellow radiance. Stripped hop-gardens and orchards blended with the furrowed fields. Naked branches stood sentinel in the spreading acres of Marston Park. A dog parked in the farmyard at Russets, and the shrill voices of children echoed in the woods bordering the lane. His daughter had walked that way this morning, and must return by that way

80

after an early tea. Cecily would drive her in the trap. His eldest daughter had strong nerves, and no fear of the long stretches of country lanes between the village and the Park. With a lantern fixed to the front of the trap, she made her way to prayer and Mothers' Union meetings, and other parochial engagements in all kinds of weather. The murder of the young school teacher had left no mark on her, but Marion was still haunted by the memory, and avoided the lakeside area of the Park when out walking with her pupils.

Under the brim of her Sunday-best bonnet, her pallid cheek was wet with tears.

'My dearest, tell me,' he entreated, and wrapped his cloak about her, as though she were a child again.

Her voice was strangled, her face buried in his shoulder. 'I love him, Father! I love him!'

'Who is it that you love?'

'Mr McKenzie.'

'Mr McKenzie?' he echoed, 'the young missionary?'

'Yes.'

'But you hardly know him. You have met but once. How is that possible?'

'My heart has its own reasons for loving him,' she whispered.

He was stunned, and totally unprepared for such a confession. He had assumed that her position at Marston Park was becoming more intolerable. There was no place for a governess outside the jurisdiction of the schoolroom. Both the drawing-room and the servants' hall were barred to a young woman who had no proper status in the house. He took her shoulders in a firm grip and her arms dropped limply from their stranglehold about his neck. They faced each other for the first time with the knowledge that another personality was dividing them.

'Has he written?' the father asked quietly.

'Yes, twice,' the daughter answered.

'And?'

She shook her head.

'You answered his letters?'

'Yes, Father.'

'My dear child, it is too soon, too sudden. How can you trust your feelings after such a short acquaintance? I couldn't bear you to get hurt.'

'I have never been more certain of anything in my whole life.'

'Then you must write and tell him.'

'Father! For *you* to suggest *that*! He will think I have no pride.'

'And have you?' he teased her gently.

Her lovely eyes flooded with tears again, and he handed her a clean white handkerchief.

'Dry your eyes. We will turn back, and you shall write the letter in my study. There is time enough to catch the afternoon collection from the letter-box in the village.'

Her step was lighter on the homeward way, but his heart was heavy with the inevitability of separation.

'There's a telegram for you, Miss,' the young housemaid said, straightening a spoon on the breakfast table. 'I 'ope as 'ow it ain't bad news, Miss?' she added, anxiously.

With a trembling hand, her cheeks ashen, the governess took up the envelope and stared at the address. Until this moment, she had never actually received a telegram personally, but there was something about the postmaster's neat script on the envelope that spelled a grim foreboding of death and disaster. Even the strongest heart would quell and hesitate to read the message contained therein.

But on this particular occasion, it was neither death nor disaster, and the housemaid, expecting the governess to faint, was surprised to see her smiling. The message was brief, but conveyed an extraordinary amount of hope: 'ARRIVING FAIRFIELDS STATION NINE THIRTY SUNDAY MORNING. REGARDS, MALCOLM MCKENZIE.''

'Is it good news, Miss?'

Starry-eyed the governess nodded. Tremulously she spoke. 'Splendid news, thank you, Ellen.'

'I'm ever so glad for you, Miss, for you ain't been looking at all well lately. We all 'as noticed it. Mrs Osborne was saying only last night at supper that it were time you 'ad a 'oliday, Miss, for the young ladies was taxing your strength.'

Marion laughed, surprised and delighted to discover her health had been discussed in the servants' hall. 'How kind of Mrs Osborne, and all of you, to be so concerned, but I do assure you I am in the best of health. One usually feels a little tired at this season of the year. There is something rather depressing about the Autumn, don't you think so, Ellen?' It was not true, of course. She loved the Autumn. It was her favourite season.

'To tell you the truth, Miss, it don't make no difference. One season is as good as another. Mind yew, there's somethink to be said for the Summer, an' feeling warm all over, an' giving yerself a proper wash of a morning, without 'aving ter break the ice on the water jug. Won't be long now, Miss. Get Christmas over, an' all them jugs will be froze,' she stated, cheerfully.

'How wretched for you, Ellen. Couldn't something be done about fetching cans of hot water from the kitchen?'

'Not for us servants, Miss. Not with all them back

83

stairs. We get enough of carrying them cans of 'ot water all round the 'ouse. What with all the bedrooms, an' the nursery, the butler an' the 'ousekeeper.'

'And me, Ellen.'

'Nn' you, Miss. We don't really mind, an' I'm not complainin'. It's our job, ain't it, like it's your job to teach the young ladies?'

Marion agreed. But why had she never given it a thought? Attic bedrooms must be miserably cold in the Winter, and uncomfortably hot in the Summer. The Parsonage's attic would be no exception. Annie had chilblains every Winter, but she did fetch cans of hot water from the kitchen for herself and Cook. With hip baths in all the bedrooms at Marston Park, what a major operation for the servants. Why had she not noticed until this moment that Ellen had such pretty hair? The nut-brown curls almost pushed off her starched cap.

'How do you manage to keep your cap on your head, Ellen, with all those curls?' she asked.

Ellen giggled. 'I gets told orf, Miss, often enough, by Mrs Osborne. I got it fastened with a couple of 'air-pins, but it don't stay straight, not for long it don't.'

Marion smiled as she tucked the telegram into her bodice. 'How old are you, Ellen?'

'Fourteen, Miss.'

Fourteen. Still a child in years, but already matured, and no doubt proud of those little pointed breasts.

'Have you got a sweetheart, Ellen?'

'Oh, yes, Miss. Me an' Sam Wallace 'as been walking out since Michaelmas.'

'Sam Wallace?'

'The undergroom, Miss.'

'Indeed?'

'Me and Sam took a fancy to one another all of a

sudden like. I were 'anging me dusters out to dry in the stable yard when I see'd young Sam a-staring at me like I was a stranger. Never said a word, jus' stood there, staring. "Seen all you want to see, Sam Wallace?" I says, cheeky like. "Aye, that I 've. I see'd you been an' growed up, Ellen Perkins," 'e says, an' goes all red in the face! Next thing I knowed, Sam 'ad 'is arm round me waist, an' was giving me a peck.' She giggled happily at the memory. '"Give over, Sam Wallace," I says, 'aughty like. "If Mrs Osborne was ter see us, I wouldn't 'arf get a dressing down." "Bugger Mrs Osborne," 'e says. Would you believe it, Miss? You could 'ave knocked me down with a feather.'

Pushing a stray curl under her cap, she concluded, artlessly, 'It's like I said, Miss, we took a fancy to one another. 'Scuse me, Miss. I gotta fly, but it's been ever so nice 'aving a little chat.'

With a darting plunge for the door handle, and a swish of a starched apron, she was gone. And the governess stood there, savouring the child's simplicity – 'Me an' Sam took a fancy to each other all of a sudden like.'

'Oh, Malcolm, Malcolm! Wasn't it so with us, my dear?' she breathed ecstatically.

It was not her free Sunday and most inconsiderate, Her Ladyship insisted, petulantly. The girls could accompany their father to church in the carriage. That was no problem. But they were not yet of an age to join him and his weekend guests for lunch. As for the afternoon walk, what did Miss Wellington propose since her daughters must be chaperoned?

Marion listened politely to Her Ladyship, but refused to be dissuaded.

Enjoying her role of semi-invalid, marital relations with His Lordship had been discarded. She had done

85

her duty, and it was not her fault that she had borne four daughters when her husband desperately wanted a son and heir. A virile, domineering husband, she had submitted to his demands because she had no choice. Each pregnancy had been endured with gloomy foreboding, and she was convinced she would die during childbirth. Nobody had ever suffered such terrible pangs. She was weak and ill for weeks after each child was delivered by the family physician. The selfishness of men was altogether astonishing. It was said, and probably rightly so, that if roles were reversed, and the male, not the female, bore the children, the world's population would be reduced to a minimum!

'Excuse me, my lady,' her personal maid interrupted, while her children's governess stood waiting. 'If you can spare me for an hour on Sunday, I will gladly escort the young ladies on their afternoon walk.'

'Very well, Simmonds,' sighed Her Ladyship.

'Thank you.' Marion smiled gratefully at the elderly maid who had spent most of her working life in attendance on her exacting mistress, but made no secret of the fact she worshipped the ground Her Ladyship walked upon.

With a light-hearted step the governess rejoined her pupils in the schoolroom, and found them bent diligently over the task she had set them. Elementary French had recently been introduced into their normal curriculum. Quite possibly they would not get beyond the elementary stage, but that at least was expected. Only two more days. Her thoughts had wings, and her plans had a daring originality. She would ask the head groom to drive her to the station in the trap. It was too far to walk, and the weather unsettled. Since Ellen had disclosed that her health had been discussed in the servants' hall, it was much easier to ask a favour, and half-a-crown would suffice for a tip. She blamed herself for the barrier that had existed between governess and servants, and her friendly smile had not passed unnoticed in the past two days.

Still blushing at every reminder of the letter she had written and posted, it now seemed, in retrospect, quite outrageously unladylike. Father had been deeply shocked but sympathetic. She could trust him to keep a secret. They had shared so many secrets of a lesser nature in the past, and he alone knew of her unhappiness at Marston Park. After she had penned the letter to Mr McKenzie, they had discussed the possibility of giving up the post and the consequences.

'Will Sir Neville be annoyed, Father? Will it make your own position more difficult?' she had asked, anxiously.

'I don't think so, my dear. He could hardly ask me to resign because my daughter asks to be relieved of her post as governess to his children.'

'You never know what he may decide. He is a very forthright person, and quite frightening in one of his rages. The children keep out of his way as far as possible. He is so inconsistent. Sometimes he will ignore their existence for days on end, then suddenly burst into the schoolroom and hand out half-crowns and kisses with fatherly indulgence. He is not to be trusted. That I do know, and I am sorry for Her Ladyship. An unfaithful husband must be so very unsatisfactory.'

'You have been listening to the servants' gossip.'

'It's common knowledge, Father.'

'So it may be, but that is no reason to repeat it. Sir Neville is a law unto himself.'

'But *why*?'

'Because he was born into the ruling class.'

'But it's so unfair. And you preach humility to the working class?'

'I am very conscious of hypocrisy, my child.'

'I'm sorry, Father. That was unforgivable.' She clung to him, kissing his furrowed brow.

'Had you been a more dutiful daughter, content with her lot, there would be no problem and no risk. I have two dutiful daughters, but a father's heart is not concerned with duty, only love. Now, off you go to post that letter. I can hear Annie busy with the tea trolley, and your mother does not care to be kept waiting.'

'Yes, Father.' Marion hurried off out of the room, donned the cloak and bonnet that hung in the cloakroom, and went on her way. Watching the youthful figure from the study window, Parson Wellington was aware of an aching sense of desolation he had neither expected nor deserved.

'Shall I wait, Miss?' asked the groom, when he had helped the governess from the trap.

'No thank you, Peters. That is not necessary.'

'Supposing your friend don't come on this train, you would have an hour to wait for the next?'

'He *will* come!'

'Very good, Miss.'

'Goodbye, Peters, and thank you.'

'It's been a pleasure, Miss.'

Smiling and blushing, she slipped the half-crown into his hand. He touched his cap respectfully, and went on his way.

How very kind they all had been in the past few days, she told herself. Even if she had wished to keep this meeting a secret it would have been impossible, with young Ellen gossiping in the servants' hall. But now she was alone to face what could only be called an ordeal.

The assurance she had known, and the strong conviction that she had not been mistaken in that mutual recognition of a kindred spirit, was dwindling – and she was afraid. No other passengers had yet arrived, and she supposed few people travelled on this branch line on Sunday. Churches and Chapels would be filled with well-dressed citizens. 'Six days shalt thou labour, but the seventh day is the Sabbath'. Yet servants still laboured in the service of their masters and mistresses on the Sabbath. It was taken for granted that cans of hot water would be delivered, fires lit, meals served, beds made, and slops emptied, seven days a week. She herself had taken it for granted until she became involved in the actual process of service at Marston Park. One free Sunday a month, and the servants had to take turns, so that the family were not even aware of the slightest inconvenience. It was a kind of slavery, yet, on the whole, they were happy and contented slaves. Only a small minority rebelled against the archaic system, and their rebellious tendencies were not allowed to interfere with the loyalty of the majority. Adventurous sons were packed off to Canada or Australia, or joined the Army. Discontented daughters married discontented sons, and they emigrated together to the Colonies, discovered they were homesick, and had to work harder for a living. Then invariably raised their families to respect the old traditions of the Mother Country!

A small girl, of 7 or 8 years, was causing a welcome diversion on the down platform. Her father, the stationmaster, was probably busy in the office, and the mother had taken her eyes off the child for a few moments. She was trotting purposefully towards the level crossing, waving her arms excitedly. Marion hurried along the platform, down the ramp, scooped up the child and carried her to the safety of the up platform with only seconds to spare before the train whistled round the bend.

Malcolm McKenzie, whose thoughts had been in a turmoil, and his mind distracted from his Christian endeavours, had been wishing himself back in the Congo, where such impetuous young women would not be encountered. Leaning from the window of the empty carriage, expecting to see Miss Wellington standing, all of a flutter, on the platform, he beheld her kneeling, with her arms enfolding a little girl, and her whole attention focussed on the child. This was quite extraordinary. Surely she hadn't brought the child from Marston Park? What would they do with her all day? He was even more surprised as the train ground to a halt and they both lifted their heads, to discover the child was an idiot. His heart contracted painfully as he set foot on the platform.

Marion Wellington was smiling, as though to be caught hugging such an unattractive child was the most natural thing in the world.

'Good morning, Mr McKenzie,' she said, without a trace of embarrassment.

'Good morning, Miss Wellington,' he answered, hardly knowing whether to be relieved or annoyed by this unexpected diversion.

Then a frantic mother came flying down the platform, picked up the child, breathed her thanks, and bore her away, babbling incoherently, struggling to be free.

'Poor wee bairn,' Malcolm McKenzie murmured sympathetically.

When they had disappeared, the man and the woman turned to face one another with a frankness that could not have been achieved without that diversion.

Gripping her shoulders, the man spoke, but it was not what she had expected him to say.

'Can ye no see this is madness, woman?' he demanded, sternly.

She shook her head, her eyes brimming with tears. Then she was in his arms, and the train thundered past.

It was a day to be remembered for all time – a day when grey skies were seen as a heavenly blue, and the chilling wind nothing more than a Summer breeze. The steep hill they climbed from the station, arm-in-arm, to the village, was no more exhausting than a gentle slope. The bells of All Saints rang out a clarion summons across the fields.

'Just time to call in at The Parsonage for a cup of coffee,' Marion decided. For of course they were going to Matins.

They still had to face opposition from their families. They still had to persuade Marion's father to call the banns for three Sundays, or they could not be married before they sailed in December. Marion must buy suitable clothes for the tropics, but only the barest necessities, since they were poor, and would always be poor. And Malcolm was not the only person to ask why Marion could not have prevented such madness. Why, indeed? Never had she known such happiness, or such an abundance of love. The love of a child for a parent, a daughter for a father, was beautiful, but not to be compared with the love of a man for a woman, or a woman for a man, Marion reflected. If spiritual love was so very satisfactory, surely she need have no fears that physical love would be equally compatible? Sex was a word that had never passed her lips at The Parsonage, and the facts of life had not been included in the curriculum of their own governess. Nature walks had not revealed anything more startling than the 'birds and the bees'. Kittens and puppies arrived overnight, and were welcomed rapturously by the three little girls. The mystery of Birth was still a mystery. The one Book with which they were most familiar since infancy – the Bible – had produced no evidence of the actual process of creativity. 'God made man in His own image'. That was plain enough, since God had already created the Universe. 'Then God took a rib from the man and made him a woman'. That was quite inexplicable. How did Adam manage without that rib? And why didn't God create Eve in the same way that He created Adam?

Marion's own curiosity in adolescence had been insatiable, and Father had done his best to answer all her questions, but had baulked at the mystery of Birth. The governess could tell you how a diamond was cut, or explain the working of the tin mines in Cornwall. She was quite an authority on the populations of India and China, could identify a number of stars through the telescope, and could add up a column of figures quickly and accurately. This was called in plain language 'General Knowledge', and text books provided such knowledge. On the question of human productivity, however, and the relationship between a man and a woman, the mind of the governess had revealed a most regrettable blankness. (Thank heavens her own pupils at Marston Park were either too young or too stupid to ask the kind of questions she had asked!)

Sensuality had been a negative experience until her lips had responded to Malcolm's first kiss, when her whole body had trembled in ecstasy. He was so thin, and she was amazed at the strength in his arms, and the hardness of his ill-clad body. Surely he could be wearing very little in the nature of underwear? She could feel his ribs under that threadbare tweed suit.

Her response had been instinctive, not questioning the right to kiss a man on their second meeting, as though they were already lovers. Some magnetic force had drawn them together on the station platform, and he had called her 'Woman'. Never had the word been so symbolic. Hitherto she had been called a 'young lady'. Women were working class. The upper classes bred only 'ladies'. So the whole nature of things had been turned inside out by a single word. So much had been conveyed in that single word – amusement, tolerance, endearment. His Scottish vocabulary and pronunciation had already surprised and delighted her. Neither her vivid imagination nor her sweet day-dreams had prepared her for the moment when she found such pleasure in being called 'Woman'. It was altogether original and charming!

'I had a mind to bring you a wee present, Marion, but there was no enough time,' he explained, as they climbed the hill.

'You brought yourself, Malcolm. That was all I was hoping for and praying for,' she assured him.

'You prayed?'

'Yes. Did you pray?'

'Aye.'

They exchanged a meaningful glance. Then he dropped her arm and took her hand in a firm clasp. With their fingers entwined, and a tingling sensation of close contact, they breasted the hill and started up the High Street. A group of children ran through the school gate as they passed.

'Good morning, Miss!' they called to her in their shrill young voices.

Once upon a time, before she had been offered the post of governess at Marston Park, she had taken a Sunday School class, and the children remembered her.

'Good morning, children,' she called back, and Malcolm raised a hand in greeting.

They stared at the stranger, then Millie Styles nudged her bosom friend. 'Miss 'as got 'erself a sweet'eart, Rube, but 'e don't look much of a catch, do'e?'

Ruby giggled. 'Our Mums won't arf be surprised when we tells 'em we saw Miss Marion a-walkin' up the 'igh Street, 'and-in-'and wiv a MAN!'

They were still hand-in-hand when Malcolm pushed open the garden gate and they walked slowly across the stable yard. Cook lifted her eyes from the pastry she was rolling on the kitchen table, and Annie nearly dropped the pot of coffee.

'Well, I never did!' breathed Cook, heavily. 'Jew see what I see, Annie?'

'Looks like they be courting.'

'What's Parson going to say – and the Mistress?'

'Dunno.'

'Well, don't say nothing. We shall know soon enough, for she looks that pleased with 'erself.'

When the door was pushed open and the young couple walked in, the two old servants stood stockstill, shocked into unaccustomed silence.

'Good morning, Cook! Good morning, Annie! This is Mr McKenzie. We are going to be married!'

'Married? Oh, *no*, Miss!' Annie protested.

'Oh, *yes*, Annie!' Marion giggled.

'You'll be the death of me, Miss Marion,' said Cook, with a sigh of resignation.

'Aye, and me too, I shouldna wonder!' The young man was smiling at his betrothed. Then he stretched out his hand in a friendly gesture, and Cook hastily wiped her hands on her apron, and Annie put down the coffee pot.

94

'It's a pleasure to meet you both,' said he.

'Pleased to meet *you*, Sir,' Annie echoed Cook's sentiments. She had liked the look of the young man on his first visit a month ago, and saw no reason to change her mind. Miss Marion was looking real bonny, and it would be nice to have a wedding in the family. Miss Cecily wasn't the marrying kind, and poor Miss Irene too delicate to think of marriage.

'If that's another apple pie on the way, I canna wait to sample it, for I mind how good it was the last time. My own mother couldna bake a better tart,' the young man was saying.

Cook flushed, for nothing pleased her more than to be told her baking was appreciated. 'Thank you, Sir, so you'll be staying to lunch?'

'Aye, and to tea, if it's no putting you out?'

'Not at all, Sir. We likes 'aving visitors, me an' Annie. It makes a nice change.'

'Come along, Malcolm,' Marion interrupted. 'We mustn't keep the family waiting. I saw Cecily at the drawing-room window as we came through the gate.'

Malcolm opened the door and she led the way, while he followed, carrying the tray, with Annie close on his heels. She had added another cup and saucer to the tray, and was looking flustered. It was kind of Mr McKenzie, but it was not his place. A *proper* gentleman, that is to say, born and bred in the upper class, would never make such a mistake. She followed them to the drawing-room to serve the coffee, more than a little concerned about the suitability of such a match. Class was class, when all's said and done. It was rammed down their throats at Day School, and Sunday School teachers made certain they didn't forget their place with one particular hymn all the children had learned by heart:

The rich man in his castle,
The poor man at his gate,
God made them high or lowly,
And ordered their estate.

And as if that wasn't enough, being in service was a constant reminder: 'Yes, Sir; No, Madam' from morn till night. Annie wasn't complaining; she and Cook were well treated. They didn't go short of grub, and they wasn't shouted at, not like some servants. Working class they was born and bred, and they would stay working class to the end of their days.

While she poured the coffee and handed round, Miss Marion was greeting her father and mother and her two sisters, but she kept a tight hold on Mr McKenzie so that he was obliged to shake hands with each person in turn, after his young lady had finished kissing. Annie was deeply shocked. No well brought up young lady should behave in such a bold manner. It was *common*. It was working class. Why couldn't she have waited to break the news when they came back from church? Parson seemed to be expecting it, but Madam was annoyed.

'You have all met Mr McKenzie, haven't you? We are going to be married!'

A dead silence followed the bold announcement, and the poor young man was obviously embarrassed. Annie could hardly wait to get back to the kitchen to tell Cook and Peg-leg how the news was received.

'You must be mad, the pair of you!' Cecily exploded, and marched out of the room, leaving her coffee untouched. Nobody seemed to notice the servant still hovering in the window recess, holding her breath at a scene she had never expected to witness at The Parsonage.

'I think I agree with Cecily,' her mother was saying.

96

'It's – it's quite preposterous!' she added, and looked to her husband for confirmation.

'My dear, they are no longer children. They are old enough to know their own minds. But I could have wished that Marion could have broken it more gently to you and to her sisters.'

'Then you knew?'

'I was expecting it.'

'Of course. I might have known you would be the first to hear of it!' she bristled. 'Haven't you always taken her part in all her naughtiness and disobedience? Haven't you pleaded with me time and time again not to use my little birch? Didn't I know you were making a rod for your own back with all the spoiling?'

'My dear, *please*,' remonstrated Parson gently.

'I think it is *most* romantic!' Irene interrupted, her cheeks flushed with excitement. 'Come here, Mr McKenzie, I wish to congratulate you!'

It broke the tension when he dropped Marion's hand and walked to the couch.

'I am allowed to kiss my future brother-in-law, am I not?' she asked, provocatively.

'I hoped ye would approve, Miss Irene,' he said, as she kissed his cheek. If there was envy in her heart, she gave no sign of it. She knew her days were numbered, and when they went away, she would never see them again. She also knew that she had an ardent admirer in Andrew Robinson, the schoolmaster, for he had made no secret of the fact.

'Isn't she sweet?' Marion demanded, giving her sister a hug.

'Aye,' he agreed, too moved to say more.

'Are you ready, Mother? Peg-leg is waiting with the trap,' Cecily announced from the doorway.

The short drive to the church, in a strained silence,

97

would soon be over, Marion reflected. She could see the two figures striding across the field to the West Gate. Only a month ago, the shorter of the two, with his narrow shoulders and wind-swept hair, was a stranger. Today he was her own dear beloved. The banns would be called for the first time. Father had promised it in a hurried whisper as they left the house. Dear Father! It would be thrilling to hear their names linked together in public and to see heads turned in their direction. Sir Neville and Her Ladyship were too well bred to turn their heads, and her young pupils would not dare. Tomorrow, with all its repercussions, had to be faced, but she was not afraid. One month's notice was legally required, and she knew already that she would not be released until every hour of every day of that final month as a governess had been worked. There would be no time allowed for shopping in Tunbridge Wells, but the village dressmaker would make her simple trousseau if she sent her measurements. Bingham's would send patterns of suitable materials.

Her thoughts had wings as she followed her mother and sisters down the aisle, with Malcolm only a couple of paces behind. His firm step on the tiled floor was most reassuring. Wrapped so securely in her own happiness, she failed to notice the smile that her sister Irene exchanged with the schoolmaster. If Irene thought it passed unnoticed, she was sadly mistaken, for her mother had been aware of it every Sunday morning for some weeks, and her heart ached for her sick daughter. Not for her the courtship of a fine upstanding man with intellectual tastes. His reputation was already established in the village. Not a breath of scandal had reached her ears – and with three unmarried women teachers it would not have taken much encouragement. From sheer mischief the children would delight in making fun of every word and gesture that passed between them. A third teacher had been engaged to replace poor Miss Mason. The crime was still unsolved, but the police were spreading their enquiries far afield, so it was rumoured. The village constable had become quite an important fellow since the murder. To be involved with Scotland Yard, even in the humblest capacity, had increased his prestige, and it required nothing more than a couple of pints of beer at The Three Nuns to loosen his tongue.

Parson's wife had much on her mind this Sunday morning. The shock of Marion's announcement, together with the realisation that her husband had known of their daughter's infatuation for the young missionary – for what else could it be called? – had left a bitter taste in the mouth. Even as a child, Marion had not confided in her. Surely a mother has a right to know what her children are thinking and planning? Father and daughter had always been close and secretive, but soon she would be lost to him for years, if not for ever. Though his heart ached with sadness, he would not turn to his wife for comfort, and there would be no pity for him in her own heart. For a parent to indulge one child more than another, unless that child was sick or handicapped, was wrong in the eyes of God, and this would be a just punishment.

Tight-lipped with disapproval, she regarded her youngest daughter's bold behaviour as disgraceful. Holding hands in public, loving glances over that shared hymn-book. And a smile of satisfaction when their banns were called for the first time! There would be the devil to pay over such a breach of etiquette with Sir Neville and Her Ladyship!

Cecily had been shocked beyond measure at such a

blatant disregard of good breeding. Her sense of duty and devoutness had been apparent from early childhood. Not a moment's anxiety with her eldest daughter, thank God. Now Irene was smiling at Marion and Mr McKenzie. Nothing would induce her to call her future son-in-law by his Christian name. It was naughty of Irene to encourage them, but her darling child was excused for she hadn't long in this world. To see Romance in such a ridiculous situation was typical of Irene, who kept a volume of poems on the table beside her couch, and was sensitive to every change of mood in those about her.

Parson's wife sighed as she regarded the tall, sparse figure of her husband in the pulpit, with mild affection. He preached such a dull sermon. Heads were nodding in the centre aisles, but she dare not allow herself such indulgence. She would never live it down.

One of the choirboys, hidden behind the high carved shape of the stall, was passing a sweet to his neighbour. His own cheek bulged. Naughty boy! She recognised the youngest of the three Blunt brothers from Russets – all three as alike as three peas in a pod.

The curate, who joined the family for lunch as usual, was somewhat reluctant to offer his congratulations to the happy couple since the family seemed to be divided on the issue. It was the parson's wife, not Parson, who had the last word on all domestic and family matters, so his loyalties were divided. A liaison with Miss Cecily was only a very remote possibility, and he would sooner remain a bachelor than risk marriage with a school-teacher or a tradesman's daughter; either would lower his prestige in the village.

Malcolm McKenzie listened to the curate's inane chatter with irritation, but kept his thoughts to himself. There had been quite enough controversy for one day, he decided, sensibly.

100

Marion was too excited to eat more than a morsel of the good roast beef and Yorkshire pudding, but her mother ignored the plate when it was removed from the table. Her obvious displeasure only added to the strained atmosphere, and it was a relief to get the meal over.

Parson had questioned his future son-in-law thoroughly as they walked to church together, and it was difficult, indeed almost impossible, to find any aspect of that far off mission attractive – the climate, the tropical diseases, the mosquitoes, the occasional hostile relations between the natives and the white men – of course Marion's father was anxious. He loved his daughter dearly.

The young couple had much to discuss on the afternoon walk, for they would not meet again until their wedding day. Malcolm would be travelling about the country with all the equipment for his illustrated talks, in church halls and village halls. Funds were urgently needed at the Mission, and he would not spare himself.

Drawing-room tea was enjoyed in a more relaxed atmosphere, with Marion and Malcolm serving the rest of the family from the tea trolley Annie had pushed in at 4 o'clock. Firelight and lamplight shed a warm glow over Parson's grey head, and Irene's flushed cheeks. Cecily and her mother, in high-backed chairs, made no further mention of 'Marion's madness'. The topic was avoided at Parson's request.

'Let us not lose our sense of family loyalty in this matter, my dear wife and daughter,' he pleaded earnestly. 'The time is short. We must send them on their way with our blessing, not our disapproval. God knows what the future holds for them. We can only commit them to His safe keeping.'

101

So they talked of parochial matters and the need to raise funds for the urgent repairs to the roof of All Saints. It was Parson's biggest problem, and the burden of responsibility was heavy. Donations were disappointingly small, and Sunday collections seldom reached his hopeful expectations. The indefatigable members of the Ladies' Guild worked tirelessly all the year to fill their stalls at the Christmas Sale of Work. Unfortunately, they lacked originality and imagination. Year after year, pin-cushions, hair-tidies, lavender bags, doyleys and antimacassars took pride of place on their stalls, and those unsold were carefully preserved and brought out again the following year. This urgent need to raise funds was a constant irritation to the upper classes who did not care to be reminded of their sacred duty.

A concert of local talent in the Village Hall from time to time would be patronised by a sprinkling of the upper classes, but the majority would purchase tickets and excuse themselves from attendance, or give the tickets to their servants. Working-class families packed the cheap seats for which they paid 2d., children half-price, and every entertainer was accorded a rousing storm of clapping and stamping. They all knew that Albert Blunt would oblige with a sturdy rendition of 'The Yeomen of England' followed by an encore, 'The Farmer's Boy', a universal favourite, Miss Letitia Langtry would be 'persuaded' to sing 'Cherry Ripe' and 'Early One Morning' in a quavering soprano, accompanied on the pianoforte by her sister, Victoria. Grocer had a fund of funny stories that never failed to amuse his uncritical audience. Ruby Simmons had a talent for reciting dramatic monologues. The members of the Ladies' Guild would act a little sketch. And Ruby's three boys had recently taught themselves a clog dance. Working at The Three Nuns, Ruby had managed to scrounge three pairs of baggy, worn-out trousers from the publican, and a few scraps of patchwork from the publican's wife. The patched trousers, together with the clogs, jerseys and caps, provided the authentic touch to their act, billed importantly, 'The Three Dutch Boys'. It takes courage to face an audience of familiar faces, and Ruby's boys had to drown the cat-calls from the back row, and suffer the jeers of their less talented school fellows the following day.

Ruby Simmons was never too busy to encourage her children, never too tired to help them. Now little Carrie was being coached in 'Little Miss Muffet' and 'Baa-baaa Black Sheep' in readiness for the next concert of local talent.

From all three classes of society, on that frosty Saturday in December, 1901, the parishioners poured in a steady stream to All Saints. Carriages and traps, normally seen only on Sunday morning and Christmas Day, were lined up tidily beyond the churchyard wall, while grooms and coachmen enjoyed a pint of beer in The Three Nuns. Even the tradesmen's wives and daughters, traditionally loyal to their Chapel, and the Misses Langtry, such devout Catholics, attended the wedding of Parson's youngest daughter. The rest of the congregation, mostly in petticoats, arrived on Shanks's pony, and many had walked for miles, from outlying farms and cottages. School children had been promised a rare treat in the shape of a magic lantern film show, followed by tea in the village hall after the ceremony.

They were ushered into their Sunday pews in the side aisle, wearing their Sunday best – the girls' button boots squeaking, the boys' hobnails clattering noisily on

103

the tiled floor. The choirboys, looking angelic in clean, starched surplices, had plastered their hair with water and scrubbed their faces. Each boy would recive a shilling, each choirman a florin, for their services. The source of the generous bounty was not disclosed. The tea was provided and served by the members of the Ladies' Guild who hovered on the fringe of the middle class because of their piety and devotion to Parson and All Saints. Flowers and pot plants supplied from the heated glasshouses of Marston Park decorated the chancel, the choir stalls, the font and the pulpit. The scent of Madonna lilies and white carnations had a drowsy effect on Marion, as she knelt to pledge her vows to Malcolm. She seemed to be moving in a dream, from which she would awaken with cruel suddenness, on the high seas.

A smart little Edwardian hat, in dove grey, to match the costume, had replaced the Victorian bonnet. She looked very young and starry-eyed when she walked down the aisle on the arm of Sir Neville, who had reacted in a surprisingly generous way over the inconvenience of losing his daughters' governess. It was all so unexpected, so heart-warming, with the packed church, the familiar, friendly faces, the choir, and the flowers.

Malcolm had no money to spare for a new suit, but Marion could not have been more proud of her bridegroom had he been attired in a frock coat and top hat. The hymn, 'Love Divine all Loves Excelling' moved her to tears, but they were quickly dried, and she walked back down the aisle on the arm of her husband with a proud dignity to the strains of 'The Wedding March'.

It was a day to remember with nostalgia during the hazards and hardships of the years ahead.

104

The moment of parting from her family and the old servants was poignant with sadness. For Irene it would be a long farewell, but they had been taught to accept Death, and whatever came in life, as but a step towards Eternal Life. Hugs and kisses were exchanged in the tearful acceptance of the thousands of miles that would separate them. 'Take good care of her, my son.' Parson's voice was choked with emotion.

'Aye. Ye can rest content, Sir. Marion will be safe with me,' he promised, earnestly.

Peg-leg was driving them to the station in the trap. A tin trunk and a leather portmanteau held all Marion's personal little treasures, and her clothes. They would stay overnight in a modest hotel in Bloomsbury, collect Malcolm's luggage from the Mission Headquarters, and travel by train to Liverpool. The following day, Christmas Eve, they would sail for Africa, and Marion would endure the twin miseries of homesickness and sea-sickness.

While Malcolm revelled in the wild waves, she lay on her bunk in an agony of doubt, weeping the anguished tears of every woman who follows her husband to the ends of the earth for the sake of love.

'Take hearrt, mae dearr woman. It canna last for everr!' Malcolm comforted.

Part II

Chapter Four

'Last Christmas we 'ad Miss Mason to 'elp us wiv these 'ere fiddling paper chains,' grumbled 11-year-old Hetty O'Brien, who would much prefer to be out with the boys gathering holly and ivy. The girls were always given the worst jobs. It weren't fair. Her brothers were not expected to make beds, empty slops, clean the privy, or mind the baby. The only girl to survive in that family, it fell to Hetty's lot, since her poor, overworked Mum had enough of scrubbing at the Blacksmith's Arms.

Back in the days of the great Queen Elizabeth, when horses were the only means of transport, there had been a forge in the near vicinity. The cobbled yard still bore traces of the stage coach, but the stables were empty. Gentlemen did not travel long distances on horseback in these enlightened days, but in comfortable Pullman coaches on the railway. Be that as it may, young Hetty O'Brien was not likely to travel on one of those noisy hissing monsters that clattered along the branch line through the Weald of Kent. Dad was a ganger, and they lived in Richmond Row which was railway property, but no free travel was accorded to families.

'I wish she were back, that I do. I liked Miss Mason. She weren't bitchy, not like our new teacher,' Hetty

109

sighed, and stuck a finger in the bowl of flour paste provided by the schoolmaster's housekeeper.

'She liked a bit o' fun, did Miss Mason, not like this new sourpuss!' volunteered Elsie Pearce. (It was noticed by teachers and parents that since her death Miss Mason had become a paragon of all the virtues.)

Hetty wiped her sticky fingers on her pinafore and reflected, 'I mind when Mister Dennis were picking 'ops in Miss Mason's bin, and she pretended not to notice 'e were giving 'er the glad eye. I see'd 'er blushing many a time, for we was picking next but one to 'er bin, me an' Danny, an' our Bert.'

'What did you say, Hetty?' Miss White interrupted. She had a sly habit of listening to the conversation of the older girls, and enjoyed a sensual pleasure in their superior knowledge of the facts of life. She had been waiting rather impatiently at her desk at the other end of the classroom to hang the chains when the girls had finished. Pretending to read a book, she was so quiet, the girls had forgotten she was there.

'What jew mean, Miss?' Hetty answered innocently.

'Kindly repeat what you said about Miss Mason and Mr Dennis.'

'It weren't nothing improper, Miss. Mister Dennis were just teasing. A rare one for teasing is Mister Dennis. But 'e were kind to us kids, Miss. Give us money to buy apples at the farm, 'e did, an' sweets when the cart came round the 'op gardens on Friday. Ever so kind 'e was, Miss.'

'I'm sure he was, Hetty. I am not questioning his *kindness*,' sneered Miss White – one of several prudish spinsters in the village who would have welcomed a little 'kindness' from the doctor's charming son.

'Yes, Miss,' Hetty agreed, mildly. You didn't contradict your betters. It was one of the earliest lessons they were taught.

110

'Bring me the chains that are finished, Hetty, and get on quickly with the remainder,' snapped Miss White.

Hetty obediently complied.

'Don't run away. I shall need your help with the step-ladder.'

'Very good, Miss.' Hetty pulled a wry face as the teacher climbed the ladder, and the girls smothered their giggles in their pinafores. Thick legs and ankles, thick woollen stockings, a skirt frayed at the hem, a patched boot, and a heavy bun of greasy hair – the back view was even less attractive than the front.

But Miss White was not thinking of Christmas decorations in the schoolroom and quite unaware of the girls' ridicule. She was thinking of Mr Dennis and Miss Mason. Why had every male in the village between the ages of 16 and 60, including her own father, been questioned by the police, yet nobody had mentioned this casual relationship between the school teacher and the doctor's son? If the children who picked hops in the home-pickers' set had noticed the playful antics of the young man, then surely their mothers would have noticed? Mr Dennis was back at the university when the body was found, miles away from the investigation.

Dismissing the girls with instructions to clean up the mess and return the bowl to the housekeeper, Miss White sat for some time on the step-ladder, pondering and planning the best move. It was not her wish to get directly involved, but she had only to mention her suspicions to her father, the postmaster, and he in turn would mention it to the postmen. Any exciting or tragic event circulated by the postmen would spread like a forest fire. A postman was generally regarded as the bearer of tidings, both good and bad, local, national and international. The master of the house in the upper classes would find his copy of *The Times* or the *Morning*

111

Post on the breakfast table, but a newspaper was a luxury few in the cottages could afford, and only a small minority of the older generation could read and write.

With sons and daughters overseas, the rare letters from Canada and Australia were eagerly awaited, and the postmen was never in a hurry, and always ready to oblige. By reading the letters aloud, he could share in the happiness and the hardships of the young emigrants from the old country. The postman was a friend to all three classes of society, and he often came back laden with gifts of fruit and vegetables. In the kitchens of the upper class he would be regaled with hot chocolate and hot buttered scones in the Winter months, and iced beer in the Summer. Christmas Day would see all the postmen reeling home in mid afternoon, as tipsy as Mike O'Brien on a Saturday night – and sick with the smell and taste of mincepies.

Miss White's vindictive nature would revel in the consequences of her suspicions. The constable's youngest sister had but recently been engaged as an apprentice in the post office. She was a bright child of 13, who kept her eyes and ears open. Climbing down from her perch on the ladder, Miss White cast a cursory glance over the sagging paper chains, took her coat, hat and goloshes from the cupboard, and hurried towards home. The constable's sister-in-law was parlourmaid at the doctor's residence, and a parlourmaid had easy access to her mistress. Such a snob, the doctor's wife, and so proud of her three handsome sons. The coming Christmas vacation would see the return of Dennis, eager as ever for some fresh diversion, and a harmless frolic with a pretty girl.

'Excuse me, Madam. Can I speak to you in private?' the parlourmaid asked respectfully one evening after dinner, a week before Christmas.

'What is it, Parsons? I am due at rehearsal in half-an-hour.' (The doctor's wife, a member of the local choral society, sang in the chorus, but saw herself as indispensable to the annual performance of 'The Messiah' at All Saints.)

'It won't take more than a minute or two, Madam.'

'Well?'

'It's about Mr Dennis.'

'What about Mr Dennis?'

'Well, it's like this, Madam. The police is still looking for the man what murdered that poor Miss Mason, and I did hear, sort of confidential like, they was going to question the young gentlemen what was away at the university when the body was found. That means Mr Dennis will be questioned, Madam, and I thought you ought to know.'

'It's kind of you to be so concerned about Mr Dennis, Parsons, but I am quite sure he will have no difficulty in explaining his movements during that period before he returned to the university. As for the school teacher, I doubt whether he has ever set eyes on the young woman.'

'Begging your pardon, Madam, but they do say Mr Dennis was picking hops in Miss Mason's bin at Monks Farm, and larking about with the young woman.'

'Who are *they*?'

'The school children and the mothers what was picking hops in the home-pickers' set. They do say Mr Dennis was giving the young woman the glad eye, Madam.'

'I am not surprised to hear it, Parsons. Mr Dennis has been giving the glad eye, as you call it, to the opposite sex, since he was at prep school. It's very naughty of him, but there it is. Young gentlemen have to sow their wild oats.'

113

'Yes, Madam. Then you don't think he ought to be warned?'

'Certainly not! My son is quite capable of attending to his own affairs.'

'Very good, Madam.' Parsons shrugged her thin shoulders and her mistress swept out of the dining-room. She had only done her duty, but she might as well have kept her mouth shut. Of course it was only natural the mistress would make excuses for her son, but she didn't know the half of what went on behind her back. It wasn't just flirting. There was that pretty little Dolly Kemp he got in the family way last Summer, and left her to face the consequences. Her Dad turned her out, and she had the baby at the Workhouse. Still there, so they said, the poor little devil. But there was something about Mr Dennis you couldn't help liking, and if she herself had been as attractive as that poor Miss Mason, then likely as not he would have been sneaking up the back stairs many a night. The mistress had taken the precaution, some years before, to engage only plain or elderly servants, and Mr Dennis looked elsewhere for his fun.

But Parsons was mistaken in thinking her mistress had taken the warning lightly. Dulcie Saunders was extremely worried. She was expecting Dennis on the 3.30 train tomorrow, and had already arranged with Doctor to borrow the trap. Roger and his wife were expected on Christmas Eve, and Lesley on Christmas Day. It was only once or twice a year that she enjoyed the pleasure of having her three sons all together.

It had never been necessary to worry Doctor over family and domestic matters, for he was a busy man, and she was a capable wife and mother. Her own small world revolved about her three sons, while her husband's world revolved about his practice and his patients. They

114

did not discuss it, and she was not concerned in the work to which he was so dedicated. They had nothing in common, and he hardly knew his sons. With a succession of young nursery maids, under the strict supervision of his wife, followed by preparatory school, public school and university, few upper-class parents had the opportunity to know their children intimately, and individually. Now it was too late.

The doctor wondered sometimes why he had married Dulcie, but then he reminded himself that she had not been afraid of childbirth, like so many of his upper-class patients, and had given him three sons. Sir Neville Franklin would probably have exchanged any one of his four daughters, none of whom had his dark good looks, for a son to inherit the vast estate as well as the London residence, a shooting lodge in Scotland, and a villa in the South of France.

'Is anything wrong my dear?' he enquired kindly, when he came upon his wife hesitating at the foot of the stairs. Dulcie was not a person to hesitate. She knew exactly what to do and where to go, *always*. She was a handsome woman, he thought, and the new Edwardian fashions suited her. Like so many of her class, she was copying the hair style and the elegance of the new Queen Alexandra. Edward, not yet crowned, but free at last of his mother's domination, was determined his reign should be different in every aspect from those sixty glorious years. He was not to know that his reign would be so short-lived, and his beautiful Alexandra left a widow in less than a decade. The Edwardian era would be remembered for its gaiety and elegance by the upper classes but, for the working class, the standards of living were practically unchanged during that extravagant decade. Wages would still be low, and working hours long and arduous. Indoor servants would still bob curtseys, and outdoor servants touch their forelocks respectfully. The widowed Queen would be photographed with her grandchildren, all dressed in white sailor suits, including the Princess Mary – and dogs, of course. Each new generation of royalty seemed to favour a different breed, it was noticed.

But Dulcie, who had recovered quickly from her slight hesitation, turned to smile and say, 'There is nothing wrong, thank you, dear,' and mounted the stairs. Her slim ankles did nothing to disturb the steady beat of his heart. Once upon a time he supposed he must have loved her, but that was a long time ago, before the birth of her eldest son, when she became, like so many of his patients, utterly maternal. They had not shared the marital bed for more than twenty years, and neither felt the need of sexual relations elsewhere.

Closing the door that cut off his private life from the public, the doctor strode purposefully down the corridor to await the first patient in his evening surgery. He had long since discovered how to close his mind on that private world as easily as he closed the door.

One of the really exciting moments in Dulcie Saunders' uneventful days, now that her boys were grown up young men, was the moment when one or the other stepped off the train. To-day, however, her joy in the occasion was marred by a premonition of trouble, and the nagging anxiety had kept her awake last night. So many memories were attached to this little country station. From here they had departed, in those early years, for their annual holiday at St Margaret's Bay. The doctor did not take a holiday, and she had not tried to persuade him to accompany his family to the seaside, even for one week of the month they were away. She just could not fit him into the picture. To have him playing on the beach with the boys, or sitting beside her in a deck

116

chair listening to the band after supper, was utterly improbable. They took the nursemaid in those early years, and the rest of the staff had to take turns with their own week's holiday because the Master had to be looked after, and the telephone manned. A doctor's house could never be closed, or his telephone left unattended.

When the surgery was closed, it was the parlourmaid's duty to take the calls and write each message carefully and distinctly on the pad provided on the hall table. The doctor answered the night bell personally, for it was switched through to the dressing-room where he slept. He was often called out in the night, and Dulcie slept on undisturbed.

One by one the boys had left home for public school, made their own friends, and their own arrangements for the holidays. They were not encouraged to bring their friends home.

As she waited for the train on this frosty day of December, she remembered that Lesley had been bored and lonely with only the nursemaid for company that last Summer at St Margaret's Bay. She remembered her own loneliness without the boys at an hotel in Worthing the following Summer, where she had spent two of the most miserable weeks in her whole life because she could not adjust to her new way of life, deprived of her children. Thereafter, she had spent her holidays with one or the other of her married sisters, but they had nothing in common, and it was more of a penance than a pleasure. She remembered now, as she watched the train coming round the bend, the anguished tears that had choked her throat when her schoolboy sons had departed, and they could not hide their eagerness to be gone. Their beaming faces would suddenly vanish in a cloud of smoke, and she would be left alone on the platform. She was probably the only mother from the upper class who

117

insisted on seeing her sons on the train, and suffering the pangs of desolation on that empty platform. Whether the boys would have preferred to take a cab and wave their mother farewell from the front entrance was not an issue. Mother had the last word, and this was understood.

When her handsome son stepped off the train as it jerked to a halt, all her fears were forgotten. He wore his clothes with careless abandon and his beaver hat at a rakish angle. The dear boy! The porter had hurried forward to carry the bulging portmanteau to the trap. Dennis was smiling. That smile of his would charm a bird off a bough – and he knew it!

'Hello, Mother!' he cried exuberantly, waving his hat.

'Hello, darling!'

Mother and son embraced as eagerly as two young sweethearts. There was no embarrassment with Dennis, no pecking at the cheek. Mouth to mouth and a warm hug.

'You are looking very beautiful today, Mother.' He had been saying it since his first vacation from public school, but it pleased her enormously. Roger would say, politely, 'You are looking very well, Mother,' after he had pecked her cheek. Lesley would mumble shyly, 'It's nice to see you, Mother.' She knew, or *thought* she knew, what to expect from them, but each in turn had cut the umbilical cord with a sense of relief. A possessive mother was a great strain on a filial relationship. They had asked each other if she would ever realise this fundamental truth.

When Dennis had tucked the rug carefully about his mother's knees, he climbed into the trap, seated himself on the opposite seat, and took up the reins.

'It's good to be back. It seemed a very long term, and I got very bored with it,' he lied, for she liked to be told he was happy to be back. Get Christmas Day over and he would break the news that he was joining a party of friends in the Bernese Oberland. He lied so glibly, he was hardly aware of lying. Lesley had often been punished for his brother's misdemeanours in childhood, but now the three brothers went their separate ways.

Dulcie Saunders loved all her sons equally, she would insist, but it was not true. This one, the naughty one, who was gazing at her with wide, innocent blue eyes, this one was her favourite – and he knew it!

The village children ran out of the school gates at the top of the hill, shouting and yelling, and frightened the mare, but Dennis soon had it under control. There was a kind of magic in those long, slender hands. A fretful mare or a frightened girl, he could calm them both. There was no evil in his mentality, only the need to satisfy his sensual appetite, and a weakness of character that was obvious only to those who knew him well. It would be unforgivable to spoil this precious half-hour of his homecoming with questions, his fond mother was thinking. She would wait until tea was served in the drawing-room. With a bright fire burning in the hearth, the red velvet curtains shutting out the darkened sky and not a soul expected to interrupt their delight in each other's company, this would be the time to ask that vital question. She had to know. Parsons had only been passing on village gossip, but even so, it had the bitter taste of scandal.

So when they were settled comfortably, with the tea trolley, and she had poured the tea from the gleaming silver teapot, she asked quietly, 'Darling, did you ever meet that school-teacher whose body was found near the lake in Marston Park?'

Dennis helped himself to hot buttered toast, spread with Gentlemen's Relish, and shook his head. 'Not to

119

my knowledge. Why do you ask? I thought the case was closed.'

'No, it's not closed.' She paused. Her mouth was dry, a pulse throbbed in her temple. She knew he was lying. Parsons would not invent such a story. Parsons was as honest as the day, and devoted to all her sons. 'The police will be questioning all the university students during the Christmas vacation, and other young men who happened to be away when the body was found – so I understand from a reliable source.'

'Really? How interesting. Our village bobby must be enjoying his new role as interrogator.'

'The constable is merely an underdog where crime is concerned. A Detective Inspector from Scotland Yard took over the case some weeks ago. A very astute man, so I understand.'

'Quite exciting, is it not? How soon should one expect to be questioned – before Christmas or after?'

'Any time, so I understand.'

Dennis shrugged and asked, 'Toast, Mother?'

'No thank you, darling. That's for you. Bread and butter please.' It was wafer thin, but even so, she choked, and covered her mouth with a dainty handkerchief. Her eyes were smarting with tears. 'Excuse me.' She was dabbing away at her eyes.

'Was it a crumb that went down the wrong way?' he teased.

She nodded.

'Do you remember that last nursemaid we had? What was her name? Carrie? Cissie? – Something beginning with C.'

'Connie.'

'Yes, that's it, Connie. A little fat dumpling of a girl with a lisp.'

'What about her?'

120

'That was one of her pet sayings in the nursery when I choked. "A crumb went down the wrong way, Master Dennis". I was a greedy little pig, and gobbled my food.'

'You did nothing of the kind! You all had beautiful table manners.'

'In the dining-room, perhaps, but not in the nursery. Will you cut me a slice of that chocolate cake, please, Mother. It looks delicious.'

'Cook made it specially.'

'Cook spoils me.'

'Everyone spoils you, darling.'

He smiled complacently, and stretched his long legs to the fire. How cleverly he had skirted round that vital question.

'Aren't you having cake? It really is delicious.'

'I've not touched a morsel of cake for a whole year. One can't afford to indulge one's appetite for cakes and pastries, not with the new Edwardian fashions.'

'They suit you, Mother. You look very handsome in that green velvet.'

'Thank you, darling.'

'What have you been doing with yourself since last October?'

'You shouldn't need to ask, not if you read my letters. I write to my sons every week. It's a habit, I suppose, but I started it when Roger went away to public school, and I've carried on writing. Am I wasting my time? Is it a bore to read your mother's letters every week?'

'Nothing you do ever bores me, Mother.'

'Flatterer! Did I tell you about my trip to London last month? But of course I did. It was so wonderful.'

'You did, and you stayed at Brown's.' (It was a safe bet. Mother had been staying at Brown's for years.)

'So you *do* read my letters?'

'Of course.'

'I do so enjoy those concerts at the Wigmore Hall, and I wouldn't miss a single performance by Paderewski if I could help it. He's an absolute wizard on the pianoforte.' She sighed ecstatically with the memory.

'And Brown's is still coming up to scratch? I find it a bit stuffy and old-fashioned.'

'The younger generation doesn't appreciate discreet service, and old-world courtesy. I simply lap it up. For one thing, I don't have to remind them. They remember all my little fads and fancies, and I feel, well, *treasured*.'

'Darling Mother! Do you have to go to Brown's to feel treasured?'

'Yes, I do, when your father is too busy to notice me, and my grown-up sons forget my existence for weeks on end.'

'That's not true! Haven't I telephoned?'

'*Twice* – the first time was the day after you left, asking me to post your pipes; though how you came to leave them behind I can't imagine. The second time was on the 13th of November when you telephoned to wish me a happy birthday.'

'But you were pleased? You said you were pleased?'

'Darling, I was delighted. It was sweet of you to remember.'

'Well, then?'

'Nothing. It's all right. I am not complaining. Don't look so worried. Will you have another cup of tea?'

'Yes, please. It's China, isn't it?'

'My dear boy! Have you ever known anything else but China tea in my drawing-room?' She shook her head, but joined in the laughter. She was a foolish, indulgent mother. Why should she expect her adult sons to remember such trivialities? The days when they accepted her authority and listened to her advice were long since past, and her clinging hands clutched at straws. When they met, they listened politely to all she had to say because they had nice manners. Then they went away and forgot her existence till one or the other remembered, and picked up the telephone. How she had treasured the few letters she had received from their public school, yet in every one she had been reminded to send more pocket money! Children were really very disappointing, and her best beloved was lying again. This time it was serious, and she felt quite ill with the thought of a visit from that police Inspector from Scotland Yard. Yet it didn't seem to be worrying Dennis.

When Parsons came in to collect the tea-trolley, he sprang to his feet to shake hands. Now how many young gentlemen would bother to be so polite to a servant, his mother wondered.

'Hello, Parsons, still hanging around with the old firm, I see.' he teased.

Parsons blushed and giggled. 'You are a one, Master Dennis! But it's nice to see you back, isn't it, Madam?'

'Very nice, Parsons.'

'So Doctor hasn't been in to tea, Madam?'

'No, it's his afternoon for the Workhouse.'

'So it is. I had forgotten. It must be very upsetting to see all those poor creatures, and some just waiting to die.' Parsons sighed heavily, but had no conception of the suffering and hardship that necessitated a prolonged stay in the Workhouse.

'At least they have a roof over their heads and food in their bellies – begging your pardon, Mother,' Dennis interrupted. 'And they are not all dying, not by a long chalk, Parsons. How about all those babies born on the wrong side of the blanket, so to speak?'

'Dennis!' His mother exclaimed in shocked disapproval.

'Sorry, Mother.'

'That will be all, thank you, Parsons.' The mistress was blushing with embarrassment.

Master Dennis was a proper scream. You never knew what he would come out with. But you couldn't help liking him. The servants had been reminded to call him Mister now he was a grown up young man, but somehow the Master Dennis slipped easy off the tongue. If Madam had already warned him about the questioning by the police inspector, he had taken it very calmly. But you never could tell with Master Dennis. He would still be joking when he was drawing his last breath!

When his father came in, some time later, Dennis was in the bathroom. It was a relief to see him, for it was a strain in the drawing-room, under his mother's watchful eye. He had been expecting her to lead the conversation back to Miss Mason, and she could still do so.

His father looked tired, and seemed to have aged in the past three months – or perhaps he hadn't really noticed. Father had always been a quiet, unobtrusive figure in their young lives. Now he was shy of his grown-up sons, and found it extremely difficult to communicate.

'Hello, Father!' Dennis called out gaily, and ran downstairs.

'Hello, my boy.' They shook hands. The father's smile was diffident, the son's smile was confident and charming, and he gestured to his father to lead the way into the drawing-room.

'Good evening, my dear.' A dutiful kiss on his wife's cheek, and the usual question. 'Have you had a good day?'

'My God! What a bloody farce. How do they stand it year in, year out?' Dennis was asking himself. Even as a boy he had wondered about this polite formality between his parents. When he visited the homes of his friends, he had seen all kinds of greetings between the parents – teasing, affectionate, casual – but never this formal, dignified restraint that appeared to hide their real feelings. But what *were* their real feelings?

'Shall I pour you a drink, Sir?' asked Dennis, with filial courtesy.

'Thank you.'

'The usual?'

'Yes, please – and your mother would like a sherry, I expect?'

She shook her head. 'No, thank you. We have only recently finished tea. Did you have tea at the Workhouse?'

'Just a cup of tea with Matron.' That was all. Neither his wife nor his son would care to hear about that unhappy place, so far removed from their own comfortable lives, so he would not bore them with details of his visit. It left a sour taste in the mouth, for he felt so inadequate, so helpless to change the archaic system with something more enlightened. How much longer would these Victorian institutions be allowed to dehumanise their unfortunate inmates? To talk about it would have relieved his mind and his conscience, but then he was not expected to relieve his mind, not here, in his wife's drawing-room.

The neat whisky warmed his chilled body, and he smiled to see his son with a whisky and soda. It seemed only yesterday that he was drinking Cook's homemade lemonade. The effort to converse was lightened, however, by his son's affability. Dennis always had something amusing to say, so he sank gratefully into the armchair, and studied the handsome features of his middle son with kind scrutiny. A doctor always knows what is happening in a village community. Friend and confidant in all three classes of society, as well as physician, he regarded himself as privileged – even more privileged than Parson, who was only called upon to minister to his Anglican parishioners. He was not unaware of the rumours that were circulating. They were saying that Dennis was no stranger to that unfortunate young woman whose body had been found in Marston Park – the body he had been called upon to examine in the mortuary. They had spent hours together, it now appeared, in the hop-garden. Of all the places where this gregarious son of his could be found in the vacation, the hop-garden seemed the most unlikely. But there it was, and mothers and children had witnessed the *rendezvous*, day after day. Apparently it had not occurred to any of them to mention the fact in the early days of the police enquiries, or to connect his son with the murder. Dennis was very popular, always had been; he was so friendly. It had been revealed that the young teacher had no close friends, and had not been seen with a male acquaintance since she came to Fairfields. According to her landlady, Miss Mason kept herself to herself, received no letters, had no visitors, and was no trouble. That in itself – to be no trouble – would recommend her to a landlady, the doctor assumed. Yet it was sad that nobody outside the school gates had bothered to get to know her, as a person – unless it were Dennis? Had he really been attracted to this young woman? Had they been meeting in secret? It was possible. This charming son of his had a reputation as a lady-killer. Lady *killer*! Heaven forbid! It would break his mother's heart.

Could a murderer be hiding behind that charming façade? It was inconceivable! So far, he was not a suspect. So far, so good. Should he warn Dennis that fresh enquiries would bring the police Inspector to this very house? No, better not mention it. Dennis was quite capable of dealing with any situation. He was no fool. As for his mother, there was no reason to suppose she had heard the gossip about Dennis and Miss Mason. Why should she, when she kept herself aloof from the villagers, and her few acquaintances in the upper class would know her distaste for village gossip? Poor Dulcie! Why did he think of his wife as 'poor Dulcie' when she had her own private income, the exclusive adoration of her three sons, a comfortable home, and servants to wait on her?

For some time past he had realised Dulcie was not a happy woman. The gradual withdrawal of the boys from her maternal wings had left her feeling bereft, and there was no substitute for this absorbing maternity. Her foolish heart had seen it as a permanent state, when nothing in this life is more precarious, more vulnerable, than the relationship between parent and child. What was she thinking now, he wondered, as she gazed at her favourite son with hooded eyes. Here they were, father, mother and son, gathered together in what would appear to an outsider to be perfect harmony. Their minds harboured thoughts that were relevant, but they were strangers one to another. It was sad.

Dennis always slept late when he was home on holiday, and the servants were told not to disturb him. The early morning was not his best time, and he would visit his local friends in the evening after dinner, and let himself in long after the rest of the household had retired to bed.

On this first evening home, after three months' absence, he spent the evening in the company of the jolly barmaid and the customers at his favourite pub. The atmosphere was guaranteed to banish any doubts or depression that still lingered from the strained

127

conversation at the dinner table. That both parents were anxious about the police enquiry was all too obvious. What else would have caused his mother to retire early with a headache, on his first evening at home, or his father to ask, 'How long are you staying, my boy?' when he had only just arrived. To be welcomed with such genuine pleasure by the customers in the saloon bar was satisfying to his ego. No mention was made of the police enquiries, probably because every man had already been questioned some weeks ago, and the murder was no longer the main topic in the pubs or on the tongues of the village gossips. Dennis contributed his share of naughty stories, and needed little persuasion to play the piano for the last hour or so before the publican called 'Time, Gentlemen. Please!' They sang all the music hall songs the Cockneys had left behind at the end of the hop-picking season. The songs had been shouted with boisterous enthusiasm by their London visitors as they drank their beer on the forecourts of the local pubs. Benches and trestle tables had been provided for the Cockneys and the gypsies, but they avoided each other and sat separately. Even the children turned their backs, and any sly glances at the other party was quickly discouraged with a stinging box round the ears. But they had long since departed, and the village settled down for the Winter – the rich in their warm, comfortable houses, with adequate food and clothing – the poor to exist in their impoverished conditions with insufficient food and fuel. The bleak Winters of the Weald took their toll of the very old and the very young and landlords were reluctant to spend money on repairs to damp walls and leaking roofs, thereby adding to the discomfort.

Already in Richmond Row the boys were spinning tops on the puddles where they sailed paper boats in the

128

Spring thaw. Little Carrie Simmons, clutching her mother's hand as they trudged to work at The Three Nuns at 7 o'clock, was huddled in a long coat several sizes too large, from the collection of discarded garments Miss Cecily had distributed at The Parsonage. A woollen scarf was wrapped twice round her neck and tied at the back, and her bonnet pulled over her eyes to protect them from the biting wind. So the poor child was gasping for breath when they arrived. They were given a bowl of hot porridge in the kitchen, however, and were luckier than most, as Ruby would remind the child.

'They give us a good dinner and tea, so we got to be grateful duckie, and we only got to walk down the path and cross over the 'igh Street and 'ere we are! Your poor Dad 'as to walk a mile to the station, and 'eaven knows 'ow far along the railway track afore 'e can start work, and nothing more than a bit of bread and fat bacon for 'is dinner. So cheer up, my duckie, and give Mum a smile.'

Carrie would sigh and wish she were back in her cosy little nest in the chimney corner. Her brothers told her she was lucky, for they slept upstairs in a big bed with a sagging flock mattress that still stank of urine, for all Ruby's airing in the Summer. It was young Freddie who had wet the bed, till the doctor prescribed a pink pill, to be taken nightly, for his weak bladder. That was several years ago, but their warm bodies, huddled together, could still revive the penetrating smell.

But nothing was farther from the thoughts of the debonair son of the kindly doctor than the misery of the poor on that cold, frosty night, as he strode towards home in his tailored overcoat and beaver hat. Thoroughly warmed by the hot fire and the convivial company in the saloon bar, he was planning his escape. His mind was most alert at this end of the day. It was late at night when he caught up with his neglected studies, and jeered at the conscientious slogging of his contemporaries. Tonight, however, his alertness was centred on the letter he must write before he packed his bag again – a letter that would shatter his mother's hopes of a united family Christmas and betray his father's privileged status in the village.

It had to be done, quickly, *tonight*.

The warm, familiar smell of home encompassed him as he hung up his coat and hat, but he pushed aside the temptation to linger over a nightcap beside the embers of the drawing-room fire. Carrying his shoes, he climbed the stairs with easy strides. The silent house slept undisturbed as he moved cautiously about his bedroom.

It was midday when the elderly housemaid tapped on the bedroom door, called twice, 'Are you awake, Master Dennis?' received no answer, and pushed open the door. The bed had not been slept in, drawers were pulled out and clothes scattered all over the room.

'Aw, my Gawd! 'e's been an' gawn an' 'opped it!' she gasped, staring wide-eyed at the confusion. Stepping carefully over a dozen pairs of shoes, she reached for the letter on the mantelpiece. 'It's like something you read about in one of them twopenny magazines,' she told herself with a shiver of excitement. 'Trust Master Dennis to give us all the colly-wobbles!'

Ignoring the untidy room – that could wait – she crept out, and hurried downstairs. Cook was busy in the kitchen, preparing lunch, and Parsons was laying the table in the dining-room.

'Jew know what I jus' found in Master Dennis's room?' Martha whispered hoarsely.

'What?' Parsons was wondering if she dare ask the mistress for a rise in the New Year. Her youngest sister had recently lost her husband, and there were four children to support on the small pension she had been allowed as the widow of the head gardener at Marston Park.

'You ain't listenin',' Martha complained.

Parsons sighed, and dragged her thoughts back to Martha.

'I found this letter, addressed to Madam, an' 'is room is turned all upside down, an 'is bed ain't been slept in. Master Dennis is gawn!' she announced, importantly.

'Give it to me.' Parsons snatched it impatiently, and her lips moved over the single word on the envelope – *mother* – 'I'll take it to Madam right away,' she said.

'But why should 'e run away when 'e only come 'ome yest'day? It don't make sense, do it?' The simple-minded Martha shook her head, but Parsons made no answer. It made sense all right, and Cook would agree that it made sense, but not in front of Martha, for her tongue was too dangerous.

'He's got wind of that police enquiry and he's scared. Wonder who warned him? Was it the Master or the Mistress?' Parsons asked herself, as she walked slowly across the hall and tapped on the drawing-room door. The mistress was addressing envelopes for a pile of Christmas cards on the desk. The cards were identical, and had been selected, as usual, from a book of samples sent by post from Harrods. She had chosen a Dickensian scene this year, with a stage coach discharging its passengers at an inn. Every window was ablaze with light, and snow was falling. The cards bore the name and address of the sender, and a simple message – 'Seasonal greetings and best wishes'. The doctor always made the same remark when she showed him the book of samples in October.

'They get earlier every year, don't they? I leave it to you, my dear.'

She sighed at his lack of interest in the Christmas

131

preparations. 'I leave it to you, my dear'. But her daughter-in-law declared that Roger behaved in exactly the same way, and she found it quite infuriating! They had agreed the spirit of Christmas could not survive without the wives and mothers to nourish it.

Dulcie Saunders had accepted the unpleasant truth that her grown-up sons came home for Christmas from a sense of duty, to please her and the servants, but they had no sentimental feelings about all the traditional trappings. Dennis and Lesley asked to be included on the greetings cards so they were spared the trouble and expense of choosing their own. Roger and his wife also ordered from a sample book of cards from Harrods.

'What is it, Parsons?' she asked when the parlourmaid entered the room.

'Excuse me, Madam. Martha found this letter in Master Dennis's room.'

'Thank you.' The face of her mistress had blanched, and the hand that reached out for the letter trembled. 'You may go, Parsons,' was all she said.

'Yes, Madam.' Parsons went out and closed the door quietly. It was not fitting for a servant to witness the anguish of a mistress.

The doctor's wife slit the envelope with an ivory paper knife and read the contents with a sense of unreality. The shock left her mind numb, and she shivered and moved over to the fire where she knelt on the hearth-rug to read the letter again.

My Darling Mother,

You are not going to like what I have to tell you, but I shall go mad if I don't tell someone. It has to be you, because you have always defended me in the past, and I know I can trust you to keep my ghastly secret.

Mother, I strangled that girl, not intentionally. It was not premeditated. We were lovers, and she had been tormenting me about a former lover, comparing my love-making to this man who was the father of her child. Yes, she has a child, a girl, boarded out with foster-parents.

I was very frightened when I realised she was dead, and dragged her body into the bushes. I am frightened now, because I'm a coward, and cannot face up to the police enquiry and a prison sentence. They would hang me, Mother, for there was no witness to prove I was provoked.

So I am going away. I shall join the party of friends in Switzerland that I was intending to join as soon as Christmas was over. Beyond that I have no plans, but of course I cannot return to the university. It may be some time before I can safely get in touch with you.

I am truly sorry, Mother darling, but that won't bring the poor girl back. I leave it to you to explain my absence.

Your penitent and ever devoted son,
Dennis

'Dear God, give me the strength,' his mother breathed. Her son was a murderer!

She huddled over the fire till the warmth crept back into her chilled body, and her numb mind was working again. It *had* to work quickly. Doctor would be in to an early lunch today, but he did not linger over his meals, and she thought he would accept the sudden departure of Dennis quite calmly. They were accustomed to his impulsive movements. He came and went as it pleased him. Roger and Lesley would think it rather odd that their brother came home for only one night, but she

133

would explain that he came home to collect clothes for his Winter holiday – which he did, of course, for he hadn't intended to stay for more than a week.

She was choked with tears, but she dare not cry. Even if her husband failed to notice her distress, Parsons would notice, and Parsons was no fool, neither was Cook. To keep her son's terrible secret would take all her ingenuity and self-control. Not for a few weeks or months, but a lifetime of secrecy. It was a ghastly thought, but she had no alternative. She was his mother.

Chapter Five

The classrooms were gay with paper chains and holly, and the children grew drowsy in the late afternoon with the fumes from the coke stove, and their stomachs warm with the hot cocoa they had enjoyed with their dinner of bread and jam. The three women teachers had to take turns for cocoa duty last Winter. The custom had been instituted by the former schoolmaster, who was sympathetic and understanding of the poverty of so many of his pupils. Hot cocoa, even made with water with a dash of skimmed milk and sugar, was nourishing, he had insisted.

For the new schoolmaster this would be the first taste of the bleak Winters of the Weald, and he had been surprised to see a deputation of senior girls at his desk one afternoon in early November, after school had been dismissed. Hetty O'Brien was the spokeswoman, as usual.

'Begging your pardon, Sir. We come to remind you that all of us children what brings their dinner 'as 'ot cocoa in the Winter. We do start with the cocoa in November, Sir, an' we finish with it the last day of March. The teachers know all about it, Sir, but likely as not they won't mention it, 'cos it's too much of a trouble, see, in their dinner hour.' Hetty paused for breath. The unflinching stare of her Irish blue eyes was somewhat disconcerting when coupled with the stares of her five companions.

Andrew Robinson stroked his beard and remarked, blandly, 'Indeed? And who suggested this excellent custom?'

'It were Mister Garston, Sir, 'im what was the schoolmaster afore you.'

The academic Robinson winced at the child's appalling English, and wondered if a second grammar lesson should be included in the weekly curriculum. He had noticed, however, that all the children from the Infants to the Sixth standard imitated their teachers in a sing-song, parrot-wise fashion, then immediately reverted to the roughness of their native tongue when they were dismissed. A pity – a great pity – but he was not a magician, and one could not hope to make silk purses out of sows' ears.

He nodded gravely, and considered the question with his usual courtesy, however. 'I will speak to the teachers on the morrow, but I cannot promise they will be willing to resume this duty if it interferes with their own dinner hour. And why should they, when you senior girls must be quite capable of making the cocoa? Do you not make cocoa at home?'

They all nodded vigorously.

'Then there is no problem. You six girls can each take a turn as cocoa monitor for a week. That means to make yourself responsible for collecting the ingredients each day from my housekeeper. The cocoa, milk and sugar will be handed only to the monitor. Then, with the able assistance of your colleagues, the cocoa can be made and distributed to each classroom. Great care must be taken with the boiling kettle in the scullery. There must be no

136

accidents, or the practice will be discontinued. Is that understood?'

'Oh yes, Sir. Thank you kindly, Sir,' said Hetty gratefully. All the girls bobbed respectfully, and walked demurely out of the classroom.

'What did I tell you? Robbie ain't such a bad old geezer if you know 'ow to 'andle 'im!' chortled Hetty, happily.

'My Mum won't 'arf be pleased.' Elsie Pearce hugged Hetty exuberantly. 'Can I be cocoa monitor after you, 'cos I'm your best friend, 'et, ain't I?'

'T'ain't fair 'avin' fav'rites, 'etty,' Susie Sparks argued, but she was shouted down.

In the cold, damp cloakroom, where puddles formed in the hollows of the brick floor, they dragged on their ill-fitting, second-hand coats and caps; gloves were a luxury, and numb fingers could be warmed with hot breath. Their stockings were darned or the holes left, according to the type of mother. Some of the boots had been roughly soled by cobbling fathers on Sunday mornings, but Hetty and Elsie had fathers who spent Sunday morning in bed, sleeping off the bad effects of their drunken state on Saturday. Their boots were stuffed with newspapers. Soon these girls would begin to criticise the second-hand clothes Parson's daughter distributed, but they were still young enough to treat the question of clothing as a small problem compared to their hungry bellies.

'I'm pleased with any old thing, Miss, s'long as it covers me decent like,' Elsie Pearce had been heard to remark to Miss Cecily, presiding over a pile of discarded frocks.

'What do old Robbie want with a fancy box of lady's handkerchiefs?' Susie wondered, as she examined a hole in her stocking.

137

'What you talking about?' Hetty demanded.

'Them 'andkerchiefs what 'e's bought at the Christmas Bazaar Sat'day af'noon, when I were buying a pennorth of 'lastic for me drawers. I were round the corner, see, an' kep' quiet. Miss Brown were servin' 'im, an' she were blushin' all over 'er silly face, the soppy thing!'

'Old Robbie's got a lady friend, a lady-friend, a lady-friend!' the girls were chanting as they marched out of the school gates.

The guests for the big house-party at Marston Park arrived on Christmas Eve, and stayed to celebrate the New Year. They brought their servants – valets, ladies' maids, grooms and coachmen – who had to be accommodated in the cottages on the estate, while nurses and nursemaids slept on camp-beds with their charges. The mansion was bursting at the seams, but it was a lively, festive occasion, and nobody complained of the extra work.

The evening of Boxing Day was traditionally reserved for the servants' ball, and the great hall, already transformed with balloons and bunting, and a magnificent Christmas tree decorated with glittering baubles and candles, was the backcloth for the happy event. The master and his guests would dance with the servants for the first hour or so with such energy and courtesy, the humblest in the servants' hierarchy would be quite overwhelmed by such a charming gesture. The old-established servants, however, knew it was nothing more than a part of the Christmas charade, and the following morning would see a return to the dutiful and dignified service to which the gentry were accustomed. Her Ladyship's delicate health did not allow for such romps with the servants, and she would entertain her

138

sisters in the drawing-room. The children had their own party in the nursery on Christmas Day, with their own tree hung with gifts wrapped in gold and silver paper. Then they all trooped downstairs to be entertained in the great hall by a magic lantern, a conjuror, musical chairs and blind-man's buff. Presents were distributed by Father Christmas from the huge pile under the tree – expensive toys for the boys, dainty party frocks for the girls. Everything was lavishly generous, for adults and children, during that festive week.

The entertaining of the gentlemen was not overlooked. Out with the guns and the dogs, horse-riding in the Park, or skating on the lake if they were fortunate enough to find it frozen. The younger ladies would join them for the skating, and they would picnic on baked potatoes, dripping with butter from a barbecue presided over by a footman disguised as a Cossack. The barbecue was a novelty at this first Christmas of the gay Edwardian decade. Hungry appetites were temporarily satisfied by the baked potatoes, but drawing-room tea awaited them when the shadows lengthened, and a six-course dinner would follow at 8 o'clock. Sated with rich food and wine, the guests would be glad to relax in comfortable armchairs, to be entertained by the delightful music of Chopin and Schubert, and the charming voice of Sir Neville's latest protégé. The master of Marston Park had quite a flair for collecting talented young singers and musicians. He collected them as some of his contemporaries collected works of art. With a delicate wife and four rather dull daughters, it was not surprising.

The customers had been generous at The Three Nuns on Christmas Eve. Little Carrie Simmons had the pocket of her pinafore weighed down with bright new pennies, and her mother's shabby purse was full of sixpences. They had been kissed under the mistletoe, and their bellies warmed with ginger wine and mincepies. But for Ruby Simmons, the wife of a railway ganger, and the mother of three young sons, the biggest pleasure would be found in the parcel of food she was taking home to the family. The publican's wife, who envied the good looks and easy-going nature of her charwoman all the year, and particularly at Christmas, had provided a feast for Christmas Day. A joint of beef, a plum pudding, mincepies and a cake. Ruby could hardly wait to get home with this wonderful bounty, but first they had to spend their money at the grocer's and the Christmas Bazaar. All four children would have small, cheap presents in the stockings they would hang over the hearth, together with a sugar mouse, an orange and a new sixpence.

Ruby was glad that her boys were still young enough to hang up their stockings, and they would encourage their little sister to believe in the legend of Father Christmas and his reindeer for many a long year. Carrie was their biggest joy, and their main reason to hurry home from work. There was Mum, of course, but they took her for granted, as children do. The pretty little sister was like a doll you could pick up and hug, and her wet kisses were as sweet as the kisses they would enjoy in the arms of their future sweethearts.

For Albert, aged 14, Freddie aged 13, and Jack, aged 12, home was a happy place. So they could ignore or accept the grim environment of Richmond Row. Jack would be working late at the grocer's on Christmas Eve, and would see his mother and Carrie at the counter, buying the few luxuries they could afford once a year, when the customers at The Three Nuns had been generous – mandarins, dates, figs, preserved fruits, a pound of sweet biscuits, and a box of crackers. It was quite unbelievably extravagant, and the boys never ceased to be surprised at the Christmas bounty – or to be sick on Boxing Day. Christmas Day was a holiday for the whole family, and the only day in the year when they all sat down together to breakfast, dinner, tea and supper.

Joe O'Brien, the eldest of the O'Brien tribe in Richmond Row, could usually be relied upon to provide a Sunday dinner for the family, and Christmas Day, of course. That was more than could be said of his father. Joe had a ferret. It was his only personal possession, and he loved it with the fierce passion of his hot, Irish blood. There was an affinity between them that was almost human, but for the rest of the family, the ugly little creature with its sharp features and sharp teeth was quite repulsive. Yet it was tolerated as a pet because it provided the Sunday dinner of rabbit stew, and the only real nourishment in that impoverished household. The ferret's name was Horace.

'Christ Almighty! Will ye get that 'orrible little beast out of me sight!' Mike O'Brien threatened on Christmas Eve. Father and son had just returned from work, and Horace was climbing all over young Joe, making little whimpering sounds of welcome.

At 16, Joe was a tall, gangling youth with a shock of red hair and freckles. He had been working on the railway with the gangers for two years now. He hated the work, and he hated his father. 'One of these days I shall murder Dad if 'e don't stop bashing our Mum,' he had told his younger brothers and sister Hetty. But they couldn't see it happening, not unless Joe put on a bit of weight. Joe was a working lad, and contributed more than his share to feeding the five younger children, but he still had his ears clouted with that heavy hand that could almost stun him. Joe was a loner. He had Horace,

141

and they were inseparable when Joe had finished work for the day. Tucked inside his shirt, the feel of the warm little body against his skin was the most comforting sensation of his young life. There was no cleverer ferret for rabbiting anywhere in the Weald, Joe boasted. The Weald was limitless to a boy who had travelled no farther than its boundaries.

Born and bred in the hovel they called home in Richmond Row, not one of the children had ever been in Ireland. There was no work, and no work meant no wages. Charity was a fine thing, but it was not for Mike O'Brien in those early days of marriage. He had pride in himself and his pretty wife before the drink became his master. His appetite for sex had always been lusty, and it still had to be satisfied by a woman who accepted her weary existence with hardly a protest.

'I'm getting out of 'ere when I leave school, as sure as me name's Hetty O'Brien,' the girl told her mother. The tired little woman shook her head at her only surviving daughter and asked, quietly, 'Where you going then, 'etty?'

'Marston Park.' There was no bigger contrast in Hetty O'Brien's small world than Richmond Road and Marston Park. You had to start at the bottom, they said, but even if you were a scullery maid you was fed proper, and you was actually under the roof of that fabulous mansion. Hetty had been warned what to expect, but she was undaunted. 'What do it matter if you starts at the bottom, as a little drudge? If you got any gumption you does your work proper, and keeps cheerful, and don't answer back, you gets promoted, see?'

'But Millie Smith 'as been a scullery-maid since she were 13, and she's 16 now and still a scullery-maid,' Hetty was reminded by Millie Smith's best friend, who was still at school.

142

'Then she did ought to be ashamed of 'erself. If the cook were pleased with 'er work in the scullery, she would 'ave been promoted to kitchen-maid, stands to reason. You got to please the cook or you don't get nowhere. But I ain't so keen on the scullery, meself, and I'd sooner be working in the laundry. Mind jew, if I was lucky enough to get took on as fourth 'ousemaid, then I could see meself climbing up the ladder, gradual like, to 'ead 'ousemaid.' And this, for Hetty, was the peak of her ambition at the tender age of 11. Marston Park, with its hierarchy of old-established servants, was the Mecca for most of the village girls leaving school at 13. Even the humblest could enjoy the prospect of future promotion and an even more exciting prospect of walking out with an under-gardener or a second groom at the age of 16. 'Once a servant always a servant', some would argue, but Hetty O'Brien was not the only girl in that group of six who had confronted the schoolmaster to know exactly where she was heading for when she left school. Farmers and tradesmen all had servants – one to each household. They were called 'generals'. The middle class had several servants, but no servants' hall, and no opportunity for promotion. You started as a housemaid or a parlourmaid and you were still a housemaid or a parlourmaid 50 years later, unless you got married. Hetty had pointed out, sensibly. 'S'posing they don't want no more servants at Marston Park when it's time for us to leave school?' Elsie Pearce had both feet planted firmly on the ground, and could foresee a little opposition.

'That'll be the day, my girl, when they don't want no more servants at Marston Park,' scoffed Hetty. 'You got to remember the oldies what get pensioned orf, and them what wants to emigrate to Canada and Australia, see?'

Elsie was still a little dubious about her chances, but the confident Hetty had no qualms. 'You 'an me will go together, Else, and ask to see the 'ousekeeper. If we take a letter from our schoolmaster what says we be respectable girls, with good manners then she 'as to see us, don't she?'

'I reckon so. Only she don't *'ave* to give us work, do she, 'et? See my meaning?'

'Stop worrying, Else, and leave it to me. In two years we ought to 'ave growed quite a bit, and we shall 'ave our bosoms to show we be women, not these flat chests what we got now.'

Elsie laughed and capitulated. 'You are a scream, 'et'. It was the highest praise from the sceptical Elsie.

'Don't forget we can read an' write, an' make ourselves flannelette nightgowns, you an' me,' Hetty reminded her.

'*When* our Mums 'as the money to buy the flannelette!' Elsie had the last word.

On this cold, frosty, moonlit night of Christmas Eve, 1901, young Joe O'Brien went off to the private woods on the Marston Park estate with his ferret tucked inside the ill-fitting tweed jacket that had once belonged to the Colonel. He brushed his mother's cheek with rough affection, and tickled the baby's bare buttocks. The baby piddled on his hand, and Joe swore an oath, but went out whistling.

He was a good boy, her Joe, his mother was thinking as she stirred the fire. They would have rabbit stew for their Christmas dinner. She had only to go next door and beg a few vegetables from Ma Simmons, who always had plenty, and never refused a neighbour. The only vegetables in the O'Brien household in plentiful supply was taters. They were practically brought up on taters.

But Joe did not come back, and neither did Horace. A

144

zealous young gamekeeper caught them red-handed. The two rabbits were confiscated, poor Horace had his small struggling body bashed against a tree, and Joe, distraught and sobbing wildly, was marched off into custody. The magistrates' court would assemble the day after Boxing Day, and Joe would be accompanied by several drunks, and two poaching gypsies who had spent Christmas in a cell at the local police station. The men knew what to expect, But Joe was a first offender.

A fine of 10s. or 30 days in custody was not a harsh sentence in that day and age. There was no money for fines, so they were taken back to the cell. For young Joe O'Brien it was a blessing in disguise, for he never went back to Richmond Row, or the gangers. He joined the Army. At 17 he was in India with his regiment, enjoying his new status as a private.

The doctor had an epidemic of scarlet fever on his hands in the New Year. It was strange how it often affected only one child in a family. There was no explanation for this; but it caused a lot of misery and heartache when a child was taken off to the Isolation Hospital for six weeks.

Young Jack Simmons was the first to develop the rash in Richmond Row, followed by Hetty O'Brien several days later. Then the baby was the next victim. It had been fretful for some days, and Hetty had been nursing it almost constantly after school till it fell asleep, sucking a dummy dipped in the sugar bowl. But it died in the hospital. Fed on 'pap' there was no strength in its puny little body. All the O'Brien children had rickets when they started to walk, and only because of the kindly intervention of the doctor in prescribing Cod Liver Oil and Stedman's Sea Salts were they spared an ugly deformity.

145

'Do she 'ave to drink the salts, Doctor?' the harassed mother had asked when she had taken Hetty to show off her bowed legs and was given two bottles at the surgery.

'My good woman, use a bit of commonsense! Would you give a child sea water to drink? Bathe her legs twice a day,' retorted the overworked doctor impatiently. She was a shiftless, pathetic creature, but what could you expect with a brutal husband and years of child-bearing? Five surviving children out of ten was average for the working class.

But now Joe was gone for a soldier and the baby dead, and there was a gap in the family till next year, when another little scrap of humanity would wail its way into a bleak, unwelcoming world. Only two people in the village were respected by the O'Briens – Father Dominic and Doctor. Their word was law. Their advice accepted. A chair would be dusted and a cup of tea offered, but only Father Dominic, closer to the poor of his parish because of his own early environment, would drink a cup of the weak, hot liquid without milk. The cheapest brand of tea at the grocer's was little more than dust.

For the girls from these impoverished families the first cup of tea they received in service was a revelation. So also was the food. Only in very rare cases would a mean mistress begrudge her servants adequate food and tea. Skinny little school leavers would be fattened up on roast beef and Yorkshire pudding, steak and kidney pie and treacle tart. The one topic of conversation when the young girls came home on their free Sunday afternoon was *food*. Older girls found their pleasure in 'walking out'.

Little Carrie Simmons cried when her brother Jack was taken away to the Isolation Hospital, and Ruby watched the child anxiously for spots to appear. Carrie seemed to have a charmed life. At the age of 3 she had been rescued from the village pond by the butcher's boy who had watched her slip away from her mother and dart towards the pond. She found the swans fascinating creatures, and had no fear of them. As she over-balanced, the boy reached her. It was a narrow escape, and Ruby dropped the packet of tripe in the sawdust as she rushed, screaming, from the shop. The second escape was in the Public Bar at The Three Nuns, when she tripped over a spittoon and cracked her head on the floor. But apart from a swelling bruise and hurt dignity, she suffered no ill effects.

Now she was 4, and lucky to escape scarlet fever. A bright, intelligent child, she was ready for something more entertaining than cutting out pictures for her scrap book, and following her mother around with a ragdoll. She would stand on a bench at the window to wave to the children as they rushed past on their way to school, longing to join them, and the hours seemed to drag interminably till the church clock struck 4, and they were running back up the hill.

'I want to go to school!' she wailed and whined, till Ruby's patience was exhausted. A few smacks on Carrie's well padded bottom had little effect, however. Carrie dragged on her mother's hand at 7 o'clock in the morning. She was fretful and naughty.

'She ain't like the same child, an' I'm proper flummoxed,' Ruby complained to Tom and the boys one evening, when Carrie had been put to bed in tears. It was Freddie, the clever one, who volunteered to call on Miss Carter, the Infants' teacher, one afternoon, as she tidied her classroom after the children had been dismissed. Would she make room for his little sister in her overcrowded classroom was a question she was not prepared to consider till she saw the appeal in the boy's dark eyes, and remembered he had been one of her most promising pupils. A grave little boy, with a fleeting smile, hungry for the limited amount of knowledge she was qualified to teach.

'*Please*, Miss,' he was pleading.

She smiled and nodded. 'Very well, Freddie. You may send her along tomorrow. Who will bring her here?'

'That won't be any problem, Miss. She can go to work with Mum, as usual. A lot of children pass The Three Nuns, and they won't mind taking her along till she's old enough to take herself. Mum will be so grateful. Thank you, Miss.' He was already speaking correctly, she noticed, but was still a little shy and nervous, twisting his cap in his hands. As a little boy he had had a slight stammer, but it was no longer noticeable.

'Where are you working, Freddie?' she asked, because she was always interested in the welfare of her ex-pupils.

'At the solicitors in the High Street. I'm the office boy, but next year I shall be promoted to junior clerk. One day I shall be a solicitor, but it's going to take a long time, Miss,' he sighed. 'Will you excuse me, please, I have to get back to post the letters. Mr Burrows, he's the chief clerk, gave me permission to leave the office.'

'I certainly will excuse you. Run along, Freddie. Work hard. One of these days we may see your name on the brass plate. Who knows what the future holds for a bright, ambitious lad?'

They shook hands gravely, and Miss Carter watched the neat little figure running down the path. They were luckier than most of the children who had passed through her class, the Simmons boys from Richmond Row. They had a wonderful mother who had somehow contrived to get all three boys into good situations. Now the little sister would be coming along. She had

148

forgotten to ask the child's name. That would make forty-one on her register.

'There is always room for one more in the Infants,' she told herself, complacently. Her small domain was her whole world, and she loved her children and wept when they were moved into Standard One at the age of 7. Freddie's little sister would be ready to move up at the age of 6, supposing she were as bright as her brothers.

When she had put on her hat and coat, her gloves and goloshes, Miss Carter picked up the gifts she had received – ten apples, twelve pen wipers, a lavender bag and a packet of hairpins – and went home. It was her 32nd birthday, and she had been teaching the Infants for nearly fifteen years.

A straggling line of poor children were waiting their turn for hot soup in the stone passage at The Parsonage one Saturday morning in January. It was one of Cook's extra duties in the Winter months, but she accepted it cheerfully. In a parson's house, a servant must expect to be overworked. Peg-leg had volunteered to serve up the soup to the children, and the novelty of being served by a man with a wooden leg was as richly rewarding as the hot soup. They giggled at his jokes and his swearing, and thought him a fine fellow.

'Bugger it!' he would mutter when he spilled soup on his green baize apron. 'I be an arkard old bugger, bain't I?' would bring a shout of denial, 'No you bain't!'

Miss Cecily would make it her duty to see the operation went smoothly, and her brusque 'Good morning, children' would interrupt a pleasant half-hour. 'Mornin' Miss,' the children would chant obediently, and Peg-leg would look as innocent as the youngest recipient of the hot soup.

'She do mean well, Parson's daughter,' was the

general opinion among the poor, the sick, and the aged of her father's working-class parishioners. It would be a fitting epitaph on Cecily's tombstone: 'She meant well'. Charity is a difficult commodity to dispense with the right amount of diplomacy, and Cecily was her mother's daughter, smug in her righteousness and a little haughty in her manner. If she found the children giggling in the passage on Saturday mornings, she would wonder what had amused them, but not one would explain it was funny old Peg-leg. He would carry out a can of beef-tea or chicken broth, and place it carefully in the trap, then hold the reins while Miss Cecily lifted her skirts and climbed in. There would be milk jellies and baked custards as well as the nourishing broth, for the invalids. Summer and Winter, in all kinds of weather, Parson's daughter was seen as a rather superior ministering angel dispensing charity to the poor and needy.

Fortified by the hot soup and Peg-leg's good humour, the children departed through the garden gate, skidding on the icy paths, and plucking frozen snow from between the rows of Brussel sprouts. Every Saturday morning till the end of March would see them back, wading through drifts of snow in the lanes, and sliding gaily behind the snow plough as it cleared the main highway. The boys were lively and carefree, the girls always burdened with younger brothers and sisters. It was their duty and their destiny. But for both the boys and the girls their childhood was brief and quickly passed. At 12 or 13 they were out in the harsh world of adults, pathetically proud and pleased to be contributing a shilling or two to the family budget. There was a toughness and a kind of Spartan endurance in these small, ill-nourished children of the Weald. Born to poverty, they seldom aspired to the flourishing ranks of the middle class.

Young Freddie Simmons would be the exception, but he might have to move away from the village that had nurtured him, and the squalor of Richmond Row in which his parents still survived, to overcome the stigma of his humble birthplace. Carrie would be accepted in any class of society because she was pretty, and had no shyness or inhibitions. She knew what she wanted at the age of 4, and was swept off to school in a group of girls all clamouring to hold her hand. The big boys would fight each other for the privilege of carrying her piggy-back up the hill at 4 o'clock. Carrie was everyone's pet – at home, at school, at The Three Nuns – but her precociousness was endearing. Carrie loved everyone, and everyone loved Carrie – well, almost. Lennie O'Brien was the exception. There had to be tears as well as laughter, even for Carrie. But when she found her missing ragdoll abandoned on the rubbish heap, soaked to her sawdust, and horribly mutilated, it was her first encounter with cruelty, and left its mark on her young mind for a very long time. It was not just a ragdoll. It was Mary Ann, a beloved and treasured possession that accompanied her to school on that first day, and got lost in the bustle and excitement of home-coming. It *had* to be Lennie O'Brien; who else would want to hurt Carrie?

It had taken the schoolmaster a good half-hour to select a suitable Christmas Card for Miss Irene that Christmas Eve, but at last he was satisfied with his choice. Back in his study at the School House, he hesitated over the signature, then, frowning thoughtfully, he signed, 'Your sincere friend and admirer, Andrew Robinson'. Tucking the card into the red ribbon that adorned the box of handkerchiefs, he found paper and string, and hurried to the post office.

Walking slowly back down the High Street, he

visualised the reactions of Miss Irene when she opened the package on the morrow. The Christmas Day postal delivery was a heavy one, and the postmen were always delayed *en route* by hospitable people offering refreshment. School had been dismissed early, after the usual joyous rendering of 'Good King Wenseslas' and ''ark the 'erald angels.' ''appy Christmas, Sir!' ''appy Christmas, Miss!' chanted the children as they filed out.

The Infants had sung 'Away in a Manger' with such innocent simplicity the sentimental Miss Carter had dabbed at her wet eyes. Each child had received an apple, an orange, and a pink sugar mouse, all forty-one gifts provided from the purse of this popular and beloved teacher.

Little Carrie Simmons, leading the procession to the door, had set the pattern for a warm hug and a wet kiss. Twenty-nine little girls followed Carrie's charming gesture, but the boys shied away.

'It were proper soppy to kiss Teacher!' Lennie O'Brien whispered hoarsely, and the others agreed.

Marching out in single file behind the girls – it was always ladies first with Miss Carter – they shook hands manfully.

'Goodbye, George. A happy Christmas.'

'Bye, Miss. 'appy Christmas.'

'Goodbye, Thomas. A happy Christmas.'

'Bye, Miss. 'appy Christmas.'

'Goodbye, Albert. A happy Christmas.'

'Bye, Miss. 'appy Christmas', . . . and so on.

Big sisters were waiting in the cloakroom to help the excited Infants into coats and caps and woolly mufflers, and to admire the pink sugar mice. The boys had eaten all the heads before they were out of the school gates, and only the tails remained to tickle the girls as they raced for home. Carrie did no more than run her little pink tongue over the pretty creature, for she wanted to share it with her three brothers later in the day. Holding it in her hot little hand, however, it was already melting when the boys came home from work. All three brothers politely declined to rob Carrie, so she finally sucked it away on her mother's lap.

When the last of the children had passed through the schoolgates, the caretaker fastened them securely with a chain. In two days they would be open again, so it was rather an unnecessary precaution. On Boxing Day he would strip the classrooms of paper chains and holly, and make a bonfire.

'That's Christmas over for another year, thank Gawd!' he would mutter, for he was a disagreeable old man with the same grudge against the whole human race as Charles Dickens' Scrooge.

Back in his study, the schoolmaster was pondering over the problem of the delicate Miss Irene. They were still worlds apart, even with this tentative approach to a closer relationship. He wondered if he had taken a liberty. Would she turn her head away when they met in church? If so, he must move to a pew on the other side of the aisle. Would she . . . dare he anticipate that she would linger for a few moments after the service? He stroked his beard. She was so frail, so feminine, he longed to offer her his undying love and protection, yet he still could not be absolutely sure that it *was* love in his heart. It could be compassion? Miss Irene had taken the place in his heart of his mother – the mother who had possessed her son for nearly forty years, and left him like a ship without a rudder.

Frowning over the problem, he ate the frugal tea his housekeeper had provided, and took a book from the shelf. But he could not settle to the peaceful solitude of his own hearth. He was restless, and his nerves were so

153

taut he jumped when the back door closed, some time later. Now he was alone in the house. The caretaker had his rooms adjoining the school, and Andrew Robinson was shy of intruding on his privacy. Surrounded by children and teachers all day, he normally welcomed his own private sanctum, but not tonight. It was his first Christmas without his mother, and he was missing her intolerably. They would go together to the midnight service, and come home to hot cocoa and a sense of spiritual detachment from their neighbours. All their habits had been regular and moderate, their quiet routine established when he left college. Her death had shattered that comfortable and complacent little world. Tears of self-pity welled in his eyes. He took off his glasses and polished them, then sat staring into the fire, wishing that Christmas was over, and the familiar routine continued in the classrooms.

His three women teachers had joined him in a glass of sherry. They had wished each other the compliments of the season, and shaken hands. All three were joining families and friends, and could not begin to understand the hideous hours of loneliness he must face before they met again.

But why shouldn't he attend the midnight service at All Saints? His housekeeper had left a cold supper on a tray. She had asked to be relieved of her duties on Christmas Day because she wished to spend the day with her sister. She would leave his dinner in a low oven, and he could help himself when he came back from church, she had explained. The prospect was dismal but he blamed himself for his lack of initiative. There had been time enough to make friends in the village, but the weeks and months had slipped away, and he had not bothered to make the effort. Avoiding the company he now desired so urgently was a sad mistake, but it was too

154

late now to expect anyone to take pity on his bachelor state on Christmas Day.

The village stirred with life as he walked up the High Street at a quarter to the midnight hour. Footsteps crackled on the frosty road, and lanterns swung in unseen hands. The church doors stood invitingly open, and the light poured out into the darkness of the churchyard. A tall Christmas tree, ablaze with candles, in the porch had attracted a group of admirers who stood chatting in hushed voices. The Nativity scene had been lovingly arranged by Miss Cecily on the steps of the font. The window sills were draped in evergreens, and Christmas roses adorned the altar. Oil lamps, suspended from the rafters on long chains, lit the shadowed hall with a faint glimmer of light, but few in the congregation would need to strain their eyes to read the hymns. The carols would be old favourites, as familiar as the hymns for Easter Sunday and Harvest Festival.

Walking slowly down the aisle to the corner seat in the pew behind the parsonage pew that he had claimed of recent months, the schoolmaster was suddenly uplifted by a glimpse of a slight figure in a velvet bonnet. But of course she would be there! Her mother and sister sat on either side of her, like supporting pillars, but she heard his step, and turned her head to smile. His heart missed a beat. He acknowledged the smile, as always, with a formal bow. More than ever tonight she seemed so childishly small and vulnerable. What would she say if she knew he had posted a gift and a card? He wished he could witness her surprise when she opened the package on the morrow. Those pallid cheeks that flushed so readily would flush with pleasure – or embarrassment? He watched her every movement with mingled joy and pain, and when he found himself kneeling beside her at the communion rail, he was so nervous he almost

155

choked on the holy wafer. She looked what she was – a lady of the much-respected middle-class society. There was breeding and refinement in every line of her slight figure, every feature, every gesture. He was very conscious of his own lack of refinement, and his clumsiness. Not all his mother's ambitious plans had succeeded in pushing him into middle-class society. They had hovered on the fringe for years, deliberately avoiding the friendly overtures of their working-class neighbours. For all his academic knowledge, Andrew Robinson was not a gentleman, and he had no claim to the class he had so long denied.

But Irene Wellington was enjoying every moment of this close contact with the nervous schoolmaster, and was fully aware of the admiration she had unwittingly evoked. Her thoughts were wandering in a way that would have shocked her mother and elder sister, who assumed such thoughts to be unappropriate to an invalid. Romance was something to be read about in the novels of the Brontë sisters and Jane Austen, not experienced by a parson's daughter inflicted with tuberculosis. She knew her span of life was short. She had envied her sister Marion that whirlwind romance with the young missionary while realising such prolonged separation from her family and hardship was not for her. It was doubtful if she would have survived the long sea voyage. But here, at her side, on this memorable Christmas Eve, knelt a man as worthy and respected as that forceful young missionary. There was a gentleness about him, and a reticence that would not be easy to overcome. But, supposing she asked Mother to invite Mr Robinson to join them for Christmas dinner at The Parsonage, would he accept? She was so weary of that insipid curate. Her heart fluttered excitedly. There could not be a better time than Christmas for such an invitation, she reflected. A few whispered words in her mother's ear after her father had pronounced the blessing, and the deed was done!

She stood aside, smiling demurely, pretending an innocence that her eager heart denied.

'Would you care to join us for dinner tomorrow, Mr Robinson? Unless, of course, you have other arrangements? One does not like to think of anyone alone on Christmas Day. What do you say?' Parson's wife was wrapping a shawl about Irene's thin shoulders. Cecily had already gone for the trap.

The question had come as a complete surprise, and Robinson stammered, 'That is m-most kind of you, Ma'am. I should be delighted to join you.'

'Splendid! That's settled then. We like to eat our Christmas dinner at midday. It is more leisurely, and it leaves the servants free after they have served tea in the drawing-room. Besides, we have to put in an appearance at the evening service, which is poorly attended. My daughters usually prefer to stay at home, so they will entertain you if you wish to spend the evening at The Parsonage.'

'Thank you, Ma'am.' Robinson bowed. Only a very courageous man would dare to disagree with Parson's wife!

Now she was straightening Irene's bonnet as though she were still a child, but there was nothing childlike in the smile she threw over her shoulder as she was bustled away. The smile had a promise of a new and closer relationship, though how it could be achieved in such adverse circumstances was beyond the comprehension of a confirmed bachelor.

The Christmas cards from the three women teachers decorated the mantelpiece in his small, crowded study. These cards were the only indication that it was

Christmas Eve. But the lack of all the traditional trappings did not disturb the village schoolmaster on this first Christmas without his mother. When he told his housekeeper he had been invited out to dinner on Christmas Day, she was obviously pleased that she hadn't to prepare a meal, and her tight lips parted in a rare smile that completely changed her expression. He was so taken by surprise, he could only stare, and wonder why he had not noticed the colour of her eyes. They were black as onyx. She must have been quite a handsome woman in her younger days. Why hadn't he tried harder to get to know her, as a person, not just as a useful pair of hands? The spirit of Christmas had been rekindled in his empty heart by that other smile from Miss Irene, and the invitation to dinner that was so totally unexpected. 'Goodwill to all men' included the housekeeper.

As she laid the table for his breakfast, he placed a little package on the starched cloth. It was tied with red ribbon.

'With the compliments of the season,' he said, and watched her reaction.

Her cheeks flushed with pleasure. 'It's very kind of you, Sir, but you shouldn't have bothered.'

'It's a pleasure. You have been very kind to me. Perhaps I have not always shown my appreciation, and I do apologise.'

She shook her head, surprised and embarrassed by his honesty. 'Can I open it?'

'Please do.'

It was a cameo brooch in a small box lined with red velvet, and the box seemed to please her as much as the brooch. 'It's beautiful. I only once had a present in a pretty box, and that was chocolates from the late schoolmaster, the first year he took over the post. He only did it that once, then he gave me money for

Christmas after that first year.'

'And you preferred the chocolates in the pretty box?'

'Yes, indeed I did, Sir. I still have the box. I keep my handkerchiefs in it. That was back in 1885.'

'But you do like the brooch?'

'Very much, thank you, Sir.'

'I had noticed that you always wore a cameo brooch.'

'Fancy you noticing that, Sir!'

They exchanged a smile of better understanding, for both had realised a barrier had been erected in the early days by a reluctance to accept the new order. It was true he *had* noticed his housekeeper always wore a cameo brooch because it reminded him of his mother's cameo. To mention it now would spoil the gesture.

'Is there anything else I can do for you, Sir?' was a question she had never bothered to ask until today. Her services to her new employer had been grudging because she was still missing that genial personality she had served for many long years. Now, at last, they would accept the change, and a more harmonious relationship would be established at the School House.

Andrew Robinson shook his head. 'No, thank you. Get along to your sister's and give her my regards.'

'Thank you, Sir. If I bank up the fires before I go, the house will feel warm when you come back. Will you be staying late at The Parsonage?'

'I don't know. Some mention was made of being entertained by Miss Cecily and Miss Irene while the Canon and his wife went to church.'

'That will be Miss Cecily playing the piano and Miss Irene singing, I expect. They do say she has a sweet voice. It's sad to think she hasn't long to live.'

'Hasn't long to live?' echoed Robinson in a hollow voice.

'It's consumption. Poor young creature. It's a shame, but it runs in families. They do say it can be cured if it's treated early in one of them sanitoriums in Switzerland. But how many could afford it, even if they wanted to be parted from their families? Parson couldn't afford it, and that's a fact. They're upper class, that family, but everyone knows they can only afford those two old servants and it's a big house. I've never seen inside, but they do say the carpets are worn thin, and the sheets are turned sides to middle on all the beds. They get outside help for spring-cleaning, and that starts the tongues wagging. Them two old servants don't gossip. Too loyal, I reckon.' Now that her own tongue had been loosened, there was no stopping her, and Robinson had heard enough. When he made no comment, she left him to finish his breakfast.

'Then I'll be getting along as soon as I've banked up the fires and washed up the dishes.' He had pushed his plate away.

'You can clear the table now. I've had all I want. I'm not hungry,' he told her. The smell of the kippers had turned his stomach – but perhaps it wasn't the kippers.

When she had thanked him yet again for the lovely present, she went away with the tray, and he covered his face with his hands. 'It's sad to think she hasn't long to live – It's sad to think she hasn't long to live.' He shivered. Did she know she was doomed to die young? And what exactly did it mean – a few months, a year? Who could answer such a question, supposing he were to ask? Time was so short. What did she want of him? That intimate, enticing smile. He was her slave. He squared his shoulders. A new year would be dawning – 1902. Would it change the whole course of his life or just provide an interlude in which to devote himself to that sweet creature at The Parsonage? The need to find a substitute for his mother was very real. It *had* to be Miss Irene. Her frail femininity appealed to his chivalry so strongly. His mother's image was fading. The umbilical cord was severed, but it was too soon to realise its loss.

160

Chapter Six

Walking back to The Parsonage with his host on Christmas morning, Andrew Robinson was very conscious of the older man's sincerity.

'That was a most inspiring service, don't you agree, Robinson?' Parson commented, as their feet crunched on the frozen snow.

'It was indeed, Sir.'

'I can never make up my mind which of the three – Easter, Harvest or Christmas – I most enjoy. All three festivals pack the church to capacity, as you will have noticed. To-day we had to provide chairs for the side aisles to take the overflow from the centre. The gentry have big house parties at Christmas and New Year, and always bring their guests to church on Christmas morning to swell the congregation in a most gratifying manner. Most middle-class families are visited by married sons and daughters and grandchildren. One sees the pews filling up with all the familiar faces, and a number of new little faces, from year to year. The children love the stable my daughter Cecily provides for their benefit. Mary and Joseph and the Baby Jesus are old favourites. So are the shepherds and the Wise Men. Do you realise, my dear fellow, that little stable has been the main attraction for the younger generation every Christmas since my own children were small?" He sighed. 'Those are the best years, Robinson, for parents, those early years. Such trusting innocence, such joy in the simplest of pleasures, and handmade toys. But children have to grow up and spread their wings. Even a daughter suddenly finds her home environment restrictive. This year we have lost Marion. We miss her sadly. She is so full of life and gaiety – but Irene will do her best, bless her. I believe she has taken quite a fancy to you, Robinson!' he teased.

'Has she, Sir?'

'You're blushing, my dear fellow!'

'The liking is mutual, Sir. But I hadn't intended to make it so obvious. I do apologise if it has embarrassed you.'

'No need to apologise. A parson often sees more than he is intended to see, from his vantage point in the pulpit. Alas, I must warn you, Robinson, there can be no happy fulfilment to such an attachment to my delicate little Irene. If you fall in love, you cannot, you *must* not betray your real feelings.'

'I think I am already in love with your daughter, Sir.'

'Then you have all my sympathy.'

'It's true, then, that she hasn't long to live?'

The older man hesitated, then turned to his companion. 'A doctor's opinion is not infallible, my son. We all are in the hands of our Maker . . . God's will be done.'

Andrew was too choked to reply, and they walked the rest of the way in silence. The peace and beauty of the snow-clad valley seemed to contradict the inevitable end to such a relationship. This short walk across the field would leave a lasting memory for both – a memory saddened by the knowledge of a parting more final than

162

the other. Five years would see Marion back on furlough with her husband and children – if God willed. A grandchild in the old nursery – for the eldest child would be left behind – would heal the wound. But that was too far distant to contemplate. Marion and Malcolm would be celebrating this first Christmas on the high seas.

Pushing open the garden gate, Andrew Robinson spoke quietly. 'Believe me, Sir, my feelings for Miss Irene are strictly honourable. Her happiness will be my first consideration. I am not a young man, or an impetuous one. My dear mother has been the only woman in my life until I met your daughter. But for your kind hospitality, this first Christmas since her death would have been quite unbearable. I am deeply grateful to you and your wife for inviting me.'

'Bless you, my son, for speaking so frankly. Come! Let us show the ladies a cheerful countenance.' And he marched purposefully towards the house. The appetising smells of roast beef and plum pudding whetted their appetites.

Peg-leg had stabled the mare with a bag of oats. With a clean white apron tied over his best suit, he was waiting in the kitchen to help Annie with the service. It was getting too much for the old servant to carry the heavy piles of plates and dishes to the dining-room. Back in the scullery, he would change into the green baize apron and tackle the huge stack of pots and pans, while Annie washed silver and crockery in the kitchen sink. Cook was too hot and flustered to enjoy her Christmas dinner till the washing up was done, but she had served up three generous helpings of roast beef, Yorkshire pudding, roast potatoes and sprouts, and popped them in the oven, together with the mincepieces. A Christmas pudding was simmering on the hob. Peg-leg had provided the cider, and the master had toasted their health in a glass of sherry before dinner was served in the dining-room. The schoolmaster had been introduced and the compliments of the season exchanged. It was a nice gesture to introduce the guest to the servants. The curate needed no introduction, of course.

'Miss Irene be talking nineteen to the dozen, bless 'er little 'eart. She do look so pretty in that blue velvet with 'er pink cheeks, don't she, Peg-leg?' Annie was panting as she slid the heavy tray on to the kitchen table.

'Like a little angel,' Peg-leg agreed, thoughtlessly.

Cook dabbed her eyes with her apron, and Annie sniffed miserably.

'You don't 'ave to remind us she could 'ave passed on afore another Christmas' said Cook, irritably.

'Sorry. It just slipped out. Cheer up, my duckies. I got a nice surprise for you when you've finished your dinner.' When he had finished his third mincepie, he belched comfortably and grinned at his two companions. Their faces were still flushed from the sherry, the heat of the stove, and the good food they had enjoyed.

'That were the best Christmas dinner I tasted since last Christmas! Thank 'ee, Cook, m'dear,' he told her.

'That were a back-'anded compliment, you silly old devil!' she chortled.

Annie sighed and patted her belly. 'I couldn't eat another crumb, not if you was to pay me.'

'Don't talk so daft, Annie. There's tea and supper, and there's all them sweets and nuts what Madam give us. If you be full up already, take a pinch of bicarb, and let out the wind.'

'Get Christmas over and we shall soon 'ave to start on the Spring cleaning,' mused Annie, with a sigh of resignation.

'Well, there's no need to introdoose it into the

164

conversation on Christmas Day, my girl!' said Cook, wagging her head at such a breach of etiquette. Cook could see no farther than tea, at the moment. The rich fruit cake had been baked in November, and lavishly iced and decorated a week ago, the large size for the dining-room, a smaller size for the kitchen. Everything had to be duplicated for the servants, apart from the master's favourite Madeira, and Miss Irene's chocolate log. Annie would cut two plates of dainty sandwiches for the drawing-room tea, and there would be wafer-thin bread and butter and home-made strawberry jam. A cold supper would be laid out on the sideboard, and the family would help themselves later in the evening. More tea could be brewed on the spirit stove when required.

Only Cecily would spare a thought for the poor parishioners for whom Christmas Day would provide a rare treat with a rabbit pie or a couple of pounds of sausages. She had distributed the money from the Christmas Fund to all the mothers of large families, whether or not they were deserving or shiftless. It was the children who mattered, and it was the children who had hung about her skirts waiting for the sweets and nuts and oranges she never failed to provide on Christmas Eve. Her father's well-to-do parishioners could expect to see Miss Cecily making her rounds in the trap in early December, to collect for the poor children. She was not very popular with the upper class, but none were spared when Parson's daughter determined on one of her charitable excursions!

The early afternoon passed pleasantly in the drawing-room, with Parson distributing the parcels that had collected about the Christmas tree in the hall, and Parson's wife presiding over the ceremony of the servants' Christmas bonus. Traditionally they received two new uniform dress, two aprons, and two caps,

165

together with half-a-sovereign. Peg-leg received two shirts with his half-sovereign. All three had washed their faces, tidied their sparse grey hair, and changed their aprons. They received the gifts with little bobs and bows, and profuse thanks. The schoolmaster and the curate added their own small tribute of half-crowns, though it must be recorded, in fairness to the schoolmaster, that he was the first to dip in his pocket.

'Peg-leg do be giving Cook and me an 'andsome pair of slippers,' Annie announced importantly, as they waited to be dismissed.

'Indeed? How nice,' murmured the ladies.

'And what did you give Peg-leg?' asked Parson.

'Pipe and baccy, Sir.'

'Splendid! Splendid!' Parson rubbed his hands and beamed on the assembled company with a geniality that was a little forced. His thoughts kept wandering away to his favourite daughter, celebrating Christmas Day on the high seas. She would be feeling dreadfully homesick, and likely as not dreadfully seasick, the poor darling. Determined to keep the spirit of goodwill to all men alive, however, he accompanied Peg-leg to the woodshed, filled several baskets with logs, and helped to carry them indoors. Then he sank gratefully into an armchair and closed his eyes.

Of recent years he had been allowed the luxury of forty winks in the early afternoon. His wife and eldest daughter, always bursting with energy, decided to take the dog for a walk, and the curate explained, with simpering self-importance, that he had promised to call on a certain lady, whose name he was not yet allowed to divulge.

When only the muted snorts and snores from the Parson's armchair disturbed the peaceful atmosphere, Irene beckoned Andrew to sit beside her on the couch.

166

Reaching behind the cushions, she took out the box of handkerchiefs and whispered, 'I hid them!'

'Why did you hide them, Miss Irene?'

'Because I love secrets, and I don't want to share you with anyone. They wouldn't understand. You see, they think I am still a child, and they treat me like a child. You must have noticed.'

He nodded gravely.

'It was such a surprise, and I nearly missed it when I sorted out all the packages the postman delivered this morning. It's such fun, piling them up on the breakfast table with all the letters and cards. Then I saw a square package addressed to me, and I turned it over wondering who had sent it. Who could it be? It was a masculine hand and a local date stamp. It was then I decided to hide it, but I had to wait ages to open it. I thought they would never leave me alone! Did you choose the card? But of course you did! Such pretty sentiments,' she sighed ecstatically. 'I am going to kiss you, Mr Robinson – Andrew.' Her lips brushed his cheek. 'There, you're blushing. Am I a very forward young lady?'

He took her hot hands and raised them to his lips. 'I am yours to command, Miss Irene,' he told her, earnestly.

'You may call me Irene when we are alone,' she whispered. Then she put a finger to her lips and shook her head. 'Hush, he's waking,' and pushed him away.

He stood there, looking down at her with mixed feelings of delight and disappointment. She was flushed and starry-eyed, and obviously happy with her secret. But when, and how, could they meet in secret? he asked himself. She would never be allowed out alone in the Winter months; only to church, wrapped in rugs on Sunday morning. She must have realised it was not

167

enough to satisfy his manly ego, for she whispered mischievously, 'Don't look so solemn. Leave it to me!'

Parson was rousing himself with a mighty yawn, but he hadn't slept a wink, let alone forty.

'Well, my dear fellow, shall we stretch our legs for half-an-hour and work up an appetite for tea?' he asked, innocently, 'if Irene will excuse us?' he added.

She nodded tremulously, and when the door closed, she slipped off the couch to watch the two figures striding across the snow-covered lawn. Both were tall, with the stooping shoulders of academics.

'I am yours to command – I am yours to command,' she repeated, softly. Her heart was racing. She must not get too excited. Dear Mr Robinson. Dear Andrew!

At Russets Farm, on the Marston Park Estate, it was lambing time, and the ewes, carrying their heavy burdens, had been driven into the shelter of hurdles as the blizzard swept across the Weald. The nation was in mourning, and the new Edwardian era had begun, but the work on a farm went on from season to season, seven days a week, and the only indication of these dramatic events was a black bow of ribbon fastened to the gilt-framed portrait over the mantelpiece in the front parlour.

Bert Blunt had married Ruby's twin sister when she was 16, and never regretted it. With three fine sons to bless their marriage, and all three looking no further than Russets for work when they left school, it seemed to Ruby, scrubbing the floors at The Three Nuns, that her sister Lucy was a very lucky woman. They did not see a lot of each other, though only a few miles divided them; the two sisters had little time for visiting, and the boy cousins hardly knew each other. But now Carrie had started school and felt the need to spread her wings still

168

further, she was escorted by her brother Freddie to the gate that led directly to Russets every Saturday morning, lifted over, and sent on her way with a reminder to be a good girl. Her Aunt Lucy would welcome her with a warm hug, for she was still hoping for a girl to complete her own family. With the youngest boy already coming up to 13, and no miscarriages, it seemed unlikely that she would conceive after so many years. The difference between their own cramped little cottage in Richmond Row and the spaciousness of the farm made a lasting impression on 4-year-old Carrie. To have three brothers spoiling her, and now her three boy cousins, did not surprise her. It was expected they would make a pet of her! Everyone said she was just like her Mum, and Mum was pretty. She hadn't to go to bed in curling rags like Freda Mason, who had long ringlets, because her short curls were natural. And because she was loved by so many people, she had love to spare for the aunt and uncle and the three boy cousins at Russets.

There was an Albert in this family also, but he was the youngest, and he was instructed to keep an eye on her that first day, and to lift her over the gate at 4 o'clock into the arms of Freddie. Thousands of boy babies must have been christened Albert after the Prince Consort long after he was dead. Victoria was another matter, and the working class would hesitate to name a child after the Queen. It was popular with the upper class, however, and seldom shortened to Vicky. Soon a new generation of little Edwards and Alexandrias would be pushed in their prams by haughty nannies in Kensington Gardens.

But for Carrie, blissfully happy and busy in her new environment, the wonderful day was crowned with a ride on Prince, one of the Shire horses that pulled the wagon.

'She's too small, Dad. She'll be scared,' Albert protested.

'I ain't scared of nofink!' said Carrie indignantly. It was not strictly true. She was scared of the big spiders in the privy, and she was scared of Lennie O'Brien.

They had a servant at Russets, and that was another surprise. Her name was Emma Smith, and she was an orphan. All the infants were christened with plain no-nonsense names on arrival, in readiness for their humble status. The babies were not all left on the doorstep, but were found in the most unlikely places. Emma had been discovered in the potting shed by the gardener early one morning in mid Summer. She was yelling lustily, and obviously hungry, for she gnawed at his earth-encrusted finger as he carried her up to the house. Nothing was known of her parents, but her preference for outdoors rather than indoors, and her black hair and eyes suggested gypsy blood. Be that as it may, girl orphans were distributed like parcels around the Weald as soon as they reached their 13th birthday. Farmers' wives, tradesmen's wives, and publicans' wives could always use an extra pair of hands, and the girls were accustomed to hard work.

The carter had dumped Emma Smith in the yard at Russets one warm Summer evening, with a small tin trunk that she was dragging purposefully across the cobbles when young Harry Blunt, the eldest of Lucy's three boys, swung over the gate.

'Hi, you! What do you think you're doing?' he called, authoritatively.

'Mindin' me own business,' came the quick retort.

Harry laughed, and snatched at the handle.

'Let be!' she snarled. 'I don't need no 'elp from you nor nobody!'

'Cheeky little bugger! That's no way to speak to your betters.'

She stared at the tall youth, with his flaxen hair and

170

fair complexion with her bold black eyes. 'You ain't me boss. I knows what I 'as ter do. It's Mrs Blunt what's 'gaged me, and I ain't takin' orders from nobody only the Mistress!'

'Mrs Blunt is my mother, and she has taught us to be polite. Get out of my way, you little shrimp!' And he picked up the trunk, and carried it easily across the yard.

Lucy was standing at the kitchen door, watching the little tableau. Harry has met his match, she thought, in this tough little creature with the glowering face. At 15 he was getting too big for his boots, and his father was too easy-going. Boys had to be disciplined, but she was the one to keep them in order. There was a time, when they were first married, that she yielded to her husband's better judgment, for she was a novice, fresh from service in the doctor's household; but she learned quickly, and soon discovered that a wife's intuition was often more of an asset than a man's experience. She smiled a welcome. She had expected a big strapping girl, and they had sent her a skinny little waif.

'Come in, Emma. You are just in time for supper,' she said, kindly.

'Thank 'ee, Ma'am.'

Emma followed her new mistress into the kitchen. It was the start of a new chapter. The first kind words that had ever been addressed to her in her short life made a deep impression. Mrs Blunt was the boss, and Emma Smith owed her allegiance to the plump, pretty woman with the golden hair, *and no other*. Lucy had found herself a loyal and willing slave that Summer evening.

'Don't let her out of your sight,' young Albert Blunt had been instructed, but it was proving a full time occupation, for Carrie was not the docile little girl he had expected to escort round the farm that first day. She had a will of her own, and a strong determination to do things her way. The first celandines in the damp ditches had held them up for half-an-hour or more while she carefully picked each flower and examined it closely, surprised and delighted to find flowers growing in a ditch. There was no flowers in Richmond Row, and the ditches contained stagnant water that smelled horrid. Only girls picked celandines and primroses, but it was too early for primroses.

Albert had so many things to show his little cousin, he grew impatient at the delay, and begged her to hurry. She took no notice. Completely absorbed in the celandines, wrapped in all her Winter clothes, she was puffing and panting as she slithered up and down the wet banks. He had taken off her mittens, and when he unwound the straggling woolly muffler, she smiled her thanks and went on picking.

At 4 years of age, when most small children were dressing and undressing without any assistance, Carrie stood and waited, he noticed. She had held out her hands automatically for her mittens to be removed, and now he was left standing there, holding the muffler as well as the mittens. He was also expected to hold the flowers when the bunch was too big for her small fist.

Girls were a nuisance, Albert had already decided, when Emma Smith arrived at the farm. Nothing had ever been the same again. But Carrie was still a baby in some ways, and he felt protective towards her. She was very affectionate. Everyone had been hugged and kissed, including Emma. Innocent blue eyes had widened at the sight of the most commonplace farm animals, such as cows, sheep and horses. He could not begin to imagine the limitations of Richmond Row and The Three Nuns, yet that had been the extent of Carrie's entire world until she had started school. The animals she now met for the first time she recognised from the picture book she had found in her Christmas stocking. With her face pressed to the gate, she had watched the new-born lambs dancing on their spindly legs, and her merry laugh echoed across the fields.

'Take Carrie to see the lambs,' Lucy had instructed, as soon as they had finished the hot cocoa and the scone spread with rich farm butter. Albert could understand her reluctance to leave the gate, for he also liked to watch the lambs. But to get stuck in a ditch picking celandines when there was still so much to see was spoiling his pleasure in the new role of escort.

From his vantage point on top of the bank, he could see his father following the plough, and Duke straining in the shafts. Where did all the seagulls come from? They were miles from the coast. Was it instinct that drove them inland at ploughing time, like the swallows returning to their old haunts in April? His brother Tom was the authority on such matters. Tom was gentle and sensitive – too sensitive, perhaps, for a farmer's son, for he shrank from killing any living creature. Even a rabbit would be allowed to escape in the hay-field. He hadn't the physical strength and stamina of his elder brother, but there was no doubt about his mental superiority. When he left school at 13, he had taken over the job of book-keeping and the farm accounts that his father had neglected to keep up to date. The three brothers had all inherited their mother's fairness, but all were different in character and temperament. Albert, being the youngest, still carried a chip on his shoulder because he had not yet displayed any particular talent or ability. He loved his mother passionately and possessively, but she showed no favouritism, and all her boys were equal in her sight. She encouraged their independence and manliness. From time to time, on that first Saturday, she

173

climbed the stairs to scan the wide acres of their valley farm from the attic window, but all was well, and Albert still in attendance on his little cousin.

When Emma rang the dinner bell in the yard, her family converged on the house from all directions, leaving their stout rubber boots in the scullery. She had trained them well. Lucy was mistress in her own kitchen, and did not care for muddied boots or the stink of dung on the red-tiled floor. Besides, it was not fair to Emma, whose vigorous scrubbing had to be seen to be believed. The skinny little waif was no weakling.

The doctor's wife, higher up the social scale, was not enjoying such maternal satisfaction in her three gentlemen sons. There was no loyalty and little affection for the mother who had indulged their every whim in boyhood.

Dulcie Saunders was a sad and lonely woman. She could not share her thoughts or her tears with her husband. They had drifted too far apart when the boys were young and dependent. The boys had been her first concern, her reason for living. Her small world had revolved around them. Doctor had always been busy and dedicated to his practice and patients. It had not mattered in those early years when he slept in the dressing-room, for she was not disturbed by the night bell. But it mattered now.

Her small world had collapsed the week before Christmas, when she discovered the horrible truth that her favourite son was a murderer. Christmas had been a terrible strain on her nerves.

'Where's Dennis, Mother?' Roger had demanded in his superior way, and Lesley had questioned her until she was on the verge of screaming. Why had Dennis come home in the first place if he intended to stay only one night? Why couldn't he wait till Christmas was over to join his friends in Switzerland? It was not like Dennis to miss the Boxing Day Meet at Marston Park, for it was one of the highlights of the festive season – and so on and so forth. Of recent years the boys had hired their mounts at the riding stables, but at one time all three boys had had their own ponies stabled in the mews behind the house.

There was nothing she was not ready and willing to provide for her sons. It was her duty and pleasure. No mother could have done more. Then what had gone wrong? Who was to blame, if not herself, for this catastrophe?

It was late March when she finally made contact with Dennis. She had lost a lot of weight, and she had aged ten years in those few short months. A letter awaited her at Brown's Hotel on her last visit to London. Dennis was working as a waiter in a hotel in some remote mountain village. He was desperately anxious to get away, right away, for he knew the police would not drop the case until the crime had been solved. There was only one safe hiding place, too far distant to be reached by the long arm of the law – the tea plantation in Ceylon. First a brother, now a son, deported in disgrace. It was heart-breaking. Money was sent to cover his expenses, and she begged him to keep in touch. Letters could be addressed to Brown's. Once every month she would spend a few days there. Nobody would suspect her real motive, since she had been attending recitals in the Wigmore Hall for some years.

But no letter came. She could not be certain that Dennis had gone to Ceylon. He was so unpredictable, and so utterly selfish. It was too late to repent of her foolish indulgence. If only she could have a second chance to redeem her mistakes.

There was no second chance for her, or her son. They

both had to live with this ghastly secret, but Dennis had left her to carry the burden of suspense, not knowing when the Chief Inspector would renew his investigation. She had lied on his first visit, and would go on lying in a desperate bid to protect a son whose weakness, and, yes, she must acknowledge the whole truth now – his *cowardice* – had placed her in such a quandary.

The servants had also been questioned. They were loyal and devoted to the boys, yet she could not feel absolutely assured of their discretion. Any careless remark could start another line of enquiry. And what of the school children who had spread the gossip so innocently?

'Mister Dennis had been larking about with Teacher in the hop-garden last September.'

The children in the late Miss Mason's class had been questioned separately, and were proud of their privileged status, boasting of the useful information they had supplied for the Deputy Inspector's notebook. The thin thread of evidence was tangible, but there were no witnesses. Nobody had seen them in the Park. Nobody knew they were lovers. Suspicion was not enough to convict a man even if he could be located. So much time had been wasted before the body was found.

But for Dulcie Saunders there was no escape from the haunting nightmare, and the heartbreak of disillusion and disloyalty.

Not all the children were marched to All Saints in a long crocodile on Good Friday. Not all the children sang 'There is a green hill far away' in shrill, happy voices. The Catholic children did no singing on this solemn day. The bright robe of the Virgin Mary and her crucified son were draped in black. Joseph and the Saints were likewise draped in black, and the altar was bare. No

176

candles illumined the dim interior of the little church, and Father Dominic moved silently on bare feet, in a long, white garment tied with a cord at the waist.

Lennie O'Brien – that irrepressible urchin from Richmond Row, peeped through his grubby fingers, and watched every movement. Why did Father wear a nightshirt on Good Friday? He would like to know, but was not going to risk a good belting by asking such a question. Dad was heavy-handed with the belt. The rest of the family had no curiosity about Father Dominic's garb, or the solemn rites he conducted on Good Friday. They expected to be impressed, and were not disappointed. Hetty was nursing the youngest boy, Mum was carrying another baby so low in her belly she couldn't get down on her knees, but she enjoyed the ritual, and shed a few tears. She wouldn't have missed it for all the tea in China.

The Chapel children boasted of a free tea with as many buttered hot-cross buns as they could tuck away. This would be followed by an hour of hearty singing in the gallery. Boys and girls were dressed in their Sunday best, but there was no sadness, and no gloomy sermon to be endured. Good Friday was recognised as the day for attracting new recruits into the Methodist fold.

Hesitating on the threshold, they were warmly welcomed and plied with buns and mugs of hot sweet tea. But there were no dissenters from Father Dominic's flock. It would be utterly inconceivable. The fear of everlasting Purgatory was too real, too awful to contemplate.

Because every day in the year, apart from Christmas Day, the little O'Briens went to bed hungry, the long period of Lent and its obligations passed unnoticed. Since the Army had swallowed the family poacher, no more rabbits came their way. Father Dominic's

177

insistence on the Good Friday fish, paid for from his own purse, was received with mixed feelings by the O'Briens. They were not even sure it was fresh, for it stank to high heaven. It was Lennie's job to collect it from the fishmonger, and it was the tail end of the cod from the back premises that was hurriedly wrapped for this particular customer. All the cats in Richmond Row enjoyed a Good Friday feast, for there is a limit to what hungry children will eat.

'Can I 'ave a bite of bread an' jam?' asked Lennie, plaintively. 'This 'ere fish don't taste of nofink.' Mum was worried about the waste, and all the children had to promise not to mention it when they attended the Saturday confession.

In The Parsonage kitchen, Cook would be frying fillets of plaice. At Marston Park, Cook would be grilling soles for the dining-room, and the kitchen-maid would be standing over a cauldron of boiling fat, dropping in generous portions of haddock, coated in batter, for the servants hall. The Easter house-party was in full swing. The grilled sole was one of several courses served for Good Friday luncheon. Sir Neville Franklin considered his duty done after attending the morning service at All Saints. Such prolonged abstinence could not be endured further. The solitary ride on his favourite hunter had given him an appetite. The solemn face of Parson, in his black cassock, and the long recital from St Matthew's Gospel were enough punishment for one day!

Easter Sunday would see the carriages rolling down the drive on their way to All Saints – the ladies in the new Edwardian fashions, the gentlemen in top hats and morning suits. Little boys would emerge in white sailor suits, little girls in flower-bedecked hats and dainty Spring clothes. Uniformed nurses and governesses would marshal their charges into church, still whispering excitedly of big chocolate eggs from Fortnum and Mason, and breakfast eggs in coloured shells.

Easter Sunday would see Parson and the choir in clean starched surplices, and the sweet scent of lilies and narcissi was quite intoxicating in the choir stalls. Easter Sunday would see the schoolmaster without his overcoat, and Irene in a freshly trimmed bonnet. But Easter Sunday would also see the tramps on the highway, *en route* to the Workhouse, still wrapped in the layers of Winter 'garments' in which they had hibernated. The stench of their unwashed bodies would not be tolerated by the haughty servants of the upper class, and the doors were slammed in their faces. It was the cottagers who filled their tea cans and cut a thick chunk of bread to help them on their way. Only the poor knew the discomfort of an empty belly. Only the poor recognised a fellow creature under a bundle of rags. The tramps avoided the farms because of the dogs. They kept to the highway, tramping the miles in silent, solitary independence. They were humble and apologetic, asking only for hot water, but hoping for a pinch of tea and sugar. They were seldom disappointed. But sometimes a cultured voice would surprise the generous benefactor.

'Thank you, Madam. You are very kind.'

'You're welcome,' came the prompt reply.

'You're welcome – you're welcome.' The muted footsteps of a pair of worn-out boots, wrapped in sackcloth, would beat out the rhythm of that heart-warming gesture.

Parson had recognised the sweet attachment between his frail daughter and the schoolmaster as a blessing, not an additional anxiety on his over-burdened shoulders.

Irene had blossomed like a rose in the adoration of her gentle admirer who had not embarrassed the family with indiscreet attentions. Parson was convinced he could trust Robinson.

There were no more lonely Sundays for Andrew Robinson since that eventful Christmas Day. Parson had intervened on his behalf.

'My dear Eleanor, with your kind approval, I shall ask Robinson to luncheon every Sunday. The Sabbath must be a long day for a lone bachelor.'

'As you wish, Archibald. I have no objection to the schoolmaster. Indeed, I find his quiet, unobtrusive manner quite agreeable. One gets a little tired of Farrow. He *is* so smug and effusive.'

'Poor Farrow. I fear he has chosen the wrong profession. He means well.'

'These well-meaning people are such bores, but I suppose we have no choice in the matter, seeing Farrow is a distant relative of Her Ladyship.'

Parson sighed. 'We dare not risk a further rebuff from that quarter, my dear. We were fortunate in getting Marion released from her post with nothing more than a reminder that it was most inconsiderate.'

'It was taking a liberty. Marion had no right to jeopardise your own position. It was selfish and headstrong. But then you have always indulged Marion.'

Parson flushed guiltily. 'If I have indulged one daughter more than the others, my dear wife, I do most humbly beg your pardon.'

'It is too late for regrets. She has gone, *with your blessing.*'

'Could I withhold my blessing from my own daughter?'

'You encouraged the liaison from the start, did you

not?' He nodded gravely. 'And punished yourself with a five-year separation?'

He nodded again. They had been over it so many times in the past few months, but it was still a bone of contention between them. Marion's impulsive marriage to the young missionary had shattered her mother's hopes of a local engagement to a suitable young gentleman. She had even visualised a romance between her lively, attractive daughter and one of the visiting gentry to Marston Park. But a governess was tied to her charges and the schoolroom, and her humble status would not encourage the attentions of eligible suitors.

'Thank God we are still blessed with two dear daughters,' she reminded her husband. 'And our little Irene has been looking so much better of late. It gave me much pleasure to see the dear child taking a quiet little walk in the garden on Sunday afternoon. It was so mild, and she had a shawl about her shoulders. She asked my permission, of course.'

'Of course.' A whimsical smile touched Parson's lips. He rejoiced in this secret liaison that brightened the days of a daughter destined to depart this life before she had savoured a normal and natural relationship with her devoted admirer. To see them together, however, knowing they shared a mutual attraction and common interests, was a constant reminder they were walking a tightrope, strained to its limit every Sunday afternoon. It was strange that neither his wife nor his eldest daughter seemed to realise the danger. But then they still regarded Irene as a child, a family pet, to be cosseted and coddled, and her every wish granted. Beneath the childish veneer, a young woman with normal emotions and reactions had been awakened. It was Irene, not Andrew, who plotted and planned those few ecstatic moments when they could be alone together.

The Spring of the year was a time for courting, and the

garden provided a number of sheltered arbours, out of sight of the house. Daffodils were spread in profusion under the trees, and tulips marched across the flower borders in stiff formation, 'like soldiers on parade', Irene had pointed out. She was a fanciful creature, and Andrew was so prosaic. In the budding lilacs and laburnums, and the chirping of small birds in the hedgerows, there was joy and hope for the future. Starry-eyed and blushing prettily, Irene stole a kiss, not once, but three times on that blissful afternoon in the garden. She could not know the torment he suffered with her arms about his neck, and her lips seeking his lips with such girlish playfulness. Latent senses of a sexual nature had to be discouraged. He had given his word to Parson. The advent of Spring, and Nature's wonderful rebirth, made his own repression seem unnatural – it *was* unnatural. Was Irene satisfied with these small crumbs of romance, these stolen kisses? Such a question must not be asked. It might provoke a dangerous situation he was too inexperienced to handle. It was an illusion, this romantic idyll. The only certainty was in its brevity.

'I love you, Andrew.'

'I love you, Irene.'

A sweet moment of close embrace, then he must put her gently away.

'I just see'd Miss Irene with 'er arms round the neck of that schoolmaster chap,' Peg-leg reported to Cook and Annie.

'Shall you tell the mistress?'

They shook their heads. 'What the eye don't see the 'eart don't grieve over,' Cook asserted.

'Maybe someone ought to warn 'im Miss Irene ain't long for this world,' Annie suggested.

'I reckon it's as plain as the nose on 'is face – the poor bugger,' said Peg-leg, sympathetically.

182

Chapter Seven

The village children were the last to discard their Winter garments. Mothers quoted 'Ne'er cast a clout till May is out', and they sweated uncomfortably in layers of ill-fitting, second-hand garments. Not all had been provided from Miss Cecily's store at The Parsonage. The children of gardeners, grooms and coachmen attached to the big estates inherited all the outgrown clothes from nursery and schoolroom. Of a much better quality and condition than Miss Cecily's, they were also more conspicuous, and these unfortunate children had to endure the teasing and tormenting the others were spared.

Lennie O'Brien, with his elbows out of his jersey, and a patch on his backside, was the first to taunt an embarrassed classmate in a Norfolk suit and a bow tie, while the older girls would pounce on a tearful child in a velvet frock with lace collar and cuffs. If only the nurses and governesses responsible for these charitable offerings could have witnessed the misery and humiliation these children suffered at the village school, they may have suggested giving the discarded clothes to an orphanage some distance from the village. But these superior members of the servants' hierarchy had no conception of the misery that each new generation of children had to endure. Parents and grandparents, born to servitude on these big estates, had forgotten their own humiliation, and cuffed their ungrateful offspring into obedience.

The children of the farm labourers did not wait for May to be out to cast a clout. They had their own celebration on May Day, when the cows plodded out from their Winter quarters into lush green pastures. Mufflers, coats and woolly caps were discarded. They were always the first to race breathlessly into the school playground to announce to their envious classmates that Summer had arrived. They had the advantage and the knowledge from their earliest years. The seasons were ruled by the elements, and a rigid conformity to an unchanging pattern. There was a time to sow and a time to reap – a time for lambing – a time for hay-making, harvest and hop-picking – a time for picking plums, pears and apples – a time for hedging and ditching – a time to make silage and a time to use it – a time for everything. Nothing they were taught at school could supplant the knowledge their natural heritage had provided. They were the healthiest and the happiest of all the children who swarmed into the crowded classrooms.

But it was Lennie O'Brien and his gang of ruffians who set the pace for marbles and tops, and his sister Hetty who set the pace for skipping and hop-scotch. There was something irrepressible about this Irish family from Richmond Row, and a cheeky self-assurance that seemed to thrive in such an impoverished environment. If a child survived to reach the village school, it would survive the rigours of Winter and epidemics of whooping cough, scarlet fever, mumps and measles. Diphtheria could be fatal. Like scarlet fever, it would often attack one particular child in a family, while the rest would escape.

184

Little Carrie Simmons, already asserting the strong independence that would see her through the troubled years of womanhood, dug in her heels one sunny morning in May, and refused to budge another step till the throttling woolly muffler had been removed. Coat, cap and mittens followed the muffler with her poor mum protesting, 'You'll catch your death, Carrie love'.

Carrie smiled serenely, tossed her curly head, and went off at a gallop down the alley. The church clock was striking 7. The village was wide awake. The milkman clattered his can on the doorsteps. The postman whistled cheerily as he tapped the brass knockers. The baker's boy was piling fresh bread into the cart, and down the bottom of the High Street Carrie could see her brother Jack sweeping the grocer's forecourt in a long apron. This was her world. She was happy and carefree – well, almost. When the church clock struck 8, she could start looking out for the big girls who would take her to school. The Three Nuns had long since lost its attraction. She shouted to Jack and he waved his broom.

When Mum came panting round the corner clutching the discarded clothes, she found Carrie astride the churchyard wall, showing her drawers.

'What's come over you, child?' she scolded.

But Carrie was too young to explain the relief and joy of stripping off those hateful Winter garments.

Spring fever affected most of the housewives in the village. In middle-class homes, one or two overworked servants were busy on the annual ritual of spring-cleaning. There was no escape. It was an unwritten law, firmly established in the Victorian era, and likely to continue till the Great War.

The master of the house, only vaguely aware of disruption, and the pervading smells of soapsuds and furniture polish, was assured of his comfort and his evening meals served with polite punctuality. The mistress was not so fortunate. She had to endure the discomfort of bare boards and stairs, while carpets were beaten, walls and shelves stripped of pictures and ornaments, and dust sheets draped over beds. Buckets and brooms had to be carefully negotiated, and lunch was a hurried meal, served by a harassed servant grumbling at the extra work.

At Marston Park the great house was spring-cleaned by an army of servants, organised and supervised by a butler and housekeeper, ready to pounce on some unfortunate maid or footman caught flirting on step-ladders. The family were not in any way inconvenienced by this major operation for they spent a month at the shooting lodge in the Highlands of Scotland. Discomfort was abhorrent to Her Ladyship, who continued to enjoy being a perpetual invalid. The malady from which she suffered, however, was incurable. No medicine would restore a happy relationship with a disappointed husband – a husband who actually envied his own tenant farmer at Russets. Why should Lucy Blunt be regarded with such favour because she had borne three healthy sons? It was a topic as distasteful as the unsolved murder on their estate, and the elopement of the second footman with the coachman's wife. Scandal and gossip should be kept to the servants' hall Her Ladyship insisted. She was not interested, and had no intention of getting involved.

The month of August would see the whole family embarking on their long journey to the villa in the South of France. Nurse, nursemaid and governess supervised the excited children. Her Ladyship, attended by her devoted maid, travelled overland in easy stages with the women and children, and a suite of rooms would be reserved for an overnight stay *en route*. Sir Neville enjoyed the sea voyage, but his unfortunate valet was a poor sailor, and a steward would be requisitioned to replace him. The skeleton staff of servants employed at the villa had to be supplemented in August by local women and girls, and a French chef was engaged for luncheon and dinner parties. Sir Neville was a popular and generous host, and the Villa Benita an excellent backcloth for lavish entertainment. His wife and children, as always, inhabited their separate little worlds. Her Ladyship would indulge her natural indolence on her balcony, while the children enjoyed the private beach below the villa, completely regardless of their parents. The ever-vigilant eyes of nurse and governess, and the unflagging energy of the young nursemaid, left no room for danger. Their happy laughter floated up to the balcony, but did not disturb the languorous figure under the striped sun canopy. She loved her children, she would remind herself, but servants were paid to look after them. If she had her way, she would keep the villa open all the year. The climate suited her. But her husband had the last word, and his authority was undisputed. To be a semi-invalid, she had long since discovered, was her only refuge from his exhausting vitality. It was here, in the Villa Benita, that she enjoyed a month of almost uninterrupted indulgence. She was excused from the luncheon and dinner parties, while her gregarious husband made merry with his guests – a cosmopolitan collection of friends and neighbours for whom the Mediterranean coast had a captivating allure. With no obligations in the Old Country, and no big estates to claim their allegiance, they had established a small exclusive community in this sunny clime.

It was here, in the Villa Benita, that certain privileged guests spent the night. Discreet servants turned a blind eye to the indulgences of their master and his guests. Hot days and sultry nights played havoc with the senses.

The bracing environment of the Scottish Highlands, and the bleak Winter landscape of Marston Park seemed very far removed from the Villa Benita. The children slept undisturbed in the nursery suite while naked figures, emerging from the warm waters of the bay, flitted across the white sand like human moths, and disappeared behind closed shutters.

It was harvest time when the family returned to Marston Park, and the nursery and schoolroom routine were set in motion immediately by a nurse and a governess who had found the month of August both tedious and exhausting. Their charges were tearful and disobedient. They had been spoiled by those foreign servants who had no comprehension of discipline and British commonsense.

The staff at Marston Park, who had taken their holidays, in strict rotation, according to status, were glad to have the family back and the normal routine resumed. Autumn was a time of mellowness, and 'walking out' a pleasant Sunday afternoon occupation.

The acrid smell of bonfires greeted the children as they bowled their hoops along the drive. There was freshly made strawberry jam for tea for good, well-behaved children, but bread and butter and no cake for a troublesome child. Nurse would stand no nonsense in her domain, and the prim, middle-aged governess who had replaced Marion suffered from nervous dyspepsia.

'What's nervous dyspepsia?' the youngest housemaid enquired of her superior.

'Bilious attacks.'

'Then why don't she call a spade a spade?'

'How should I know? Get on with your work!' came the sharp retort.

Her Ladyship was suffering from fatigue after the long journey, and the state of acute depression she always 'enjoyed' at this season of the year. Leaving the Villa Benita was such a wrench, and the drifting smoke of the bonfires was a reminder that Winter followed close on the heels of Autumn in the Weald. There was really no need for Her Ladyship to start worrying about the Winter, since she hadn't to endure its hardships. A coal fire would keep an even temperature in her boudoir, and her breakfast would be served after she had taken her bath. Sir Neville's dressing-room had been cleverly converted into a bathroom. Her personal maid would run her bath and drape fresh towels over hot pipes. The fragrance of lavender scented the water and the soap. It was her favourite, and the children knew exactly what to give their mamma for Christmas. The older girls would remind the younger.

But now, in early September, the sadness of Autumn fell heavily on her spirit and her idle hands, and she blamed her husband for insisting that she return home as always with her children.

There was a season for each separate establishment, he had explained, impatiently. August was the season for the Villa Benita. There was a London season, a season for the Scottish Highlands, and certain seasons in the year when his obligations to the big estate and his tenants had to take priority. He liked to watch the hay-making in the month of June, and apple picking in October. But one unchanging and beautiful scene in the farm calendar he would not have missed for any other event: sheaves of corn, stacked in stooks, in a stubbly field, with the horse waiting patiently in the shafts of the wagon, and the labourers busy with their pitchforks.

This was a scene that Constable left to posterity, but Sir Neville Franklin was no Constable, and had no creative talent. His senses were those of a virile and energetic nature. The Villa Benita was dismissed from his mind as soon as he embarked on the return journey.

The first morning back at Marston Park, the groom would lead out the restive stallion it had been his duty to exercise daily for a whole month. The great house was astir, and the Master had enjoyed an early breakfast of bacon and kidneys, toast and marmalade. There was something to be said for an English breakfast, he contended, with such a choice of dishes on the sideboard. Continental breakfasts had no substance, but it was an understanding with the servants, 'When in Rome, you do as the Romans'. It was oatmeal porridge and Finnen haddock in Scotland. The children, he supposed, ate boiled eggs for breakfast at the Villa Benita. It did not occur to him to enquire. It was not his province.

It was good to feel the freshness of early Autumn on his sun-tanned cheeks, and the strong flanks of Jasper moving rhythmically under his own strong body. They would spend all day riding round the estate, interrupted only with a cold buffet lunch at midday and hot, strong coffee. He would leave Russets till late afternoon, as usual, because he never tired of watching the Blunt family at work. At each of the farms on the estate he would be received with constrained courtesy, and invited to drink a measure of home-brewed cider. He would listen to complaints about his bailiff, and promise to rectify any injustice, for he was a fair landlord. But he sensed their relief when he bade them farewell.

He came to Russets with a sense of happy anticipation, for here, in this pleasant valley, the Blunts had made their roots for several generations. Fathers and sons seldom had need to employ outside labour. Together with wives and daughters, they worked the farm between them. The present family was particularly blessed with three boys, all as keen on farming as their parents, but not yet of an age to marry. A typical farmer's wife was Lucy Blunt. She employed a young servant girl for scrubbing and other household chores, but she managed the dairy single-handed, bottled her preserves in season, and fed her family like fighting cocks. Bert Blunt was a lucky man, and he knew it. Lucy was a woman in a million, he had told Sir Neville on more than one occasion. She was plump as a spring chicken, and that was the way he liked his woman. He couldn't abide a skinny woman in his bed! There was no restraint in Bert's vulgarity, and it amused his landlord.

So, on this mellow September day, he reined in his horse on the edge of the copse and gazed down on the pleasant pastoral scene. They were working on the last load. The barometer was falling, and a heavy shower could ruin those golden sheaves. Bert Blunt's sturdy figure was balanced precariously on top of the wagon, directing operations with a pitchfork. The three boys, healthy and sun-tanned, all had pitchforks and kept their father employed from below.

But it was Lucy Blunt who held his attention. She was gleaning some distance away, her buxom figure stooping and stretching with an easy grace that many a slender woman would envy. Her rounded arms and her throat were bare. She worked with the deftness of long experience. The sun caught the golden strands of her piled hair, and when she turned her head to smile at her husband, the watching man could see the hollow between her swelling breasts. His hands clenched convulsively on the reins, his loins ached and trembled in frustration.

191

Tragedy struck in a split second. He watched horrified and helpless in the shade of the copse. A young rabbit, racing terror-stricken from a disturbed stook, collided with the hooves of the massive Shire. With a jerky, impatient movement, the horse moved a pace to rid himself of the tiresome creature. The wagon rocked. The sturdy figure swayed and fell, head first, with a terrible scream. The pitchfork flew away. The man lay still.

The human tableau, shocked into stillness for a brief moment, suddenly came to life. Lucy Blunt dropped her apron, and the gleanings fell to the ground. She sped across the stubble on winged feet, gasping and sobbing.

'Bert! Bert! Oh, my God!'

The youngest boy ran to meet her, and she took his hand and they ran together to the prostrate figure in the shade of the wagon. The other boys dropped their pitchforks and stared, hypnotised. The younger of the two retched, and was violently sick.

The man on the horse moved out from the shadows and took command.

'Here, boy. Hold my horse,' he told the youngest, who was crouched on the ground beside his mother. The boy obeyed automatically, gulping back his tears.

'Fetch a hurdle. We will carry your father to the house,' he instructed the others, brusquely.

They ran off with the same automatic obedience.

Gazing down at the weeping woman stretched across her husband's body, Sir Neville found his own eyes smarting with tears. Bert Blunt was dead. Such a fall would have broken his neck. But when the woman lifted her stricken face to ask, pleadingly, 'He's not dead, is he, Sir?' he could not tell her the truth.

'It could be concussion. He fell heavily. I will get in touch with the doctor. Try not to worry.' He knelt beside her. She knew he was lying, and she stared at him with streaming eyes. A wave of tenderness, completely foreign to his nature, engulfed him. He put his arms about her, and her heavy body slumped on his chest. She smelled of sweat and earth and urine. She had wet her drawers. There were seeds in her hair. Her hands were rough, the nails broken. But she was all woman. The warmth of her sagging body only confirmed what he had known for a very long time. He wanted her.

The boy cried quietly now, sniffing in his misery. It was strange to see Sir Neville kneeling on the ground, holding his Mum, but everything was strange today. Nothing would ever be the same again after today. A new chapter had begun, and changes were inevitable.

Prince was standing quietly, the splayed body of the baby rabbit under a shaggy hoof. Albert shuddered and wiped a hand across his eyes. Away in the distance he could see his brothers running with the hurdle. He felt very small and frightened.

'Mum,' he called, entreatingly, 'Mum, they're coming.'

With a shuddering sigh she scrambled to her feet and dried her eyes on a corner of the long white apron. She was maternal now, loving and protective, and quite unconscious of any emotion other than a stunned awareness of her children's need of her.

Tom was staggering under the weight of the hurdle. His stomach was sick. He was shivering and sweating. She took his end of the hurdle and kissed his cold cheek. Harry's mouth was thin and stubborn. She could depend on her firstborn, but he was still only a child in years.

They put down the hurdle. Once again the landlord took command. It was natural. 'Take his feet. I will take his head,' he told Harry. And they lifted his father from the stubble, and laid him gently on the hurdle.

'Can you help your brother, boy?' he asked Tom kindly.

Tom nodded, and took his place beside Harry.

'Lead the way with Jasper,' he told Albert. 'And you, Mrs Blunt, could lead the horse with the wagon.'

'Yes, Sir,' she agreed. One did not disagree with Sir Neville Franklin. Picking up the scattered pitchforks, she carried them carefully in one hand and led Prince with the other. One did not leave tools lying around. It was one of the first lessons the boys had been taught – as she herself had been taught when she married Bert.

The little procession wound its way slowly to the back of the house. The kitchen door stood open. The mellowed walls were bathed in sunshine. Brown hens clucked in the scattered straw. Pigeons cooed in the loft over the stables. It was very peaceful till Emma appeared in the doorway, wide-eyed, and screamed in panic.

'Be quiet, girl!' The authoritative voice carried little weight with Emma, however. She went on screaming.

'Shut up!' barked Harry, impatiently.

'Come here to me, child.' It was the only voice she recognised. She flew across the yard, skirting the still figure on the hurdle, panting with fear. Her mistress propped the pitchforks against the wall and, still holding Prince, gathered the frightened servant girl to her motherly breast.

It was cool in the parlour, but remote from the rest of the house in its prim arrangement of starched antimacassars and muslin curtains. Lucy used the room only for important visitors, but Bert would have nothing changed.

'What was good enough for Mum and Dad is good enough for me' was Bert's simple philosophy. He could be stubborn as a mule, and young Harry was the same.

The red chenille cloth with bobbles had been draped over the table since grandmother's day. A few of the bobbles were missing. The mantelpiece was crowded with two china dogs and a collection of ugly vases that Bert's father had won at the hoopla stall on Fair Day. That was Michaelmas, and the only treat in the year for the boys.

Lucy wrinkled her nose and pushed open the window. Bert would feel stifled in this musty room, but Harry had led the way, taking it for granted that the parlour was correct, not the kitchen. Already aware of his new responsibilities, her firstborn was frowning thoughtfully.

Albert was still obediently holding Jasper's reins, and Tom was holding Prince. They stood there, in the sunny yard, too stunned to speak, waiting for further instructions. Emma had been sent to the kitchen to brew a pot of tea. Hot, sweet tea for shock. That was another of Grandmother Blunt's remedies.

Sir Neville would have recommended brandy, but he was not consulted. He waited in embarrassed silence, his hat tucked under his arm. His smooth hair shone black as a raven's wing. His dark eyes followed the woman's every movement. There was no brandy – no spirits of any kind, since Grandfather Blunt, blotting his clean copybook, came reeling home dead drunk one market day. It was home-brewed cider for the men, lemonade for the children, and tea – gallons of tea – piping hot, straight from the pot, or stone cold in a bottle on a hot day in June at hay-making time.

When they had laid Bert on the stiff horsehair sofa, Harry quietly removed the hurdle to the yard and stared glumly at his two brothers.

'What are you waiting for, Tom? Take this load into the barn. Then unharness Prince and make him comfortable in the stable.'

195

'I feel sick,' mumbled Tom, miserably, but he did as he was bid. The big Dutch barn was a haven after the nightmare of the past hour. Dead was dead. That terrible scream would ring in his ears for many a long day. Mum was so brave, but then she never panicked not in any emergency, and there were plenty on a farm. Broken bones had been put in splints, sprained wrists and ankles soothed with witchhazel. Harry's painful boils dressed with hot flannels. Albert's chilblains rubbed with raw onion. Boils and chilblains were not an emergency. They happened every Winter like his own bout of bronchitis after Christmas. A steam kettle, and his chest rubbed with linament, and he was back to work in a couple of weeks. Accidents and ailments had to be expected in every family, Mum insisted. She managed. Mum always managed. Would she manage now, without Dad? If only Harry had been 18. A boy became a man at 18. If only he, Tom, were not such a coward? Who ever heard of a farmer's son who shrank from wringing the neck of a chicken, or watching the birth of a calf? Yet Russets was his whole world. He would die if he went away.

He leaned against Prince's massive flanks and asked kindly, 'Why did you have to move, Prince? It was such a little rabbit.' It could have been Duke, not Prince, with the wagon today, and Dad would still be alive. Duke wouldn't budge an inch in the shafts of the wagon, not if a whole littler of baby rabbits ran between his legs. He had a different temperament. Even a Shire can be temperamental. No two animals were alike, any more than two human beings, Dad had insisted. But Dad was dead. How could they manage without Dad?

The big stallion was getting restive, and Albert was having some difficulty in controlling it.

'Mum! Where are you, Mum?' he was calling urgently.

But it was Sir Neville who came striding across the yard

and took the reins. Without a word he handed the boy sixpence, and leapt on the horse with the easy agility of one who had been riding before he could walk. They were gone and out of sight in a matter of seconds, the three boys staring after them.

One by one, Harry leading, they filed quietly into the house, averting their eyes from the parlour door. Emma was pouring tea from the big brown teapot. Her face was swollen with crying. Their mother was rocking gently to and fro in Grandmother's rocking chair, her blue eyes bright with unshed tears. The seeds still clung in her hair. She smiled wistfully at her three sons.

'Come and sit down. You must be tired,' she said – and Albert went to sit on her lap.

The lamp burned low in the parlour. The grandfather clock struck 3. It was the longest night she ever remembered, even longer than the night Albert was born. Slumped in the chair beside the sofa, her head sunk gradually on to her chest. She slept fitfully, for an hour or so, and woke, shivering, to stare at that dear familiar face on the cushion. Hot tears pricked her eyes, but she forced them back. Tears would be a luxury she would only indulge in the privacy of the bedroom. That big marriage bed, in which Bert and his father and her own three boys had been born, would be so lonely.

She had stayed with Bert, tonight. She could not leave him alone. There had really been no need for the doctor to call, but she supposed he had to sign the death certificate. Sir Neville had taken a lot of trouble. A lad had delivered a note from the Big House. The funeral would be arranged at All Saints, and a wreath ordered. The farmers and their wives on the estate would already have been notified, and a retired cowman from Lovell's Farm would be coming to lend a hand for as long as he was needed. His name was Fred Wallace. He was 70, but still hale and hearty, and a widower, so he hadn't to return home at night. He could sleep in the loft over the stables. The note was signed 'Yours sincerely, Neville Franklin'.

The boys had been eating their supper when the lad brought the note, and he was invited to join them. There was always enough and to spare at Russets, and the lad was thin and undernourished. Another mug of tea was poured, and a generous helping of home-cured ham and pickles was piled on his plate. With home-baked bread, fresh farm butter and cheese, it seemed like a feast to the orphaned lad, apprenticed to the miserly old carpenter.

Lucy had only glanced at the note, then slipped it in the pocket of her apron. Now she took it out to read again in the dim light of the lamp. She had to keep awake to call Harry at 5 o'clock. They would do the milking together, this first morning. She supposed Fred Wallace would arrive in time for dinner, and would take over the evening milking with Tom. It was only a matter of three miles or so from Lovell's Farm, and that was no distance to a man born and bred in the country. Her own boys had walked long distances since they started school at the age of 5. Shanks's pony was the only means of transport unless you were going to market.

It was usual for the landlord to make funeral arrangements for his tenants. In fact, it was taken for granted that he would do so. Then why did she feel uncomfortable, even a little resentful that she had no voice in the matter? She had her pride. As Bert's wife she had enjoyed the respect of her farming neighbours, the tradespeople, and the servants at the Big House. She saw herself as indispensable in her small world – as indeed she was. In her opinion, the good yeoman stock of the farming Blunts was every bit as important as the aristocratic Franklins. The Blunts had worked hard for their inheritance. The Franklins hadn't lifted a finger. It was there, waiting for each new generation – the wealth and the big estates. Bert had laughed at such revolutionary independence. There was nothing subservient in Lucy Blunt's manner when Sir Neville called on them, and she knew he spent more time at Russets than the other farms, because the bailiff had told her so.

'Yours sincerely, Neville Franklin'. She reminded herself to be grateful. He was only doing his duty as a good landlord. But now she was remembering the way he had looked at her, as they knelt on the stubble beside Bert's broken body, and the way she had reacted to that look. It seemed the most natural thing in the world that his strong arms should hold her close, and that she should weep on his chest. She remembered that her sobbing breath had been smothered by the pressure, and her wet cheeks bruised by the hard buttons on his riding jacket. They had clung together for a long moment without embarrassment, almost as equals, yet her dusty garments and sweating body could have kept him aloof. In his fastidiousness, could there be an earthiness to complement her own? Looking back, it was not inconceivable. There *was* something between them – a physical attraction that was shameful and disloyal to Bert. There could be no love in such an attraction. She was no fool. It was dangerous. She shivered and stretched her stiff limbs.

The kitchen was warm and welcoming. She pulled out the damper and the black coals burned red in a matter of moments. A singing kettle on the hob; it was the start of a new day. Life went on . She would take a mug of tea to Harry, and another to Emma, who slept in the smallest attic and felt like a queen in her solitary state. Lucy supposed it must be very pleasing to an orphan, after the

199

crowded dormitories. The poor little waif was one of the family now. She ate her meals at the family table. Lucy would not have her banished to a servants' table, though it was customary. Bert never interfered with her domestic affairs, and he had always been kind to Emma.

She knew exactly what Emma would say when she saw the mug of tea. 'Oh, Ma'am, you shouldn't 'ave. It ain't your place to wait on me.'

'Just for today, Emma,' her mistress would remind her, quietly – and the girl would gasp, 'The Master! Oh, Ma'am. I just remembered . . .' and burst into tears.

Fred Wallace arrived before they had finished breakfast; a short, stocky figure with a drooping walrus moustache and a face as lined as a walnut. Dressed in corduroys and an open-neck shirt, his Adam's apple wobbled in his scraggy neck. But his eyes were as blue as Lucy's. He carried a carpet bag containing his black suit to attend the funeral, his best boots, a clean shirt, a change of underwear and socks.

'Mornin' Ma'am.' He walked straight into the kitchen, dropped the carpet bag on the floor and looked about him as though comparing it to Lovell's – as indeed he was. He nodded approvingly, hung his cap on the back of the door, and sat down.

'It was good of you to come at such short notice,' Lucy told him kindly, filling another mug with tea from the pot on the hob.

'Glad to oblige, Ma'am. Bugger retirement. I ain't ready for it, not now nor never . . . My ole Dad dropped dead when 'e were mucking out the cowshed and that's what I 'opes to do when me time comes.'

Lucy's lips twisted in a wry smile. 'Don't talk of dying, Fred. We shall need you here for many a long day.'

'That's the best bit of news since they pensioned me orf at Lovell's last Michaelmas. Nigh on sixty years I bin

200

with Lovell's, for I started work when I was 9 years old, picking up stones in the fields afore the plough come along. Then over to the orchard with them black-'eart cherries, scaring orf them buggering starlings with tin cans. Many a time I dropped orf to sleep on top of that gate, pulling them strings. Shilling a week they paid me, but a shilling were a lot of money in them days when I were a little nipper. You lads don't know the meaning of 'ard work, I'll be bound.'

'That's what you think,' scoffed Harry, indignantly, already annoyed by Fred's assumption that old age gave him the right to walk straight into his mother's kitchen and make himself at home.

'You'll be ready for your breakfast, Fred, after that long walk,' said Lucy, getting up to fry more bacon and eggs.

Fred nodded. 'I do feel a bit peckish, Ma'am.' He ate noisily, in the manner of a man who had no wife to remind him of his table manners; taking draughts of tea with his mouth full of food, spearing the fried potato on his knife, clearing his plate with a crust.

Emma and the boys regarded the old man distastefully, for Lucy had always been strict with the boys, and Emma had learned quickly. Three rashers of bacon, three eggs, and fried potato disappeared before you could say Jack Robinson. Belching comfortably, Fred grinned, and wiped the egg from his moustache with a calloused hand.

'That were proper gratifying, Ma'am,' he declared. 'Now I'm ready to start work. You don't 'ave to tell me what 'as to be done. I bin at it long enough to be buggering well acquainted. So don't you fret, Ma'am. Jus' you show me round the place, boy, an' leave me to get on with it. I won't need no supervising,' he added, meaningly.

201

'The name's Harry,' muttered Lucy's firstborn, sulkily.

'Sorry, Fred, I should have introduced you properly. You must excuse me. We have all been rather upset. It was such a terrible shock.' Since Fred made no comment, she indicated Tom and Albert. 'Emma helps me in the house. She's a good girl.'

Fred nodded affably and pushed back his chair.

'I hope you will find the loft comfortable, Fred. It's warm and dry, and Emma did her best up there before breakfast. Of course it's only for sleeping. You can wash in the scullery, and there's always room in this big kitchen when you've finished your work,' Lucy explained.

'Thank you kindly, Ma'am. I couldn't wish for nothing better.'

'Albert will take you up to the loft, then you can leave your bag.' Lucy smiled persuasively at her youngest. He was still tearful, and clinging, but he was only a little lad, and it would take time to recover from such a shock, she reminded herself.

Surprisingly it was Tom who had accepted the tragedy most calmly this morning. He was dressed and downstairs an hour earlier than usual, and helping Emma to carry up the truckle bed and blankets to the loft over the stables. It had been Tom who had been waiting to kiss her cold cheek when she closed the parlour door.

'Don't worry, Mum. We shall manage,' he told her quietly.

'We *have* to manage, Tom.' Her voice was choked.

'I'm sorry I let you down yesterday.'

'But you didn't let me down. You were very brave. I was proud of you, Tom.'

'But I was sick. The others weren't sick.'

'They haven't got your sensitive stomach.'

'I shall be all right now.'

She hugged him affectionately. She loved her boys. Her only disappointment in her married life was not being blessed with a daughter. It was too late now. There would be no more children. She was still a young woman, but Bert could never be replaced.

The tolling bell could be heard faintly in the valley as the cortège moved out of the cobbled yard. The handsome Shires, Prince and Duke, harnessed to the wagon, had been groomed by Tom and Albert till their coats shone. Black bows adorned their brass-studded collars. Their shaggy hooves had been washed and combed. The wagon had been freshly painted, and Emma had scrubbed the floor in her eagerness to be included in the sad preparations for the master's funeral. The coffin was piled with wreaths. The scent of lilies, roses and carnations mingled with the stench of steaming dung, for Duke had lifted his tail as the cortège moved off.

'Bugger it!' muttered Fred, irritably, at the horse's head. In his black suit and best boots, with a borrowed bowler falling over his ears, he was proud of his allotted task to lead the procession.

The three boys, in their Sunday suits, with their smooth fair hair and scrubbed faces, tanned by the sun, walked immediately behind the wagon. Harry looked grim. Tom was determined not to be sick, Albert was sniffing miserably. A few paces behind the boys, Lucy and Emma followed in the governess-cart a young groom had delivered from the Big House. The sombre black garments enhanced Lucy's fair complexion. Her freshly washed golden hair was piled under a black straw hat. Her blue eyes glistened with unshed tears. The wide, braided skirt and the high-necked blouse had been hurriedly run up on the machine by the sewing-woman at the Big House. A black frock and a bonnet had been found for Emma, and she was wearing gloves for the first time in her life. While her fair mistress looked so enchanting in her mourning clothes, the little servant, with her sallow skin and black eyes, looked more than ever like a gypsy.

Behind the governess-cart walked the farmers with their sons and labourers from the other farms on the estate, all attired in black suits. The farmers and their sons wore bowlers, the labourers wore cloth caps, and their cheap boots squeaked as they walked. Wives and daughters followed in wagonettes, all suitably clad for the sad occasion. It was a rare treat for the little girls, who could not hide their excitement. Grooms, gardeners and footmen from the Big House had been instructed to follow the cortège on foot to the church. It would be a long hot tramp on this warm September day, and all the men and boys would be sweating in their black suits, and strangled by their collars and ties.

The coachman had been delegated to drive the brougham in which the housekeeper, the governess, the lady's maid, the head housemaid and the parlourmaid sat in solemn state. Other servants of lower status could walk across the Park to attend the funeral service if they felt inclined. So also could the tenants of the cottages on the estate.

At the tail end of the procession, adding a touch of glamour and dignity, Sir Neville Franklin sat stiffly erect on his splendid black stallion. His brows were creased in a frown of deep concentration, his dark eyes intent on the woman in the governess-cart. She was lovely. Had she been born in his own class of society, he would not have hesitated to arrange a divorce from his lady wife. He wanted her, but there was a limit to the price he would pay. He must bide his time, wait for an opportunity. The easy conquests that had so delighted him at the Villa Benita held no significance now. The young girls, with their charming ways and childish adoration were put aside, like discarded toys. There was no place for them now, since he had held this woman in his arms and smelled the sweat of her strong, healthy body.

To have such thoughts as he followed the cortège was altogether outrageous, but his thoughts were private, and he did not feel ashamed. His natural virility could not be restrained for long, and his own strong healthy body yearned for the other with mounting desire. Beyond that exquisite moment of her surrender – and he had no doubt that she would eventually surrender – he had no plans. A mistress, actually living on the estate, would be an open secret. His pride and dignity would suffer from such an association. Yet to take her but once, and forever forfeit the right, would be intolerable.

Now the tolling bell could be heard quite distinctly as they turned into the High Street. The horses' hooves and the wagon wheels echoed to the rhythm of the tolling bell. It was very impressive. Blinds were drawn in all the shops and houses. Little groups of villagers stood silently and reverently, the men bare-headed. There was no other sound but the tolling bell and the ringing of hooves and iron wagon wheels – nothing to disturb the passing of that respected farmer from Russets.

Another group of mourners stood waiting at the church gate, but these were family mourners. Lucy's twin sister, Ruby, in her borrowed black garments, had Carrie by the hand. Her husband and her own three boys stood stiffly at attention. All had been allowed to take time off from work, but Tom Simmons would have a shilling deducted from his wages.

205

The neighbouring farmers stepped forward to shoulder the coffin. Lucy was helped from the governess-cart. The two sisters embraced, but could not speak a word, for their hearts were too full. Carrie hugged her aunt and whispered, excitedly, 'I got a new frock an' bonnet. Mum got it for nofink from Miss Sisly at The Parsonage.'

Lucy smiled with misted eyes. 'Hush, child,' Ruby admonished, and Tom Simmons looked embarrassed.

Parson was waiting in the church doorway, and when all were properly assembled, he led the cortège slowly down the long aisle. Parson's wife and eldest daughter occupied their usual pew. They attended all the funerals; it was one of their parochial duties. It often happened, when the mourners were pathetically few, that they followed the coffin to the grave. But not today. Farmer Blunt was well accompanied on his last journey.

The two sisters, standing side by side in the front pew, were strikingly alike in their mourning clothes, but their sons were different. Three fair, sturdy boys, and three thin, dark, little lads, staring solemnly at the piled wreaths on the coffin. Ruby had added their tribute at the last moment. A shilling a week, for five weeks would be deducted from her wages, for she had to borrow the money from the publican's wife. Five shillings was a lot of money, but she would not have her family shamed by a lesser tribute to her sister's husband. The boy cousins, almost strangers, had nothing in common. It was true Ruby's eldest boy worked on a farm, but a labourer has no status. Lucy's boys would inherit the tenancy of Russets one day, and Harry, at 15, was ready to step into his father's shoes. The only link between them was Carrie, who was everyone's pet. She had been given the privileged seat at the aisle end of the pew, where she could watch the entire ceremony with avid curiosity.

Emma sat immediately behind with Tom Simmons and his three boys. They had not met before. Surprisingly, it was Freddie who was most attracted, and her bold glances brought a blush to his cheek. Emma enjoyed every moment, and her singing of Bert's favourite hymn 'Abide With Me' brought fresh tears to Lucy's eyes. Her little waif was always singing about the house, and it was usually hymns. She knew every word, and did not need a hymn-book. The six boys stood mute, in embarrassed silence, while Emma's voice rose clear and pure, for she had no shyness. But then, she was full of surprises and contradictions. So proud of her tiny attic bedroom, with the sloping roof, yet she could not bear the kitchen door shut, and often disappeared in the midst of her chores and came running back, some time later, with glowing cheeks, quite unconscious of disobedience. Emma was still a child in years, but her budding breasts had captured the attention of Harry, and she flaunted her new maturity.

The service over, the solemn procession proceeded slowly down the aisle, out into the sunshine. Birds twittered in the eaves, and rooks squawked in the tall elms that bordered the churchyard. A dog barked in a nearby cottage, and a horse neighed.

Over the churchyard wall, Fred was holding the horses in the farm wagon. The head-groom from the Big House was walking Jasper up and down, while the under-groom was in charge of the brougham. A gardener's boy held the reins of the quiet mare in the governess-cart while the youngest sons of the neighbouring farmers were responsible for the wagonettes. All were glad to be spared the tedium of the funeral service.

'Take Carrie to the governess-cart and sit there quietly,' Emma was instructed. An open grave was no place for a 5-year-old child.

'Where are we going, Em?' asked the child, skipping happily down the path.

'Back to the farm o'course, to the funeral tea. Me an' the Mistress got it all ready afore we left, an' everythink is covered over in the big larder with clean cloths. The taties is baking in the slow oven. There's cold roast beef and pork, with pickled onions and chutney, sausage rolls, veal an' 'am pie, fruit salad an' cream. The Mistress baked the bread last night, an' there's fresh butter an' cheese. Nobody won't go short, Carrie, don't you worry. It's going to be the best funeral tea folks ever remember in these parts.'

Carrie looked suitably impressed. 'Can I eat as much as I want then, Em?'

'You can stuff yerself till you're ready to bust!' They were laughing as they reached the church gate.

''ere, whatcher think this is then – a bloody wedding?' Fred demanded irritably. 'I be ashamed of you, Emma Smith. Thought you 'ad more respect for the Master.'

'So I 'ave then! You mind your own business, Fred Wallace. I don't take no orders from you!'

'Cheeky little bastard!' muttered Fred.

'And I ain't a bastard, neither. I'm a n'orphan, see!'

They glared at each other – the old man who had seen so many seasons come and go at Lovell's, and the young servant girl whose first Summer at Russets had been the happiest she had known in her short life. The grooms were chuckling at the sparring match. All the horses were getting restive now. Carrie took no notice. This was nothing compared to the fights and quarrels in Richmond Row. She was trying to imagine the lavishness of a funeral tea at Russets. It was such an exciting day, full of new experiences, and Carrie could never get enough of new experiences.

Since she had started school, her avid curiosity was

constantly surprised and gratified. Now she could hardly remember the time when she had been happy to play with her ragdoll, and cut out pictures for her scrapbook, while Mum scrubbed the floors at The Three Nuns. But today was almost unbearably exciting. She clutched Emma's arm and whispered, hoarsely, 'Em, I want to pee.'

'You would.' snapped Emma, still smarting from that hateful word – bastard! Would she never hear the last of it?

'I know where the lavtry is at the pub. I bin there lots of times,' Carrie prompted helpfully.

'Well, come on then. What are we waiting for? We got to buck up, or we shall be left behind,' Emma threatened, and they sped towards the inn.

Fred shook his head sadly. 'The worst day's work Mistress Blunt as ever done was to take that little bugger in from the orphanage, in my opinion. Gypsy blood, as plain as plain, an' gypsies spell trouble.'

'Cheer up, mate. She's not your responsibility,' the headgroom reminded him.

Little groups of mourners were straggling back across the grass. The wreaths had been admired, and all the inscriptions on the black-edged cards duly examined. Parson was waiting in the church doorway to finish his pastoral obligations. A few well-chosen words to the widow and the fatherless boys, then to shake hands and watch them depart. There was no hurry. Everything must be conducted with due reverence and solemnity. Lucy would thank him, on behalf of the family and the husband they had laid to rest beside his forebears.

Sir Neville Franklin stood waiting impatiently, his hat tucked under his arm. He, too, had done his duty to a respected tenant farmer, but now he wanted to get away. He took Lucy's gloved hand.

'Goodbye, Mrs Blunt. You have been very brave. If you need any help, in any way, just send a message,' he told her, quietly.

'Thank you, Sir, for everything.' Her voice broke. 'I shall always remember today.'

'So shall I,' he said, meaningly. He was still holding her hand.

'Then you are not returning with us, Sir?'

'No. I shall take the short cut across the Park. Goodbye.' He dropped her hand and strode away, covering his handsome dark head with the grey topper. In a matter of seconds he had mounted the stallion, and he rode away almost unnoticed, and was instantly forgotten in the clatter and clamour of departing vehicles.

The six boys had climbed into the empty wagon. Emma and Carrie had been instructed to join them. Lucy, Ruby and her husband, Tom, would ride in the governess-cart. There was plenty of room in the wagon for the grooms, gardeners and footmen from the Big House. They had walked far enough, and were glad to sit down. A mug of home-brewed cider would be welcome at the end of the journey, they all agreed.

The female staff, back in the brougham, resumed their seats with the gravity and decorum the occasion demanded.

'A cup of tea will be nice,' the housekeeper whispered, and they nodded agreement. Their tea would be served in the parlour, still smelling faintly of lilies and carnations in spite of the open window.

While Fred hurriedly cleared away the heap of dung in the yard, the younger boys stabled the Shires. There was no time for tears, not for a busy hostess.

It was Lucy's big day. She felt like a queen, a tragedy queen. Emma was back where she belonged, shiny-eyed with pride; a long white apron draping her black frock.

210

When the horses had been stabled comfortably, Freddie slipped away quietly into the kitchen and watched Emma covertly. He envied his cousin, Harry, who was teasing her as though she were a sister. A sister? No, a boy did not look at his sister in such a way.

Fred and Harry donned their white coats and went to drive in the cows for milking. Plentiful helpings of food were put aside for them. They had swallowed a cup of tea and a couple of sausage rolls.

'That were a mighty perty funeral, lad,' Fred commented, dryly.

'What's so pretty about a funeral?' snarled Harry, holding back the tears. 'Dad's gone, and he was the best Dad in the world. So shut your mouth! I don't want to talk about it.' And he hurried away and left the old man gaping with astonishment.

'There weren't no call to bite me 'ead off, lad,' he reminded the boy, some time later, but Harry made no answer. Lad! Lad!

Stepping into his father's shoes, he felt he had grown several inches. Nearly 16, then only two more years to manhood. Would his mother hand over the reins when he was 18? It was not uncommon for an elder son to take over the responsibilities at that age. But Mum would still be a young woman. In a sense, she had always been the guiding hand, the strong, sturdy figure on whom they all depended. He was proud of the way she had conducted herself today. Only once had he seen her dabbing her wet eyes. Why did that skinny little waif have to spoil it by singing that hymn like a blinkin' choirboy? Showing off, as usual. He would have it out with her when he got her alone. He knew where to look for her later, when she collected the eggs. The hens laid all over the place, but her sharp eyes would find the eggs, or most of them.

'Abide with me; Fast falls the eventide.' The clear

pure notes still rang in his head insistently. 'Abide with me; Fast falls the eventide; In cloud and sunshine, Lord with me abide.' Abide with whom – Mum or Dad? Dad was dead. He had seen the coffin lowered into the grave, seen Parson sprinkle a handful of earth, seen Mum step forward to drop a a single red rose on the coffin. It was all wrong. Dad should never have died such a violent death. Not such a quiet, easy-going man. He should have lived to a grand old age, and died peacefully in his sleep, like Grandad.

They would not speak of it because they were shy of sentiment and emotion. Tom was the sensitive one, but he was plucky today. Near to fainting in that front pew, he had held his head between his knees for a long moment, then looked up, and smiled bravely at his elder brother. Albert was still young enough to cry. He was Mum's baby. 'Abide with me.' Dad, or Mum?

'Last 'oppin' we 'ad Teacher an' Mister Dennis, didn't we, Mum?' Elsie Pearce remembered as the home-pickers settled down to their first long day in the hop-garden.

'That's right,' Mum answered absently, rocking the iron-wheeled pram-cart with one foot. The baby was fretful, cutting teeth, but the dummy had been dipped in the sugar basin before they left home, and she hoped he would soon drop off to sleep.

'They never found that man what killed Teacher, did they, Mum?' Elsie persisted.

'Well, t'ain't no use to keep 'arpin' on it.'

'No, only we liked 'er better than the one we got now. She were *fair*.' Fairness was a virtue more desirable than cleverness when estimating the value of a school teacher. 'Did they ever find 'er drawers, Mum?'

''ow should I know?' Elsie's curiosity on sex was

insatiable, yet the word was never actually mentioned.

'I jus' wondered,' she sighed, and stripped off the hops in clumsy fingers. Hop-picking wasn't going to be much fun this year, what with the fretful baby, and Mum with her sore gums after having all her teeth out.

'Just a whiff of gas and you won't feel a thing. They're rotten, and rotten teeth are bad for the constitution,' the dentist had told Mum brusquely.

'But I won't be able to eat nofink in the 'op garden, an' I'm partial to a nice bit of cold bread pudding.'

'Make up your mind.' The dentist was a busy man.

'Get on with it then,' said Mum, with the usual resignation of the poor to what seemed an ultimatum.

They had walked more than four miles to the market town of Oakhurst because no dentist had yet put up his brass plate in the village. The upper class travelled to London to visit a dentist and did not trust a man who threatened to draw all your teeth with a whiff of gas. After a cup of tea at a tea-shop in the High Street, where Elsie had been allowed a halfpenny bun with pink icing as well as a cup of tea, they started for home. Mum was looking proper poorly, and ever so old without her teeth, but it was a mistake to mention it, for Mum lost her temper.

'A fat lot you care! I might as well 'ave managed on me own.'

Elsie had taken the day off from school for moral support. It was a nice outing for Elsie and the baby, who had enjoyed bouncing over the bumps in the rough track through the forest in his little pram-cart.

'Why don't we stop for a rest, Mum? It's nice and cool in the shade,' Elsie had suggested, after they had covered about half the distance.

''Cause if I sits down, I won't ever get up,' came the prompt retort.

213

So on they went. That was three weeks ago, and Mum was still wondering whether it had been a mistake. 'It's upset me nerves,' she complained bitterly. Living on slops till her gums had hardened was a penance she had not foreseen. And there was no money to pay for a nice new set of teeth.

The bines were dripping with early morning dew, and a cascade of water showered the pickers as the bines were pulled. Elsie laughed as the children squealed and darted away. It was her last year in the hop-garden. Next year she would be in service at The Parsonage. It was a bit of a let down when she had been expecting Marston Park, but Mum said beggars can't be choosers, and what did it matter when you could earn twelve pounds a year just for helping the two old servants? Everybody knew they lived like fighting cocks at The Parsonage, and that's more than could be said of some of the upper class. Strong and willing, these were the only credentials required, and Elsie was tough as a little mule, but a poor scholar. To stay on at school for another year, messing about with ''istry, jogrufy and sums was a shocking waste of time,' Mum had argued, vehemently.

'Do I 'ave to live in?' Elsie had enquired, timidly, at the interview.

'Yes, indeed, child. The sole purpose of engaging a young girl is to make life easier for Cook and Annie. Serving the early morning tea to the family will be one of your first duties after lighting the fires.'

'Yes, Ma'am.'

Parson's wife was a rather formidable lady, but Cook said she was kind.

'It's a good place,' Peg-leg had confirmed over a cup of tea and hot buttered scones, after the interview.

'Keep a civil tongue in your 'ead, an' do your duty, an' you'll 'ave no cause to regret it,' said Annie.

214

But Elsie was more concerned about the lack of young society. These three old servants would keep her nose to the grindstone, and all work and no play wasn't much of a prospect. The gardener's boy was too young. Besides, his Dad was the village constable. They said the schoolmaster was courting Miss Irene. What a lark! Not any of the senior girls could imagine Old Robby kissing anyone.

'Maybe they just 'old 'ands?' Elsie had suggested.

'That ain't *courting*!' scoffed Hetty O'Brien, a bright spark if ever there was one, and not likely to find herself in the Workhouse with a baby she hadn't expected. 'What you an' me 'as in mind, Elsie, wouldn't do for Miss Irene. I reckon she'd die of shock!' said Hetty. And they all had a fit of the giggles.

Still, it was romantic, and watching developments would enliven the dull routine. As for her own chances of a bit of a lark, there was always the butcher's boy and the grocer's boy, both likely candidates for a romp in the hay next Summer.

'Mum!' Elsie's voice was plaintive.

'What now?' sighed Mum, impatiently.

'What age was you when you started walking out with Dad?'

'Bout your age, but I was out to service when I were 11 years old. We started work much earlier in my young days. You bin lucky, Else.'

'Me lucky?' choked her daughter indignantly. ''ow about all them lines of washing I been 'angin' out afore I went to school, an' the times I 'ad to stop 'ome from school to mind the baby. Ain't that working?'

But Mum had the last word. 'You was born on a Sat'day, Else, an' "Sat'day's child works 'ard for a livin'." You couldn't get away from it. There it was, year after year, in *Old Moore's Almanack*.

215

The village children went back to school in late September, looking fit and healthy after six weeks in the open air. There was seldom an epidemic at that season of the year, and Doctor could concentrate on his patients in the upper class. Her Ladyship was suffering from 'nerves' – a vague malady that only the ladies of the upper class indulged in. It followed on from the bout of depression she suffered in September, after their return from the Villa Benita. Her personal maid, so devoted to her exacting mistress, encouraged the general assumption of her being a 'martyr to ill health'. Nobody, least of all her husband, could understand her reluctance to make an effort of some kind, if only for the sake of the children.

In the lovely month of October, with the Autumn glory spread out across the acres of parkland, Her Ladyship reclined as usual, in her boudoir, in an atmosphere of scented luxury. It was difficult to maintain a fondness for a husband with such rude health who disturbed her privacy. He seemed to flaunt his robustness. But thank goodness he had not wanted to share her bed since their youngest daughter was born. It no longer troubled her that Neville was unfaithful. It was not uncommon in society, and not in any way abnormal. The gossip in the servants' hall did not concern her, any more, for she was immune to the slings and arrows of scandal. Should he attempt any amorous advances, which seemed unlikely after such a long period, she would plead a sick headache.

The tragedy at Russets had hardly disturbed her complacency. She had listened to her maid's graphic account of the funeral while her hair was being dressed, but Neville did not refer to it at dinner that night. He had seemed in a strange, sullen mood, and scarcely aware of her. But then, a husband was entitled to his moods. It

216

had been one of the lessons her own mother had taught her marriageable daughters, so it hadn't surprised her. The servants indulged these moods in the Master, for it signified his manliness and his absolute authority.

When she ventured a comment that the weather had been agreeable for such an unhappy event, he looked at her with dark resentful eyes, and made no answer. How could she know he was so obsessed by the woman in deep mourning, with her brave smile, and tremendous courage, he could think of nothing else? How could she know that her lord and master had already lost interest in his latest protégé from Drury Lane, and the attractive wife of the well-known actor had rejoined her husband for a tour of the United States of America?

Lucy Blunt, so long admired and coveted, was no longer unobtainable. Impatiently he reminded himself he must bide his time. Six months, a year perhaps. Her loyalty to her husband would be absolute, for they had always been a devoted couple. He must guard against a sudden, impulsive word or gesture whenever he visited the farm. With a family of three boys, the servant girl and the old man all about the place, what opportunity would there be, at any time in the future, for that sweet intimacy he had known for a brief moment beside her husband's body? He wanted her, with a desperate urgency, but he had to wait, and waiting was a penance.

Martha Carter, that beloved teacher of Infants, was pregnant, and unashamedly proud of her state. Speculation on the father of the child was the main topic between the senior girls. Everyone expected to hear she had been dismissed from her post when the bulge under her dress became embarrassing, but the schoolmaster, averting his eyes whenever they came into close contact, was postponing the inevitable decision.

217

Miss Carter had all the qualities desired in that particular classroom – patience, tolerance, kindness, and discipline. To replace such a treasure would be a problem. So the weeks went by, and she continued to smile happily and join in the chanting of 'Twice one are two. Twice two are four.'

Little Carrie Simmons was her brightest pupil, but Miss Carter had no favourites, and dunces were regarded as clay to be moulded into shape, with infinite understanding. The bright scholars were not allowed to feel proud of their superior knowledge and showing off was frowned upon.

'What do 'er Dad make of it, I wonder?' Elsie Pearce reflected.

Sam Carter was the wheelwright, a widower, and a strict Methodist, and Martha was his only daughter. They enjoyed a comfortable prosperity in one of the solidly built cottages in Station Road. Sam Carter was a craftsman, and he carried on a craft handed down from father to son for several generations. He employed two men and a boy. The farmers over a wide area had nothing but praise for the quality and durability of the wagon wheels, and the upper class had no cause to complain on the refinement of the wheels for their carriages and governess carts.

'Sam Carter won't ever turn 'er out, I reckon. 'Twould be a terrible disgrace for 'is daughter to 'ave the baby in the Workhouse,' Hetty O'Brien asserted.

'But ain't 'e already disgraced?' Elsie argued. 'They do say 'e don't go to Chapel no more, an' nobody don't dare to mention 'er name. Mum says she's a brazen 'ussy, but she ain't. She's jus' the same as she always 'as been since we were in the Infants.'

'That's true,' Hetty agreed. 'Only it do seem as if our teachers is slipping from the straight and narrow, for it

218

were only last year when Miss Mason got herself murdered up in Marston Park.'

'It's Miss White's turn to blot 'er copybook,' another senior girl suggested, hopefully.

'What! That soppy 'apporth! I'll bet she ain't never walked out with nobody, only 'er Dad, an' she goes as red as a beetroot every time Mr Robinson do speak to 'er – the soppy thing,' Hetty pointed out.

'Still waters run deep,' Elsie reminded her.

'So blinkin' deep a bloke could fall asleep while she's making up 'er mind,' tittered Hetty. But she added kindly, 'Miss Carter's the one we've got to worry about. I wish we knowed the chap what got 'er in the family way. We could tick 'im off proper. I only 'ope she won't 'ave the baby in the Workus. She's too nice for the Workus.'

'Yes, she's too nice.' They all agreed.

It was all so quietly arranged that it came as an unpleasant shock one Monday morning to be lined up in the playground by a young pupil-teacher in place of their beloved Miss Carter. They marched in sullenly, scuffing their feet. Before the poor girl had finished calling the register, she was rudely interrupted by a voice from the back of the class.

'We want Teacher!'

In a matter of seconds, the whole class was chanting, 'We want Teacher! We want Teacher!'

'Stop it! Stop it! I say!' The girl's voice was shrill with vexation. She had lost control and she knew it.

Andrew Robinson, obliged to engage a replacement for Miss Carter at short notice, with no time to consult the School Governors, had been listening for the children's reaction, and was horrified to hear the rising hysteria in the girl's voice. He pushed open the door and stepped inside – a frowning formidable figure who

219

seldom intruded in the Infants' domain. The chanting stopped abruptly, the young teacher burst into tears and fled. The Infants trembled and waited. Teacher was gone. Lambs without a shepherd, they were lost and frightened. Several little girls wet their drawers and began to cry, quietly. The schoolmaster spoke, and his voice carried weight and conviction.

'Now, we will have no more of this *disgraceful* behaviour! You will copy out on your slates all the sums on the blackboard, *silently*. Is that understood?'

'Yes, Sir,' piped the Infants, obediently.

'One of the senior girls will be sent in to supervise. You may start.'

Their covert glances followed him as he flung open the door and left it hanging open. Five minutes later, Hetty O'Brien walked in with a confident swagger.

Only a week before this minor rebellion, Andrew Robinson had received a polite note from Miss Carter, with apologies for the inconvenience, and sincere regrets at being obliged to leave her Infants. The note was headed 'c/o Mrs Martin, 3 Richmond Row'. So the rumour that was circulating had some foundation, and young Dick Martin was the father of the child. A mere boy of 17, and one of several new recruits for the West Kents, since drafted to India. What on earth had possessed an intelligent young woman, so many years his senior, to throw away not only her good reputation, but a solid, respectable background, and a job for which she was ideally suited? It was inconceivable, and he would never understand the vulnerability of the female sex. They seemed to be swayed by their emotions. Silly little creatures!

He was very conscious of his manliness, the following Sunday afternoon, as he strolled in The Parsonage garden with Irene, and told her the full story. She was very sympathetic to his problem, and listened attentively. He had persuaded an elderly teacher, living in retirement in the village, to take over the Infants temporarily. He had not liked her brusque manner or her dowdy appearance, but there seemed to be no alternative under the circumstances. She was a pallid-faced woman with pale eyes and a disfiguring mole on her cheek, and she ruled her small domain by fear.

The children had not been accustomed to threats, or the sudden, painful rapping of their knuckles for minor offences. It was little Carrie Simmons who ran sobbing across the playground, and shut herself in a lavatory after her initiation to the new disciplinary order. Hetty O'Brien was sent to get her out, but the poor child was too frightened to be taken back to the classroom, and had to be taken to her Mum at The Three Nuns. Never, in her short life, had Carrie been chastised with a ruler. What had she done? Had she been naughty or disobedient? Mum wanted to know.

Carrie shook her head and went on sobbing. Her drawers were soaked, and this further humiliation only added to her misery. Hetty had been delegated to escort the child she normally regarded as a spoilt little brat, but her warm Irish heart melted with compassion as they hurried towards the shelter of The Three Nuns, and the comfort of Mum's loving arms.

'She do seem awful strict with them Infants, but some don't get upset like Carrie,' Hetty explained.

'My Carrie is 'ighly strung, an' she don't go to school to be punished for nothingk. She's never been no trouble, not Carrie. She loves school, but I ain't sending 'er back, not till you lets me know it's safe. What a pity that nice Teacher got 'erself in the family way, but there 'tis. An' 'er Dad says she's made 'er bed an' must lie on

221

it. But it's a bit of a come down, living with the Martins, ain't it, 'etty? I mean ter say, you an' me is used to it. Them privies do make a nasty stink and there's no getting away from it, and Ma Martin ain't all that perticler where she chucks 'er slops. I feel real sorry for that nice young woman. I 'ad a little chat with 'er last night. She says she ain't given up teaching for good. She loves teaching, and anyway, she 'as to make a living for 'erself and the child.'

Ruby was still on her knees, hugging Carrie, the bucket of soapsuds forgotten in the unexpected diversion. A sticky peppermint had been discovered in her apron pocket, but Carrie had outgrown sticky peppermints.

'A nice cup of tea, then, eh, my luv?' Mum suggested.

Carrie nodded, and Hetty ran back to school, eager to impart the knowledge she had gleaned from Carrie's Mum.

'She'll be back, you'll see,' she announced dramatically to the chosen few. 'I reckon she's about seven months gone, don't you, Else?'

Elsie agreed.

'So them poor little buggers won't 'ave to put up with that spiteful ole bitch for more than two months, maybe less if the baby comes before its time?'

'Shall you tell Master that Teacher would be willing to come back if she were asked?'

'I shall that,' said Hetty, decidedly.

But the baby was not premature, and it certainly healed the breach between father and daughter. Sam Carter's curiosity had to be satisfied when the midwife, who happened to be the wife of one of his employees, reported to her husband that it was a bonny boy. The young apprentice was despatched with a note to Richmond Row, summoning the errant daughter. One glance at the infant was enough.

'Put him down on the sofa, Martha. The boy will keep

an eye on him. Go right back and collect your things. I don't care what you tell the Martins. This is his home and this is where he rightly belongs.'

'What about Dick? I have to know, Father. Will he be welcome here when he comes home?'

'Time enough to worry about that, my girl. The regiment's been drafted out East for five years.'

'I still want to know if my baby's father will be welcome.'

'Drat me if you're not as contrary as your mother! Very well, you have my word. My son-in-law won't have no cause to complain about his welome. I've missed you, Martha. I'll be glad to have you back. There now, don't cry. I had to be harsh, but I never intended you should spend the rest of your life in that stinking slum.'

'They have been kind to me, Father – and they are Dick's people,' she added, meaningly.

an eye on him. Go right back and collect your things. I don't care what you tell the Mudras. This is his home and this is where he rightly belongs."

"Watch out Dick? I have to know, Father. Will he be welcome home when he comes home?"

"Tibbe simply, 'Of worry about that, my girl. The neighbours been drifted out East for five years."

"I still want to know. If my Baby's father will be welcome..."

"Tell me, if you're not as courtesy as your mother? Why, well, you have my word. My son-in-law won't have no cause to complain about his welcome. I've missed you, Martha. I'll be glad to have you back there now, don't say I had to be told all, but I never intended you should spend the rest of your life in that stinking slum."

"They have been kind to me, Father — and they are bit expensive," she added meaningfully.

PART III

Chapter Eight

The young O'Briens ran barefoot in the Summer months, but were compelled to wear their boots for school and for Sunday Mass. Carrie sighed with envy, and she watched them scampering down the dusty alleyway and wished she might be allowed the same freedom. Mum was adamant. They had always behaved respectable, and no child of hers would be seen running around on bare feet. Only gypsy children, and poor Irish immigrants like the O'Briens had no pride, Ruby insisted.

To see the young O'Briens paddling their dirty feet in the village pond, one sunny Saturday afternoon in June, was too much for Carrie, however, and she promptly sat down, took off her boots and stockings, and wriggled with pleasure as the slimy green water slid over her toes.

'I'll tell,' threatened Lennie O'Brien, still the only real menace in Carrie's young life.

But Lennie could be bribed to keep his mouth shut, and never missed a chance of robbing some unfortunate victim. The boys were robbed of marbles and spinning tops, conkers and caterpillars, according to season. Little girls had only one alternative – a

227

half-penny, or torment. Most little girls preferred to hand over the half-penny, and Carrie was no exception. Two farthings would do. There was a good choice for a farthing at Mother Morgan's sweet shop. Carrie usually had a few farthings in her pinafore pocket, for she was allowed to keep the change when she was sent on an errand to the haberdashers or the bakery. The milkman also obliged with a farthing change when Carrie paid the bill for the daily delivery of skimmed milk every Saturday morning, according to Mum's instructions. Not many little girls of 6 could be entrusted with such a transaction, but sums presented no problem to Carrie.

'What be the total 'mount for this week then, my clever little maid?' the milkman would tease.

Now their beloved Teacher was back in the Infants, harmony had been restored. New talents were discovered in the bright children, and the dunces were encouraged to try harder. So Carrie promptly handed over two farthings, and Lennie ran off to Mother Morgan's on his bare, wet feet. He was quickly back with two bags of sherbet and two sticks of liquorice that he shared with the two little brothers he was minding for the day. Nobody could accuse Lennie O'Brien of selfishness, for he always shared his spoils. His sister, Hetty, an authority on the religious rites and dogma of the Catholic church, had assured him it was not a crime and therefore no need to mention it at the weekly confessional. But Lennie was taking no chances with Father Dominic refusing to believe that a boy could get through a whole week without some misdemeanour. A little sly prompting on the part of the priest would eventually discover most boys of Lennie's age had suddenly acquired a curiosity about the 'private parts' of little girls.

'How many times have you peeped up a little girl's

228

frock this week, Leonard?' Father would enquire blandly – and Lennie would confess to not more than two times, and get away with half-a-dozen Hail Marys.

It was only innocent fun at present, but the little girls would not be safe much longer from such avid curiosity. Lennie had never quite recovered from the shock and surprise of having the tables turned on his crafty tactics, last hop-picking season, when all the children raced off to the woods in the dinner hour, to pick and eat blackberries and nuts.

'I got some'at to show you, Len, an' I know of a nice little 'iding place,' 9-year-old Cissy Harris had invited, with a gracious air of bestowing a favour.

Lennie followed her with a readiness that delighted her sense of self-importance. But when they were comfortably settled in the hide-out, Cissy announced artfully, 'I charges a n'apenny a peep – an' I don't wear no drawers.' Lennie had not stopped to argue, but had hurried away quickly after the peep, to rejoin the gang who were stuffing themselves with blackberries. He was still wondering whether it had been worth a half-penny.

Carrie sat quietly and contentedly on the low wall in the warm sunshine. It was Saturday, the only day in the week when few questions were asked by working-class Mums, providing the eldest girl took charge of the baby. The village held no attraction for Hetty or Elsie, however, and they carried the babies to a nearby sand-pit, and dumped them unceremoniously in the sand with a couple of empty cocoa tins. The girls relaxed with sighs of relief, to chat about the future. Their brief childhood was almost over, and schooldays would soon be forgotten in the demanding world of service. Separated by a wide gulf between the established servants' hierarchy at Marston Park and the old-fashioned pattern of service at The Parsonage, the two bosom friends would meet only once a month, for an hour or so, on a free Sunday afternoon. There was sadness as well as excited anticipation in these last months of childhood.

'I wish I were coming with you, 'etty, that I do. It ain't going to be much fun at The Parsonage, not with them two old servants,' sighed Elsie, not for the first time.

'There's old Peg-leg, and 'e's not such a bad ole codger,' Hetty reminded her, handing over a bullseye.

Miss Victoria and Miss Letitia Langtry watched the blind piano tuner in their comfortable drawing-room with absorbed interest, and never failed to marvel at the touch of his sensitive fingers. Joseph was an established institution, and had been visiting the homes of the upper-class for many years. His radiant smile and unfailing courtesy had endeared him to a whole generation of young ladies with little or no talent for the pianoforte. Only rarely on his travels about the countryside had he encountered real talent, and the Misses Langtry, with whom he had been acquainted for the past thirty years, were not included in this particular category. Miss Victoria always insisted on playing one of her 'little pieces' when he had finished, in order to satisfy herself that the job had been done properly. Joseph would listen politely, his noble face lifted, his sightless eyes bright as onyx. Sun, wind and rain had given him a healthy complexion, for he depended entirely on Shanks's pony.

'The tone is much improved. Thank you, Joseph,' Miss Victoria acknowledged, graciously.

'Thank you, Ma'am. Then I'll be getting along.'

No mention of payment was ever made in the

drawing-room, but the half-crown would be waiting in the kitchen, where Cook would welcome him with a cup of tea.

The two ladies had no intention of letting him go, however, until they had satisfied their curiosity on certain rumours that were circulating in the village. Since Joseph had access to both upper-class drawing-rooms and kitchens, where he enjoyed light refreshments and a gossip with Cook, his visits were regarded as something of an event.

Was it true, Miss Victoria asked, bluntly, that the doctor's son, Dennis, had been located on a tea plantation in Ceylon, and charged with the murder of the young school teacher?

'It do seem as if there was some foundation in the rumour, Ma'am, for it hasn't been denied by Doctor or Mrs Saunders,' Joseph replied, cautiously.

'The poor dears. How dreadful! Always so respected in the village. Such a tragedy! Will he be brought home to face trial? Isn't that the usual procedure?' Miss Victoria persisted, with morbid curiosity. Her own sheltered, uneventful life with her sister had been much enlivened by the hunt for the murderer, and this new development would be followed to its tragic end with only superficial compassion for the victims.

The sisters' eccentricities were regarded by the servants with tolerant affection. It was the right and privilege of upper-class society to behave in any way they desired, within certain limits, of course. Dennis Saunders would pay the price of stepping outside those limits. The law did not recognise such class distinction.

'And how did you find the young ladies at Marston Park on your last visit, Joseph?' prompted Miss Letitia. 'I understand they have another new governess?'

'That is so, Ma'am,' Joseph agreed, wishing he could

231

escape to the kitchen. 'She is quite a talented pianist, so the young ladies should benefit from her tuition. She played a Chopin Nocturne for my pleasure when I had finished the tuning, and I must say the performance was most professional.'

'You tune the drawing-room piano as well as the one in the schoolroom?'

'Yes, it's a lovely instrument with a mellow tone.'

'Does her Ladyship play?'

'Not to my knowledge, Ma'am.'

'Poor dear. She seems so frail since the birth of her last daughter, and Sir Neville enjoys such excellent health. There are so many rumours of his infidelity, one wonders if he deliberately encourages such tales from sheer devilment. I wouldn't put it past him,' Miss Victoria hinted darkly.

'That I couldn't say, Ma'am.' Joseph refused to be drawn into any criticism of the local landlord. Sir Neville Franklin was a law unto himself, and it was no secret that his ex-mistress had rejoined her actor husband, and that his latest protégé had been little more than a child.

'Such a handsome man, one could forgive a little indiscretion,' sighed Miss Letitia.

Miss Victoria played her last card with a subtleness that did not deceive Joseph. His senses were more acute than the majority of sighted people, so he recognised this avid curiosity for scandalous gossip that spinster ladies of his acquaintance often indulged in.

'We understand Sir Neville is quite a frequent visitor at Russets Farm these days. Such a tragic death last harvest, when that poor man fell off the wagon. They say Sir Neville has provided an extra pair of hands with one of the retired labourers from another farm on the estate, but of course he has a reputation, as a kind

232

and generous landlord, and would feel sorry for the widow.'

Joseph shook his head, for Russets Farm was not included in his territory, or any other farm, for that matter. Farmers' wives and daughters had little time for playing the pianoforte.

Miss Victoria continued with hardly a pause to take breath. 'We happened to be passing the church on the day of the funeral. It was most impressive. Was it not, Letitia?'

Her sister nodded agreement. 'We thought the widow looked extremely attractive in her mourning clothes, quite distinguished in fact. One could almost have taken her for upper class. With Sir Neville riding at the rear of the cortège, it was really *most* impressive.'

'Yes, Ma'am, so I understand. Now, if you will excuse me, I must be getting along, or else I shall be late at Woodlands, and the Colonel does not like to be kept waiting.'

'No, indeed,' Miss Victoria agreed, somewhat disappointed in Joseph's mild observations. She took his arm, hurried him along to the kitchen, and handed him over to Cook, who had just taken a fresh batch of scones from the oven. She greeted him warmly, and sat him down at the open window. He could smell the new-mown grass in the paddock, and hear the shrill whistle of the gardener's boy. He could also sense another presence in the kitchen.

'You've got company, Cook?' he questioned.

'I ain't company.' Peg-leg protested. 'I jus' 'appened to be passing, so I called in to 'ave a word with my sister.'

'Cook your sister?'

'Aye, that surprises you, don't it? Thought you

233

knowed everything what was going on in this village, eh, Joseph?'

'I was under the impression you had no relatives hereabouts.'

'He's a crafty old bugger, this brother of mine,' chuckled Cook, amiably, pouring three cups of tea and buttering hot scones. 'Never calls in but what it ain't time for a cup of tea and a bite of something. Anybody would think they starved 'im at The Parsonage. Tell Joseph what you just told me, Peg-leg.'

'Miss Irene is breaking 'er poor little 'eart over that schoolmaster, 'cause they can't get married. Parson won't agree to it, neither will the Mistress, for they both knows she ain't long for this world, and the shock might kill 'er.' Peg-leg sighed, and sipped the scalding tea.

'But hasn't she been a semi-invalid for years? I've never known her in any other place than on the sofa in the drawing-room, in all the years I've been acquainted with the family, and she always seems cheerful enough.'

'But you ain't seen 'er lately, not since she lost 'er 'eart to this schoolmaster chap?'

'That's true. Has her health deteriorated?'

'Don't repeat this, Joseph, not to nobody, but Annie says there's blood on 'er 'andkerchiefs.'

'I'm sorry.'

'So be all of us, Joseph. Sorry for both.'

There was no longer any need to hide their love from the rest of the household. It was common knowledge, and regarded with obvious disapproval by Irene's mother and sister. Parson could feel only a sad resignation for a relationship that could end only in heartbreak. In reminding Andrew Robinson of the risk

234

he was taking in the early days of their acquaintance, and the need to guard against intimacy, Parson had not foreseen the rapid development of the relationship, or the sad predicament of the hapless man in love with his sick daughter. Irene's precarious health had grown steadily worse in the past few months, and Andrew was blamed. Yet to cancel the open invitation to join the family after morning service, and to prevent that happy interlude in the drawing-room or garden on Sunday afternoon, was well nigh impossible. It was too late. The damage was done. Such an emotional creature, adored by family and servants since early childhood, and her every wish granted, had found romance. It would be cruel to rob her of such unexpected delight in the person of the grave schoolmaster. It was now that Irene found her reactions more disturbing than anything she had ever known. Embraces and kisses were not enough, but Andrew was adamant. He, too, was tortured by a relationship that hovered precariously on the borderland of intimacy. Sexual intercourse could be fatal, yet he had no experience of the wiles of a woman in love, or her determination.

In the privacy of the Summer house, sheltered from the cool breezes of early Autumn, one Sunday afternoon, Irene lay passive in the arms of the man who steadfastly refused to become her lover. In all the romantic novels she had read so avidly on the drawing-room sofa, the two main characters lived happily ever after, but only on the last page. For such a gentleman, Andrew was surprisingly stubborn. She had offered herself and been refused. Neither her tears nor her temper had any effect on his strong principles. Her moods were as variable as the winds that blew across the Weald, and her wilfulness surprised and frightened him.

'You don't love me.'

How many times in the past months had he listened to this petulant accusation and denied it? In some ways she was still the spoilt child.

'Why can't you be honest with me and admit you're afraid of infection?' she demanded irritably.

He looked down at her with compassionate tenderness – the flushed cheeks and feverish bright eyes – so much a part of this wasting illness.

'Because I'm not afraid of infection, my love. I am afraid of losing you.'

'You have to lose me sooner or later. What are a few short weeks or months?'

He sighed and smoothed the hair from her damp forehead.

'Sweetheart, they would never forgive me.'

'What is there to forgive? Whether I die in my bed or in your arms concerns only two people – you and me.'

He shook his head.

'So there is another reason? Perhaps you think me a forward hussy for offering myself? Perhaps you think a woman should wait to be courted with restraint and delicacy. Oh, Andrew, my dearest, there is so little time left to us. Would you have it on your conscience for the rest of your days that you denied me the consummation of our love? Take me. Take me now,' she whispered, and her blue-veined hand stroked his beard.

'No, sweetheart, no.'

'*Yes. Yes.*' she urged. Her thin arms slipped round his neck. He could feel the heat of her frail body, the frantic beat of her heart. Her mouth was wet and soft. His loins quivered with tormenting frustration. He had never known such a moment of sweating indecision. His own mouth was wet and soft. There was no hardness,

236

no mastery in his lips, only the sensual acquiescence of a man tempted beyond his scope of endurance.

One blue-veined hand still clasped his neck while the other fumbled at the buttons of her blouse and camisole. She had no shyness. He was agonisingly shy. She was smiling as she placed his hand on her fluttering heart. There was no drawing back now. He was too deeply involved to remember his promise to Parson. With an anguished groan he buried his face in her bared breast.

She died the following day. It was her father who held her in his arms while her life's blood drained away. Too weak to speak, she was smiling and happy.

When he laid her back on her pillows, he kissed her cold brow and fell on his knees in prayer. He could hear Peg-leg beating mats in the yard, and smell the baked potatoes on the dinner wagon Annie was pushing in to the dining-room.

His wife had gone upstairs to wash her hands and tidy her hair. Cecily would soon be back from a round of visits to sick and aged parishioners. Life went on.

He did not blame Andrew Robinson. This tragic end to their relationship had been a foregone conclusion. He may have been the only witness to his daughter's starry-eyed adoration, as she clung to the arm of her lover when they left the Summer house. Be that as it may, it would not be the first time a parson had wavered in his principles in a father's love and understanding.

It was highly improper, and altogether ludicrous, Miss Letitia Langtry insisted, to turn the Infants' classroom into a nursery. The Colonel agreed, because it was less trouble to agree with the Misses Langtry than to oppose them. Sir Neville Franklin, who usually had the last word as Chairman of the Board of Governors, was surprisingly in favour. As for Parson, he would not have opposed Sir Neville even if he objected to the arrangement.

Andrew Robinson was taking a firm stand for once. 'We have tried a young pupil-teacher and an elderly retired teacher, and both have failed regrettably. 'Tis true the Infants are quiet and well behaved, but the atmosphere in the classroom whenever I make an unexpected visit is one of sullen and subdued submission. The children have lost their lively interest in their lessons. They have no respect for this woman and no affection. They love Miss Carter and she loves the children. In my opinion, it would be sheer folly to lose her to the school at Tonbridge which is advertising for an Infants' teacher. I have spoken to her, and seen the baby. She has assured me it is a good child, and will not disturb the children's lessons. With your approval, therefore, I should like to re-instate Miss Carter forthwith.'

The schoolmaster had surprised them with such strong views on the matter, since he normally had little to say and acquiesced most obligingly.

Sir Neville nodded agreement. 'Robinson's right. The young woman should be re-instated. Surely such a young infant sleeps for the best part of the day, or have I been misinformed?'

'In a quiet nursery an infant will sleep, but not in an Infants' classroom, unless the children are to be trained to speak in whispers,' Miss Letitia scoffed. 'It's quite ridiculous. And how does she propose to feed the child?' she added, addressing herself to the schoolmaster.

'There will be time enough in the dinner hour to feed

238

both herself and the child. She lives but a bare ten minutes' walk from the school. She has always been free to go home in the dinner hour. The Infants are well looked after in the adjoining classroom by elder sisters. The senior girls make cocoa and supervise the younger children. This is no problem.'

'I still think we should do better to advertise,' argued Miss Letitia, obstinately. 'Has anyone given a thought to the child's growth and development? In a couple of years or so it will be climbing out of the bassinet and trotting about the classroom.'

'Sufficient unto the day,' murmured Parson soothingly.

But Miss Letitia, as the only female on the Board of Governors, was still determined to oppose the motion, and rallied the Colonel to her support. He was inclined to drift into forty winks these days unless something stronger than tea was provided in the way of refreshment.

'Quite so,' said he automatically, wondering why Letitia didn't do something about that moustache on her upper lip. She was not a bad looking woman, but the moustache was becoming a disfigurement. They had been near neighbours for some years, and shared a fondness for Siamese cats and an obsession for bezique.

'Colonel! You were not listening!' admonished Letitia, playfully.

'My dear, I haven't missed a word,' he objected, stifling a yawn. He had a habit of smoothing his bald head as though he were smoothing the thick auburn curls that once had covered it so effectively, some forty years ago, as a dashing lieutenant. There was little to remind his long-suffering wife of that handsome young officer who had courted her so ardently in the hill station of Bangalore. She supposed the Colonel found

239

little to remind him of the pretty girl he had married; a wrinkled old hag, with parchment skin, gazed back at her whenever she powdered her nose.

'You *are* on my side, aren't you, Colonel?' prompted Letitia impatiently.

He smiled, and nodded agreement. In that sudden smile, the boyishness that lingers in every man was revealed. It could take the sting from his brusque manner and soothe a frightened child. But this was a boring subject to a man not blessed with children or grandchildren. As for Letitia, if she had any sense, she would admit absolute ignorance on the question of whether or not an infant in the Infants' classroom would be such a disturbing element. Sir Neville would have the last word anyway, whatever the opposition. That was a foregone conclusion. He patted Letitia's hand affectionately.

'It's three to one, my dear, so we may as well capitulate gracefully. Come along. I'll walk back with you.'

They shook hands with Sir Neville, Parson and the schoolmaster, and bid them good-day. 'Robinson seemed quite determined to get that young woman re-instated. I suppose we should give him the benefit of the doubt under the circumstances,' the Colonel reflected as they walked down the path to the school gate.

'He has hardly recovered from the shock of Irene's death. I thought he was looking very sad.'

'You think he was seriously in love with that poor girl?'

'It was obvious, and Irene was radiant. Everyone noticed her sudden blooming. She was such a romantic little creature, and so lovable. One can only assume it was too much for her, all the emotional excitement, in her precarious state of health. Poor little Irene.'

'What happens now? Will Robinson eventually marry a strong healthy woman or remain a bachelor?'

240

'I think he will be true to her memory. He is not a young man, and her death must have affected him deeply.'

'Quite so. Shall you invite me in for a glass of sherry?'

'Of course, *dear* Colonel.' Her gushing affection often jarred on his nerves, but she was a part of his small world of retirement, and he had to bear with her. He was out of his true element in his declining years, and Peg-leg was the only reminder of those memorable days. He often wished he had not been so generous in parting with his old batman, but he seemed to have settled down happily at The Parsonage.

He followed Letitia into the drawing-room and greeted her sister Victoria with a kiss. Victoria liked being kissed.

'Teacher's back! Teacher's back!' squealed Carrie Simmons excitedly, proud and pleased to be the first to have seen her. Carrie was always an early arrival, for she no longer had to wait to be escorted to school by the senior girls. To race down the alley, into the High Street, past the village pond, the Haberdashery, the Newsagents and Tobacconist, and the Fire Station to the school gates was a matter of ten minutes or so, unless she was delayed on the way. Avid curiosity had to be satisfied, an enquiring mind had to know the whys and wherefores of the small, interesting world in which she found herself.

Sometimes she stopped to inspect the baker's shop window, and the tempting display of rich cakes he was arranging with an artistic eye for colour and effect. He would raise a hand in greeting, and was tempted to offer the child a sugar bun, for she was a pretty child, with winning ways, but his wife would say it was a mistake.

'Do it once and you do it day after day,' she insisted.

241

She was right, of course. When she was busy in the house, he would invite a young customer to choose a biscuit from one of the glass-topped display tins on the front of the counter.

So Carrie did not really expect to receive a sugar bun. For a small girl who tasted only the plainest home-made cake for 363 days in the year – Christmas Day and her birthday they were treated to a cake from the baker's shop window – it was a fascinating game to pretend she could choose, and had money to spend. But the few farthings she carried in the pocket of her pinafore often dwindled away on bribes for Lennie O'Brien. If she told Jack, there would be a fight, and her brother in disgrace at the grocer's shop with a black eye. Not any of the little girls dared to tell tales on Lennie O'Brien. If Jack was sweeping the forecourt at the grocer's, Carrie would stop to coax him into lending her the broom for a few minutes.

'You'll get me fired!' he would grumble, but he couldn't refuse her anything, and neither could Albert or Freddie. She had her way with them. Stifling his giggles, he watched her sweep a couple of yards before she tripped over the unwieldy object and had to be rescued.

'Get along to school now, there's a good girl. I got no time for larking about,' he told her, with a businesslike air. Jack was very conscious of his new status, for he had recently been promoted to serving behind the counter at busy periods of the day. It was one step up the ladder, and another sixpence a week on his wages.

But today there had been nothing to delay Carrie, and she skipped happily through the open gates, across the playground, and into the Infants' cloakroom where the pegs had been placed conveniently low. The door of the classroom stood wide open, and Carrie peered cautiously inside, expecting to see 'old sourpuss' writing the sums on the blackboard in readiness for the first lesson, after calling the register. A short dumpy figure, so much like Mrs Noah, was bending over a bassinet, tucking in a shawl. Carrie crept on tiptoe, bright-eyed with wonder.

'Teacher,' she whispered.

Teacher turned her head, a warning finger to her lips. 'Hush, Carrie. He has just dropped off, and I am hoping he will sleep all morning. I know he has to get used to noise, but just for a day or two he may be a little startled.'

Carrie peered under the hood and spoke with awed reverence. 'It's like the Baby Jesus in the manger at Bethlehem.'

Teacher smiled at the child.

'Is it yours?'

Teacher nodded.

'Has it got a name?'

'Philip.'

'Have you come back for always?'

'Yes.'

'Oh, *Teacher!*' Carrie hugged her exuberantly.

'And the baby? Will you bring him every day?'

'We shall see. I can't promise.'

'I'm going to tell. I'm going to tell everybody!' She raced away.

Teacher closed the door softly and followed the child to the cloakroom. Instantly surrounded by a crowd of clamouring excited children, she shook her head, her eyes wet with tears.

'There's a baby! Teacher's got a baby!' Carrie announced importantly.

'A baby? Teacher's got a baby?' they echoed, staring at her flat stomach with wide-eyed interest.

'We knowed Teacher 'ad a baby, you soppy lot!' scoffed Maggie McKenzie with all the aplomb of a 6-year-old authority on such matters. 'It weren't no secret. We sawed it under 'er skirt afore she left,' she added.

There was no embarrassment. Neither birth nor death held any mystery for these children. They were too familiar with both.

'Hang up your clothes and get into line.'

Teacher was back. They obeyed because they loved her, not because they were threatened.

She pushed open the door and they marched in on tiptoe, glancing covertly at the bassinet under the window.

'You may look quietly, one at a time,' said Teacher. And they filed past, then went to stand behind their desks.

'Good morning, children,' said Teacher.

'Good morning, Teacher,' they chorused happily. The new day had officially started.

Slate pencils were scratching busily on the slates at mid morning, after the short break in the playground. The whimpering cry from the bassinet was the signal they had all been waiting for. Even the Infants knew better than to expect a baby to sleep for hours without a whimper, so they showed no surprise, only a natural curiosity.

'Maggie McKenzie, you may rock the pram gently,' said Teacher as calmly as though it was no novelty to have a baby in the classroom.

Maggie stepped forward, flushed with importance. Carrie, Dorothy, Phyllis, Rose and Winifred pouted with disappointment.

'You will take turns,' Teacher promised, with a smile and a nod. 'The rest of the class carry on with your

244

copying. There is no need to wait,' the quiet voice prompted, and the scratching continued.

''e's dropped off, Miss,' whispered Maggie a few minutes later.

'Thank you, Maggie.' For all her calmness, Martha Carter was very much aware of a sense of anxiety, for so much depended on her baby's good behaviour. It was too soon to predict their future, but she hoped they would be allowed to have a trial period of one month to settle down without disturbance. She had no previous experience of babies, and was too proud to ask advice. If Philip disturbed the lessons with his crying, there would be no alternative but to leave him in the care of the elderly housekeeper, but she was deaf as a post and crotchety. It was not what she would have chosen for her firstborn, but she had only herself to blame. Dick had not replied to her cablegram, informing him that he had a son, but she was not unduly worried. Already it was difficult to recapture the face and the voice of her young lover. In five years she would be marrying a stranger, and Philip might resent sharing her with a strange man. Such thoughts would often trouble her in the night, when she lay awake, listening to the chimes of the grandfather clock in the hall, while her son slept in the cradle her father had carried down from the loft. She kept such thoughts to herself.

So the weeks slipped away, and it almost seemed the baby understood their future depended on his good behaviour. His whimpering cry, when he was hungry or uncomfortable, could be quickly hushed with a gentle rocking.

'It's my turn, Teacher,' one of the girls would remind her, when she forgot. And when she started back to school after the dinner hour, she would find a group of girls waiting at the gate.

'It's my turn to push the pram.' One or several would step forward eagerly.

But still the nagging anxiety persisted, for nothing had been said. The School Governors could change their minds. Their authority was absolute. The schoolmaster could only abide by their decisions. He often slipped quietly into the classroom, and only once had he discovered Carrie Simmons rocking the baby. When Teacher had bid the children rise to acknowledge his presence, he had bid them be seated with his usual brusqueness. As for Carrie Simmons, she was senior girl in the Infants now, and would soon be moving up into the adjoining classroom, for she was a bright child, ready for a higher standard.

It was 3.30 on a Friday afternoon when the door opened and Master came in. A sigh of disappointment ran through the classroom, for it was customary for Teacher to read a story at the climax of the week's curriculum.

'Proceed,' said schoolmaster, seating himself in the chair the monitor brought forward.

Teacher cleared her throat, her cheeks flushed nervously. 'Once upon a time. . . .'

Andrew Robinson's lips twisted in a wry smile. The children sat enthralled. There was something very homely and comfortable about that dumpy little figure. Carrie Simmons could have told him why it seemed to evoke memories of early childhood. Teacher was like Mrs Noah! He was wondering, not for the first time, what an intelligent young woman had found in a 17-year-old youth. It could only have been physical attraction, and physical attraction could be tragically impermanent, sexual intercourse but a bitter reminder of a brief moment of ecstasy and torment that he had no desire to recapture, even if Irene had lived. His conscience gave him no peace. Compassion for her frailty and a natural tenderness as her health deteriorated, had resulted in a climax of which he was deeply ashamed. No matter that Irene had used all the wiles of Eve to tempt her reluctant Adam, he should have resisted. She had left him restless and dissatisfied. Sexual intercourse had awakened latent senses in his own virginal body. He would never be the same man again. It was too late. Now his relationship with Irene had taken on a new image, as ethereal and insubstantial as a dream. Yet that moment of consummation had not been imagined. He had only to close his eyes and his loins began to tremble. How long would it last, this tormenting contradiction of mind and body – of bitter remorse and agonising frustration?

So, on this Friday afternoon, listening to Martha Carter reading the story to a hushed, attentive class, Andrew Robinson had a sudden inspired thought. Would she allow him to stand godfather to her son? He had to find a new, absorbing interest or the future was bleak.

But when he asked her to report to him when school was over her calm eyes were startled, and she stammered, 'Yes . . . Sir. Certainly . . . Sir.' He could not know that she expected her worst fears to be realised, and that her heart sank at the brusqueness of the command.

When she had helped the younger children into their coats and tied on the little girls' bonnets, she waved them away and walked slowly back to the classroom. Philip was awake, and she picked him up and sat down to wait till the older scholars had left. For such a young child he was very alert, and he smiled readily. If anyone had complained that her baby was a nuisance, it was not true. Why, he even slept to the stamping of marching feet as the children entered and left the classroom, and the chanting of tables and the tinkling of the piano for exercises. It was amazing how soundly he slept now that he was accustomed to noise. The children adored him. He was surrounded by love. She cuddled him close. She would defend his right to his place in the classroom with her last breath.

When the shouting had died away, the silence reminded her that the moment she had been dreading had to be faced, bravely. She had faced the consequences of that brief enchanted hour, suffered the misery and humiliation of banishment from her father's house, and borne the child in the squalor of Richmond Row. Everything had gone well in the past weeks, however. She was back in the Infants' classroom; Philip was such a happy baby, and she was reunited with her father. It was too good to last, she reminded herself. With Dick thousands of miles away, she had a double role to play, for her child would not know a father till he was five years of age. It was no secret that her child was born out of wedlock. An unmarried mother carried the stigma for the rest of her days. One day, when her son reached the age of understanding, she would tell him the truth, but she flinched at the thought that he, too, must suffer when he learned the meaning of the word bastard.

She was pale and trembling as she carried her precious bundle through the empty classrooms. The schoolmaster was not seated at his high desk, but pacing up and down in nervous agitation. Poor man! He was obviously reluctant, but he had a duty to perform. He stopped his pacing, waved her to a chair, and sat down, staring intently at the child in her arms.

'It's all right, Sir. I understand. It was kind of you to allow it, but no mention was made of it being a

248

permanent arrangement,' she told him, in her calm, quiet voice.

'What *are* you talking about?' he demanded irritably.

She was puzzled by the question. 'Why, bringing Philip to school. It's not convenient, is it, Sir? You wish to make other arrangements. Isn't that why you sent for me, Sir?'

He smiled at her and stroked his beard. She could not understand why his manner was suddenly so friendly and amiable.

'I do apologise, Miss Carter, if you have been unduly disturbed by the summons. I should have explained it was a personal matter, in no way connected with school, on which I wished to speak to you. I have a proposal to put to you, but you are under no obligation to accept. Would you consider me a suitable candidate to act as a godparent to your son? It would give me much pleasure.'

'Godparent?' she stammered. 'I should be deeply honoured, Sir.'

'You would?'

'Yes, indeed, Sir.'

'Splendid! Then that's settled. You see, Miss Carter, I am not unaware of your problem, and I admire the way you have conducted yourself in the face of such adverse circumstances. As a godfather, I should wish to make myself responsible for Philip's education, if you are agreeable? I was thinking of Grammar School. What do you say?'

She shook her head. 'What can I say, Sir? I am completely overwhelmed. You must forgive me, but it's all so wonderful, so unexpected.' She was crying quietly. She looked so young with tears on her cheeks.

'You were expecting something different, were you not?'

249

She nodded tremulously.

'May I hold him? Would he be happy with me?'

She began to wonder why she had always thought of him as unapproachable and insensitive. It was just his manner. Shyness was his worst enemy. She placed the bundle in his arms. Philip was awake. One tiny hand reached out of the shawl.

'You see, he wants to make my acquaintance!' The schoolmaster was extraordinarily pleased with the gesture, and he examined the baby's fingers carefully. This was something beyond the scope of his brilliant mind. No text book could do justice to the perfection of a baby's hand. The tiny fingers curled and clutched.

'Amazing,' he said. 'And such a handsome little fellow. I am going to enjoy being a godfather. Thank you, Miss Carter.'

'Thank you, Sir.' She took the baby and waited to be dismissed.

'Good afternoon, Miss Carter,' said he, with a grave little bow.

'Good afternoon, Sir.' She walked away with a wonderful sense of purpose. All her anxiety had been quite unnecessary.

'Miss Carter?'

She stopped, and her heart raced. What now?

'You will let me know the date of the christening?'

'Oh, *yes*, Sir! Goodbye, Sir.'

She was humming as she tucked the baby into the bassinet and walked briskly away. Andrew Robinson stood watching till she was out of sight. Was it only the child he wished to befriend?

Chapter Nine

Five years have passed since the christening of young Philip Carter. He is one of the brightest pupils in his mother's classroom because he has been listening and memorising since the age of 3, and had his own little chair in the class, joining in lessons and games with a lively interest, and adored by all the children.

Philip Carter was the schoolmaster's godson, a privilege not extended to any other child. No favouritism was shown to the child, however, in school hours, but out of school, he was fully aware of the special place he held in the heart of that grave, kindly man. Sixpence a week pocket money had been allocated since his 4th birthday. He received Christmas and birthday presents from his godfather, and enjoyed an outing to the zoo and the seaside in the Summer holidays. Wherever they went, Mother had to accompany them. Philip loved his mother passionately and possessively, and he loved his grandfather. But the strange man in soldier's uniform that he had to call Daddy was a hateful person, with a rough voice who used bad words that upset his grandfather who went to Chapel every Sunday and couldn't abide swearing. This stranger he must call Daddy had boxed his ears on the wedding night because he refused to obey an order to go to bed in the boxroom where the boxes had been stacked up to make room for a small bed and a chair. His calm, quiet mother had flown into a temper, her eyes blazing.

'If you dare to strike my son again you can leave this house for good!' she threatened.

'*Your* son?' he jeered. 'A fine job you've made of it – spoilt little brat! The sooner we get away from here the better.'

'We are not going away, not Philip and me. We are staying here.'

Philip was clinging to her skirts. He could feel her trembling, and he started to cry. Harsh words and stormy scenes had not been a part of his young life. Surrounded by love, he was gentle and loving.

'What did you say, Martha?' Dick Martin demanded.

'I said, we are staying here, Philip and I.'

He laughed. 'My, my, quite the little madam! Supposing I remind you, my dear wife, I could claim the boy if you refuse to move. He bears *my* name now.'

'You wouldn't? . . . You couldn't?'

'Just try me.'

She wrapped her arms protectively around the small, shrinking figure. 'I would never part with him. *Never!*'

'A father has first claim on a child, by law.'

'I don't believe it. You are just trying to frighten me.'

'I'm just reminding you who's the boss. This happens to be our wedding day, in case you have forgotten. With that gold band on your finger, and the marriage certificate, I've made an honest woman of you, Martha. You should be grateful. And the boy is safe from persecution. Bastard is not a nice label to be attached to a child, but he would have to live with it if his mother had no husband.'

252

'I've had no husband for five years, and I have never once heard that word.'

'You've been lucky. Now look here, Martha. I'm not standing for any more nonsense. I've been patient. Why do you think we were married by special licence? Because I couldn't wait three weeks for the banns to be called. It's been a long time, Martha, since I last had you in my arms. Get the boy out of this room. I want my wife to myself. And we are getting out of here next week, whether you like it or not. You're an Army wife now, my girl. Three years at Tidworth, then another overseas posting, and next time we go together. No more separation. It's a good life, Army life. You are going to enjoy it. No more bloody teaching.'

'Give up teaching? I couldn't, Dick. It's my life.'

'It was your life. Now you follow the drum. Where the regiment goes, we go. Now, for the last time, get that boy out of this room, and tell him to stop snivelling.'

Philip would never forget that first night in the cold little bed. As far back as he could remember he had slept with his mother, curled into her plump warm body. He could hear a man's rough voice and a sudden bellow of laughter. He pulled the blankets over his head and lay there shivering. Then all was quiet. Lonely and miserable, he cried himself to sleep.

For the second time in five years the Infants waited for a new teacher, but the present-day children did not remember the previous disturbance. They were not yet born. All the original children had long since been promoted to the main school where the teachers were strict, and punishment severe.

Those five years had slipped away so pleasantly, the schoolmaster could have wished for nothing better than

253

that the situation in the Infants' classroom would be permanent. But it was not to be. The day that had seemed so remote five years ago had suddenly arrived. Dick Martin was there in the flesh, no longer a slim shy attractive youth, but a broad-shouldered, hefty fellow, coarsened by the rough and tumble of the ranks, and over indulgence in drink and sex. Dick was a stranger – a blustering, masterful man with a special licence in his pocket, and no time to waste on getting acquainted. Time enough to get acquainted in the marriage bed, he declared.

Martha was shocked and embarrassed. She shrank from his lewd jokes and pawing hands. There was no escape, or so it seemed to her overwrought nerves. Without love or respect, what could the future hold for herself and Philip. It was for Philip's sake, she reminded herself. She could not bear to think of that day when her son would be labelled a 'bastard', by some cruel or thoughtless person. Marriage was the only assurance, the only safeguard of her son's reputation. So Martha Carter became the lawful wife of Dick Martin within a week of his homecoming. In a matter of hours she had realised her mistake in clinging to the image of her young lover. For the second time, a disappointed father had to remind his daughter she had made her bed and must lie on it. It was not his intention to interfere between husband and wife. In the eyes of God they were joined together till Death, and beyond. So he watched his daughter pack her bags with a scowling acceptance of a long separation. He had no liking for his son-in-law, and little hope of seeing his grandson in the near future.

Dick Martin would be a possessive husband. Already there had been evidence of the bitter jealousy between the man and the boy, both demanding her full

254

attention. Poor Martha! Poor, unhappy little boy! Sam Carter reflected sadly on the mystery of God's purpose in this marriage during that busy week of preparation, but he was a good Methodist, and could only assume there was a pattern and a purpose that would be revealed in time.

The schoolmaster was not so readily persuaded that such a hasty marriage was unavoidable. He saw it as a terrible mistake. Martha Carter's behaviour in the past five years had been so exemplary, not a breath of scandal had reached the School House, and her child was loved for his own sake. What would become of the gentle, intelligent little boy in that strange new world of soldiers and barracks and rough Army discipline? He was fond of the boy, and his mother. It had been a time of quiet contentment and mutual understanding. The boy was the go-between, the human link in a relationship in which sex played no part. To lose them now, after enjoying five years of their companionship was heartrending.

'I don't want to go, Sir. I want to stay here with you,' the child had protested when they came to say goodbye the day before they left for Tidworth.

'I wish you could, Philip. I am going to miss you. But don't forget you are still my godson. I shall write you a letter once a month and send your pocket money, and you must write to me, and tell me about your new school.'

'Yes, Sir.'

Martha was too choked to speak. They shook hands gravely. It was doubtful if they would meet again. Dick had decided to make a clean break from his family in Richmond Row.

He had quarrelled with his mother and walked out, he told Martha, and swore he would never set foot in her house again.

Three years at Tidworth, then another posting

overseas. It could be Singapore or Aden. There would be no Grammar School education for Philip now. The future was taken out of their hands. The Army had the last word, and Dick was a soldier of fortune. He was in his right element.

Andrew Robinson looked down on the woman whose face had been a feature of his life for so long, and gripped her hand in his sweating palms. Her eyes were brimming with tears, her mouth trembling, and he knew she was afraid of the future and what it would do to them. He smiled reassuringly, wishing he had the right to kiss that trembling mouth. They would keep in touch through the boy.

'Give my kind regards to your mother,' he would say. Not even the most possessive husband could object to that.

'God bless you both,' was all he said, and it was not enough. Those pleading wet eyes had betrayed the secret she had not dared to divulge until today. She loved him.

Ten-year-old Carrie Simmons had grown into a pert, independent child, spending the school holidays at Russets where she was still a great favourite, and acting nursemaid to Charles, a handsome little boy with dark eyes and hair, and a striking resemblance to Sir Neville Franklin. Carrie was too young to question this strange coincidence, or to remember that her Uncle Bert had been dead for almost two years when Charles was born. As for Lucy's three boys, they were shocked and disgusted by their mother's disloyalty to a father they had loved and respected.

They were not the only ones to be shocked when Bert's widow became pregnant. She carried her child proudly, and had no shame. It was not her nature to be

256

humbled by a condition that was neither intended nor desired. That the landlord had been a frequent visitor to the farm since Bert's death was considered to be nothing more than a natural interest and concern for a woman so suddenly responsible for a farm on his estate.

Lucy Blunt was soon established legally as the tenant farmer of Russets, and provision made for her three sons to inherit the tenancy jointly (with a farm bailiff until Harry became of age), in the event of their mother's death. Money had been spent on new fences and urgent repairs to outbuildings, and that, too, was taken for granted since Bert Blunt had always postponed asking favours of Sir Neville's farm bailiff. Lucy had no such qualms. Now that she was responsible for the upkeep of the farm, she had no hesitation in stating her requirements. Sir Neville vetted all expenditure on his big estate, and seldom disputed an item. It was an authentic excuse for a good landlord to inspect the nature of the repairs and improvements. His manner was courteous. He was liked and respected as squire and landlord. With nothing more obvious than an appraising glance in Lucy's direction in the months following Bert's tragic death, his motives were not questioned. They were never alone. Her three boys and old Fred Wallace were always in the near vicinity, and the servant, with her gypsy black eyes, came and went with the cunning of a little fox. The only day in the year when farmhands and servants were entitled to a holiday was Michaelmas. Lucy's boys had never missed the Michaelmas Fair since they were old enough to accompany their father in the wagonette. This year Harry would be in charge, and they would take Fred and Emma. With the cows milked and driven out to pasture, they all sat down to

257

an early breakfast, then set off, leaving Lucy alone for the first time in her married life. She had the dogs and cats for company, horses to stable, pigs and chickens to feed, and the milking, single-handed, in the late afternoon. She decided to pickle onions and make more tomato chutney, both enjoyed by her family with cold pork and home-cured ham. She hadn't to cook a dinner for her hungry brood, and a snack lunch of bread and cheese with a pot of tea would make a nice change.

She had been pouring a second cup of tea at the kitchen table, feeling rather lonely, but reminding herself of the fun the boys would be having at the fair. They deserved a treat, for they worked hard, and seldom grumbled. Suddenly a man's figure darkened the open door.

'Why, Sir Neville!' she gasped, and stood up shakily, wide-eyed with shock and dismay. There could be only one reason that had brought him to Russets on this particular day, when she was alone. He walked in slowly, laid his hat carefully on the table with the riding crop, and peeled off his gloves.

'I have waited a long time, Lucy, my dear. I want you,' he said with quiet authority.

'No, Sir, no!' She backed away, putting the table between them.

He smiled disarmingly, reached out and caught her wrist with a grip of steel. She struggled and turned her head away.

'Look at me! Look at me, Lucy! he commanded.

She was sobbing now, but he had no pity for her tears, only impatience. His dark eyes held a magnetism that was irresistible.

'I take what I want, my dear,' he reminded her, as his arms closed round her. His mouth was hard. There was

258

no gentleness in his strong, enfolding arms, only a desperate eagerness. When her lips had parted and her body slumped, he whispered, 'Come'.

And she went with him, climbing the stairs slowly, his arm about her waist. An hour or so later, sated and satisfied, he rode away. Whether or not she became his mistress was still a matter for doubt. He was a proud man, and such a relationship on his own estate would soon be discovered. So he stayed away. Rumour said that Lucy Bunt was pregnant, but that was her affair.

Several months later, his farm bailiff reported that Mrs Blunt had given birth to a son, and the whole nature of his relationship with Lucy was changed. As the mother of his son – his only son – nothing was too good for her. In vain Lucy protested that the baby was *her* child, and she alone had the right to decide its future. She was fighting a losing battle from the moment he saw the child and recognised in the handsome little head, with its cap of black hair, a tiny replica of his own. Blue eyes turned dark in a matter of weeks.

'A proper cuckoo in the nest, that little bugger!' chuckled old Fred.

'You'd better not let my mother hear you talking that way,' Harry threatened.

But it was true. How could three grown lads, still faithful to the memory of a working farmer, ever be reconciled to a half-brother fathered by Sir Neville Franklin? Even his name had been chosen by his father. There had always been a Charles in every generation of Franklins until the present Lady Franklin produced only four daughters. His pride in his son held no embarrassment. Why should he apologise? A generous allowance was agreed and his solicitor was instructed to make it legal. His Will was altered in favour of Charles who would be heir to the estate. It was altogether most irregular, it was argued, but Sir Neville was a law unto himself. His four daughters would each receive a handsome dowry on marriage to encourage reluctant suitors. Servants would be rewarded according to years of service. He knew his duty and had no need to be reminded. But a son was a son.

For the first time in his life Sir Neville Franklin knew the meaning of love and tenderness. For the first time since the birth of his fourth daughter he took his pleasure not in the arms of a woman, but in the growth and development of the handsome little boy at Russets. The child's wilfulness was encouraged by his father, who delighted in any characteristic that reminded him of his own early childhood. Lucy was determined not to spoil her youngest son, but she had reckoned without his father, who gave orders that Charles was not to be punished for his naughtiness. In any case, Lucy had soon discovered that even a smack on his small bottom before he was out of petticoats was a mistake. The child went stiff with rage, choking with sobs. She had to cuddle him in her arms and whisper endearments. And when he had got his breath, he was bribed with his favourite sweet – home-made toffee.

'You never had time to make sweets for us when we were little,' Albert reminded her sulkily, for he was jealous of the baby who had so much attention, so soon to grow into a self-important, undisciplined little boy.

At the age of 3 Charles had his first pony, and a young groom was sent from the Big House to escort the child. Even at that early age he sat his pony with arrogant assurance that pleased his father enormously. At the age of 4 he was riding round the estate with Sir Neville, and a year later, sharing the governess with his two half-sisters in the schoolroom at Marston Park.

His future had been decided as he lay in his cradle at Russets. He would spend his early years at the farm. At the age of 7, he would be sent away to boarding school, to start the formal education of an upper-class male child. From his seventh year Marston Park would be his home, and the farm a place for brief visits during the holidays. But his father would also discover that he too had reckoned without the child's strong, rebellious spirit. Charles adored the pretty mother with the soft bosom and plump arms who smelled of sweat and curds, and had learned to laugh at his wilfulness. At an early age, a child's character is formed, and it has accepted its environment and its immediate family. For young Charles Russets was home. He belonged in the midst of his three half-brothers, for whom he had a certain affection in spite of their discouraging resentment. Old Fred Wallace was a funny old fellow with dirty habits and swear words the child delighted to imitate. Wallace never used a lavatory when he wanted to pee, but went behind a tree or a bush. Handkerchiefs were wasted on him; he squeezed his nose with finger and thumb. Lucy had been horrified to discover her small son practising these dirty habits, and Fred was threatened with dismissal. It was going to be a life-long tussle with conflicting loyalties for Sir Neville Franklin's bastard son.

The boy was not actually aware of the conflict until he reached the age of 7 and was told to say goodbye to Russets and shown the room that had been prepared for him at Marston Park. On his last evening before leaving for school he dined with his father in solitary state, with a liveried footman to wait at table. At Russets they ate all their meals in the kitchen, and Charles had no hesitation in deciding which he preferred. The following morning, he embarked on the

261

first stage of the long journey to school in the West Country, in charge of the guard to Victoria Station, then handed over to a young master to be escorted to Paddington where a hundred or so other small boys were lined up on the platform, waiting for instructions to board the train. Once aboard the train, supervised by the irate masters, Charles soon realised they would stand no nonsense. To have his ears boxed for the first time was a shattering experience, but it was even more shattering to have his companions jeer at his tears. It was a hard lesson to learn on his first encounter with an alien world. But Charles was intelligent enough to understand he must either conform to pattern, or suffer the penalty of public disgrace and lose the privileges he most enjoyed.

He now had three distinct worlds in which to live for certain periods of the year, until he came of age and could decide for himself. Till then – and it seemed a far distant horizon to a 7-year-old schoolboy – he would waste no time in tears. In this teeming new world he had no status, but he knew his value in the other two worlds, back in the Weald, the one so homely, the other so grand. He enjoyed both the warmth of his mother's arms and the firm grip of his father's hand. He could be what they most desired him to be, his proud father's son, and his mother's adored baby. He could tease the one servant at Russets with his naughty pranks, and have the deferential butler at Marston Park refer to him as 'Master Charles'. It was great fun, but a little confusing to belong to the farm and also to the Big House.

When he tried to explain such an unusual situation to his best friend some weeks later, it was received with embarrassing silence. It was even more difficult to explain to that same 7-year-old boy, on his first visit that Summer, that his mother was a farmer's widow.

*　　　*　　　*

'I don't know what I be going to do with you, my girl, when you leave school, that I don't,' Ruby Simmons had admitted with doleful uncertainty, for Carrie was a problem with her airs and graces. 'You're proper spoilt, that's your trouble, and I been making a rod for me own back all these years,' Ruby continued.

With her 13th birthday only a few months away, the question of Carrie's employment should have been settled. Her three brothers would never allow their sister to go into 'service', and Ruby was reluctant to have her only daughter following in the footsteps of all the other village girls when they left school at 13. As for Tom Simmons, he left it to his wife to settle such matters, and took the line of least resistance.

'I wouldn't go into service anyway. I'd run away!' Carrie had threatened. It was no idle threat, and Carrie was quite capable of looking after herself if she did run away, but it had to be prevented at all costs, and her poor mother was worried to death.

When Jack bespoke the cashier's job for his sister, since Carrie was a bright girl at school, and the grocer's three daughters too stuck-up to help in the business, Ruby thought that her troubles were over, but Carrie had refused the offer, and Jack was annoyed for it made him look like a fool. He had conscientiously worked himself into a position of trust and responsibility, and the grocer always referred to Jack Simmons as his right-hand man. At the age of 17 he was entrusted with the important job of calling on the cooks and housekeepers in the upper-class establishments to discuss the weekly order, and to advise on the various brands of cheese and butter, tea and coffee, and the quality of Danish and English bacon. His polite manner and ready smile had endeared him to several young servant girls over the weekly cup of tea and gossip in

263

the kitchen, when the business had been transacted, but it was Elsie at The Parsonage who took his fancy. She was cheeky and cheerful with a hearty laugh that indicated a good temper and a sense of humour. All these qualities, in Jack's opinion, were most desirable in a wife, but it was not his nature to hurry. They were walking out for two years before Jack suggested they visit his family in Richmond Row, not that he was ashamed of his home environment, but simply that he had to be quite certain he was not making a mistake – and his Mum would know.

So the courtship had developed with steady but reliable progress. Jack could be stubborn when he made up his mind – as stubborn as young Carrie. Unlike her bosom friend, Hetty O'Brien, Elsie had no ambition to better herself in service. Hetty had her eye on the housekeeper's post at Marston Park. In five years she had climbed the ladder to the position of head housemaid, for she was quick to learn and to imitate her superiors. Elsie had only one ambition, to marry a decent, respectable, working-class chap, have a little place of her own, and raise a family.

At one time, when the courtship seemed to be lagging, Elsie had wondered whether to ensnare her steady-going swain with the age-old wiles of Eve, but Jack was no fool. Too many decent young fellows had been obliged to lead their pregnant brides to the altar. His own mother and his Auntie Lucy had been two of the naughty girls who could not wait for the sanctity of the marriage-bed. It had been quite a shock to discover, at the age of 10, both his eldest brother and his cousin had been born out of wedlock. As for the scandal of recent times with his Aunt Lucy pregnant two years after the death of Uncle Bert, that was still being talked about and a topic of much speculation

264

among all classes of society. Only his mother and sister visited the farm these days, but the boy cousins had never been close.

Jack would make a good husband and father, for he was the most like his own father. He did not drink or smoke, paid his mother what he considered fair and reasonable for his board and lodging, gave his sister threepence a week pocket money, saved a shilling a week in the Post Office Savings Bank and a shilling in a clothing club. His carefulness would complement Elsie's tendency to extravagance, and that was a good thing – unless there came a time when carefulness merged into meanness, when the sparks would fly.

Carrie collected threepence a week from all three brothers, and threepence from her father. It was a lot of money, and she spent it lavishly on anything that took her fancy.

'Easy come, easy go,' Ruby scolded, but she was proud of her pretty daughter, remembering her own longing for fripperies at the same age.

The problem of what to do with Carrie when she left school had been settled in a most unexpected way, as such problems often are decided. She had kept in touch with her beloved Teacher and Philip, when they moved away. Letters had been exchanged, also small gifts for birthday and Christmas. It was sad that Teacher and the child were not allowed to visit her old home, or her many friends in the village, but it seemed that her husband kept them both under his thumb. Not that Teacher complained. She was too loyal, but Carrie was intelligent enough to guess what the situation was.

It so happened that the wife of Dr Saunders' youngest son, Lesley, now a captain in the regiment in which Dick Martin was a sergeant, was looking for a nursemaid for their first baby. Although an officer's wife did not normally associate with the wives of the rank and file, and snobbery was an inherent part of Army life, Captain Saunders' wife had defied protocol and made a friend of Martha Martin who was certainly superior in manner and intelligence to the majority of Army wives stationed at Tidworth. The boy, Philip, had been the means of bringing them together, when she had knocked him down outside the barracks a few months after their arrival.

Felicity Saunders rode her bicycle with careless disregard of pedestrians, and her husband had warned her on more than one occasion that she would end up in court. The accident was not serious enough to be reported, but it taught her a lesson, and gave her a nasty shock to see a small boy lying in the road with books spilling from his new school satchel. There was nothing to choose between them, both were pale with shock and trembling. The captain's wife knelt down in the dust and cradled the sergeant's child in her arms.

'Darling, I'm so dreadfully sorry. Are you hurt?' she asked anxiously.

Philip shook his head. She was a pretty lady, she smelled nice, and he liked being called darling. But he was a nervous little boy since he made the acquaintance of the hateful man he must call Daddy.

'I'm going to be sick,' he told her, and the nice smell was instantly evaporated in the sour smell of his vomit. 'I . . . I . . . couldn't help it,' he faltered, expecting an angry reaction, but the pretty lady wiped his mouth and mopped up the mess with two clean handkerchiefs.

'Don't look so worried. It's an old skirt. It will wash,' she told him, kindly. 'What's your name?'

'Philip Martin.'

'You're a new boy, aren't you? I haven't seen you around here until today.'

266

'I don't think I'm very new. I can't remember.'

'Are you going to like living in Army barracks?'

'No. We didn't want to come here, my mother and me, but my father said we belonged to the regiment now, and we must follow the drum.'

She smiled at the child. He was obviously recovering. 'It's strange at first, but you will soon get used to it.'

'I won't,' he said decidedly. 'I want to go home.'

'But this is your home now, darling. Hasn't your mother explained?'

'Yes, she always explains everything because she's a teacher.'

'I see.'

'She's the best teacher in the whole world. When I was a baby, she took me to school in my pram. When I was a big boy, she explained about my father being in the Army, and that he would be coming home when I was 5, but I didn't want a father. I had a nice godfather. He was the schoolmaster at our school. I wish he was my real father, then we could go home,' he sighed, and picked himself up. She helped him to collect the scattered books, pushed them into the satchel, and hung it over his shoulder. Then she picked up the bicycle and took the child's hand.

'I'll take you home. I have to apologise to your mother for knocking you down. Besides, I should like to meet her.' She was intrigued by the child's story. Children were so honest. You always got the truth from them. They walked on together. Children rushed past, then turned to stare.

Martha Martin opened the door. 'Good afternoon,' she said. 'Is there anything wrong?'

'Nothing seriously wrong, Mrs Martin, but it might have been. I knocked Philip down, but he doesn't appear to be hurt. It was my fault. I do apologise.'

'Won't you come in?'

'Thank you. May I introduce myself? I'm Felicity Saunders. My husband is Captain Saunders.'

'How do you do.'

They shook hands. 'I was just making the tea. Can I offer you a cup?' The sergeant's wife had yet to discover the conventional barrier that divided them, but Felicity Saunders, who came from an Army family and had spent her early years in India, was fully aware of the controversy such an acquaintance would provoke.

'Thank you, I should like a cup of tea,' she said.

'Mother, I was sick all over her skirt,' Philip interrupted importantly.

'Philip! How disgusting!' His mother shuddered. 'Please let me clean you up, Mrs Saunders. I'm ashamed of my son.'

'Don't scold him, please, Mrs Martin. It was just a natural reaction from the shock. It's only an old skirt.' The Captain's wife followed the sergeant's wife to the kitchen, and her skirt was sponged with a clean cloth. So they had no bathroom. The rooms were small and shabbily furnished, but spotlessly clean. The last tenants had left their mark, however. Cigarette burns on the faded carpet in the sitting-room and sagging springs in a sofa not always used for sitting on. Philip had followed them into the kitchen.

'Take off your cap, Philip, and wash your hands,' his mother prompted automatically.

'Is it strawberry jam for tea?' he asked eagerly.

'Not if you're sick.'

'I'm not sick, I'm hungry.'

Both women laughed. So started a friendship that would serve to smooth the difficult path of a woman totally unsuited to the rough discipline of barrack life.

She did not visit her new friend, so had no opportunity to make comparisons of their style of living, but Felicity was a frequent visitor to the small, shabby rooms allotted to the wife of a sergeant.

'You're asking for trouble, my girl!' Dick Martin threatened. 'What's wrong with the sergeants' wives and kids?'

'Nothing. I just don't like to see women drinking and smoking, and Philip is quite happy playing on his own.'

'You coddle him. He's turning into a bloody little cissy!'

'I don't think so.'

Sometimes he was so infuriated by her calm, superior manner he slapped her face, but he had to be careful to keep his hands off her when the boy was around. There was nothing of the cissy about Philip when he saw his mother abused. He flew at his father, sobbing and screaming, 'Let her alone! Stop it! I hate you!' and got his ears cuffed for insolence. It was a tricky situation with the Captain's wife so fond of his wife and child, and Dick Martin was a little afraid of a relationship he could not handle. If his Captain's wife chose to defy the conventions, a sergeant had no alternative but to accept the situation. There were no more children, for which Martha was grateful. He was a lusty, demanding lover, and she often wondered about the women he had known during his five years in India, and was more than a little afraid of contracting some horrible disease. She need not have worried. The British Army had its own strict rules and regulations. Brothels were carefully vetted, and standards of hygiene were strictly enforced. Dick could have put his wife's mind at rest had she asked, but it never occurred to Martha to discuss such an intimate subject with her husband. They had nothing in common, and their marriage was a sad mistake.

269

Only two events brightened the days for the ex-schoolteacher and her small son – a visit from the Captain's wife, and a letter from the schoolmaster – always addressed to Philip. He wrote with an easy flowing style that pleased and surprised Martha, for he was not a very articulate person. Philip's pocket money arrived regularly from his godfather, and a five shilling postal order for birthday and Christmas. The letter concluded, 'Please give my regards to your mother. Your affectionate Godfather, Andrew Robinson.'

There was nothing that Dick could object to in the letters, but they warmed Martha's heart. She was conscious of a tangible bond that held them together, the three of them, out of reach of the demands of a possessive husband and a jealous father. She could not foresee the future, but she lived for her son. They shared everything, and had no secrets from one another. In some ways Philip was mature for his age, she noticed. He had never again attempted to climb into her bed, or protested at being obliged to sleep in another room, not since the wedding night.

'I hope we have a son, and I hope he will love his mother as Philip loves you.' It was a nice compliment from Felicity Saunders when she became pregnant, five months later. She was delivered of a nine-pound boy, and nearly lost her life.

'No more children!' the Captain decreed. It was then that Felicity was persuaded to look for a nursemaid. Protocol expected it, and in this respect it was more sensible to comply with the conventions. Martha recommended Carrie Simmons.

When the baby was a month old and the Captain was due for a week's leave, they came to stay with his parents at Fairfields. Felicity's parents had died of enteric fever in India when she was 13, and she had

270

been sent back to England to finish her education and make her home with an elderly aunt. On the few occasions they had stayed with Lesley's parents, Felicity had found her mother-in-law a silent, withdrawn woman, and they had made no contact. But now, with the first grandchild to bridge the gap, she was hopeful of a closer relationship. Doctor Saunders was a dear, and regarded her as a daughter. Once in the week she accompanied him on his regular visit to Lady Franklin at Marston Park.

'Mother was not always so withdrawn. Her whole personality seemed to change after that sad affair with my brother Dennis,' Lesley had explained.

'What affair?' Felicity had asked, innocently, and was deeply shocked by the sordid story. Dennis had escaped the penalty of hanging, but would spend the rest of his days in Ceylon. No extradition order had been issued, and the case was eventually dropped.

'He always was a lucky devil,' his younger brother declared. 'Think of all those dusky maidens on that tea plantation – and he doesn't even need a marriage licence!' he added.

'Darling, spare my feelings' his wife protested, laughingly.

'Not you, my sweet. You were born and bred to such interesting situations.' He took her in his arms and kissed her with tenderness. They were ideally suited, and very happy. Now they had a son they were proud parents. The Army was their life. They followed the drum as naturally as other young couples stayed at home.

The baby was christened by Parson at All Saints. He was named James Ernest after his two grandfathers, and called Jimmy. It was a splendid christening, and the church was packed. There had been trouble enough in

271

Doctor's family, and this was a special occasion to mark the start of a new and happier era – it was universally hoped. Service overseas would mean a long separation but this was inevitable, as Parson knew to his cost.

The years had brought many changes. Marion and Malcolm had been home on leave from the Congo with three young children. The eldest boy had been left behind to make his home with his grandparents and to start his formal education at boarding school at the age of 7. His sisters would have their mother to give them lessons. But the second parting from his favourite daughter had all the poignancy of the first. In another five years, Parson would not be there to welcome the little family, and Cecily and her mother would be living in a cottage on the Marston Park estate.

Chapter Ten

Changes were not welcomed at The Parsonage, but had to be endured, for the years took their toll of old servants who had worked hard all their lives. Cook had collapsed and died of a heart attack in her own kitchen, leaving Annie distraught and quite incapable of boiling an egg. Who would prepare the good, satisfying meals to which family and servants had long been accustomed? Who would make all the preserves in due season? Who would boil marrow bones from the butcher and add the vegetables that made such nourishing soup for the poor and needy?

These were the questions that Parson's wife asked herself as she rolled up her sleeves and donned the white starched apron on the day after the funeral. But she was a resourceful woman, and had already set about finding a replacement for Cook. An advertisement in the Parish Magazine brought several eager applicants for an interview, including Ruby Simmons from Richmond Row. In spite of her lack of experience, she appeared to be the most suitable. She had always fed her family well, and Parson's wife would not expect miracles from an ex-charwoman. Ruby was clean and presentable, cheerful and willing, and had an excellent reference from The Three Nuns. What more could one expect? But Ruby insisted on living out and having free Sundays, for she had no intention of neglecting her family. Saturday would be 'baking day' at The Parsonage. Elsie would cook Sunday breakfast. The traditional Sunday lunch would be a thing of the past. In future they would be served with cold meat and baked potatoes, followed by a fruit pie that Ruby would prepare on Saturday.

Annie took the opportunity during this period to plead for an early retirement, and was allocated one of the almshouses endowed by Sir Neville Franklin's father. The Parsonage kitchen without her old friend and companion was dismal and lonely, and Annie had no heart for anything. As for Peg-leg, he sadly missed the two old servants but was still hale and hearty, and quite capable of doing all the odd jobs to which he was accustomed. He took his time. There was no hurry. After supper, he walked along to The Three Nuns for a pint of beer, but not on Friday when he went to sit with the old Colonel, now confined to bed and very testy. They talked of the old days, and relived the exciting years of their Army service. The past was recalled with poignant nostalgia, and the two old men, master and servant, seemed to communicate with a mutual understanding that was lacking in other relationships. When, at last, the Colonel died after falling out of bed in a vain attempt to reach the chamber-pot, Peg-leg felt his own days were numbered, and he aged ten years in the weeks that followed.

Elsie stayed on for six months as house-parlourmaid after Annie's retirement, to oblige, but she was already carrying her first child, and anxious to settle down in the small terrace cottage that Jack was renting for 3s. 6d. a week in Chapel Road. All the cottages had long gardens and earth closets stuck right at the bottom. Husbands and children complained bitterly of this inconvenience in the Winter months, but the landlord's agent demanded indignantly, 'What do you expect for 3s 6d. a week? Marston Park?'

A rather dour young woman replaced Elsie when she finally got away, and Parson sighed for the old days that were gone for ever. Elsie had done her duty as a servant, and had no regrets, but now she was a married woman and had her duty to a husband to consider. She was glad now that her steady-going Jack, with his high principles, had not succumbed to the tantalising glimpse of her knees when they were walking out together. Now she could truthfully claim that her first child was conceived in wedlock.

Hetty O'Brien, on her first visit to the cottage after Elsie had settled in, regarded the matronly figure of her bosom friend with a disparaging nod.

'You want to watch out, Else, or you might get landed with a kid every year. Still waters run deep, and Jack didn't waste much time, I reckon, once he got you in the marriage bed.'

'That won't worry me, Het. I love kids, and I want a big family.'

Both young women, it was noticed, had learned to 'speak proper' in service, and it pleased Jack, who had long since mastered the art of picking up his aitches.

'What about Jack? Does he want a big family? Too many mouths to feed keeps a man poor,' Hetty reflected.

'I dunno. I've not asked him. There's no cause to worry a man about the kids. That's a woman's job. We shall manage fine, for Jack don't spend anything on beer or baccy, and he's got quite a bit saved. Since Parson asked him to be a sidesman Jack never misses a service at All Saints. I tell you, Het, there isn't a more decent living chap in all Fairfields than my Jack.'

Hetty smiled, in a superior way. Time would tell if the couple could rise above their circumstances and bring up their children decently. She remembered the sordid, overcrowded cottage in Richmond Row where her own mother had been defeated. She, too, had started married life with good intentions, but that was before her husband took to drink and gave her hell every Saturday night. A baby every year, even if half of them died in childbirth, was too much for any woman, and her poor Mum had not lived to see the youngest surviving boy out of petticoats. Things had gone from bad to worse when Hetty left home. Dad had been killed on the railway one foggy November day.

'Mike must 'ave been drinking something stronger than tea not to 'ear that bloody goods train,' his mate asserted bluntly.

The dirty, rat-infested cottage stood empty, and Hetty spent her free half-days in Tunbridge Wells. Of course it could be argued that the Simmons family had managed to rise above their sordid environment, and Tom and Ruby had reared a family of decent, respectable citizens. They had all turned out well, and now that Ruby had settled young Carrie in a good post, she had given up charring and taken on the job of Cook at The Parsonage. One had to admire such a woman, Hetty admitted, rather grudgingly.

The twin sisters, Lucy and Ruby, might look alike, but there the resemblance ended. Lucy Blunt had lost her reputation. It was disgraceful for the mother of three fine sons to be laid by the Landlord. She would never live it down *in her own class*.

'My, but 'e's a fine big boy, Ma'am!' Carrie exclaimed when she was introduced to her future charge at the interview in Doctor Saunders' drawing-room.

Felicity Saunders smiled at the child and thought it was such a pity the rough speech of working-class children was not corrected at the village school. However, Carrie Simmons had been one of Martha's brightest children in the Infants' classroom, so she understood from the ex-teacher at Tidworth, and had high marks in every standard of the upper school. Jimmy was still too young to imitate his nursemaid. By the time he started to talk, she would have Carrie nicely trained in speech and deportment.

'Will 'e come to me, Ma'am?' Carrie was asking eagerly, holding out her arms.

'I'm sure he will. He's a friendly baby,' his mother said, handing over the heavy infant.

Carrie seemed to sag with the solid bundle in her arms, but soon recovered when a pair of blue eyes gazed at her with the solemn stare of very young infants.

'The little love,' she breathed. 'I do declare 'e seems to know I be going to look after 'im. Bless 'is little 'eart.'

'Perhaps he does, Carrie. Who can tell what a month-old baby is feeling? It's all a profound mystery.'

'When did you want me to start, Ma'am? That is, if you think I be suitable,' she added anxiously.

'I think we shall suit each other very well, Carrie, but first we have to get you fitted out with uniform. There is no time for the dressmaker, since we are here for barely a week, so we must go shopping tomorrow, you and I. We shall find all we need at the big drapers in Tunbridge Wells. My mother-in-law has volunteered to look after Jimmy, and we will go by train. Can you be ready by 9 o'clock?'

'Yes, Ma'am. I'll be ready. I ain't never been on a train and I ain't never been no farther than Goose Green.'

'Then you will enjoy the outing. Have you quite made

up your mind, Carrie? It's a big step to take for a girl who has never been farther than Goose Green. What did your mother have to say? Does she approve?'

Carrie nodded emphatically. 'She's ever so pleased, Ma'am, for she were getting proper flummoxed 'cause I wouldn't make up me mind. Me brother Jack, 'e were rare put out when I told 'im I I didn't want the cashier's job at the grocery, but I couldn't see meself sitting on a stool all day in that poky little cubby 'ole. Why, Ma'am, I should go clean off me rocker, and that's a fact!'

Her new mistress laughed as she gathered up the baby. 'Your ex-teacher was right to recommend you, Carrie, for it's important for a baby to have someone young, and of a happy nature. After all, you will be spending a good many hours together. Has Mrs Martin mentioned in her letters that the regiment will soon be posted overseas, and that the families will be going with their menfolk?'

'Yes, Ma'am.'

'It could be for as long as five years, and certainly not less than three years. You could be very homesick, Carrie.'

'Then I should 'ave to put up with it, Ma'am. Our Mum says she would miss me something shocking, but she won't stand in me way, not if you was to engage me, Ma'am.'

'Actually, I had almost decided to engage you, Carrie, even before we met. You see, I know quite a lot about you and your family from Mrs Martin and Philip, who are both very fond of you. We shall be seeing quite a lot of them, so you won't feel you are entirely among strangers. Now, I should like you to meet my husband.' She opened the door, called 'Lesley! Are you there?' and a tall, handsome man in immaculate uniform strode into the room.

278

'Give me that child! Haven't I told you repeatedly, darling, you are not to carry him until you are stronger,' he scolded. Then his glance ran over the sturdy little figure with the flushed cheeks and bright curls on which her Sunday best hat was perched precariously. His mouth twitched as Carrie curtsied. Then he held out his hand and demanded with brusque good humour, 'So you think you are strong enough to manage this hefty son of mine?'

To a working-class girl at her first encounter with the upper class, the clipped voice and the Captain's uniform could have been rather intimidating, but Carrie was not lacking in confidence. 'I'll manage 'im fine, Sir. Don't you fret. I be ever so strong and 'ealthy, even if I ain't all that big.'

'Splendid!' said he approvingly. He liked the look of her, and if Felicity had engaged her, he had no intention of interfering. She was a good judge of character, and they had no trouble with their servants. He held the baby awkwardly, but he was a little wary of infants since the christening of his god-child, when she wet his best pair of trousers!

They moved over to the window to watch the new nursemaid walking sedately across the road, but when she had turned the corner, she took to her heels and ran all the way to The Parsonage. Mum must be the first to know about this wonderful job! Mum would want to see the mistress, for that was right and proper. Sometimes a girl of 13 took her Mum to the interview, but not Carrie.

'I don't want nobody to speak for me. I got a tongue, ain't I?' she had reminded Mum. When she burst into the kitchen, she found Peg-leg drinking a cup of tea and her mother taking a batch of scones from the oven.

'She looks as though she lost a farthing and found a

279

sixpence, don't she, Ruby?' he chuckled. 'Come and sit down, young 'un and tell us all about it.'

Carrie snatched off her hat and coat and the white cotton gloves specially bought for the occasion, pulled out a chair, and sat down. With her elbows on the table, she held her flushed cheeks in her two hands and began her story. Ruby and Peg-leg exchanged a meaningful glance as the hot scones were buttered, and the tea poured, but Ruby's heart was aching long before the tale was finished. Five years! It was a lifetime. What would her Dad have to say – and her three brothers, who thought the world of her? Nobody in the family had ever thought of emigrating, yet many parents had said goodbye to sons and daughters and had grandchildren growing up in Canada and Australia. But Ruby was not concerned with other families, only her own, and she looked at her only daughter with her bright eyes dimmed with unshed tears.

So began the new chapter for Carrie Simmons that would change the whole course of her life. Yet few of her ex-school friends would have changed places with her even if they had the opportunity. This new chapter was as hazardous and unpredictable as emigrating, and separation was a heart-breaking experience. Carrie was still an ignorant child in spite of her dauntless spirit and determination. She saw only the wonder and felt only the excitement of such an adventure, and none of its pitfalls. She was too young to visualise a strange new world in which her family could play no part in her protection. Whatever had been her objection to 'service' in her own village, Carrie would still be a servant with no status. The nursemaid's uniform would set her apart from the college-trained nurses and the governesses who would turn up their superior noses.

The native servants would treat her with caution, not knowing whether she could be trusted. Master Jimmy Saunders would claim all her attention and devotion. She would be on duty day and night under the supervision of her mistress. Felicity Saunders could be a fair and reasonable mistress but she could also be demanding and disagreeable. Just because she had behaved kindly and generously on this first day of their acquaintance was no guarantee that it would last. A mistress was not required to produce credentials, only the maid-servant, yet the risk was greater for the servant.

So Carrie embarked on this new chapter without a backward glance, and went off to Tunbridge Wells in grand style the following day, with the doctor driving them both to the station in his trap. It was altogether too overwhelming to have so much money spent and so many garments spread on the counter. Carrie was too surprised and too impressed to say anything more than 'Oh, *Ma'am*. I could make do with 'arf of them print dresses and aprons, for I be quite able to wash 'em out when they gets grubby. Me Mum 'as been learning me to wash and iron since I left school.'

'It's not an extravagance, Carrie, to buy six of everything because they last longer if they are not constantly in the wash. Besides, we may not always be living in a place where washing facilities are available. On board ship, for instance, you will have to take your turn with other nursemaids in some crowded little wash-room.'

Carrie nodded, undismayed. She had no conception of the poor facilities provided on a troopship or the tiny, stuffy cabin in mid-ships in which she would find herself installed with her charge. To carry the heavy baby up and down shuddering companion ways and

281

swaying passages would take all her strength. It was too far removed from the present day to bother her.

Standing at the counter beside her mistress, for whom a chair had been fetched, Carrie sighed with pleasure and gratitude. Six pairs of black stockings, six pairs of white stockings, four pairs of shoes, two black, two white. Frilled cuffs to wear over the rolled-up sleeves of her print dresses, and white starched caps. A grey overcoat and matching hat for the first Winter at Tidworth, and thereafter on the early part of the long voyage between Southampton and Marseilles. Carrie knew where to find Marseilles on the globe that stood on the schoolmaster's desk, and she remembered that Port Said and Aden were located at either end of the Suez Canal and the Red Sea. Geography had been one of her favourite subjects but never in her wildest dreams had she imagined herself actually seeing all these fascinating places. Eagerly she questioned her mistress on the return journey. The uniform would be delivered by the carter the following day.

'I will ask my mother-in-law if she will spare one of the tin trunks the boys used for boarding school in their young days. I expect they are lying around in the attic,' Felicity promised.

Carrie had tasted coffee for the first time in a tea-shop in the Pantiles, and a generous slice of cake called 'gateau' that had to be eaten with a fork, not the fingers.

'I be proper flummoxed, Ma'am,' Carrie exclaimed over every new experience, and Felicity Saunders felt her heart warming to the child. Her mother-in-law, who would not hesitate to write a cheque for charity or church funds, could have offered to pay for the nursemaid's uniform, but it did not occur to her. She was fond of her son's wife, and knew the importance of

282

a well-dressed nursemaid for her first grandchild. She reminded Felicity however, that it was customary for the mistress to deduct the cost from the first year's wages.

'Then the poor child would have nothing left to spend,' Felicity protested.

'Don't spoil her, dear. It's always a mistake to spoil a servant. They should be kept in their place.' She was a hard woman beneath that veneer of upper-class reticence, her daughter-in-law had long since discovered. But there was an excuse for a fond mother with a black sheep in the family. The disgrace had not been forgotten. The first grandchild had not softened the hard core of bitterness and disappointment for which her favourite son was responsible. It was no secret that the doctor and his wife occupied separate bedrooms. Much of upper-class behaviour was revealed by servants' gossip that would not be disclosed of the lower class.

The tin trunk brought down from the attic was a shabby affair, not surprisingly, after several years of rough treatment by careless porters.

'Me Dad will give it a coat of paint. Don't you worry, Ma'am. T'will look as good as new when it's finished,' said Carrie decidedly.

In the February twilight, the echoing notes of 'Lights Out' startled the young nursemaid in the nursery of the house overlooking the barrack square. She clutched the baby to her breast, and peered anxiously between the curtains. Nobody had explained about 'Lights Out' at sundown and 'Reveille' at sunrise. Nobody had really prepared Carrie for this strange new world of men and horses, of marching feet, and the raucous voice of a sergeant bellowing orders. The ugly barracks had the

283

grim aspect of a fortress, and the lone bugler added an eerie finality to the closing day.

She shivered, and whispered, 'We 'as to get used to it, me little love. We're in the Army now.' So many new impressions had crowded into the hours since they left Fairfields, there had been no time to feel homesick. Only her brother Freddie had been free to see her off at the station, and she was proud of Freddie in his dark suit, shining boots, and bowler hat. As a solicitor's clerk he sat all day on a high stool in an office stacked with musty law books. He was pale, and his slight figure seemed to sway in the wind that swept across the fields. As the train moved away from the platform, he stood bareheaded, smiling his shy, charming smile, waving his hat till he disappeared into a cloud of steam. He had kissed his sister affectionately, and promised to write. Carrie knew she could depend on that promise. Albert and Jack had also promised, but they hadn't the knack of putting words on paper, not like Freddie. As for Mum, she was a poor scholar, and had not penned a letter to anyone in all her married life. Why should she, when all her near relatives lived within walking distance? A pen and a bottle of ink on the mantelpiece had been utilised by her clever daughter who liked to draw maps and practise her sums in the long Winter evenings. All three brothers had given their sister five shillings, and Freddie had stood over her while it was invested in the Post Office Savings Bank, for he knew she would be tempted to fritter it away if she kept it in her possession.

'You never know when you might be glad of those few shillings in some emergency. Take my advice, Carrie, and save a small amount of your wages every month. You won't ever regret it,' he told her, gravely. Then he added as an afterthought, since she looked so young and vulnerable, 'Be sure to let us know, dear, if you are not being treated well at Tidworth, for it's a big risk to go overseas if you feel unhappy, or at all doubtful in your mind.'

But she smiled and shook her head. 'I ain't affeared, Freddie. Don't you fret,' she whispered as they parted.

As the train gathered speed, she had caught a glimpse of Dad with a group of gangers standing on the bank with their picks and shovels. She had waved frantically from her corner of the first-class carriage, but he had not seen her, and her mouth dropped with disappointment.

The Mistress was nursing the sleeping baby on her lap, the Captain reading the headlines in the *Morning Post*. The rattle of the iron wheels beat out a steady rhythm that was music in her ears, as the familiar countryside slipped away. A mist hung over the fields, and the naked branches, etched against the grey sky, had a kind of beauty, she noticed for the first time in her young life. But this eventful day would still be remembered when Carrie was an old woman. Her blue eyes shone with wonder and excitement, and she rubbed a clear space on the steamed window with a gloved hand and stared at the flying landscape. Her mistress watched the trim little figure approvingly. She had been relieved there had been no tears at parting from her brother, but she was wondering afresh if it had been wise to engage a child of 13. If she had engaged a young woman with some experience, then her own authority might be questioned. A young girl could be moulded into the shape and nature of a kind mistress with patience and tolerance. It was a challenge. Most village girls, born and bred by solid working-class parents, had a healthy respect for the upper class. Only rarely did a girl rebel against her

285

birthplace and seek her fortune in the city, but if she did her reputation was lost. As for the unfortunate servant girls who found themselves in the family way, they were quickly dismissed, and threatened with the Workhouse.

What of Carrie in a world of men? her mistress was wondering with some misgiving. The child had matured early. She was pert and pretty. It would be quite a responsibility, but her ex-teacher would help. The sergeant's wife and her charming little boy would welcome the girl. A telegram had been despatched, and she was expected.

So the journey had passed pleasantly, and when the baby woke, he was handed over to his nursemaid who pointed out the interesting objects flying away in the distance – moo-cows, baa-lambs, chick-chicks and quack-quacks.

'My God!' breathed the Captain, from behind the *Morning Post*.

'Don't worry, darling. Once upon a time you and I were listening to baby talk. It's natural,' his wife whispered soothingly.

That same evening, with Jimmy tucked up in his cot and the door of the night nursery left open to warn the servant if he should wake, Felicity Saunders stood waiting in the hall for Carrie to join her. She had promised the girl a visit to her old friends, and her sense of responsibility recognised the risk in leaving the young nursemaid to find her way to the barracks. That there *was* a risk in this world of men was acknowledged by all the officers' wives who employed young servants, and they all had a duty to safeguard their own particular servants. After today, Carrie would meet Mrs Martin by daylight. They could push the pram together on the afternoon walk, and meet Philip from school. It would pass the time pleasantly, and Carrie would not feel lonely in her new environment. The Captain had joined his brother officers in the Mess. They both were glad to be back in their own familiar world. Even with the baby, the week at Fairfields had been rather a strain. It was almost impossible to penetrate the closed mind and heart of a fond mother still grieving for a banished son. She was living in the past with her memories of their boyhood, and her own importance in their young lives. Her loneliness was intensified by her husband's dedication to his practice and his patients.

'Master Jimmy be fast asleep now, Ma'am,' Carrie whispered, as she joined her mistress in the hall.

'There is no need to whisper, Carrie. He must get used to noise, and if he cries, Susan is quite capable of soothing him. The Captain is anxious that his son will not be spoiled by too much fussing and attention. By all means take good care of him, but he mustn't be coddled.'

'No, Ma'am,' Carrie agreed obediently, but kept her thoughts to herself. Surely the Captain should be minding his own business and not interfering in domestic matters. 'I be beholden only to Mistress,' she reminded herself, so her loyalties would not be divided.

Now she stepped out with a fine sense of importance, not in the least intimidated by the mild rebuke. Master Jimmy was a cuddlesome baby, and cuddling he would get when they were alone in the nursery. Carrie was proud of her small domain – a day- and a night-nursery and a bathroom. Because she regarded it already as her own personal property, she would enjoy keeping it neat and clean. The lone bugler would not startle her tomorrow when he sounded Reveille, for she would be expecting it. Bill Jenkins, the Captain's batman, had taken the trouble to explain it when she made his acquaintance in the basement before supper. It was strange to see a man pegging up a line of washing.

'Come on in,' he invited, with a friendly grin. 'I've left you plenty of room. Want any help?'

'No thank you,' said Carrie, on her dignity. A cheeky fellow, judging by the way his dark eyes ran over her trim little figure. She was vaguely reminded of Lennie O'Brien, but it was a long time since she had to escape the attentions of Lennie. To discover the Captain had his own personal servant had been yet another surprise to add to the many surprises of that first unforgettable day.

'Did that bugle give you a bit of a shock?' he asked, taking a peg from his mouth.

She nodded.

'Your first encounter with the Army, I take it?'

'Yes.'

'You'll soon get used to it, my girl.'

'I'm not your girl! Me name's Carrie.'

'Take it easy,' he grinned. 'No offence meant.'

'None taken!' she snapped. But her curiosity got the better of her dignity. 'What was 'e doing, then, blowing that bugle all on 'is own?'

'Sounding Lights Out. The flag comes down at sunset, and it's hoisted again when the bugler sounds Reveille at sunrise.'

'I see.'

'Where do you come from, Carrie?'

'Fairfields.'

'Where's that?'

Surprised at his ignorance, for she thought everyone should know her village was situated in the Weald of Kent, she retorted, 'That's a stoopid question when you knows the Captain and the Mistress is just back from there!'

288

'Sorry.' He was still grinning, and much amused by this pert little addition to the household. 'How old are you, Carrie?'

'Fifteen.'

He knew she was lying, but he let it pass. 'Weren't you afraid, coming away from home?'

Carrie shook her head.

'You've got some pluck,' was all he said, but he wondered if she was as innocent as she looked. Susan would be jealous of this pretty little peach from the country. He must watch his step. They were engaged to be married.

'I got to go now. The Mistress is taking me to visit me friend. I ain't seen 'er since she left Fairfields soon after she were married,' Carrie confided.

'Who's that then? Anyone I know?'

'Mrs Martin. She's the wife of Sergeant Martin.'

The corporal whistled. 'That bastard!'

'Is that what they call 'im?'

'That, and a few other choice names not to be mentioned in the presence of a young lady!'

'I didn't know. Mrs Martin ain't never mentioned 'er 'usband in 'er letters, only Philip.'

'Poor little blighter. We all feel sorry for the kid, but the Sergeant wouldn't thank you to interfere. Mrs Martin don't complain, you see. She's too loyal.'

'She's me best friend. I love 'er, and I loves Philip.'

'Then she'll be right glad to have you around, for she don't seem to mix with the other sergeants' wives, and as far as I know, the kid doesn't mix either. It must be difficult, keeping themselves to themselves in the barracks, but they just don't seem to fit in somehow. You'll soon see what I mean. Watch your step with Serg. He's got a nasty temper, and it don't take much to upset him.'

289

'I ain't afraid.'

'I still say watch your step or you might find yourself in trouble.'

'What sort of trouble?'

'He can't keep his hands off anything in petticoats, and you're a pretty little piece!'

'Thanks for the warning.' She tossed her curly head and ran up the basement stairs, leaving him gaping at a plump little backside the Sarg would soon be slapping.

'Good evening.' Martha Martin greeted them from the doorway at the top of the scrubbed steps. Philip stood beside her. Three years had changed them both. The ex-teacher had lost the bloom of youth, and the gaslight picked out the silver hairs in the smooth brown head. But the smile was the same smile that had welcomed her Infants in the village school.

'Here she is, safely delivered as promised.' said the Captain's wife gaily – and Martha opened her arms. The child's warm hug brought tears to her eyes. The boy stared and drew back a pace. His 8-year-old dignity shied away from hugs and kisses. He had grown tall and thin, and his eyelids twitched nervously.

''ullo, Philip, luv. My, ain't you grown a big boy!'

'Good evening,' he answered her politely, and offered his hand. She took the small, limp hand and shook her head, teasing him with such a gesture.

'Why, you ain't shy of Carrie? That would be stoopid, luv, for I rocked you in your pram when you was a baby, and I were the first to take your little 'and when you started to walk.'

He shrugged. 'I don't remember.'

'Philip was too young to remember, Carrie,' his mother reminded her gently, as she ushered her

290

visitors into the tiny lobby, hung with coats and hats. A new scooter was propped against the wall.

'A present from Grandad for my birthday,' Philip explained proudly. 'See, it has a pedal. It's one of the latest models. I work it up and down, then I can travel quite fast. Can I show Carrie how it works, Mother?'

'Not tonight, dear. It's too late.'

His mouth drooped with disappointment, and Felicity Saunders, who was fond of the child, suggested kindly, 'If you wait till tomorrow, darling, Carrie can meet your mother with the baby, and they could take a walk together and bring the scooter to the school gates. That is, if this arrangement would be convenient to you, Mrs Martin?' she added, diplomatically.

The ex-teacher smiled at the girl. 'We should both enjoy it. Thank you for suggesting it. I will push the scooter to the school gates, and you can ride back,' she promised her son.

'*Thank* you, Mother.' The sulky mouth was smiling now, and the worried little frown smoothed away for the present, but his small world was a very worrying place, and he always anticipated trouble.

A bright fire in the polished grate distracted the visitors' attention from the faded wallpaper and the threadbare mats. The curtains were drawn, and a tea-tray laid ready on the red plush cloth. A reminder of those happy days in the Infants' class were a number of small ornaments of Goss china, carefully arranged on the mantelpiece. These had been parting gifts from teachers and children who knew she collected them. Because of its shabbiness, it reminded Carrie of home, and she shivered with the first twinge of homesickness. They would be missing her tonight. Her ears were burning. 'They're talking about me now, as they eat their supper,' she told herself, and caught the

291

sympathetic glance of Teacher's eyes. She still thought of her as Teacher, but would soon get used to calling her Mrs Martin. The few text books on the single shelf told their own tale: history, geography, grammar and other subjects of interest to a bright, intelligent child. Martha Martin was teaching her son all she knew, whenever they found themselves alone on these long Winter evenings. Philip was an apt pupil, and loved his mother dearly. Education was so important to a boy, she had insisted, and she was not satisfied with his progress at the local school. Although she had not dared to mention it yet, either to Dick or to Philip, she had not given up hope of Grammar School, and a future that would still depend on the generosity of his godfather, and the goodwill of his grandparent. It would mean a heart-breaking separation, for Philip would be living in Fairfields while she travelled to the Far East, with Dick and the regiment. To separate the man from the boy was a kind of escape from the misery they endured as a family. It would never solve itself while she battled with the possessiveness and jealousy between her husband and son. Determination and desire for her son's happiness was the only lifeline on which to cling in a world almost completely dominated by Dick's contempt and cruelty. The deep understanding that existed between mother and son infuriated Dick Martin. They had no armour against his sullen moods and violent temper. The neighbours could not guess the half of what the sergeant's wife suffered in the privacy of the marriage bed, but they could hear the boy crying when the shouting had stopped.

But Carrie had yet to discover the true picture behind the homely façade that Martha Martin presented to her visitors that first evening. It was not often that Dick disturbed them at this early hour, for he

292

preferred the noisy atmosphere of the Sergeants' Mess, and beer suited his palate rather than the tea Martha was brewing at all hours of the day. A heavy smoker, the sergeant kept a rack of pipes on the mantelpiece, and the smell of stale tobacco still lingered in the room, in spite of the window open all morning.

Carrie chattered happily about the baby and the nursery, while Philip listened with a puzzled frown, for he had forgotten the rough dialect of the village children.

'Why doesn't Carrie talk properly?' he asked his mother after their visitors had left.

'You mustn't be critical. It's not fair. Carrie is intelligent enough to realise her defects and will learn to think before she speaks. Besides, Mrs Saunders will correct her. It's not our business to do so,' she added, meaningly.

The weeks slipped away in the regular routine of the nursery, to which Carrie had quickly adapted. Now she could be trusted to bath and feed the baby without supervision. Feeding bottles were diligently scalded, and the baby food recommended by the doctor carefully measured. Jimmy was clean and sweet-smelling whenever his mother picked him up, for the young nursemaid had soon realised that cleanliness played an important part in the training of children of the upper class. Fresh air was another obligation, and the baby's parents were quite fanatical on this particular point. In all kinds of weather, the child must be pushed out in his pram every afternoon, and the window of the night nursery left open. Carrie had grown up in Richmond Row, where an open window was a hazard, and the stink of the neighbours' privy was a constant reminder of a squalid slum.

This alarming initiation into the Spartan environment of the middle-class nursery, was truly discomforting. In all her short life, Carrie had never been subjected to 'draughts'. They were frowned upon by the working class. Huddled under the blankets on the little iron bedstead in the corner of the night nursery, the hard mattress was a poor substitute for the feather bed to which she was accustomed. Health and Hygiene had been discussed with much gravity during those early weeks of training, and Carrie had listened attentively, and done her best to adjust her own limited standards.

At the end of the day she was tired, and glad to tumble into bed by 8 o'clock, but she took the precaution to undress beside the dying embers of the nursery fire, and not to remove her long woollen vest for fear of catching a chill. She moved about the room quietly, in the dim light of a gas lamp in the street, but Jimmy slept soundly in his cot, and only grunted a feeble protest when she lifted him out of his warm nest to hold him over the chamber pot. This was her last duty of the day and her first duty in the morning.

'Poor little fellow, why can't 'e do 'is pee in 'is nappy?' she asked herself, when she was instructed on this cruel procedure.

'Good habits must be encouraged from the start, Carrie,' she was reminded when she seemed doubtful.

'Yes, Ma'am,' she would agree obediently, and remembered that Mrs Martin had advised acquiescence on such matters and discouraged the tendency to air her views. Still a child in years, and lacking experience, it would be presumptuous, Martha insisted kindly.

They met every afternoon for a walk, and Carrie spent Sunday afternoon and evening with Martha and Philip. It was a nice change to stay indoors after six days of compulsory exercise in the now familiar streets

294

of Tidworth. They would take turns to read the books that Philip had won for Sunday School attendance. These were naturally of a religious nature with a good moral, and included *Pilgrim's Progress*, a heavy-going saga for a young nursemaid. But Martha had been brought up strictly, and still managed to read a passage from her Bible every morning when Dick had left.

In the privacy of his little box-room, Philip treasured the old favourites his mother had brought from her home at Fairfields: *Black Beauty*, *Robinson Crusoe*, *Uncle Tom's Cabin*, *The Swiss Family Robinson*, *Treasure Island* and *Tales of King Arthur and his Knights of the Round Table*. Such stirring tales for a nervous little boy who shrank from his father's punishment, seemed to provide an antidote to the reality of his daily combat with a harsh parent. Mother and son attended Sunday morning service at the Methodist Chapel, while Carrie followed the marching column of men to church parade in company with the other nursemaids and a swarm of children of the rank and file. Jimmy would wave his arms excitedly, for he loved the sound of drums and bugles, and Carrie would find herself keeping step with the column – left, right, left, right. Propped up on his pillows, the baby needed no encouragement to shout as they marched along. He was a lusty child, healthy and strong, but a heavy weight to be carried up and down stairs, and to lift him from the bath, stiff with protest, was a nightly battle.

'Master Jimmy do seem to know. HE is going to follow the drum, don't he, Ma'am?' Carrie reflected one Sunday morning, as they watched the parade forming on the barrack square. Her mistress smiled approvingly. The child was quick to learn and Martha Martin was a good influence. She hadn't to worry that her pretty nursemaid might be molested on Sunday, for

Philip and his mother walked back with her after an early supper.

The sergeant's wife had disclosed her plan to leave the boy with his grandfather, but Dick had not yet been consulted. They would travel to Fairfields one weekend, and Carrie would accompany them to bid farewell to her family. Only once had Dick Martin surprised them by arriving home early one Sunday evening, but apart from teasing Carrie and rumpling her curls, he behaved with surprising decorum. Perhaps it would be a little risky to pinch the bottom of a nursemaid to the son of an officer. Dick Martin was no fool, for all his bullying and blustering. Between the two – the Captain's wife and the sergeant's wife – Carrie was carefully protected, and guarding her innocence was an obligation not to be taken lightly.

To find a letter from home propped against the Toby Jug on the nursery mantelpiece was the highlight of her regulated day, and she enjoyed answering the letters. Freddie wrote precisely. Mum wrote laboriously every Sunday afternoon, believing it to be her duty. It was a labour of love, encouraged by a kindly husband who would put on the kettle and make a cup of tea. But it was her cousin Albert who surprised her with her first love letter on her 14th birthday. The grammar was poor, but the sentiments rich.

'Dere Carrie,

I be riting to tell you I miss you, and it don't seem the same place since you went away. There ain't nobody else I would ask to be my sweetheart, but since we shan't be walking out, or corting in the proper fashion, I be proper flummoxed, and that's a fact. Mum says to wait for there be plenty of time, and it ain't fair to tie you down to making a promis, but Aunt Ruby says you mite be going to

296

India for five years, and that's a lifetime, and you mite want to marry an army bloke. Please let me no what you think about it. I won't never change my mind, for I been luving you, Carrie, since you was first cuming to Russets and I took you to see the lambs. Do you remember. Mum sends her luv, and a postal order for five shillings.

Yore luving cousin Albert.'

'Well I be jiggered!' Carrie exclaimed, blushing with surprise and pleasure. It would do no harm to accept the proposal. She liked Albert, but she could not see herself as his sweetheart. A lance-corporal would be more to her liking! Uniform did something for a man, and when heads were turned in her direction as she walked proudly along with the Captain's baby in his shining pram, her heart fluttered excitedly. All the girls in the sixth standard at the village school had sweethearts, and she had been called 'a snooty Miss' for tossing her head at the village boys. Her cousins were different, she was reminded again as she considered her first proposal. She had seen them working as hard as labourers and dressed as labourers, but they had status and respect in the farming community as their father's sons.

It was understood and accepted that childhood, for the working class, ended at the age of 13, when earning a living was a very serious matter. A whole year had passed since she had left school, and Carrie saw herself as an adult, able and willing to take responsibility, and make her own decisions. But her mistress would regard the young nursemaid as a child till she reached the age of 17, and would always have the last word on everything that concerned her son.

It was a tedious and frustrating period, and the close contact with the upper class still had its limits and depended solely on her care and devotion to Jimmy. There were compensations, and Carrie was mindful of her good fortune in being engaged as a nursemaid in the household of an Army officer. If she behaved herself, and improved her speech and habits, there was no reason why she would be dismissed till Master Jimmy was sent off to boarding school.

Carrie's determination to 'speak proper' was matched by the strong desire to leave behind for ever the stench and depravity of Richmond Row. To feel ashamed of her home and her birthplace was a new experience, but it was inevitable once she began to compare her present environment with the past. As yet, she could not actually visualise the heartache she would leave behind when she finally embarked on that adventure, or her own reactions when she found herself on the high seas, bound for some vague destination on the other side of the world. Five years would seem an eternity. In the past few months an occasional pang of homesickness had been quickly dispelled, but she was unprepared for the emotional disturbance of such an unforgettable experience. Her new, exciting world had captured her imagination, and she no longer belonged to that small, confined world of childhood. But Richmond Row was still there, waiting to shock her fastidious senses and disturb the harmony of the forthcoming weekend.

Dick Martin had shown no objection to Martha's plan, but Philip was torn between the sudden and surprising end to three years of persecution, and the parting from the mother he adored. The sadness was there, as well as the happy anticipation, as they travelled back to Kent. He would be back where he rightly belonged, in the security of the wheelwright's shop, and his grandfather's gruff kindliness. And his godfather would be pleased to see him back at the village school, and would help him in his studies later. To pass the entrance examination to Grammar School was his mother's fond hope, and he must not disappoint her. Their homecoming was an event to be celebrated with a mixture of smiles and tears. It was altogether too short, yet too prolonged for both Martha and Carrie, who would be glad to get it over with, and on their way back.

When Martha caught a glimpse of a tall, bearded figure on the station platform, her thoughts were confused. She had not expected that he would meet them. The hired cab from the station hotel was waiting outside the gates. His kindness brought the tears to her eyes, for it was so long since she had known a man's kindness and courtesy. He waved his hat, and smiled at the two eager young faces in the open doorway as the train jerked to a halt. Then his eyes sought the familiar little figure in the background, who followed them out, unsmiling, and obviously nervous. She was changed, grievously changed. She had suffered. Something had died in her bright personality.

He took her hand and asked, 'Did you have a good journey?'

She nodded. 'Very good, thank you, Sir.'

He wished she would stop calling him 'Sir' since she was no longer a teacher on his staff, but a married woman, independent of his jurisdiction. Yet the sight of her was so disturbing, he was tongue-tied, and he turned to greet the children, who stood quietly, side by side.

'So there you are, Carrie and Philip. How are you?'

'Quite well, thank you Sir,' they answered respectfully, and shook his outstretched hand.

299

The porter hurried down the platform, touched his cap, and picked up the bulging Gladstone bag that contained Philip's few precious possessions, his clothes and books. He was holding the scooter, and Carrie carried a bag filled with presents for the family. The schoolmaster donned his hat and escorted them to the cab. They climbed the hill slowly, the coachman leading the mare. They passed the school gates and the pond. The swans were still sitting majestically on the slimy green water.

The wheelwright stood waiting in his stained leather apron, and Carrie's brother Jack lifted a hand in salute from the forecourt of the grocery. It seemed they had put back the clock three years, Martha was thinking, as she hugged her father.

The six months for Carrie had seen many changes, but here was Jack, still a little self-important in his starched white coat, pecking her cheek, and patting her shoulder affectionately.

'Nothing's changed, Jack. It's still the same,' she told him.

'That's what *you* think. I'm a father now,' he reminded her.

'But you don't *look* any different.'

'You wait till you see me pushing the pram down Richmond Row tomorrow afternoon. We always visit Mum and Dad on Sunday, and Mum gets a special tea. She's cooking all the week at The Parsonage, but she don't object to cooking for her family on Sunday, and she's proud as Punch of her first grandchild.'

'I've brought her a rattle, and I've got presents for everyone in this bag. How soon will you be finished work, Jack?'

'Half-an-hour. I'll take you home, but I can't stay. Elsie will be expecting me back to supper, and I like to nurse Rachel while I eat my supper.'

'I was surprised when you called the baby Rachel. It's in the Bible.'

'That's why we chose it.'

'It's a pretty name. I like it, Jack.'

'Well, you're an aunt now, Carrie, whether you like it or not. What's the schoolmaster doing at the wheelwright's?' he added, staring at the little group crossing the yard.

'He *is* Philip's godfather, and they have a lot to discuss.'

Jack grinned. 'And Teacher has been working on your dropped aitches, I'm glad to hear!'

'She's still my best friend. I love her. I see her every day. She's sad because she's leaving Philip behind. She's so *unselfish*, Jack.'

'So's our Mother, Carrie, and so is Elsie, and one of these days, when you're a mother, you will feel the same.'

'Shall I?' asked the youthful Carrie, doubtfully.

Dick's name was not mentioned, and since he had lost touch with his family in Richmond Row, it was not necessary for Martha and Philip to call on the Martins. The schoolmaster stayed to supper, and was invited to join them for dinner the following day, after Chapel. Andrew Robinson still attended All Saints on Sunday morning, but sat in a back pew to avoid meeting Parson's wife and Cecily. He placed flowers on Irene's grave on the anniversary of her birthday, and on Easter Sunday, and a holly wreath at Christmas. But that short period of his life had no substance, he had long since discovered. It was the sturdy little figure of Martha he had remembered in the three years since she went away with her husband and son. To meet her again in her home environment was pleasantly nostalgic, and he accepted the invitation gladly, anticipating the traditional Sunday roast such as he once enjoyed at The Parsonage.

As a schoolmaster, he had seen many changes in the past three years, particularly in the Infants, where a succession of young pupil teachers left a trail of incompetence and disinterest. It was not entirely their fault, he had to admit, for it was a mistake to expect the loving dedication of a Martha Carter. His housekeeper had retired, and he was blessed – or cursed – with a houseproud widow, who spread newspapers on her floors, and had strong views on the punishment of small boys who broke windows with flying peg-tops. The boys were caned and their tops confiscated, but still an occasional window was broken. It was natural, the schoolmaster argued defensively. Boys could not be so readily subdued as the girls, and the cane was a mild form of chastisement to the offspring of working-class fathers who invariably took off their belts.

That Martha was shy of being left alone with him was obvious, for when he suggested a walk on Sunday afternoon, they were accompanied by Philip, though the boy would have preferred to curl up on the sofa with a book while his grandfather enjoyed his forty winks. Prompt obedience was second nature now to Dick Martin's son, and he fetched his cap and followed them out with a sigh of resignation. Mother was quiet, and her eyes were sad. She was already looking ahead to the morrow. He took her cold hand and asked, gravely, 'Mother, if Father gets killed, you will come back to live with grandfather, won't you?'

'What a question!' she said, her mouth trembling.

'Soldiers *do* get killed when they go to war,' he persisted.

'Your father has already served five years in India, and came back unscathed.'

302

'But next time he might get killed, and then you would come back, wouldn't you? Wouldn't you, Mother?'

'I suppose so. Where else should I go?'

'I want him to be killed. I *hate* him!'

'Philip.'

'It's true, only I couldn't ever say it aloud in Tidworth. I could only whisper it to myself. I don't have to see him again, not ever, do I, Mother?'

She turned her head and met the steady gaze of the boy's godfather. 'It depends on circumstances, dear. I cannot promise anything. You should know that now. You're a big boy. It also depends on whether you pass the examination to the Grammar School, and whether your grandfather is still willing to provide a home for you.'

Philip sighed. It seemed he might still be snatched back by that hateful man, and he had thought he was safe, for ever. A worried little frown puckered his eyes.

'I don't want to be a soldier when I grow up. I don't have to be a soldier, do I, Mother?'

'Of course not. Don't worry, dear. Nobody is going to force you into uniform if you wish to be a civilian.'

'I think I should like to be an engine driver when I grow up.'

They laughed at him then, and his godfather pointed out that most small boys had that ambition.

'Did *you* want to be an engine driver, Sir?'

'I did, but it was a long time ago.'

They walked on in companionable silence, till Andrew Robinson asked quietly, 'Has the posting come through?'

'Yes, it's Aden. But it could be changed *en route*, so I understand from our Captain's wife. With any fresh disturbance on the North West Frontier, a battalion of

303

our Light Infantry would be sent to reinforce the garrison at Peshawar. That would be under the command of Lieutenant-Colonel Bradley.'

'Your husband's battalion?'

'Yes.'

'I see. It's nothing new, is it? We seem to have been hearing of skirmishes on the North West Frontier for years.'

'I know where to find it on the globe, Sir,' Philip interrupted importantly. 'It's next to a country called Af . . . Af . . .'

'Afghanistan?'

The boy nodded. 'I like geography. It's my favourite subject, Sir. Mother has been teaching me, and I've brought all my text books.'

'Splendid. We must see what we can do together, you and I. There are still two years before you sit for that examination, and you mustn't disappoint your Mother.'

'No, Sir. Can I start back at your school tomorrow, please Sir?'

'But won't you want to accompany your Mother and Carrie to the station?'

Philip looked from one to the other appealingly.

'I don't mind, dear. I shall be all right with Carrie.'

His mother's smile was wistful, but in a sense it would be a relief.

The cab was ordered for the 9 o'clock train, so they could drop him off at the school gate. In his excitement to get back to his old school, he would not realise they were saying goodbye for *years*, not days. They had never been parted for a single day in those eight years. Her heart ached, but there would be time enough for tears on tomorrow's train. Carrie would be upset at leaving her family. They would comfort each other.

'I shall pick you a bunch of wild flowers, and you can take them back to Tidworth. You'll like that, won't you, Mother?' her son was asking.

'Thank you.'

He dropped her hand and ran on ahead.

'It's a lovely month, Martha, the month of May,' said Andrew quietly.

'Yes,' she agreed, a blush spreading over her pallid cheeks.

'Will you write to me?' He was asking the impossible, and he knew it.

She shook her head. 'I shall write to Philip. You *will* see that he writes to me?'

'Of course.'

She sighed. 'Thank you, Sir.'

'The name is Andrew.'

'It would seem strange, presumptuous.'

'Not at all. It would please me. Our time is so short. You *do* care for me? I have not been mistaken?'

'I have always cared,' she told him, simply, her voice choked with emotion. And when she turned her head, her eyes swam with tears. 'Don't make me cry, Andrew, *please*. I mustn't cry, not today,' she pleaded.

'Forgive me.' He pressed her gloved hand, then dropped it quickly as the boy ran back with the flowers he had gathered.

'Will you hold them, Mother, while I pick more?' he asked, breathlessly, 'and will you hold my cap?' He snatched it off and pushed it into her hand and ran away.

'He's happy again. I'm so glad, so grateful.' Her voice faltered. 'Your friendship, it means so much to me. I can never repay you for your kindness to Philip.'

'I'm fond of the boy – and his mother,' he added. 'Take care of yourself, my dear.'

305

The dirty, rat-infested cottage in Richmond Row, once the home of the O'Briens, had been rejected by several young couples engaged to be married, and looking for a place of their own. The girls had shuddered at the damp, crumbling walls and the stinking privy hung with cobwebs, and the young men refused to be compelled to work on the railway in return for the privilege of living in such a hovel, so they looked elsewhere, discovered the farmers could offer only seasonal work, and were sadly discouraged by the lack of opportunity to earn an honest wage in their native land. So they joined the ranks of young emigrants to the Colonies and left behind the aching hearts of parents who would never see their grandchildren.

Carrie had no sense of belonging to Richmond Row as she walked down the cinder path that evening in May with her brother Jack. But when she saw her mother standing on the freshly whitened doorstep, she ran on ahead, ashamed of such feelings of disloyalty. Enfolded in Ruby's arms, and cradled on that soft, warm bosom, she could not speak for the tightness in her throat. They were so alike, these two, and never more so than at this emotional moment of reunion, with their blue eyes wet with tears, and their sturdy bodies locked together.

Tom Simmons stood waiting patiently in the background. He was not a man to assert himself, and content to have his pretty wife 'wear the trousers', so to speak. It saved a lot of trouble.

'Hullo, Dad,' said Jack, with a grin. 'Can't stop. Just brought Carrie along.'

Ruby lifted her head and regarded her son with affectionate tolerance. He was so smug! 'Be off with you, then, and be sure you come along early tomorrow af'noon then Carrie can take a walk with you and Elsie and the baby afore tea.'

306

'Yes, Mum,' Jack answered, obediently, and hurried away.

'Thinks 'isself no end of a toff, since Parson made 'im a sidesman at the church, an' Miss Cecily stood godmother to little Rachel.' Ruby snorted indignantly. 'T'ain't no use for the likes of us getting ideas an' swollen 'eads. We be good, 'onest, working class, and proud of the fact. Ain't we, Dad?'

'You're right, Rube,' Dad agreed, not for the first time.

'Hullo, Dad.' Carrie hugged him exuberantly. He smelled of Lifebuoy soap and his hair was plastered with water.

'It's good to see you, Pickle,' was all he said, but she was a child again, not a grown-up young woman earning her living. Dad had always called her 'Pickle'.

'You're thin as a rake, Dad. What have you been doing with yourself?' she demanded.

'I've always been thin. You've forgotten.'

'That's right. You would think I never fed 'im proper, but there ain't nothing wrong with your Dad's appetite,' said Mum.

'What's for supper, Mum? It smells good.'

'The usual Sat'day supper, luv – sausages an' mash an' fried onions.'

Nothing had changed; only she had changed, Carrie was thinking. 'Where's Freddie?'

''e should be along any minute. Been working late again, but 'e don't seem to mind. If 'e were courting it would be different, but Freddie don't seem to take no interest in young women, not yet 'e don't. One thing I will say. We ain't reared no lazybones in this family. You be all good workers. Take after your Dad and Mum, I reckon.'

Tom was smiling his slow, contented smile. Few men

could claim to be as happy at middle age as the day they married. It had been a bit of a gamble, with Ruby only 16 and the first baby on the way, but they had shared all the ups and downs, all the joys and sorrows of married life. They were proud of the children they had reared, but did not neglect the tiny graves in the churchyard.

'What's Albert doing then? I thought he was free on Saturday afternoon?' Time was so short, and her brothers were not hurrying themselves.

'Don't ask me. Albert don't tell us nothing these days. Shuts up like a clam if you jus' so much as want to know what 'e's been a-doing of. Wouldn't surprise me if Albert ain't courting that Eva Smith, what was Eva Monk before she married. Even when they was at school 'e were dead keen on Eva, but a bit too slow for that little Madam. She took a fancy to 'arry Smith, an' a fine lot of good 'e did 'er. There she is, a widder at 25, an' three little children. Fell off a ladder, thatching a roof, an' that were the end of 'arry Smith. Albert reckoned 'e'd been drinking too much of that 'ome brewed cider.'

'Where do they live, the widow and the children?' Carrie interrupted.

'In one of the farm cottages. They don't go short of nothing, not with Farmer Monk.'

'Will Albert marry Eva, do you think?'

'Sure to, but it's a load of trouble for a young chap what's only earning a small wage. There 'tis, luv, an' there ain't nothing we can do about it, not if 'e's made up 'is mind. Stubborn as a mule, our Albert. Three little children, all under five. A ready-made family, as you might say,' she added with a sigh. 'Jack reckons Albert's a fool to get mixed up in it, but Jack don't know nothing about trouble, not yet 'e don't. Everything 'as gone 'cording to plan for Jack an' Elsie. They been lucky.'

Did Mum always chatter nineteen to the dozen?

Carrie was wondering as she hung her hat and jacket on the back of the door, and took her place at the table. It was hot and stuffy, and the pungent smell of onions seemed to penetrate every crack and corner. The smell of cooking was confined to the kitchen in the Captain's house. She ate her meals in the nursery where she rightly belonged. But Mum was not always right, she decided. She was already reaching out, like Jack and Freddie, to a wider world beyond the limitations of her class. She must be careful not to mention how much she enjoyed her new environment, and her lessons in English grammar from Mrs Martin. If Mum had noticed the improvement she would make no comment, and neither would Dad. Escaping from Richmond Row had been the first stage of an education the village school had not completed. Learning was fun.

Her plate was piled with mashed potatoes and fried onion. She shuddered, and helped herself to mustard. Cook always served her vegetables in small dishes on the tray the housemaid carried up to the nursery. How quickly she had adapted to her new way of life.

Comparisons were not kind. She must be careful. Even the presents she had chosen might not be suitable. What would Mum do with a pink satin cover for her flannelette nightgown? It would be much admired, then tucked away in a drawer. Dad would smoke his new pipe, just to please her for tonight and tomorrow, but the old favourite would not be discarded.

'Eat up, luv. There's trifle for afters,' said Mum.

'Trifle for *dessert*,' Carrie was thinking in her superior enlightenment.

They dropped Philip off at the school gate the following morning. He was proud of his new satchel, a parting present from the Captain's wife, and the new pencil box, complete with pencils, pen-holder, nibs, rubber and ruler. His godfather was waiting to welcome him back to the village school. No mention had been made of the long separation that lay ahead for mother and son, and the weekend had passed quickly and happily, with Philip enjoying the reunion with his grandfather and the young apprentice, now grown into a gangling youth already 'walking out' with the servant girl at the grocery store.

The schoolmaster, with a strained smile, hurried to the station cab to shake hands with Martha and Carrie, then stood back to wave, his arm laid protectively across the boy's shoulders.

Whether or not Philip suddenly realised at that last moment his mother was not coming back, she would never know, but he did not return the wave. Her handkerchief fluttered from the door till the two figures were out of sight, then she turned to Carrie with streaming eyes, and the girl's mouth quivered as she struggled to control her own tears. Philip had not noticed her swollen eyes in the few yards he had travelled with them in the cab. Now she clutched Martha's hand and told her, chokingly, 'I've been crying half the night. It came over me suddenly when I was kissing little Rachel goodbye after supper, that she would be going to school when I saw her again. And Albert would be married to that Eva Smith and likely have children of his own. And Freddie will have his name on the brass plate of the solicitors in the High Street. But that's not all,' she gulped. 'I've got an awful feeling I won't see Dad again. He's so thin, and he's always tired. I know Dad has never been fat but . . . but . . .' The awful possibility that Dad would die while she was thousands of miles away was too much for her overwrought state, and she sobbed despairingly.

310

'Why did I ever think I wanted to leave home? I don't! It's not true. Poor Mum. Poor Dad. They went off to work as usual, and left me with Freddie. He was crying too. Freddie is so sensitive, not like Jack. When we said goodbye, last night, Jack just pecked my cheek. "So long, Carrie. Have a good time", was all he said. You would think I wasn't going any farther than Tunbridge Wells! As for Albert, he didn't even wait to say goodbye to me, but went off to work on his bike while I was calling on the neighbours. But he could have waited, couldn't he? Mum was cross with him, but he told her he had to get back because Eva's little boy was poorly, and she thought he was sickening for something. I never thought to see Albert so taken up with that woman and her children to have no time for his sister.'

'There comes a time, dear, when a brother finds his pleasure elsewhere, and you have been away from home for six months. I'm quite sure Albert is still very fond of you.'

'Well, he's got a funny way of showing it, going off like that without a proper goodbye,' sniffed Carrie, miserably. 'For two pins I would change my mind. It's not too late, is it? I don't want to follow the drum. I want to go home!'

'If you went back now, you would not find anyone at home, for they have all gone to work, and what would you do all day? Be a sensible girl, dear. You love little Jimmy, and his mother depends on you. There is no time to train another nursemaid. Besides, you would be letting me down badly, for I recommended you, Carrie. Have you forgotten?'

The girl shook her head, the tears still falling. She was only a child, with a child's reluctance to look beyond the present moment.

311

'I didn't know I would feel like this when I said goodbye to Mum and Dad,' she sniffed.

'Of course you didn't, but it will pass, dear. Be brave. If you give up now, such a wonderful opportunity is not likely to come your way again, and you would regret it for the rest of your days.'

'Should I?' asked Carrie doubtfully, but she dried her tears.

In comforting the girl, Martha's own sadness had not been forgotten, only put aside. A mother's tears could be shed in private. She was dreading this first night alone with Dick in the flat. He would make a great fuss of her now that he hadn't to compete with Philip for her affection. She shivered at the prospect. What a mentality for a grown man. As if a man's love for a woman could be compared to a mother's love for her son! But was it love, this jealous possessiveness that frightened her into submission? Their marital relationship was something to be endured, not enjoyed, and she wondered how other women managed to control the demands of their over-sexed husbands. Dick swore he loved her, and that he had never looked at another woman during that long period of separation, while their child was growing up. She couldn't believe it. He was such a lusty man.

In all fairness, she supposed she was partly to blame for the animosity between the two. Philip had been her constant companion for five years. Her joy and delight in his bright intelligence, and his popularity with her infants had been such a happy, settled period. But it had passed all too quickly, and Dick came home and claimed her. It was a grave mistake, that hurried marriage, for she had no need of a husband or a father for her child. That he was born out of wedlock had long since been accepted. It was too late. 'Teacher' was loved and respected for her own sake. She had become an institution in the Infants' classroom. The schoolmaster thought very highly of her service. The schoolmaster? 'The name is Andrew,' he had reminded her kindly, only yesterday. 'Take good care of yourself, my dear.'

She sighed, still clasping the hand of the girl as the cab turned into the station yard. She was leaving behind the three she loved best for an uncertain future with the man who was her husband. 'A wife's first duty is to her husband,' her father had reminded her when she had ventured to suggest a separation. He was shocked and angry. 'Those whom God hath joined together let no man put asunder,' he quoted piously.

He was right, of course. Father was always right, but it was difficult to live up to such high principles. She had shamed him once. He would never condone a second fall from grace.

Neither the woman nor the girl would ever forget that journey back to Tidworth. They gazed at the flying landscape with unseeing eyes, looking inwards at their own heartache. The lovely month of May would always bring disturbing nostalgia for both, when they were thousands of miles from that village in the Weald, where both had been born and bred. But it was people who mattered – a few very special people, to whom they were connected by birth or by the ties of friendship. The years had no real meaning as yet for the girl who lived in the present, but for her companion on that journey, they were fraught with such anguish, she had to close her eyes and pretend to take a little nap while the hot tears scalded her eyelids.

In the opposite corner of the carriage, the child who would grow into a woman in the years that lay ahead, twisted her wet handkerchief and sucked aniseed balls

313

from the small paper bag in her lap. Martha had been offered the bag, but shook her head. She was long past the age to enjoy such aniseed balls. Automatically, the girl turned the sweet on her tongue, took it out to examine its change of colour, and put it back. The gesture only emphasised her childishness. Had she made a mistake in recommending Carrie to the Captain's wife? Because she was so fond of the girl, it was partly for her own sake, to keep in touch, to have a young, familiar face to accompany them on their travels. Now she was feeling a little guilty and apprehensive. Would Carrie recover her initial delight in her new way of life, or would the pangs of homesickness spoil her first venture into a wider world? Did one really know what went on in another person's mind, even a person as young as Carrie? Her figure had matured early. She was like her mother, plump and pretty, and would grow more like her with the passing years. Heaven forbid that her working life should follow the same pattern, or that she should know the poverty and drudgery the older woman had endured with such cheerful fortitude. According to Carrie, her mother never complained. She was still a pretty woman, with a happy nature, and if, at one time, she had envied her twin sister at Russets Farm, the boot was on the other foot since the tragic death of her brother-in-law and her seduction the following year.

Carrie had explained about that sad situation on one of their afternoon walks together.

'Aunt Lucy looks much older than Mum now, and she often looks as though she has been crying. She is not allowed to see much of Charles, and she loves him as much, if not more, than her other boys. I suppose I am too young to understand, but Mum says she was a fool to get herself in the family way when everybody knows what Sir Neville Franklin is like.'

314

'Perhaps when you happen to live on Sir Neville's estate it's not so easy for a woman to refuse his advances, especially when you are left a widow and as pretty as your Aunt Lucy.' Martha had suggested.

'It's not the same place. They used to be such a happy family, but it's done something to my cousins. It's a shame. They seemed to quarrel a lot after Uncle Bert was killed, and Harry became very bossy. Having another baby when they were all grown up, and knowing Uncle Bert was not the father, only made things worse. The boys were jealous. Charles was such a lovely baby, with dark eyes and black hair, and they were fair. Aunt Lucy made such a fuss of him. I suppose they felt neglected. I was sorry for Emma, because I think Harry would have married her if this hadn't happened to split the family. He's quite fond of her in his funny way. She likes being bullied by Harry, and only pretends to struggle when he gets hold of her. I've seen the way he looks at her. I wouldn't want to be Harry's sweetheart. He's too rough.'

'Emma must enjoy his roughness. Didn't you tell me she was like a wild little gypsy when she first arrived from the Orphanage? Who knows what that girl has inherited.'

'She's still wild, though not nearly as bad as she used to be, and she works hard. Aunt Lucy has trained her well, but she can't stop her running away when she feels she wants to escape. Sometimes she runs away in the middle of the night, and when Aunt Lucy finds her bed empty in the morning, she sends Harry to fetch her back. "One of these days I shan't bother. Let her go, the silly little bitch!" That's what he told his mother one Sunday morning when I was staying there for the weekend.'

'Where would she go? Russets is her home, and your

315

aunt has been good to her. I expect she is just teasing Harry. It's another way to get his attention. If she really has gypsy blood in her veins she would naturally be happy outdoors. Poor Emma!' Martha had concluded, sympathetically.

To be estranged from one's own people, and to be constantly reminded she was still a gypsy by the eldest son, was cruel. Yet, because of her strange heritage, she obviously found Harry's cruelty more congenial than the kindness of his younger brothers. Human nature had a tendency to revert back, and parents were surprised and shocked by behaviour they neither recognised nor understood. She herself had been responsible for shocking her father with such high principles. Now she was responsible for Carrie's estrangement from her family. It was a solemn thought. Torn between the urge to get away from Richmond Row and the strong ties of her home, the child sucked her aniseed balls, confused and uncertain. Her wide blue eyes, still blurred with tears, were so innocent, so honest.

'Come and sit beside me, dear,' she invited gently. And Carrie tumbled on to the seat, nestled comfortably in the warm, protecting arm, and dropped her head on her companion's shoulder with a sigh of relief.

'Thank you, Teacher,' she murmured, drowsily, and fell asleep.

Teacher? What precious memories were evoked. It was three years and more since a child had called her Teacher. To stop at the school gate and drive on to the station, leaving Philip behind, had been almost unbearable, but he was in good hands. She thought of him proudly displaying the contents of his new pencil box in Standard Two. There had been no time to meet Miss Gaynor, but Andrew had described her briefly as 'a sensible woman, but not very intelligent'.

Dear Andrew! He was rather prejudiced.

PART IV

Chapter Eleven

Sometimes it was difficult for Sir Neville Franklin to realise the handsome boy who rode beside him round the estate was born out of wedlock. He had inherited all the family traits, and his father's arrogance. Not a breath of scandal had reached his own ears, but it was unlikely that a servant or a tenant would be foolish enough to gossip in his hearing. A servant could be instantly dismissed, or a tenant obliged to leave at Michaelmas when a tenancy was renewed. Sir Neville was considered a good landlord, but his quick temper was easily roused, and he had always been impatient of fools.

When the boy was home from boarding school, the Big House revolved around him. Servants loved him for his own sake, and three of his sisters found him adorable. Cynthia, the second daughter, was the exception, but she had developed a naughty tendency of being different and difficult after their first governess had left so suddenly. She had been very fond of Parson's daughter, and found her desertion quite unforgivable. A governess should be too devoted to her pupils to want to marry, she had insisted, and her own young life had been blighted as a result.

'What utter nonsense, Cynthia!' her elder sister,

Beatrice, had retorted. 'One governess is as good as another. We only have to put up with them for a few years. It's just part of growing up, you ninny! Think of the marvellous time when we have finished with the schoolroom for ever. I can hardly wait to be 18! To be presented at Court, and make your curtsey to their Majesties, and the London Season, with all those fabulous balls Mama has told us about. I know I'm not pretty, and not at all clever, but Papa has promised us a good marriage dowry, so I'm sure to find a husband. I like to imagine a handsome, eligible young bachelor asking Papa for my hand in marriage. I shall probably swoon with happiness!'

'The only eligible young bachelor ever likely to ask Papa for your hand in marriage – or mine for that matter – will be a penniless young officer of His Majesty's Guards!' scoffed Cynthia who had no desire for the London Season, or a husband of any sort. If their parents were a typical example of wedded bliss in their class of society, then she would remain an old maid, she had long since decided. Perhaps she had seen more than a child should be permitted to see, that moonlit night at the Villa Benita, when she couldn't sleep, and had crept out to the verandah. She had never forgotten, never would forget, the extraordinary sight of Papa, hurrying across the beach with a girl in his arms – and both stark naked! They had disappeared behind the closed shutters, and she still shuddered at the memory. It was ugly, hideously ugly, and terribly disloyal to poor Mama, who was so refined, so ladylike and gracious. No wonder she chose to spend most of her days in the privacy of her own apartments, and only played hostess when Papa insisted.

The mystery of marital relationships would only be disclosed on the wedding night, according to Beatrice, who showed little curiosity in the nature of the disclosure. Innocence was expected and encouraged. They were protected from the facts of life with the utmost discretion. All would be revealed, and the veil of mystery would be lifted, on that romantic wedding night.

'Innocence is ignorance!' Cynthia had argued. 'Even the youngest housemaid who cleans out the ashes and lights the schoolroom fire would be better informed. Why should this one subject be taboo when it concerns us so deeply?'

'Because we have to conform to the standards of our class of society. A housemaid has no standards. The working class are not expected to have our sensibilities. There is no comparison, Cynthy.'

'You're such a horrid little snob, Trice. Of course they have standards, far more strict than ours. Do you suppose a coachman or a groom or a gardener would behave like Papa? They would be loyal to their wives.'

'We should never know if they were unfaithful, should we, because it doesn't concern us?'

'I suppose not,' her sister admitted.

'Servants are so clannish. They stick together. We don't really know what goes on below stairs, and neither does a governess. I do wish our dear Welly hadn't married that missionery. She was the best of the lot, and she *might* have been a little more informative on this very interesting subject had she stayed. At least she didn't insult us with silly references to the birds and the bees. Why is the word SEX a dirty word, Trice? Old Dottie avoids it like the plague.'

'Because she can't explain it, I suppose. Who said it was a dirty word?'

'Nobody actually *said* it, but it sounds dirty.'

'Honestly, Cynthy, you should do something about

321

that imagination. One of these days it's going to land you in terrible trouble,' her sister predicted, more than ready to drop the subject, but the younger girl worried it like a puppy with a bone.

'Have you noticed that Charles never bothers to cover his private parts when he's getting undressed? Mama would die of shock if she could see him prancing about without his knickers. I don't think he knows the meaning of the word modesty, but it's rather embarrassing to girls who had no brother, not until Charles arrived, and he's not a *real* brother. Papa makes such a fuss of him. I suppose I'm jealous. Papa always wanted a son, didn't he? And Charles doesn't seem to mind in the least that his mother is one of Papa's tenants. It's all so *sordid!*' she declared, vehemently.

No, Charles didn't mind. In fact, he was rather proud of the fact that he had two homes. He had been christened Charles Franklin Blunt, but when he started school, the Blunt was dropped. Nobody had yet dared to call him a bastard to his face. That would come later, at public school. But Neville Franklin's son was quite capable of defending his honour! For all the spoiling, Charles Franklin was nobody's pampered darling, and his undisputed claim to leadership at his preparatory school was decided, as always, on his manliness and the natural ability to handle a ball on the playing fields. Few small boys could face up to a flying cricket ball as fearlessly as young Franklin. He saw it as something to be whacked, not dodged. It was no accident that he was voted captain of the junior eleven in his second Summer. They could depend on him to make the runs, and he delighted in the cheers and yells of encouragement, and the flattery of the small boys in their first term. The high principles on which the youth of upper-class society had been reared for generations had to be accepted and

322

defended. Tradition was an important element. The laws of the Medes and Persians could not have been more strictly defined than the rules and regulations governing the system of upper-class education. From father to son, the rules were handed down, and only rarely discarded. The herd instinct was so much stronger than isolated rebellion. One exception had been Dennis Saunders, the doctor's second son, but his recklessness had brought nothing but shame to his long-suffering mother, and a way of life that could result in a steady decline of health and a growing obsession with women and whisky.

The young Charles Franklin was not destined for such obscurity in a foreign land. He had been told of the murder on his father's estate before he was born, by the doddering old labourer at Russets. Fred Wallace was a mine of information about the estate, the tenants, and the village. His memory was quite phenomenal, and he gloated over the details of a crime that no longer raised an eyebrow in the public bar of The Three Nuns. The boy was an avid listener, and his dark eyes widened with excitement as the tale unfolded. A shiver of sympathy for the unfortunate victim, hidden in the bushes, was quickly dispelled on the arrival of the Detective Superintendent from Scotland Yard.

'Every man jack of us was questioned, but the murderer was sitting pretty in one of them colleges – Oxford or Cambridge – one's as good as another, I reckon. And what was the purpose of all that education when 'e chucks it all away and murders a nice young woman what never done nobody any 'arm?' the old man demanded.

Charles shook his head. It did seem rather a waste. He had listened with bated breath, and related the tale with gruesome embellishments in the school dormitory after lights out. The garrulous old man had died in his sleep a few weeks later. A funny way to die, Charles thought. It made him a little nervous for a few days till he discovered he was still very much alive each morning! Mother said it was a nice way to die, when you were old, and your working days were over. Work must never be regarded as a duty or a drudgery. It was the very breath of life. But of course she was speaking of the working class, not the upper class, she explained with a whimsical smile. Then she gave him a hug, and told him he would understand everything later. He loved her dearly, but she sometimes contradicted his father's views, and this was a little confusing. Father had never worked in his life. He would hardly know the difference between a rake and a hoe. He was waited on hand and foot by a valet who went down on his knees to pull off the tight-fitting riding boots. Once he fell over backwards, and Charles yelled with laughter. He looked so funny, sprawled on the floor, still holding the muddied boot, red in the face with embarrassment.

'One does not work because one pays servants to do the work,' had been Father's simple explanation.

'But I like doing things for myself,' the boy objected. 'That's why I like being at Russets. Mother lets me help myself to vegetables, and she never stands over me while I dress or take a bath. She's too busy. Besides, they have only one servant at Russets, and Emma sits down at the same table in the kitchen to all her meals. Emma calls me Charles, not *Master* Charles, like your servants, Father. Why must everything be so different, Sir, between the working class and the upper class? It doesn't seem fair. When I'm a man I should like to be a farmer and marry someone as nice as Mother,' he added innocently.

Sir Neville Franklin was livid. 'If that's the sort of

influence your mother inspires, then the sooner you forget her existence the better!' he stormed. 'In future, you will spend your vacations in your proper environment or you stay at school. Is that understood, Charles?'

'Yes, Sir,' the boy answered dutifully, but he had no intention of hurting his mother by neglecting her. She was so kind and loving, and she always tried not to cry when they parted. Her blue eyes would swim with tears, and once she reminded him sadly, 'Don't ever be ashamed of us, Charles. You belong here as much as you belong at the Big House.'

That was one of the days when he believed his mother was right, and when the young groom came to escort him back to his father's mansion, he was rude, and refused to ride with him. It was one of those days when the sweet smell of hay in the big barn was sweeter than the scent of lilies and carnations in the glasshouses at Marston Park – and the pump in the yard more to his taste than the heated bathroom he shared with his two half-sisters.

Ruby Simmons was proud of her son, Freddie, who had not swerved from his original ambition since he joined the firm of solicitors in the High Street as office boy, at the age of 13. Always a studious lad, it was no hardship to spend the evening hours after supper poring over the dusty old law books he was permitted to borrow. His industry and intelligence had surprised his superiors, and it was suggested by the head clerk that it was unnatural, and that young Simmons would find himself a sweetheart, and eventually marry the girl. He was wrong. Freddie Simmons hardly noticed the village girls, and had no desire or intention to start courting. The teachers at the village school remembered him as a bright, intelligent lad, with a thirst for knowledge they could not satisfy. A gentle, serious boy, he was teased and tormented by the majority of his school mates because he was quite incapable of playing any sort of game, other than marbles. There was nothing to suggest in his appearance or behaviour that he harboured any driving ambition in his breast.

For three years he had polished that brass plate six mornings a week, and in his mind's eye saw his name engraved thereon as junior partner. Only the senior partner had recognised in the lad from Richmond Row the potential raw material on which to build a worthy successor to an old-established firm. Sons and grandsons had automatically followed in the family tradition, but their path had been made easy by a public-school education and an upper-class background. Old Hardcastle could well afford to finance the youthful protégé, for certain examination fees and travelling expenses had to be met during that slow but determined climb up the ladder. But the old man had no intention of making the climb any easier. Extra hours must be worked to compensate for such encouragement, and Freddie often found himself cycling long distances to visit clients who insisted on a personal representative attending to their business rather than the impersonal telephone call.

It was ten years now since he first stood before that brass plate, and hesitated on the freshly whitened doorstep before ringing the bell. Ten years of hard slogging and dedicated application to a goal. He was feeling a little queasy in his stomach that afternoon in June, as he pedalled slowly down the long drive to Marston Park. His final examination was pending. He knew he could do no more, that he had reached the limit of his endurance. His mind boggled with the mass of facts assimilated in the past twelve months, and his pale

326

ascetic face was twitching with nervous tension. His dark suit was shiny, but well brushed, and his bowler hat was uncomfortably tight on this warm day of early Summer. He was grateful to his mother for her firm refusal to accept any money for his keep since he first climbed on that high stool as a junior clerk. Unlike his brother, Jack, who wore his oldest clothes under a starched white coat, or his brother Albert in corduroys and hob-nailed boots, Freddie had always to present himself in a dark tailored suit and a white shirt. He was grateful and appreciative, but he was wishing his hard-working mother would stop worrying about his improved status, for he was quite able to cope with a situation that had taken ten years to achieve. She would never fully understand this urge to rise above the environment in which he was born and bred. Why couldn't he be satisfied with a job as a clerk in the firm of solicitors? Why spend years of his young life and ruin his health to pass a lot of silly exams? she had argued. If other young men with a Grammar-School education were satisfied, why not Freddie? Like most working-class mothers, Ruby believed profoundly in the class system that divided them from their 'betters', and she hadn't failed to notice that each successive year had seen the gap widening between them. Not that Freddie had ever shown the slightest indication of being ashamed of his parents, he was too loyal. He accepted his family background with a natural dignity and restraint. The neighbours had long since ignored the slight figure in the dark suit and bowler hat, hurrying back from the office to take his dog for a walk before supper. Freddie Simmons was a bit of a freak, and they felt sorry for Ruby and Tom who seemed to be unlucky with the way their children had turned out. There was Freddie getting ideas above his station, Albert married to a widow with

327

three kids and a bad reputation, and Carrie gone off to some foreign clime with the British Army. But they could depend on Jack, a steady, reliable, decent bloke, not likely to prove a misfit, or to disappoint his parents. Jack had chosen his partner sensibly, a village girl, most suitable to be the wife of a grocer's assistant and the mother of his children.

Elsie knew where to find her husband in any emergency, and had no real problem in managing to keep house on Jack's small wage because she had never known a time when women hadn't to count their pennies. Jack came straight home from work six days a week, spent a busy couple of hours on his vegetable allotment after supper during eight months of the year, and filled in the rest of the time white-washing walls and laying cinder paths for Elsie to hang out the washing in comparative comfort. No puddles, no stink of earth closets or rat-infested rubbish heaps in Jack's small domain. His memories of Richmond Row left an unpleasant taste in the mouth. As a dutiful son, he took little Rachel to visit her grandparents every Sunday afternoon, and enjoyed the high tea that Mum provided. Rachel soon had to make room for her little brother, Matthew, in the old-fashioned second-hand pram that had once been the pride and joy of The Parsonage nanny. When Matthew was still clutching at his mother's breast and Rachel clinging to her skirts, Ruth arrived. The Sunday afternoon walk had to be taken slowly, for Rachel would refuse to walk and had to be carried. She was a heavy child, and they would often arrive at Richmond Row with the sulky little girl perched precariously between Matthew and the baby. Only once, when their firstborn was the only occupant of the pram, had they walked as far as Monks Farm and called on Jack's brother in one of the farm cottages. It was a mistake. Albert had got into bad habits since his marriage, and Sunday afternoon was as good a time as any for a little cuddle while the kids were running wild in the woods!

'Didn't even offer us a cup of tea!' grumbled Elsie on the return journey. In future, the two families would meet once a year in Richmond Row, on Christmas Day.

Now, with three young children, Jack was beginning to wonder if Elsie's desire for a large family was a mistake. There was no peace, no time to enjoy his supper, with the demands of his noisy brood. 'Thank God for Mum,' he would be thinking, as he pushed the heavy pram down Richmond Row on a Sunday afternoon.

A letter from Carrie was an important event in Ruby's day, but she had soon discovered the rest of the family quickly lost interest when she had passed the letter round after tea. Carrie's way of life had changed so dramatically, it was quite beyond the scope of their understanding. If she was homesick, she managed to hide it, but Ruby and Tom still missed their only daughter, and never tired of talking about the early years – the best years for parents.

Jack went off to church soon after tea, to attend his Sabbath duties as sidesman, accompanied by his brother Freddie, who took a back seat in a side aisle to avoid meeting any of his ex-schoolmates. He was particularly shy of the servants from Marston Park, who came in force, both male and female, and seemed to regard this compulsory obligation as a weekly outing to be enjoyed to the full.

Conspicuous among the females was Hetty O'Brien, once a frequent visitor to Jack's place on account of Elsie being her best friend, but long since bored with Elsie's noisy brood. Tunbridge Wells with its shops and cinemas was a bigger attraction for servants who had no family responsibilities. Once a month Hetty was now entitled to a whole day free, because in her own particular way, Hetty had also climbed the ladder of the servants' hierarchy. Her services, as assistant housekeeper, were both efficient and devious. The elderly housekeeper, soon due for retirement, could spend more time in her cosy little sitting-room with the sure knowledge that nothing was being neglected under the capable supervision of Hetty. A sad mishap to the former head housemaid, when Hetty was her conscientious understudy, had resulted in early promotion, leading eventually to the much coveted post of assistant housekeeper. The young woman in question had blotted her copybook, and was instantly dismissed as soon as her condition became too obvious to hide under a starched apron. There was no room for bastard babies in the servants' hierarchy. The second footman flatly denied he was responsible, but they had been known to linger near a remote corner of the estate after church on Sunday. Be that as it may, he suffered only the indignity of a lecture from the butler, and a warning to be more careful in future. A male servant could only be dismissed for theft or insubordination. It was hoped, however, that he also suffered a guilty conscience when the postman reported, some weeks later, that the poor girl's body had been dragged out of the river.

Working-class parents had little patience or sympathy with erring daughters who had been acquainted with the facts of life and its pitfalls at an early age. They held strong views and high principles on moral issues that were not fully appreciated by the upper class. The incident was nothing more than a fresh topic in the public bar of The Three Nuns, and a welcome diversion for the village gossips.

Hetty O'brien had automatically stepped into the shoes of the head housemaid, and enjoyed her new status with smug satisfaction. She had the same tenacity as Freddie Simmons, and the same background. Richmond Row was responsible for breeding several very determined characters. Young Joe O'Brien had quickly recovered from that thirty-day jail sentence for poaching, and his subsequent Army career could only be described as spectacular. The last time he spent his leave with his family in Ireland, he was proudly displaying three stripes on his sleeve. As for Lennie, the arch enemy of innocent little girls in those far off days, he was making a fortune as a junk merchant. Lennie never refused a reasonable offer, and never made the same mistake twice. He had a horse and cart that he stabled free of charge in a convenient mews in return for cleaning and servicing the cars of the rather superior residents. The cobbled yard that once stank of dung, now stank of petrol. Lennie had the same shrewd bargaining instincts as the born Cockney, but lacked the Cockney humour. He made no friends among the street traders, and shared a basement flat with a prostitute. It was a satisfactory arrangement for both parties had a lusty sensuality, and no silly inhibitions.

Whether or not the Martins were proud of their son Dick was a matter of speculation. His name was never mentioned in Richmond Row.

'Can you understand it, Tom?' Ruby Simmons would puzzle over the queer nature of a mother who could apprently forget she ever had a son called Dick.

'She was always a contrary woman, and Dick wasn't her favourite, if you remember, Rube?' the peaceable Tom replied, quietly, and added, with a rare flight of fancy, 'I been meaning to tell you, Rube, but keep forgetting. I planted a rambler rose last Sat'day when you was down at The Parsonage.'

'Did you luv, where?' asked Ruby, with some surprise. Tom wasn't a one for flowers, as a rule. His allotment provided all the vegetables, and more than she could use, with her family so depleted.

'Alongside the privy.'

'Well I never did! Isn't that just like you, luv, to think of it. I'm a very lucky woman to 'ave such a thoughtful 'usband.'

'And I be just as lucky to 'ave such a good wife, for what I should do without you, Rube, I daren't think,' said Tom, picking up the empty scuttle.

Ruby stared after him with tenderness. Not many husbands would notice when the coal scuttle was empty, and not many husbands would think of planting a rambler rose to hide the ugly privy!

'Watch out! Bloody young fool!'

Freddie had been cycling, head down, thinking of that final examination that was so important to his future prospects. The groom and the girl had suddenly appeared at a bend in the drive, and were there, almost on top of him, before he could brake. The girl's horse plunged and reared in terror, then bolted down the drive, followed by the cursing groom. But Cynthia Franklin was an expert horsewoman. It was one of her few accomplishments, and she was enjoying that wild gallop. She made no effort to stop the terrified animal, but let the rains go slack, waiting the eventual exhaustion. It came sooner than she expected, and she slid to the ground and stood there, making soothing noises, caressing the trembling, beautiful flanks.

The four girls had all been mounted on their ponies at an early age, but only Cynthia had shown any real aptitude and enjoyment in this daily exercise. Her elder sister, Beatrice, was too nervous, and the younger girls preferred to ride in the governess-cart. Sir Neville had little imagination where his daughters were concerned, and simply took it for granted that riding was a natural requirement for children living on a big country estate. Cynthia had to wait a long time for her beautiful Jason, and might still have been riding the pony but for the timely birth of Charles at Russets. Sir Neville had to be in the right mood to spoil one of his daughters, and on this particular occasion, he was prepared to spend money lavishly on all four!

When the irate groom caught up with her and blurted out, 'You all right, Miss Cythnia?' she replied, 'Perfectly. I have never enjoyed anything more.'

'You had me worried, Miss. That blasted young idiot! Begging your pardon, Miss.' He was running an expert hand over the trembling, sweating animal, while she still talked soothingly, her arm flung over Jason's neck. She was a strange girl, he thought, to treat it so calmly, but then Miss Cynthia was not like her sisters. She was odd one out in the family, and a bit of a rebel, the servants had discovered of recent years.

'We'd better get back, Miss, then I can give him a good rub down before he gets a chill.'

But Cynthia was not listening. She was remembering the startled face of the young cyclist, and the gasp of horror as the horse plunged and reared.

'Was he hurt?' she asked.

'Who?'

'That young man.'

'God knows,' he shrugged indifferently.

'Then we must find out,' she told him, and hurried back down the drive. The groom followed, leading the two horses. They walked for a mile or so, then suddenly came upon him in the bend of the drive, sprawled on the gravel beside his bicycle.

'Have we killed him?' Cynthia gasped, and ran forward with a thumping heart, to kneel beside the slight, prostrate figure.

'Is he dead, Lindridge?' she asked, with a choked voice.

'I'll soon tell you, Miss, if you hold the horses.'

Lindridge was beginning to wish it was not one of his duties to escort Miss Cynthia. He would be blamed for the accident. Servants always had to take the blame. He handed over the reins, knelt down, unbuttoned the jacket, waistcoat, shirt and vest, and laid his hand on the flat chest. The heart seemed to be beating quite normally.

'Concussion,' he told Cynthia, 'but I wouldn't say it was serious.'

'How can you tell when he's unconscious? What do we do now?

'Get him to a doctor, Miss.'

'How? He can't ride your horse and he can't ride his bicycle. What do you suggest?'

'We are not very far from Russets. I could get help there. I'll take the horses back to the stables. Blake will attend to Jason. He's a good lad. Then I'll ride over to the farm. We shall need a couple of men with a hurdle. Will you stay with him Miss? I'll be as quick as I can.'

'Of course.' She watched the short, bandy-legged figure walking away between the two horses, then looked down on the calm young face. Lindridge had not fastened his clothes. He would be embarrassed if he suddenly recovered consciousness. She knelt down beside him, fumbling with the buttons. It was her first close encounter with such a person. The dark suit, of poor quality material, was shiny, the shirt and vest spotlessly white. He wore hand-knitted socks, and his boots were polished. Obviously a clerk. The bowler hat

334

had rolled away on the grass, and she left it lying there while her hands fumbled, and a strange sense of pleasure enveloped her young virgin body.

When she had fastened all the buttons, she smoothed the hair back from his high forehead, and saw the bruise. It was a nasty bruise, but the skin was not broken. Very gently she took his head in her lap. His slight weight was no burden, but the sense of pleasure was increased. That it was a sensual pleasure and had come about because of his maleness, she was fully aware. Once upon a time they were so ignorant, she and her sisters, she would not have recognised the sensuality. Charles had changed all that. His nakedness had surprised and shocked them. She remembered it now, most vividly, the first time she had chased and caught that naked little body in her arms. But that close contact with the boy had not fully prepared her for the melting sensation or the sweet delight in holding the young stranger.

The mystery of marital relationship; the differences in the male and female – had she discovered the first clue? His utter stillness and dependence on her mercy was the sweetest sensation she had ever known. Tenderness was not a quality that she recognised, because she had never known it from her parents, or those who had charge of her early training. A mild affection for her sisters, and a schoolgirl 'crush' on that first governess, could not be compared with the passionate love for Jason. But this new sense of gentle protectiveness was tight in her throat. They seemed to be the only two people in the world – her own small world of Marston Park. The silence was disturbed only by the squawking of a pheasant and the barking of the dog at the farm. That meant they must be on their way. Time had stood still. She would never know whether it was one hour or more that she sat there, so quietly, with his head in her lap.

When she heard voices, and the thud of hooves on the turf, she laid him gently back, and sat there, waiting, hugging her knees.

The groom was the first to appear, looking very pleased with himself. He slid off his horse and stood over them with a proprietary air.

'Lift him gently, lads,' he ordered.

'Why, it's Freddie!' the elder of the two exclaimed. 'It's our cousin, Miss Cynthia, Freddie Simmons from Richmond Row.'

Cynthia had never heard of Richmond Row, and was only vaguely acquainted with the family at Russets. The first governess had allowed them to walk in the direction of the farm, but the others had preferred the shore of the lake. Since they had discovered Charles to be their half-brother, Russets had been avoided.

She greeted the two sturdy young men cordially. In corduroys and open-neck shirts, with their sun-bleached hair and vivid blue eyes, a bigger contrast to the young man on the hurdle could not be imagined.

'Will your Mother mind if we take your cousin to the farm? It won't upset her?' she asked.

'Not at all, Miss. Mother is too used to accidents to get upset. There is always something happening on a farm.' It was the eldest brother who answered her. The younger had turned pale and was looking worried.

'Is there a telephone at the farm? We shall need to call a doctor?'

'Yes, Miss. Mother will attend to it.'

They lifted the hurdle gently. Cynthia picked up the bowler hat, dismissed the groom, and walked beside them, pushing the bicycle. They took a short cut across the Park, then suddenly there was the farm, cradled in the hollow of the land as though it had grown there. A hay-wagon stood partly loaded. Beyond the hay-field, the sun reflected on the taut wires stretched across the hop-garden, and smoke curled lazily from a tall, Elizabethan chimney. Cows were standing placidly in the pond, and brown hens scratched in the loose straw under the rick. It was a peaceful, pleasant scene, and the woman who came to meet them was part of it. She belonged here, as the two sturdy young men belonged, and a third, who was holding a big Shire horse in the distance, and only glanced in their direction. So this was the woman her father had chosen to be the mother of his son. He could hardly have chosen more wisely, the girl was thinking. She was a picture of health and beauty. The buxom figure and rounded arms, the shining hair, and those intensely blue eyes, the full bosom, under the tight bodice of the print dress, the very essence of womanhood, and so far removed from his delicate lady wife.

'It's Freddie,' her elder son called out to her, as she hurried forward.

Cynthia stood back, feeling her presence might be an embarrassment, but Lucy Blunt was concerned only for her nephew. Smoothing his hair with a gentle hand, she examined the bruise, then turned to the girl to ask, quietly, 'Was he kicked?'

'I don't think so. It all happened so quickly. My horse was frightened and bolted. I just had to hang on till he pulled up. When we got back to the spot where the accident happened, we found your nephew lying there, unconscious. Lindridge seemed to think it was only mild concussion. I do hope he is not seriously hurt. I feel responsible, though Lindridge insisted I was not to blame.'

'I see, so it could have been caused by being knocked off his bicycle?'

Cynthia nodded. One thing was certain. This woman

was talking and behaving as though to one of her own class. There was no shyness or embarrassment in her manner, no subservience to Sir Neville's daughter. Was it because she had the right to speak freely, as the mother of his only son? Or had Lucy Blunt always regarded herself as superior to the other tenants on her father's estate? Cynthia was wondering, as she followed them through the kitchen to the cool parlour. Harry and Albert lifted their cousin on to the sofa.

'He's not dead is he, Mum?' The younger brother spoke for the first time, and his mother laid a comforting arm about his shoulders.

'No, dear. He will be all right. Don't worry. Do you remember when old Fred slipped on the ice and cracked his head on the cobbles? I had to call the doctor then, but he was sitting up and asking for a cup of tea by the time the doctor arrived!'

A wan smile flitted across the boyish face. He *did* remember, and he had thought old Fred Wallace was dead.

'I'll get on to the doctor right away,' said Lucy, bustling out of the room. Her two sons hesitated, then followed her out. they hadn't acquired their mother's easy-going manner with the gentry, and felt shy of being left with this elegant young lady in her stylish riding habit. Once again she was left alone with the young man, but now he was no stranger. She knew his name, knew he was related to this capable, motherly woman. Her small, exclusive world had suddenly widened, and she wished she might be allowed to further the acquaintance of Lucy Blunt and Freddie Simmons.

'How very fortunate that you have the telephone connected, Mrs Blunt. It's so useful in an emergency,' she whispered when Lucy came back in a few minutes later.

'It is indeed. I sometimes wonder how we ever managed without it, yet we had to depend on messages delivered on horseback in my husband's time.' Sir Neville had ordered the telephone to be connected soon after Charles was born. 'It may be some time before the doctor gets here. Would you care for a glass of lemonade? That is if you wish to stay,' Lucy prompted.

'Thank you. I should like the lemonade, and I should like to stay if I won't be a nuisance?'

Lucy smiled. 'You are most welcome. I expect Lindridge will tell them where you are?'

'I expect so.' She took off her hat and shook out her short lank hair. She was a plain girl, with one redeeming feature – her father's dark eyes.

'She's shy of me,' Lucy was thinking as she filled the glass tumbler with ice-cold lemonade. They drank a lot of lemonade at hay-making time. It was thirsty work.

When she had seen the girl comfortably settled in the parlour, drinking the lemonade, she excused herself to check on Emma in the dairy. Emma could not be relied upon to fashion the pats of butter in uniform size for the market stall. Her gypsy blood still ran in her veins, and on hot Summer nights Harry would take her, as normally as the animals with which they were surrounded. You could not change human nature, Lucy had long since decided, and she was already well acquainted with the facts of life when Bert brought her to Russets as a bride at the age of sixteen. The sweet smell of hay reminded her of Charles, who had revelled in the hay-making every Summer till he was sent away to boarding school. Her blue eyes clouded. She still missed him unbearably. Just an occasional day at Russets in the school holidays, and that only because the boy insisted. Charles was loyal. He loved her dearly, but his father provided so many distractions, and of course he spent

339

the month of August at the Villa Benita with the rest of the family. Last year he had been invited to spend the Easter vacation with his half-sister, Beatrice, who had married a wealthy widower, old enough to be her father. He had a big estate in Norfolk, and Charles was quick to learn to handle a boat on the Norfolk Broads. Beatrice was expecting her first child. She was lonely and homesick for Marston Park. Poor Beatrice! Her London Season had been chaperoned by her father's sister, who had discouraged the attentions of a handsome young Guards officer with no prospects.

Lucy received an occasional picture postcard from Charles, but it saddened her to be reminded of the widening gap between them. His father was determined to separate them eventually, of that she was certain.

Harry and Albert had wasted no time in getting back to the hay-field. She could see all three of her sons in the distance, and forgot her sadness over her youngest (and dearest) in the affection of the three born in wedlock. They were good sons, and she counted her blessings, for it could have been so different if Harry had emigrated to Canada with his friend. Perhaps if Bert had lived her eldest son might have been tempted to seek his fortune with others of his generation. She could see him balanced precariously on top of the hay-wagon, and she shivered at the poignant reminder of that other Summer day, at the end of harvest. Would she ever forget it? Would she ever be reconciled to life without Bert, or her lonely nights in the big marriage bed? She was a sensuous woman, and she needed a man. How often had she wondered, guiltily, whether Sir Neville would return, as a lover, not as a landlord, or the father of her child. She knew, even to this day, that she would lie with him again, even if it meant having another child. A girl child would grow up at Russets. She had always envied her sister Ruby, and loved her nice, Carrie. Every Michaelmas, when her three sons went off to the Fair for the day, taking Emma, she waited for him to come, restless with her longing for his lusty love-making and strong, virile body. But she waited in vain. He had used her for one purpose and when his dearest wish had been gratified, he had discarded her. It was humiliating because she saw herself as desirable, as indeed she was. She supposed he had a mistress somewhere. It was a gentleman's privilege.

But she had her pride. Not once, since that fateful day, had she made any demands on him as the mother of his son. That he gave generously and willingly as soon as Charles was born, and continued to be generous, was to be expected.

She sighed, and went on her way to the dairy.

Chapter Twelve

Freddie was unconscious for three days. He lay on the sofa in the parlour where he could be watched by one or other of the family, who took turns to sit with him. Lucy had gently removed his clothes, and he was dressed in a nightshirt of Bert's, covered with a sheet.

Cynthia had offered to take her turn in the parlour every afternoon, for two hours, and Lucy had accepted the offer gladly because they all were anxious to get the hay carted before the fine weather broke. So Cynthia rode over every afternoon on Jason, but was still an outsider and had no real knowledge of the seasonal changes which governed the life style at Russets, or the hard work demanded of the mother and her sons. She took a book to read, but found herself reading the same page several times over. Sitting quietly in the open casement window, she could see the young waxen face on the pillow, but his breathing was so shallow she unbuttoned his nightshirt from time to time to make quite certain that his heart was still beating. At least, that was the excuse she would offer if anyone walked into the room.

In the silent house – for Emma was helping in the hay-field – the sense of isolation was complete, and the

342

distant sounds seemed far removed from that cool room, where the muslin curtains barely stirred in the draught. It was but an interlude, however, she reminded herself, and when Freddie had recovered conscousness, they would no longer need her. The thought was intolerable. In sharing the anxiety of the aunt and cousins, she was wishing his recovery might be delayed for at least a week, but until he regained consciousness not even the doctor could be certain whether he had suffered any brain damage. That would be appalling, simply appalling, for she still blamed herself for the accident and relived her part in it over and over again. Because they had been cantering on the turf, and only turned on to the gravel drive at that hairpin bend, Freddie had not heard their approach – she thought of him as Freddie now. The groom had obstinately refused to take his share of the blame. Why should he, when neither Miss Cynthia nor Jason had been injured? Every afternoon he offered to accompany her to Russets, since the squire had given strict instructions that his daughter must always be escorted by a groom. The memory of the murder on his estate still rankled. An innocent young woman had been strangled, and her body dumped in the bushes. It was a long time ago, but he was taking no chances.

Cynthia had surprised him of recent years. When Charles was away at school, he had found his second daughter to be a lively and interesting companion as he rode around the estate. But she flatly refused the groom's escort, and since the master was visiting his London property, there was no risk of a confrontation. Besides, Cynthia liked to ride bare-headed, in breeches and shirt, but seldom had the opportunity. The conventional side-saddle and the ridiculous riding habit had to be endured when Papa was in residence. Mama

343

never enquired what her daughters wore, or how they spent their time. She had gradually succumbed to the indulgence of being a permanent invalid, and was no longer expected to take an active part in entertaining Sir Neville's guests, or to join him for meals. Father and daughter ate their meals in a more congenial atmosphere. It was a relief to all three parties, and had actually encouraged a closer relationship between father and daughter. When Charles was home, meals were conducted with less formality, and often concluded with a lively debate between father and son. But the Summer term was now in full swing, with cricket and tennis taking precedence over lessons for young Charles Franklin.

The glorious month of June seemed more beautiful, the splendid trees in the Park were gloriously decked in their Summer dress as Cynthia rode towards the farm after lunch in that memorable week that would change the pattern of her life. Birds sang in the orchards, and sweet-scented roses trailed over the stone walls of the old farmhouse. The accident had changed her whole conception of the familiar surroundings. She saw it with a new, surprising valuation, and came to Russets in a humbler frame of mind, longing to be received into that close community.

Lucy Blunt welcomed her with a grateful smile and a glass of ice-cold lemonade, then she bustled away. She had not spoken to the two young men or their brother since the day of the accident. They kept their distance. The class barrier was erected between them in early childhood, and could not be dislodged by a few days acquaintance. That they shared a half-brother was quite incidental to Lucy's three sons. They were proud of their heritage, and had no reason to envy Charles.

In the cool sanctuary of the parlour, watching over the

344

unconscious young man on the sofa, the girl discovered a kind of quiet happiness she had never known with her parents or her sisters. To touch his bare flesh, to listen to the faint beat of his heart, was an emotional experience. Her hand would tremble over the hidden organs she knew existed because she had seen them on Charles. To lift the hem of the nightshirt and intrude on his privacy would be a deplorable lack of decency. Yet the urge was there, and her latent curiosity was intensified by his helplessness and by her own throbbing senses. Unwittingly, she had found in this unremarkable stranger the answer to her future. She would fight for the right to please herself.

'Who are you?'

The question surprised her on that third afternoon till she saw that he was gazing at her with troubled eyes. Then she left the window seat and went to him, still holding the book.

'Cynthia Franklin,' she told him quietly.

'Cynthia Franklin?'

'Yes.'

A puzzled frown creased his forehead, then he looked about him at the room, recognised his aunt's parlour, and seemed to relax a little.

'What happened? Why am I lying here? I can't remember.' His voice was a whisper, and she lowered her own voice which was apt to be rather loud and authoritative.

'There was an accident. You almost collided with my horse. You were riding your bicycle through the Park. Your aunt thought you must have been on your way to see my mother about some business or other. Mama fusses over her Will. She seems to think she is not going to live much longer. I believe she has some private property and investments that my father cannot touch, but of course you would know about it.'

345

He shook his head. The puzzled frown still puckered his eyes. 'Who brought me here?'

She explained about the groom and his cousins, and that they were busy in the hay-field, and that she had volunteered to sit with him for two hours every afternoon.

'*Every* afternoon?'

'This is the third.'

'*Three days!*' He was astounded. Throwing off the sheet, he tried to struggle to his feet, but he hadn't the strength, and sank back exhausted on the pillows, weak tears pricking his eyes.

'You are not to worry. The doctor said you must rest after you regained consciousness. Your employer and your mother have both been informed of the accident. Your aunt has attended to everything. She is quite a remarkable woman, is she not?'

He nodded. 'Three days.' His troubled mind groped for the incidents to fill the gap in his memory, but he had no recollection of anything that had happened for some days prior to the accident. It was so frustrating he wept quietly, and her heart ached for him. Slipping to her knees beside the sofa, she took his limp hand in a strong clasp. It was a small hand for a man, but then her own hand was big. She was a big woman, not dainty like her sister Beatrice. Through his weak tears, Freddie Simmons saw a tanned, boyish face, a pair of dark, discerning eyes, a firm chin, and a wide, generous mouth. It was a strong face, full of character, and the warm pressure of her hand had a comforting reassurance.

'You will remember everything soon. It was only slight concussion,' she told him, soothingly. 'This is the best place for you. It's such a peaceful atmosphere.' She sighed, wishing it might have been prolonged so that she

346

could still watch over him every afternoon, touch his bare flesh, feel the quiet rhythm of his heart under her fingers. Such tenderness was new to her. The daughters of Sir Neville Franklin had been reared in all the stern conventional standards of their class, but they lacked the parental love and the bond of a close family relationship. Their disciplined lives had allowed little scope for individuality. First in the nursery, then in the schoolroom, a code of conduct had been enforced. And the nursery and the schoolroom were worlds apart, each with a separate routine strictly enforced. The only thing they shared was the diet of plain nourishing food, as unvaried as the routine. The younger girls were almost strangers during these early years, when they occupied the nursery wing, and nurse ruled their small domain. A succession of governesses had ruled the schoolroom after Marion Wellington went away. They invariably showed a tendency to regard Sir Neville with languishing sighs and humble adoration. To discover tenderness in her autocratic person only added to the confusion of emotions already evoked by newly awakened senses. Since a young man's head had rested in her lap, and his slender body draped across her thighs, there had been no rest from the disturbing sensuality. But Freddie could not know her thoughts or her feelings, for her strict training had not encouraged the childish inclinations to tears and tantrums in the nursery, or the feminine emotional disturbances in the schoolroom.

Uncomfortably aware of his undressed state, and puzzled by the loss of memory, he was feeling wretched. 'Where are my clothes?' he asked, tentatively.

'I don't know. Your aunt undressed you after the doctor had examined you.'

'Could I have a drink of water? I'm so thirsty.'

'Of course. I should have thought of it. Would you

prefer the lemonade? It's quite delicious.'

'Water, please.'

She scrambled to her feet and hurried away. Cynthia Franklin of Marston Park. What was she doing here? She had explained, but he was still puzzled. Surely Emma could have sat with him for a while if he had to be watched. The daughter of Sir Neville Franklin was doing her best to convince him that she belonged in this environment. Why, he asked himself, but his head was throbbing, and he couldn't think clearly. He picked up the book she had dropped on the bed – a novel of the controversial authoress, George Sand, in French. It only served to emphasise his own limitations.

He sipped the ice-cold water gatefully, and asked, 'Do you always read books in the French language?'

'More often than not. It's a beautiful language. I am teaching myself German. I find I miss my sister and the schoolroom routine. One gets accustomed to a disciplined way of life, and when that discipline is removed, one just drifts aimlessly, like a boat without a rudder. Now the last governess has departed, I should be enjoying my freedom and independence, but the days are long, and I am terribly bored. That was one reason why I volunteered to sit with you in the afternoons.' She sighed. She had drawn up a chair. The big, capable hands resting in her lap could control a temperamental horse, but had never wielded a broom or a duster, never made her own bed, never boiled an egg or brewed a pot of tea, never laundered a blouse, never laid a table or washed the dishes. Freddie was only vaguely associated with the gentry because of the nature of his work, so he could not comprehend such a way of life.

'Bored?' he echoed. 'Isn't there something you could do? I mean, it must be so tedious not to have a purpose?'

She shrugged. 'I suppose I should be grateful for these

348

few months of independence, for it's probably the last I shall ever know. Next year I have to endure that awful London Season. I hate London, and I dislike my Aunt Agatha intensely. She's an old bag. So what can she know about the feelings of young girls? Beatrice fell in love with a handsome young Guards subaltern. My sister is very romantic, and I am sure she would have been perfectly happy to marry her Julian, but my Aunt, aided and abetted by Papa, of course, decided the poor fellow could not adequately provide for a wife on his Army pay, so the match would be quite unsuitable. They married her to a stuffy old banker, who must be at least 50, and reads nothing but the financial press. Why is money so important, Mr Simmons?'

'The lack of it can be quite a problem, Miss Franklin.'

'I suppose so, but surely happiness is not entirely dependent on the state of one's purse?'

'Not entirely, but an empty purse can be quite an embarrassment.' His mouth twitched in a wry smile. How could you explain the poverty and hardship of the working class to Sir Neville Franklin's daughter?

'I know I could be happy without all the luxuries to which I have been accustomed,' she insisted. 'It's just a question of adjusting oneself to a different environment. And I don't intend to be bullied into marriage by Papa because he would find unmarried daughters a strain on his resources. Papa can be an absolute darling, but one is never allowed to forget the sole purpose of our education has one ultimate goal – the acquisition of a suitable husband. The London Season is nothing short of a marriage market. You have no idea how devastatingly competitive it can be. All the prettiest debutantes claim all the titled and most eligible suitors, and it's terribly embarrassing for the unattractive girls. Beatrice found it so. I think that is why she gave in to

349

persuasion so soon after losing all hope of marriage to Julian. We are not pretty, you see. Not one of us girls, and it's such a pity. Poor Papa. I think he could have forgiven Mama for producing four daughters if only one had been pretty. We are so *ordinary*. It must be such a bitter disappointment because he *is* so handsome. They tell me I have his eyes, but one redeeming feature is poor consolation.' She sighed, and he lay back on his pillows and watched her mobile face. She had something more than mere prettiness. It was an interesting face, full of character, and he found her account of the 'marriage market' rather pathetic.

'Of course, I might be able to persuade Papa to allow me to stay at home. Now that he has Charles, he is so much more amenable. Indeed, he often seeks my company since Charles went away to school. Do you know, I have always wondered what Mrs Blunt was really like, but now I have met her, I can better understand Papa's infatuation. I suppose it *was* infatuation, and not a preconceived intention to beget a son? What do you think?'

Her frankness was a little disconcerting. His Aunt Lucy was a very pretty woman, and a very nice person, but why had she betrayed his Uncle Bert's memory and so embarrassed his cousins?

'I don't know what to think. It was certainly a shock to all the family at the time. Whatever the reason, Sir Neville was blessed with a son.'

'But your aunt has been obliged to conform to my father's wishes. It's not fair! She has no real authority. Now that I have made her acquaintance, she has all my sympathy. It's not an enviable position for any woman, and according to the gossip in the servants' hall, she is not even his mistress. That strikes me as being peculiarly distasteful, but then Papa has never cared two hoots what people think. He is so utterly selfish. I suppose most men are selfish?'

Freddie shook his head. 'My father and my two brothers seem to me the most unselfish of husbands, but it's not conclusive, and it may be more a question of heredity. The working class are slow to change. They tend to follow a pattern, from father to son.'

'But so do we. Papa is behaving with exactly the same arrogant selfishness as Grandpapa. I remember him quite well, but Grandmama stood up to him. She was not at all intimidated, not like Mama. Am I tiring you with all my chatter? You are looking rather pale.'

'It's nothing. Just a slight headache.'

'Tell me about yourself. I have never met a budding solicitor. You must be very clever.'

'If having a one-track mind is cleverness, then I do fit the pattern, but I couldn't have managed it on my own. I've had a lot of help and encouragement, and I have to thank my hardworking mother for providing me with food and clothing.'

'She must be very proud of you?'

'She is, bless her heart.'

'And your father?'

'Dad is a man of few words, but he usually agrees with Mum, and she certainly has the last word in everything.'

'Is that unusual?'

'Not where I come from. It's the mothers who really bring up the children, and the mothers who scrimp and save to feed and clothe the family on the meagre wages. Most working-class husbands hand over their wages to their wives every Saturday and receive a shilling back. This is known as beer and baccy money, and has to last all the week. There are exceptions, of course; the hard drinkers who spend too much on Saturday night. Then the children go hungry to bed and there is no money for

351

boots. Sometimes the men are not entirely to blame. The women are shiftless. They beg and borrow from the neighbours. They live on charity and have no pride. The Church has a fund called Parish Relief, but Mum always swore she would work her fingers to the bone rather than ask for a penny. And she very nearly did, with all that scrubbing. Mum was the charwoman at The Three Nuns for years. That's the public house at the top of the High Street.'

Cynthia nodded. She had noticed the curious inn sign, but had not enquired how it came to have that name. Their carriage was usually drawn up on the forecourt on Sunday morning, and the horses tethered to a stake in the churchyard wall. Their coachman naturally assumed the foremost position should be reserved for Marston Park. Cynthia wondered why Freddie Simmons was explaining about the way the poor eked out a living, and his own mother scrubbing the floors of that public house. Was he doing it deliberately to emphasise the class barrier that divided them?

'What is your father's occupation,' she asked, for she really wanted to know.

'Dad is a ganger on the railway.'

'What is a ganger?'

Freddie explained.

'I see.' But she didn't see. They always travelled in a reserved Pullman compartment and would not have noticed a gang of labourers working on the line. 'Does your father receive only a shilling a week pocket money?'

'Yes. All his married life.'

'Does he never ask for more?'

'No. It wouldn't occur to him. He has no expenses. Mum buys his boots and my Uncle Bert always passed on a jacket or corduroys when he had finished with

352

them. When he died, Dad had all his clothes. Mum gets most of her clothes from Aunt Lucy. They are twin sisters, you know.'

'I didn't know.'

'This branch of the family has always been more prosperous. The tenancy of Russets will be handed on to my cousin, so I understand.'

'Do you envy them?'

'No, why should I? We can't all be farmers.'

'No, but it's such a good outdoor life. Your cousins look so strong and healthy.'

'So they should. They were born and bred here. But my elder brother, Albert, enjoys the same kind of healthy outdoor life as a farm labourer. Naturally he has no status, and no prospects. He lives in a tied cottage and would be evicted with his family if he lost his job.'

'That's not fair!'

'It's the custom.'

'Is Albert your only brother?'

'No, there's Jack. He works at the grocery shop in the village. He often cycles through the Park to see the housekeeper who places a small order. The bulk of the provisions is sent from London – Fortnum and Mason, so Jack tells me.'

'And your brother has to cycle all this way just to have a small order confirmed?'

Freddie nodded. 'It's customary.'

'But it's such a bother. Is it worth it?'

'Jack thinks so. It's the prestige. Actually, as far as the village traders are concerned, it's the upper class with small establishments who spend more, not the gentry. The working class can only afford to spend pence, whereas the others spend pounds, but even so, their custom is not despised. Unfortunately, there are some, not all working class, who live on credit.'

353

'Then why are they served if they cannot pay?'

'They pay in small instalments. In the meantime, they have to live.'

'I suppose so,' his companion agreed. It was all so *sordid*.

'Tell me about the village school. Papa is one of the Governors, but we have never been invited there. We should be better informed about our own village, should we not?'

'There is not much to tell. The teachers do their best but the classrooms are so crowded and there are never enough text books. We learn the three Rs, recite our Catechism and Gray's *Elegy*, and sing 'Land of Hope and Glory' with tremendous fervour on every possible occasion. It's not a bad system, and I enjoyed it most of the time. I was 13 when I left, and I cried. So did my young sister, Carrie, but I know my brothers and my cousins were glad to leave.'

'I didn't know you had a sister. Tell me about her.'

She was hungry for information. They were still strangers making polite conversation, separated by a palpable gulf. She listened to his quiet voice reflecting on the sister he obviously adored. She could not visualise Richmond Row, or parents that were called Mum and Dad, not Mama and Papa.

When the door opened and Lucy Blunt bustled in, she brought the very essence of a Summer day in her glowing cheeks and bright eyes, and the crumpled print dress, dusted with pollen. Her piled hair was sprinkled with hay seeds, and when she saw her nephew had recovered, she exclaimed, 'Freddie! You're better', ran to him, and cradled his head on her breast. Her strong maternity was one of several good qualities she shared with her twin sister, Ruby. They both were born mothers, and their children had enjoyed an endearing warmth and

354

love that the children of the rich would envy. Cynthia Franklin had never known the comfort of a mother's breast, or the warmth of loving arms.

'How long has Freddie been awake, Miss Cynthia?' she asked, as though he had merely been taking an afternoon nap.

'About an hour, I think. I didn't really notice.'

'It must have been your quiet presence,' she told the girl with her melting smile.

'Can I get up, Aunt Lucy?' Freddie interrupted.

'Indeed you can't. Not till the doctor's seen you and given his permission. Don't you feel anything at all?'

'Just a slight headache, but I can't remember what happened. My mind seems to be a complete blank, and Miss Franklin tells me it's three days since the accident?'

'That's right, but don't let it worry you, dear. It's just nature's way of healing. Damaged tissues will benefit by a few days' rest, so will the nerves that have suffered a nasty shock.'

'You speak as though you had a certain knowledge of such injuries, Mrs Blunt?' Cynthia suggested.

'Yes, it's not an uncommon accident on a farm. My husband was unconcious for three weeks, in hospital, when the wagonette turned over on an icy road on the way to market, but he recovered with no ill effects, other than headaches. It's just as well to be prepared, for there's always something happening on a farm. I have all the usual remedies handy for bronchitis and influenza, and I don't need to bother the doctor. I have always been interested in medicine. Had I been born in upper-class society, I would have studied, but there was no money and no encouragement for a working-class girl. Besides, I loved a farmer, didn't I?' she chuckled, her blue eyes soft with memories of those happy years with Bert. 'I remember when I was expecting Harry. I had to stay in bed for several weeks with swollen legs. I was so bored with the rubbishy novels Bert brought back from the market, I asked the doctor if I might borrow his text books on anatomy. He wasn't too surprised. You see, I worked for Mrs Saunders as a house-parlourmaid, when I left school, and Doctor let me help in the surgery with the children. Do you know, Miss Cynthia, I found those text books quite fascinating, and I even neglected the mending and the knitting I got so carried away. Bert thought I had taken leave of my senses. He was quite worried.'

'I should think so. What an extraordinary taste in literature for a farmer's wife, expecting her first child.'

'They do say a little knowledge is a dangerous thing, but I haven't found it so, and I've managed to cope with all manner of accidents till the doctor could be located. With that useful knowledge I gleaned from those text books and a bit of common sense, a life could be saved in an emergency.'

'I think your family have been fortunate, Mrs Blunt. You are a very remarkable woman,' Cynthia was pushing back her chair. Freddie was leaning comfortably against his aunt's shoulder and she was smoothing his damp hair. He did not need her any more. The thought was intolerable, for she had allowed her imagination to run wild in these quiet hours together. She had visualised a permanent injury, and herself as his indispensable nurse. It would be her salvation, her destiny. No more boredom. No need to fret over that London Season and that ghastly marriage market. They would be married, of course, and Papa would find them a cottage on the estate. She would have her dowry. That had been promised. Now all her dreams had no substance, and she felt very young and foolish as she shook Freddie's limp hand and bade him 'Goodbye'.

'I'll see you out,' said Lucy politely. And when the girl had swung easily into the saddle, she called after her, 'Freddie will be staying here for at least another week. You are welcome to call any time.'

'Thank you.' There was no warmth in that stiff smile. She lifted a hand in salute and rode away, choked with disappointment and a bitter sense of defeat. They were just being polite. She could understand Lucy Blunt's reluctance to make a friend of Sir Neville Franklin's daughter. It would be embarrassing. There had been trouble enough with young Charles.

'I feel sorry for that girl, Freddie. She's lonely since her sister married, and Charles went away to school,' Lucy mused, as she wandered back into the parlour. 'We could invite her to spend a day here, but I'm not too sure of her father. Would he think it presumptious? What do you think?'

'Why not? Surely she can please herself where she spends her time? She's not a child, and she's finished with the schoolroom. Why should we feel inferior, Aunt Lucy? It's not her fault; it's her misfortune that she was born at Marston Park and not Russets – or even Richmond Row!'

'Freddie Simmons! I'm surprised at you. I thought you had more respect for your betters.'

'What I say in public, Aunt, and what I feel in my heart are not compatible. I believe all men are equal in the sight of God. I believe in the working class, and when I have qualified I shall move away, possibly to London. My clients will be working class. I know what I want to do, Aunt Lucy. Mother thinks I'm attracted to the upper class, but she's wrong. If Cynthia Franklin wants my friendship, she will know where to find me.'

When Parson died in his sleep in the Summer of 1913,

everyone but Parson's wife thought it was a just reward for his Christian ministry. 'Such a nice way to die.' 'Such a worthy man should not be allowed to suffer,' they said. Parson's wife was vexed. It was a nasty shock, and when she realised Doctor Saunders had warned her husband of a heart condition some years previous to his death, her vexation was acute. Why hadn't she been informed? It was a wife's prerogative, she insisted, but Doctor Saunders disagreed – one of the few people in the village who dared to disagree with Parson's wife! A patient's wishes were sacred, he told her, precisely, and her husband had asked for the information to be kept secret. But since he had never complained about anything in all their married life, it would have been completely out of character to mention the 'tired' heart. It would have seemed that he was excusing himself from the rigours of Winter in his spreading parish, when he cycled for miles to visit his sick and aged parishioners. He was, perhaps, one of the few completely dedicated ministers of the gospel, deeply concerned for his flock, his beloved church, and his family, in that order.

Since the marriage of his favourite daughter and the death of Irene, his depleted family seemed so capable, managing their lives without his assistance that they had drifted further apart. Cecily was so like her mother, so self-sufficient and smug in her good works. It was unkind to be critical, he had reminded himself, since they both were indispensable to the parish, and he could not have managed without them. If *only* they would show a little more Christian humility, and little less of their strong personalities.

The years had brought so many changes in the village and at The Parsonage. He had accepted the changes as inevitable, but he still missed the lively daughter who had gladdened his heart, and the two old servants who had known all there was to know without being told.

'We must be thankful for small mercies, Archibald,' his wife had reminded him, tartly, soon after Ruby Simmons had taken over the kitchen, and he had dared to comment on the strange flavour of the cake that was served for afternoon tea. Not a complaint, only a comment, he hastened to explain.

'Too much vanilla essence. She hasn't read the directions on the bottle. I suppose one shouldn't expect miracles of culinary art from an ex-charwoman.'

'Indeed not, my dear, and she is so willing and cheerful,' Parson pointed out, carefully, since he had no desire to discredit the good woman.

'Why must he always agree with Mother?' Cecily wondered irritably. When Marion was here, we often had quite a heated argument. I suppose he misses her moral support.

'Do you know, I once discovered Father weeping over Marion's photograph in the drawing-room,' she blurted out one Sunday morning on their way to church in the trap.

'Really, dear? What did you do?'

'I crept away. It was Marion he wanted, not me.'

'My dear child, you are his daughter and he loves you dearly.'

'As a dutiful daughter, yes, but it's not the same as being a *favourite* daughter, is it? Of course I'm jealous. She's married and she's left him, but he still hasn't turned to me for companionship, has he? We share no confidence. Our conversation is always impersonal – the Sunday School, the Mothers' Union, the Missionary Society, the poor, the aged, the sick; any good cause you like to mention we can discuss till the cows come home. But not ME. Don't you see?' Her tear drenched eyes turned away, and she flicked the reins impatiently on the mare's broad flanks.

'You must calm yourself, dear. We are nearly there,' her mother reminded her, surprised by the outburst. Cecily must be sickening for something. It was so unlike her. She had always felt so sure of her eldest daughter. They were two of a kind, two extroverts, outspoken and definite. Not mincing their words. But in all the years of their married life, she had not known the half of what went on in her husband's mind. It was inconceivable that a whole lifetime together had not been long enough, yet it was a fact, and she had always faced facts squarely. She had no illusions about their relationship. Like Cecily, she was indispensable to his parish, and his parishioners, but they moved on a different plane. They were worlds apart. She saw only the obvious, while he saw beyond the reach of her limited vision. His intellect had always been a barrier, his knowledge inexplicable. She was amazed at the hundreds of books stacked on the shelves in his study. She never listened to his sermons; her mind was busy on more practical matters. She had been too busy to worry over their incompatibility. There was no time for heart searching.

Now he was gone, and it was too late. It was cruel of God to snatch him away without warning, and cruel of Archibald to keep such vital information to himself. Had she known he was so afflicted, she could have insisted that he took the trap for his visiting. But if he never complained, how could she know the bicycle was to blame for this sudden collapse? Now, of course, a dozen or more people had confirmed that they had seen Parson leaning breathlessly against a wall, or a tree. 'Puffing an' panting 'e were, Ma'am, like my ole bellows,' was Widow Hawkins' definition. Too late! Too late! Like the tolling bell on the day of the funeral, it rang in her head persistently. The shock would have shattered some women, but not Parson's wife.

360

'Life went on,' she told Ruby, who was crying over a fresh batch of scones she had taken from the oven.

'Yes, Ma'am, but it won't never be the same again, not without the Master,' sniffed Ruby, miserably.

'We must be sensible. God moves in a mysterious way, Ruby.'

'Yes, Ma'am,' Ruby agreed, because she never argued with Madam.

The changes were sudden and drastic, and their small, safe world completely disorganised. The curate had waited a long time to step into Parson's shoes, and his eagerness to do so was positively indecent. When he was summoned to Marston Park the day following the funeral, and received the living from Sir Neville Franklin, he seemed to swell with importance, and immediately decided on the wife he would choose as a useful partner in his ministry. He hoped that Cecily Franklin would live to regret the day she had refused his hand in marriage, for it would have been such an ideal arrangement. Life could have continued in the same pleasant channels. His mother-in-law would have her separate apartment and her daughter step into the limelight as Parson's wife. It was regrettable, but they had to move out, and his new wife would reign in their stead. If they wished to continue with their good works in the parish, they must do so as unobtrusively as possible, for he would not stand for interference or for condescension. Such thoughts were uncharitable, but typical of a man so lacking in the human qualities of his predecessor. To engage a new young curate would further increase his status, and he would enjoy instructing the fortunate young man in his parochial duties. To see *him* at the bottom of the table for Sunday lunch while he himself sat at the head was a pleasure to anticipate; and his whole demeanour was changed towards the widow and her daughter. He came and went with an air of ownership and authority, uninvited, walking about the grounds with his hands tucked under his jacket and a simpering smile on his thin lips.

'I b'ain't staying 'ere, Ruby, not to take orders from 'im after the Mistress has left,' Peg-leg declared. 'It's time I retired anyway, for I be getting too old to carry them buckets of coal and beat all them carpets at Spring cleaning time. It do give my rheumatism a fair pasting, all that exercise. Bugger me if I don't deserve to 'ave a bit of a rest!'

'So you do, and you see you get it. Why not ask the Mistress to find you a place in the Almshouses afore she moves away? I don't trust this 'ere new parson, Peg-leg. Reckon 'e would try to keep you 'ere once 'e takes over the place.'

Peg-leg nodded agreement. 'What 'bout you, then. You staying on?' he asked, sipping the hot tea Ruby had brewed for their elevenses.

'Don't know. Nothing ain't been said, but I got to know one way or t'other, though I reckon we could live on Tom's wages now we ain't got Freddie to keep. But what should I do with meself all day? I been going out to work ever since I left school.'

'Something will turn up, Rube. It always do.'

Ruby smiled. 'I'm going to miss your funny old face,' she told him, gently.

When Eleanor Wellington and her daughter, Cecily, were invited to call at Marston Park the following week, they were received with much cordiality by Sir Neville Franklin, and drank tea in the drawing-room with their host and his daughter, Cynthia.

'There is absolutely no hurry, my dear ladies. You must take your time, but I expect you will wish to get settled comfortably in your new home as soon as

362

possible.' Sir Neville suggested affably. 'When we have finished tea, my daughter will show you over the cottage you are at liberty to accept or refuse. It is one of the larger cottages on the estate, and conveniently situated but a bare half mile from the house. You could use one of our stables for your mare and your trap. The cottage was allocated to my butler on his retirement, and an unmarried daughter came to keep house for him. Unfortunately the poor fellow only lived for a few months to enjoy his retirement after serving the family for more than forty years. His daughter has since married and moved away. I think you will find it quite adequate, though nothing like your present abode of course. One must be realistic. The pension is small, and would hardly cover all your expenses if you lived elsewhere and had to pay rent. My bailiff will attend to any repairs or decorations before you move in. I would suggest that you select the wallpaper to suit your own taste.'

'Thank you, Sir Neville. You are very kind,' murmured the late parson's widow, feeling her own status slipping away.

'There are two good attics that will accommodate the servants,' Sir Neville added, as an extra bonus.

'I have not yet decided about a servant. We shall only need one, of course. My present cook would have been an ideal person as a cook-housekeeper, but she cannot be persuaded to live in. Our man-servant will be retired to the Almshouses.'

'The indispensable Peg-leg we heard so much about when your daughter was our governess?' Cynthia interrupted.

'Yes. We are going to miss him.'

They were going to miss a whole lot of things. It would be an entirely new way of life. She sighed, then

363

straightened her shoulders. Sir Neville must not think her ungrateful. She smiled bravely, and assured him they would manage. It was just a matter of adapting themselves to their changed circumstances.

'A very sensible outlook, dear lady.' The squire nodded approval, then excused himself from the tea-party. He had done his duty to his late parson, but found the widow and her daughter rather tedious. Bowing and smiling over their hands, he assured them with a heartiness they found embarrassing, 'Do not hesitate to ask for anything. I am yours to command!'

They thanked him politely, and toyed with the last morsel of Madeira cake on their plates. But as soon as the door had closed behind him, they were surprised to hear the note of mischief in his daughter's voice.

'Take no notice. Papa means well!'

Eleanor Wellington coughed discreetly. It was disrespectful. Cecily laughed delightedly. A spark was kindled between the two younger women that would change the course of their lives.

'Are you ready? Shall we look at the cottage? It's only a short walk.' Cynthia pushed back her chair and led the way. They were still wearing their hats, as was customary for taking afternoon tea in any house but their own. Their shabby, old-fashioned clothes contrasted so conspicuously with the new style of casual elegance Cynthia Franklin had adopted. She wore no hat or gloves.

They took a short cut across the Park, and came upon the cottage suddenly. It was sheltered by high hedges and several silver birches. Somebody had trimmed the hedges and tidied the flower beds. Pansies bordered the front path, and the air was sweet with the scent of stocks and pinks. Roses climbed over the porch, and wistaria trailed over walls and windows.

'It's charming,' Cecily exclaimed, darting round the side of the cottage to inspect the back garden. 'Only a yard, a parch of grass and a few shrubs. We can easily manage that.'

Cynthia shrugged. She never noticed what was growing in the formal gardens of the Big House. She pushed open the door and they followed her in. A flight of steep stairs led straight up from the tiny hall. It was typical of working-class homes. The late parson's wife shuddered involuntarily, but Cecily seemed not to notice and hurried through the open doors.

'Three small rooms, a kitchen and scullery, and a closet next door to the scullery,' she announced importantly, while her mother waited in the hall as though transfixed by that ladder-like stairway. She could hear the two younger women talking excitedly and their voices echoed through the empty rooms. Then they rushed upstairs, giggling like a couple of schoolgirls. What was so funny about a situation that left her stunned with misery and dread?

The front door was hanging open, and she was standing there, gazing forlornly across the Park when they clattered down the stairs. She had been wondering whether to use the small annuity she had happily regarded as her private means to pay the rent of a house in the village, but her practical commonsense reminded her that it would be unwise to refuse Sir Neville's offer of the cottage, and to lose touch with his influential patronage. No, they must manage in this tiny place, and count their blessings. It could have been worse. It was secluded and private, and if she suffered with claustrophobia, she could go for a walk in the Park.

'Three small bedrooms but no bathroom. Miss Franklin says she will mention it to her father. She thinks the scullery could be converted into a bathroom,' Cecily explained.

A converted scullery? Her mother shivered.

'The attics are dry, and they might be quite useful, Mother, when you have found a cook-housekeeper to live in.' Cecily was being extraordinarily cheerful under the circumstances, yet she had started out in a disagreeable mood, reluctant to drag herself away from The Parsonage.

'Why not offer the two rooms, furnished, one to be used as a sitting-room, the other as a bedroom? Would it not be an inducement? You could advertise in the Parish Magazine,' her daughter suggested eagerly.

'Don't rush me, dear. I will think it over.' Her voice sounded peevish.

'Sorry, Mother. I was only trying to be helpful.'

'I know, dear, but it's not something to be decided in a hurry.'

'There's a wonderful view from the window right across the Park for anyone who likes a view,' Cecily persisted.

'Yes, dear, but I shall be engaging an elderly woman, possibly a widow, and the state of the bed will be more important than the view.'

'What are we doing about all the furniture and stuff that we shan't have room for?'

'I thought an auction sale. We could get a man out from Tunbridge Wells.'

'Good idea. It's going to be fun sorting it out.'

'Fun? It's going to be heart-breaking,' her voice was choked, but she braced her shoulders again in a gesture that had served her well through the troubled years. 'We must not keep you hanging about any longer, Miss Franklin. Thank you for your kindness. Come, dear, we will call in at the general store on the way back and ask Jack Simmons to deliver the book of wallpaper patterns, then when we have made our selection, your father's bailiff can get a man started on decorating. The sooner the better, don't you think?'

'Jack Simmons? Is he not related to Freddie Simmons?'

'Yes, they are brothers. Their mother is my cook. The Simmons are a most respectable family. All the children have done well. The girl was engaged as nursemaid to Doctor Saunders' first grandchild. The parents are Army people, and when Captain Saunders regiment was drafted overseas, they took Carrie with them. Rather a risk, we thought, for she was nothing but a child. However, she seems happy enough. We get all the news from her mother's letters.

'Do you get any news of Freddie?' Cynthia prompted, for she was not particularly interested in the girl.

'Yes, his mother was sadly disappointed when he moved away to London after passing his final examinations. She couldn't understand it, for his prospects seemed so bright locally. A very determined young man, apparently. One needs determination to struggle out of the mire of Richmond Row. So you have met the young man, Miss Franklin?'

'Only briefly. He was staying at Russets for about ten days after the accident, and all the family were busy with hay-making, so I offered to sit with him for a couple of hours every afternoon, but he recovered on the third day.'

'That was kind. I remember hearing about the accident. His mother was very anxious, but she knew he was being well cared for by her sister at Russets. We are going to miss Ruby Simmons and all the gossip she collects in the village. The Parsonage has always been a focal point, and my daughter and I have always seen ourselves as indispensable. A sorry mistake, Miss Franklin. Nobody is indispensable. The new parson and

367

his new wife will soon be taking over all our duties. But I shall insist on keeping an eye on the aged inmates of the Almshouses. They look on me as a friend, and two of our own retainers are housed there. Annie is over 80, and delighted to have Peg-leg living nearby.'

'And I shall carry on teaching at the Sunday School, no matter if I do meet with opposition,' Cecily declared emphatically.

'Are you expecting opposition?' Cynthia asked.

'Yes, we are – aren't we, Mother?'

Eleanor Wellington shrugged. 'New brooms sweep clean. They will want to sweep us out of the way, but I doubt whether they will succeed.' The bitterness in her voice was not lost on Sir Neville's daughter, but she was too young and inexperienced to understand the implications of such a drastic change of circumstances. In Cecily Wellington she had recognised a woman of strong character and resourcefulness. They met at a time when her own future was uncertain, when she was expected to conform to the standards of her class, to endure the London Season and the agonising suspense of the marriage market. Forced into marriage, she could only expect to find herself as lonely and miserable as her sister Beatrice. So she saw in the daughter of their late parson a means of escape, a friend of her own sex, who would know the answers to all her questions: 'What shall I do?' 'How can I break away from this deadly future they have planned for me?' 'Where can I find a purpose?'

They shook hands formally; but a smile passed between them as Cecily gathered up the reins, and the wheels rattled over the cobbles.

'Au revoir, Miss Wellington!' Cynthia called after her. And back came the answer, 'Au revoir, Miss Franklin!'

It was a physical attraction she felt for Sir Neville's daughter, an attraction she had never felt for any man, and there had been a number of eligible bachelor clergymen taking Sunday lunch at The Parsonage during the years. In that first meeting she had recognised the nucleus of a devoted disciple. The girl was obviously bored, eager to attach herself to a stronger personality, to have her future decided since she had neither the initiative nor the vision to take the first step.

Driving back through the Park, Cecily had little to add to what had already been said about the cottage, and her thoughts were busy on her own plans, not to be divulged until Mother was nicely settled at the cottage with her new cook-housekeeper and her little King Charles spaniel for company. She knew exactly what she would do, and now she had little doubt, after that brief conversation in the attic, that Cynthia Franklin would be joining her. Mother would be annoyed. She would raise all manner of objections, but they were well matched, and she was determined to get her own way.

When she had stood beside the open grave and dropped a rose on the coffin, the past was finished, the chapter closed. She could not face a future without the respect and affection she had enjoyed as Parson's daughter. 'Miss Cecily' would become a nonentity, another typical spinster to add to the ever-increasing number in the village. She could see herself, at that moment of revelation, growing old and peculiar, like the two Miss Langtrys, Victoria and Letitia, whose eccentricities were widely discussed at the Ladies' Working Party every Tuesday afternoon. To be suddenly deprived of her status and her parochial duties, to stand aside to watch the new mistress at The Parsonage stepping into her shoes, would be too humiliating. Her ego had been sustained by the flattery and appreciation of her father's parishioners since she left the schoolroom. She *had* to be indispensable to someone, somewhere. It was her nature. It was not too late to start a new chapter.

In her late 30s, enjoying the best of health, she was already acquainted with the rudiments of first aid as practised by the Red Cross Society. Doctor Saunders and the village midwife held a weekly class during the Winter months. So what better future could be anticipated than nursing? And what more obvious institution than the Elizabeth Garrett Anderson Hospital for Women in London? This remarkable woman had made history when she broke into the exclusively male medical profession, and Cecily was one of her most ardent admirers, In that surprising burst of confidence in the attics, she had revealed her intention to request an interview with the matron, and Miss Franklin had pleaded most earnestly, 'Take me with you, *please*, *please*, Miss Wellington!'

'You will never persuade your father to allow you to train as a nurse,' she had reminded the girl.

'Then I shall run away, for I cannot endure all that paraphernalia of the London Season. You *must* help me, dear, dear, Miss Wellington!'

'I will do my best, but I can't promise you will be accepted as a trainee. You do have one thing in your favour, your extreme youth,' she added, in all fairness.

So it was with barely concealed impatience that she pored over the heavy book of wallpaper patterns Jack Simmons delivered to The Parsonage that same evening. Since it now seemed unlikely she would ever be living in the cottage, she flicked over the pages much too quickly for her mother, who was giving the matter her full attention.

'Two heads are better than one, dear, and we both have to live with it, do we not?'

370

'Yes, Mother. I do think the Regency stripe will be better suited to the drawing-room since the room is so small, and the rose pattern for your bedroom, to match the curtains Miss Styles will be making.'

'Of course, dear, I had forgotten the curtains. My head is in such a whirl, and you are so calm and sensible about the whole business. What should I do without you?'

Cecily had the grace to blush. What a hypocrite! All her Christian values were being ruthlessly discarded in this deceitful pretence. Poor Mother!

Chapter Thirteen

If young Carrie Simmons had known the half of what she must endure, it was doubtful whether she would ever have left the village. She was 15 when the regiment finally embarked from Southampton, *en route* to Aden, and her first glimpse of the troopship brought home the fact there was no turning back. Her heart sank. The avid curiosity to sample life in a wider world, and the urge to spread her wings now seemed to be nothing more than a foolish mistake. She was afraid – fear of the unknown, fear that disaster might overtake them, fear that she was saying goodbye to her family, her village and her country for ever.

All these fears combined to upset a stomach that was normally capable of coping with anything in the nature of food. But eating a meal seated comfortably at the nursery table was one thing, and eating a meal in a crowded saloon with the floor tilting giddily was another. They ran into heavy seas almost immediately, for it was mid January.

In the tiny, stuffy cabin where a fan stirred the stale air, she clutched little Jimmy in frantic anxiety, convinced they were going to be shipwrecked. But Jimmy was enjoying himself enormously. He had no fears, and his stomach was hungry for food. It was a new game, to be played with all the energy and enjoyment of his lively, intelligence.

No longer a baby, he struggled fiercely against the clutching arms of his young nursemaid, and demanded imperiously, 'OUT! OUT!' He was a heavy child, and Carrie was no match for him now. Staggering along the shuddering alleyways, up and down the companionways, was a feat of endurance, yet she could not keep the child amused in such a cramped space, and they were obliged to join the noisy crowd of children and agitated mothers and nursemaids, four times daily, in the crowded dining saloon. It was also her duty to exercise her charge on deck, for she had long since discovered his parents' obsession with fresh air. Wherever they went, one of these terrifying stairways had to be negotiated, but she was not alone in her misery and terror. Other girls were struggling with their charges, but Carrie was the youngest of the nursemaids attached to the regiment. All her adult assurance deserted her completely in this first taste of a situation her wildest imagination could not have envisaged. She lost her status, and her pert individuality. She was one of a crowd, battling to get the best for their charges – the food to which they were accustomed, the daily bath, the clean clothes, and enough space on deck to take exercise. Jimmy refused to be hampered by the reins, and his screams of rage brought so many diverse opinions from the interested spectators, Carrie gave up the struggle.

'It's the thin edge of the wedge, my girl. Now he's got you where he wants you,' an elderly nurse who was making her third voyage with an Army family prophesied darkly.

'But what can I *do*?' wailed Carrie. 'He's so strong and determined, and I feel so sick.'

'Give him something to push or pull. I always bring a

373

little wooden horse on wheels for my youngest boy or girl, it makes no difference.'

'I've brought all his toys. Usually he likes his red engine, and never tires of dragging it around, but now he won't look at it and he won't play with any of his toys. He just wants to run about.'

'That's because he's lost without his usual routine. Everything is strange. Little children are creatures of habit. Leave him here with me, I'll keep an eye on him while you fetch his red engine.'

'Thank you all the same, but I daren't leave him even for a second.' Carrie backed away, clutching the child's hand. The wind tore at her clothes. They rolled about like drunken sailors. Jimmy shrieked with excitement, his face glowing with health. But the tussle over the reins, coupled with the ferocious wind, had left her feeling quite unable to cope, and her blue eyes swam with tears at the thought of yet another perilous journey to the cabin.

'I'll take him,' offered a familiar voice, and her beloved Teacher suddenly materialised from a lower deck. They were separated now by protocol, in a manner they had not been obliged to obey at Tidworth. Her husband's rank as a sergeant entitled them to certain minor privileges, but the upper deck was reserved for the officers and their families.

'Will you get into trouble?' asked Carrie, who had been carefully instructed on the protocol so strictly observed on a troopship.

'I'll take a chance. I thought you might be finding things a little difficult with young Jimmy. He's such a hefty lad to carry around,' she laughed, indulgently, as she gathered him up and followed Carrie to the cabin. 'You'd better lie down, dear. You look ghastly. I'll take him back on deck. Don't worry, I won't let him out of my sight.'

'Will the Mistress mind?'

'Why should she? You can't help feeling sick. I'm surprised she hasn't checked up on you.'

'Compliments from the Captain, Carrie,' the batman interrupted. 'The Mistress is sick, so you must manage without her. You don't look too good yourself.'

'I . . . I . . .' she gulped, and fled to the nearest bathroom.

'Poor kid. It's a shame. She's too young for this sort of lark. It was all right at Tidworth,' he told Martha Martin.

'She wanted to come. She's so fond of Jimmy, she couldn't bear to leave him. Tell Mrs Saunders not to worry. I'll take charge of him during the day, till she gets her sea legs. I seem to be one of the lucky ones. I'm quite enjoying it.'

'Me, too,' he grinned.

They waited till Carrie had staggered back from the bathroom, and collapsed on the bunk, whimpering miserably, 'I want my Mum'. Then Martha made her comfortable under the blankets with a hot water bottle, while the batman tossed the boy over his head and he shrieked for more.

'Try to sleep, dear. It will pass.'

The kind, familiar presence bent over her, then she was gone, leaving the imprint of a kiss on the girl's wet cheek.

'I am going to die,' Carrie told herself, as the door closed behind them – and it seemed not to matter.

A buxom stewardess, rushed off her feet with seasick women and children, bustled in with a small cardboard box, fixed it to the side of the bunk, and remarked cheerfully, 'It's got to get worse before it gets better. Be all right when we're through the Bay and round the other side of the Rock.'

Carrie was feeling too ill to enquire which Rock, and she gasped feebly, 'What's that for?'

'Vomit.'

375

Carrie shuddered. She would rather die. This dominant person seemed to fill the cramped space, and the strong smell of antiseptic hung over the cabin when the woman had left. Weak tears wet her pallid cheeks. In all her short life she had never known such misery, but she would not use the little box and staggered repeatedly to the bathroom, clutching her stomach. The big, exciting world she had been so anxious to explore was reduced to the size of the airing cupboard in the house at Tidworth. It closed about her throbbing head. There was no escape. At every shuddering convulsion, the great ship seemed doomed to sink – like the *Titanic*! That terrible disaster had been depicted in all the horrifying detail by every artist in Fleet Street. The *Titanic* had been on her maiden voyage. The *Titanic* had been indestructible. But she sank, and 1500 lives were lost. The horror was real. She cowered under the blankets, shaking with terror. There were no icebergs on this perilous voyage, but the sea was still a deadly enemy.

The days passed in a nightmare of misery and self-pity. She was hardly aware of the child when Teacher carried him back to the cabin at bedtime, smelling fresh and clean from his bath. He shrank from the sour smell of the young stranger on the lower bunk. This was not his Carrie. He turned his head away and clung round the neck of the woman who had invented new games in a sheltered corner of the deck, and allowed him to eat a second helping of his favourite chocolate pudding. Then he climbed the little ladder to the top bunk, cuddled his teddy and fell asleep, exhausted by the strangeness of his new world, the tearing wind, and the roaring sea.

The Captains's batman looked in every day, but whether it was morning or afternoon, Carrie could not have told you. Bill Jenkins was a different person, a kinder, more thoughtful person than the man who had teased her at Tidworth. When he knelt beside the bunk, she could see his brown eyes warm with compassion, and feel the gentleness of his touch when he dried her wet cheeks.

'Poor little girl. It's not fair. Here am I, enjoying every second.' His glowing face, smelling faintly of shaving soap, swam into focus then receded, till only the two brown eyes remained, soft as velvet, holding her back from the brink of oblivion. He persuaded her to sip a little water, and when her stomach heaved and she struggled to get off the bunk, he held her there with the hateful little box under nose, and his hand on her forehead, while she retched and spat. She was like a little child in her weakness, and he like a father or an elder brother, or something between the two she could not identify. It seemed that he deliberately insisted that she drank the water, knowing her stomach would reject it, and it was contrary to the compassion and the kindness, but she was too ill to reason or to understand why he should do it. Humiliated, choked with her vomit, she could only wonder at his gentleness. Drained and exhausted, her head sank thankfully on to his shoulder. Then he pushed the offensive box out of sight, and cuddled her in his arms. It was the most comforting sensation she had ever known. He was so clean, so immaculate in his serge uniform. She was shamed by her own condition.

'The Mistress had been very ill,' he told her. 'The Captain has been worried. But the worst is over. After today, we should begin to notice a difference.'

'How many days since we left Southampton?'

'Four.'

'It feels like forty.'

He was twirling a damp curl round his finger. 'Baby's curls,' he said. 'But then you are nothing but a baby, and

377

much too young to be let loose with the British Army. What made you decide to come to Tidworth?'

'Because Teacher was there. We had kept in touch by letter. She had married Sergeant Martin and moved away. She's my best friend. I love her.'

'She's a nice woman. Can't think what she saw in that bastard.'

'She hadn't seen him for five tears. He was completely changed, but she had to marry him.'

'Why?'

'Because he was the father of her child and he insisted.'

'Young Philip?'

'Yes.'

'I didn't know. He's a grand little kid. A pity she had to leave him behind.'

'It broke her heart, but it's for his own good. He will be happy enough with his grandfather. He was always in trouble with his father. Besides, Teacher has always wanted Philip to go on to the Grammar School later, and the schoolmaster at the village school will coach him for the entrance examination. They are very good friends. Teacher and the schoolmaster.'

'You are feeling a little better, aren't you?' Bill had heard enough of Teacher and her affairs.

Carrie nodded. 'Thank you, Bill.' She stroked his cheek. He kissed her dry lips and tasted the sourness of her breath. She was nothing but a child, and he a grown man with a woman who had expected to be his wife before they left Tidworth – but it was the child he loved.

'Letters for you, dear.' Teacher dropped them into her lap. She was sitting up, drinking a cup of tea, the first since leaving Southampton. A wonderful stillness enveloped them.

'What's happening? Why is it suddenly so quiet?' she asked.

378

'The engines have stopped. We are docked at Marseilles, and we have picked up the mail. I have been queueing in the alleyway outside the office, Such excitement! Four for you, Carrie, and two for me.'

'Only two for you? That's not fair.'

'I was not expecting more than two, one from Father and one from Philip.' She was hiding her disappointment, for she had hoped Andrew would take the risk of addressing a letter to Mrs Martha Martin, but he hadn't, and he was right, of course. Supposing her husband collected the letters and opened them? Nothing was private with Dick. There would be a scene, and how she dreaded those scenes. She had gradually succumbed to his dominating personality. To oppose him was to let loose the demon of ill-temper that could only be mollified by sexual intercourse. She hated herself and she hated Dick, because she had lost her own identity in slavish subjection.

No, Andrew would not write. He was not a person to take risks. She scanned Philip's letter and found a message from the schoolmaster. 'PS. Mr Robinson sends his regards. He says to tell you we have started on English and Maths. He bought me a puppy. It's a little girl spaniel. I have called her Lucy because that is my favrit name.' The letter was neatly written, and signed, 'Your loving son, Philip', followed by a row of kisses. There was no mention of his father. Would that upset Dick? She never could tell what would spark off that hot temper. Yet why should the child mention a father for whom he had nothing but fear? Even a child as young as Philip must have been aware of a sense of relief at the separation. He was an intelligent little boy, and sensitive to her suffering on his behalf. How could she bear this long separation? She had asked this question repeatedly since she left her son standing at the school gates. But he was not alone.

The schoolmaster stood beside him. The man and the boy had drawn closer together as the cab moved away. She *had* to bear it, for it was a penance she had to pay for her mistaken belief that to marry the child's father would rectify her fall from grace eight years ago. It could never be rectified, for as long as they lived, because Dick would not let her forget. His sexual appetite had to be satisfied at any hour of the day or night. He took her with the thrusting impatience of an animal with its mate. She was shamed and degraded by her own submission. There was anguish in her trembling thighs that his hands could manipulate into complete subjection. Time and again she had stiffened every muscle and every quivering nerve against his dominance, only to be defeated, weeping in a kind of hopelessness while he laughed in mocking delight at her futile attempt to escape the demands of his strong, virile body, and his hard, persistent hands.

Her thoughts had strayed unwittingly. She sighed and asked the girl, 'What news from home?'

'Another baby on the way for Jack and Elsie. They haven't time to write, and that's not surprising. They sent their love in Mum's letter. Poor Mum. She says she feels lost without a regular job now she has finished at The Parsonage. Miss Victoria Langtry is worrying her to take over the job as daily cook at The Grove, but they are fussy old things, those two sisters, and Mum's not keen. Dad likes to have her at home because it pleases him to know he's the breadwinner. Men are funny that way, Mum says.' A wave of homesickness swept over Carrie as she looked at the sprawling, illiterate epistle. It was a labour of love and would have been written with the pen from the mantelpiece and the bottle of ink provided for the use of her two clever children. Mum was not ashamed that she had no 'book-learning'. Why should she be ashamed when all that splendid zest and energy flowed from her work-worn hands? She could not begin to describe the heartache they endured since Carrie went away. She could only say with simple truth, 'We miss you, luv, Dad and me'.

'They miss me.' The girl's voice was choked. The little boy looked up from the floor where he was building a house of bricks. His 'Cawie' was crying. He was still puzzled by the stranger who had taken the place of the pretty, happy companion of the nursery at Tidworth. But he got up and went to stand beside the bunk, screwing up his eyes.

'Oh, Jimmy!' she sobbed. 'I wish we were back there you and me and Teacher.' And she hugged him so passionately he pushed her away and went back to his house of bricks.

'You haven't read your other letters, dear,' Teacher reminded her quietly. 'Why not get washed and dressed. You will feel better. I'll take Jimmy on deck, and you can join us when you are ready. Bring the letters. I should like to hear all the news from home. Who has written to you besides your Mother?'

Carrie scanned the writing on the envelopes. 'Aunt Lucy, Freddie and Aunt Lucy's Albert,' she said.

Jimmy had been running up and down the deck, pulling his red engine on a string, but when Carrie joined them, Teacher persuaded him to sit down on the deck with a slate and a box of coloured chalks. She still had this gentle, persuasive manner with little children, and they obeyed her automatically. It surprised Carrie, who often had to resort to bribing her small charge with a piece of chocolate. For one thing, the ex-mistress of the Infants' class fully realised that the attention of little children quickly wanders if a lesson or a game lasts for longer than half an hour, and she was prepared for this and the little boy now played happily with the slate. She had even

381

provided a tiny sponge so that he could rub away the scribbles and start afresh. They watched him completely absorbed in his own artistry, then Carrie began to read her letters aloud. Bill Jenkins had carried up a couple of deck chairs and rugs to a sheltered corner. A chill wind was blowing across the harbour and the sky was grey, but it was good to feel the fresh air again, and to get away from the stuffy cabin.

Some time later, Captain and Mrs Saunders appeared, and Carrie and her companion prepared to rise to their feet respectfully.

'Stay where you are. Don't move.' The Captain's brusque voice instructed, and they obeyed. His wife was looking rather weak and wan, but she insisted she was feeling better. Jimmy was reminded his parents were waiting, so he scrambled up reluctantly, gave them his pursed mouth to be kissed, and went back to his slate and coloured chalks.

'It was kind of you, Mrs Martin, to take charge of him. My husband and I are extremely grateful,' Felicity Saunders was saying.

'It was no trouble. We have kept each other company.'

'With Carrie and myself both laid low, we were fortunate to have a friend who was such a good sailor. Yet it was your first voyage, Jenkins told us.'

'Yes, it was. I didn't know I was a good sailor. It just happened that I was one of the lucky ones who actually found the rough sea splendidly invigorating. I was quite fascinated.'

Felicity Saunders shivered at the memory and smiled at the young nursemaid. 'We didn't really appreciate its fascination, did we, Carrie?'

They all laughed.

'Carrie had four letters from home,' said Teacher, conversationally.

382

'Did you, Carrie? How is everyone?' Her mistress was genuine in her interest and concern for the girl, and very conscious of her responsibility.

'Quite well, thank you, Ma'am. Mum says they miss me.' She sighed, and then squared her shoulders. 'Jack and Elsie are expecting another baby. If it's a boy, it will be called Mark and if it's a girl, it will be called Rebecca. They all have Biblical names.'

'What happens if they run out of Biblical names?' the Captain asked.

'I don't think that is likely to happen, Sir. I can think of quite a number,' said Teacher quietly.

'Ah, the authority on such matters,' he teased.

'I can only think of Salome, and that wouldn't do,' his wife reflected.

'Why not?' The Captain was getting a little tired of the subject.

'Because Salome was the girl who danced for Herod at a banquet, and he was so enchanted by her performance, seeing she was covered only in a veil, he rashly promised to reward her with anything she liked to mention. She asked for the head of John the Baptist.'

'How revolting,' the Captain murmured.

'Yes, but it wasn't really her fault, darling. Her mother prompted her. Even so, I don't think your brother and his wife are likely to settle for Salome, are they, Carrie?'

'No, Ma'am.'

'There's David and Jonathan, both nice names and linked together so to speak. Then we have all the disciples.'

'Not Judas,' said Carrie, decidedly.

'No, not Judas,' her mistress agreed.

'We seem to have wandered away from the most important topic of the day,' the Captain reminded his wife.

383

'Tell them,' she said, and they looked at him expectantly.

'We have received an urgent despatch from Whitehall. We are not to disembark at Aden as planned, but we are ordered to proceed to Bombay and from there to Peshawar in Northern India. More trouble on the Afghanistan frontier has depleted the garrison at Peshawar. Since they also have to defend the Khyber Pass, all the year round from raiding Pathans, it doesn't surprise me. There were rumours of fresh disturbances on the North West Frontier of India before we left Tidworth.' The Captain paused, then asked, irrelevantly, 'By the way, Carrie, have you heard from that clever brother of yours, the one who passed his final law examination some time ago?'

'Yes, sir. I've had a long letter from Freddie. He is living in furnished rooms in Soho and he has an office there. He calls himself a poor man's solicitor.'

'Really? I wouldn't have thought he could make a living in that particular sphere?'

'Freddie says he gets plenty of work with the Trade Unions because the workers often need to be represented at court when they have been dismissed for minor offences, and cannot get another job without a reference. That's when a solicitor is called in, Sir,' Carrie explained carefully.

The Captain yawned. Unlike his father, he had little sympathy and understanding of the working class. All three of the doctor's sons had their mother's upper-class snobbishness.

'Glad to hear all those years of swotting dusty old law books haven't been wasted,' he said, laconically. 'Well, darling, shall we take a turn round the deck?'

His wife nodded, and they walked away together, stepping out with military precision.

'Do you mind that we are going to India and not Aden?' asked Carrie.

'No, I think it might be more interesting, and less monotonous. The families seem to spend several months of the year in one of the hill stations, either Simla or Bangalore, when the men are defending the frontiers, according to a novel I've been reading. We will have another look at the atlas some time, Carrie, and find the places the author mentions in the book. She is writing about an earlier period, the Victorian era, but I don't suppose it has changed very much. I've heard of the Khyber Pass. That often crops up in books, but for the rest I must confess my geography of India is a little vague.'

'It will be a long way from England, much farther than Aden, won't it?'

'Yes, a few thousand miles east of Aden, but we may as well see a little more of the world, dear, now we have actually started, and you will enjoy it now we are past that rough passage. It's one of the advantages of following the drum, and we mustn't allow our homesickness to spoil our pleasure in such an experience. How many girls of your age, or women of my age, in our class of society would have such a wonderful opportunity, Carrie? I can't think of anyone in the village?'

Carrie shook her head, not entirely convinced by Teacher's sensible outlook.

'Aren't you going to read the other letters?' prompted her companion. It was good to receive letters from home, but she knew the girl would be upset whenever the mail arrived from England. The letter from her Aunt Lucy contained a full account of the Christmas festivities at Russets, and a visit from Charles who was allowed to spend only one day of the school vacation with his mother and half-brothers. She had tried to hide her disappointment, but the sadness was there, the sadness of a mother

385

wishing she could put back the clock to those happy early years, before the father claimed his son. She insisted, however, that Charles was loyal to those early memories, and would never forget them.

'Poor woman, she has all my sympathy. Enforced separation from one's child is a heart-breaking experience,' Teacher interrupted. 'One loses so much of those interesting years when a child, especially a boy child, is developing as a person. Is Charles allowed to write to his mother?'

'He does write a letter occasionally, but she doesn't say whether there has been any objection. He always sends picture postcards from France when he goes on holiday with the rest of the Franklins, and also when he stays with Miss Beatrice – I don't know her married name – but she lives in Norfolk. One year he went to Interlaken in Switzerland with his best friend, and the boy's parents. She is very proud of the cards, all arrayed on the mantelpiece in the parlour. When she showed them to me, she said, 'You see, Carrie, Charles doesn't forget his mother." I wanted to cry. She looked so sad. She's not like she used to be when Uncle Bert was alive. They were such a happy, united family. Charles has divided them. You see, my cousins dislike him. They can't forget he is not Uncle Bert's son, or the attention he received as a little boy because he was Sir Neville Franklin's child. Aunt Lucy didn't spoil the older boys, but she did spoil Charles, so it was natural they resented it. Of course it was an awful shock to all the family when Aunt Lucy was pregnant, and she didn't hide the truth, not from anyone. It was a nine days' wonder, but it blew over as Mum said it would when the tongues stopped wagging. My youngest cousin, Albert, was the most upset because he was so jealous of the baby, I like Albert. He's my favourite. Did you know he had asked

386

me to be his sweetheart on my 14th birthday?'

'Yes, dear. You told me.'

'And he sends me Valentine cards. They are not signed, but it couldn't be anyone but Albert because I don't know any of the village boys, I mean, not well enough for them to send a Valentine card. Mum wouldn't let me mix with them. She was very strict about that.'

'Well, see what he has to say. He may have changed his mind. Five years is a long time for a young man to wait for his sweetheart.'

They smiled at each other, the woman and the girl, with a mutual understanding and affection that bridged the gap of the years between them. The small boy at their feet was still engrossed, but would soon be tiring of the slate and the coloured chalks. Then it would be put away till the morrow, and some new diversion would be found to keep him busy till it was time to take their place in the dining saloon.

Albert had surpassed himself, and surprised them both, with his first letter to his absent sweetheart. He must have spent all of Sunday afternoon compiling a composition that would have earned him full marks at the village school, yet he hadn't been a clever scholar, or shown much interest or aptitude for anything other than nature study and drawing. Now he wrote of everyday happenings at Russets with such natural fluency, they could almost have taken part in it. The early lambs, the new litter of kittens in the chimney corner, and Betty's calf, all came to life for the two who had left the village behind. He was proud of the pile of logs he had sawn for the parlour on Christmas Eve. They had taken Emma to sledge in the Park on Boxing Day, and they had seen Charles and Miss Cynthia, but they hadn't stopped. It was rather odd just to wave to your half-brother in passing, and Mum was cross because they hadn't stopped to

387

enquire if Charles had liked his Christmas present. Harry had broken his right arm, and Doctor Saunders had put it in splints. Mum was helping with the milking. The pump was frozen in the yard. The big barn was the warmest place with all the hay, and the coldest place was the dairy. Emma liked having Harry sitting around in the kitchen with his broken arm. Why didn't they get married? 'I hope you are well and having a good time. I will write again soon, so you should get another letter at Port Said. I made enquiries at the Post Office about the mails.' The letter was signed, 'Your loving cousin, Albert.'

'Three pages! He must be very fond of you, Carrie,' Teacher reflected as the girl wiped the tears away with the back of her hand in a childish gesture. Nostalgic tears. She was reminded of her first visit to Russets at the age of 3, when Albert had been instructed to look after her and to show her all the animals. He had taken her hand and led her away across the yard. She remembered pressing her face to a gate to watch the lambs skipping about in the field. She laughed, because they were so funny, but Albert didn't laugh. He was a very serious boy and very patient, waiting a long time at the gate till she was ready to move on to see the rest of the animals. She remembered every detail of that first visit to Russets. It must have been one of the really important events in her early childhood like the day she started school and met Teacher.

'Walkie!' demanded a small boy, pushing a slate and a handful of chalks on to her lap.

'Yes, my love,' she smiled, and kissed his shining face.

Now the days slipped away, and they used the cabin only for sleeping, and Carrie was back on duty with her small charge. With the influence of the Captain's wife, however, Teacher was still permitted to join them on the deck normally reserved for the officers' families, and her gentle presence made the task less exacting. For one thing, he was persuaded to rest in a deck chair for an hour or so in the afternoon, and would curl up under a rug with his teddy. In this brief respite, they read their books and listened to the teeming life all about them. The men were engaged in routine drills and exercises to keep them fit and healthy and maintain discipline on the long, tedious voyage. Orders were barked, and boots clattered on the decks as relays of men were put through their paces.

In their crowded quarters, at the end of the day, every man loosened his collar, reached for a cigarette, and cursed the sergeant! Decks were scrubbed and brasses polished six mornings a week. Sunday was different, and the difference was felt and welcomed. Instead of the usual church parade, the men massed on deck for a service conducted by the commanding officer. Uniforms had been sponged and pressed. Buttons, belts and boots had been polished to a perfection that dazzled the wives and children, all arrayed in their Sunday best clothes. The band played 'Rock of Ages' and 'Fight the Good Fight' with due solemnity.

'Last Sunday they played "Eternal Father",' Teacher whispered. 'It was most impressive with the wind howling and the waves roaring.'

Carrie shivered and clutched Jimmy's hand. Every inch a soldier's son, part baby, part boy, he stamped his feet in time with the big drum. He was puzzled and disappointed to discover they were not going to church, and that everyone was standing still and not marching away. But then he had been puzzled, one way and another, since he was carried up the gangway at Southampton, and he was still upset by all the changes in his nursery routine. The barrack square had disappeared, so had the nursery window. The ship had stopped rolling, but it was still not safe to run, and running was a new achievement. When he fell, he picked himself up, laughing at Carrie who would have spared him every tumble, every bruise. It was fun to run and tumble. Everything was fun, though a little puzzling in this new world. His familiar world was turned upside down, but since he was still surrounded by familiar faces, he accepted it. Never in all his short life had he liked to be left alone, and when it happened, he yelled for attention and the company of another human being. Born into a world of men, he preferred the company of men – his Daddy and Bill the Batman and every uniformed figure that strutted past. Unconsciously he was storing up impressions of smartness and disciplined behaviour while still too young to emulate his elders. When he was naughty, punishment was swift. Carrie smacked his bottom, and his dignity was outraged. He beat at her starched apron with his small fists and screwed up his face.

'Behave yourself, James!' the Captain would roar if he happened to be anywhere in the near vicinity. The voice of authority was recognised and prompt obedience expected.

'Don't let him bully you, Carrie,' the Captain would insist.

'No, Sir.'

She was still a little afraid of the Captain, and automatically stood to attention when being addressed, wondering if her cap was straight.

At Port Said, the men discarded their serge uniforms for khaki shorts and shirts. It was strange to see all the bare knees. Now the officers' batmen would be kept busy washing and ironing their white uniforms. It was a matter of personal pride and satisfaction for a conscientious batman to see his well-groomed officer at the head of his company.

After they sailed from Marseilles, however, Bill Jenkins had no further excuse to visit the young

390

nursemaid in her cabin. There were no messages to convey, and his sympathy was wasted on a girl so obviously enjoying the calm seas and her first glimpse of the coast lines she had found in Teacher's atlas. Bill was feeling depressed and more than a little guilty. Susan was expecting his child. It was the old story of a batman and a maid-servant thrown together in Army quarters where it was all too easy to share a bed. But there was no security or permanence in a situation in which the batman moved on, and the maid-servant was left behind to cope with a new mistress, a new family, and a new regiment. Now Bill would be obliged to make Susan an allowance or she would be writing to the Captain. He was trapped, and he cursed himself for a fool, and awaited the next letter from Tidworth with sulky resignation.

The scene was constantly changing now, and Port Said, they told Carrie, was the Gateway to the East. It was fascinating to watch all the native salesmen swarming like ants on the quayside. Those who could find a place in one of the tiny craft plying between the quay and the anchored ships hurried up the gangways, chattering in shrill excited voices. When they approached, they carried a musky smell, and an assortment of cheap toys, jewellery, souvenirs and sweets.

The first to arrive bowed low and enquired in wheedling pidgin English, 'Will little sahib like toy?' – careful not to insult the sturdy little boy by calling him 'Baba'.

Jimmy found the smell of his first native so foreign to the fresh, astringent smells of the nursery, he stepped back a pace and took Carrie's hand. Feeling very travelled and worldly, Carrie purchased a windmill for Jimmy, and a box of Turkish Delight to share with Teacher who had gone ashore, but this was not enough for the persistent little salesman.

391

'Lovely bracelet, memsahib, pure gold.'

Carrie shook her head, and he fastened a bracelet on her wrist so quickly, she gasped, 'No! Take it off!' Now she was frightened, for she hadn't enough money in her purse, and she glanced about desperately for help.

One of the ship's officers had been watching from the boat deck. Suddenly he stood beside her, snatched off the bracelet, tossed it back in the tray together with a few annas, and barked an order. The little man rolled his eyes to Heaven and protested he had been robbed, but was waved away haughtily.

'You should never buy anything from these natives. They are just a pest,' the superior one told Carrie. Immaculate in the white uniform that had replaced the blue serge only that morning, the young novice was not to know that his status as fourth mate was almost as humble as her own.

'I couldn't get rid of him, Sir. Thank you for coming to my rescue.' The dimpled smile, the bright blue eyes, and the curls escaping from the starched cap, made an instant appeal to his chivalry, and he waved aside the purse she offered.

'Allow me. It was a pleasure.'

Jimmy was running up and down the deck with the windmill, but there was no breeze to stir the paper sails. He threw it down in disgust and stamped on the useless object.

'Jimmy! That was naughty!' Carrie admonished, but the superior one was laughing.

'It's rubbish. See how easily it breaks. And go easy on that Turkish Delight. Heaven knows where it's made or what it consists of. Nobody buys the stuff after their first voyage.' So he knew she was a novice. She wished now she had been allowed to go ashore with Teacher and the other families, but the Captain would not allow it, and his word was law. Carrie had been instructed to take Jimmy to the stateroom reserved for officers and their families when he tired of the deck.

'There's plenty to watch. It's a novelty when it's your first voyage,' the superior one was explaining. 'We shall be taking on fresh fruit, and it's my job to supervise the unloading. Can't trust these native bastards. But at least it's clean produce. Wait till we get to Aden. That will surprise you. Everything covered in coal dust, and all the portholes shut tight. It's like something out of the Bible, with scores of little figures carrying baskets of coal on their heads, walking up one plank and down another, hour after hour, chanting a sort of dirge. It gets on your nerves, I can tell you. If they don't let you go ashore, it's going to be darn uncomfortable.'

He was rather nice when he smiled, she thought. It was just his manner. She didn't realise he had to throw his weight about with the natives, since his humble status in his particular hierarchy kept him subservient to his superiors. The system was one of disciplined protocol, and the Medes and Persians could not have been governed by stricter rules and regulations. Carrie had a lot to learn.

A steward served them lunch in the saloon, and a double portion of strawberry ice-cream helped to compensate for being deserted by the rest of the nursemaids and children.

'My husband may seem to be fussing, Carrie, but it's so easy to pick up germs going ashore in a place like Port Said. And I must warn you, for this is important, he will not allow Jimmy to be left in the care of native servants in India. That is why we brought an English nursemaid. When you are off duty, I shall be on duty, so he says!' her mistress had explained whimsically.

'Yes, Ma'am,' Carrie had answered obediently.

393

Sometimes she felt sorry for her mistress. In a sense the Captain's wife was more subservient to Army discipline than the sergeant's wife, and the friendly association she had enjoyed with Martha Martin was discontinued when they left Tidworth. Formalities had to be observed.

While Jimmy scribbled happily on his slate with a new box of coloured chalks. Carrie read her letters from home, keeping Albert's letter to the last. Her cousin would remind her that she was 4, not 3, that first Saturday at Russets, that she was put in his care, and that they had wasted a lot of time while she picked celandines in the ditch!

'What can you do with celandines? They fade and die before you can get them home, like bluebells,' he reminded her.

She smiled at the memory. It was just the sort of thing her brothers would have said. Boys could never see the sense of picking wild flowers. She had thought she had remembered everything, every detail of that eventful day, but she was wrong. Albert had a memory like an elephant!

'Freddie says there is going to be a war with Germany,' Carrie told Teacher complacently, when they had welcomed her back and she had distributed the gifts she had bought – a tinkling brass bell for Carrie, and a fort for Jimmy that had to be assembled. But Teacher had her mind on the letter she was reading, from Philip, and she turned over the single sheet to read, 'PS. Mr Robinson sends his regards. He says to tell you the Infants are growing mustard and cress on the saucers.' She smiled nostalgically. Each generation of Infants had grown mustard and cress on those cracked saucers lined up on the window sills around the classroom. She was remembering those happy days that had gone for ever, and wondering who had encouraged the Infants to resume this particular custom. A new teacher, with time to listen to the requests of little children? It had taken a long time to find a suitable substitute after she had left – according to Andrew.

Dragging her mind back to the present, she looked down at the young nursemaid, absorbed in the task of marshalling the tin soldiers on the battlements, and asked, 'What did you say about a war, Carrie?'

'A war with Germany.' She did not look up.

'It's probably only a rumour, dear. The War Office would not have sanctioned our embarkation if war in Europe is threatened.'

Carrie sat back on her heels, her face flushed with hopeful anticipation. 'Will they send us back if we have to fight the Germans?'

Teacher shook her head. 'Too expensive, and it could be over in six months. What else did Freddie say?'

'He said he had seen Miss Cynthia Franklin in a tea-shop in Oxford Street, and they shared a table and had tea together. She is training to be a nurse in the hospital for women.'

'Miss Cynthia *working*? But that's incredible. Whatever possessed her to take up such an arduous profession?'

'I don't know. Freddie doesn't say. If there is a war, nurses will be needed, won't they?'

'They certainly will.'

'But isn't it strange that two people from our village should meet quite by chance in a tea-shop in London?'

'It's a small world, as Father would say.'

'Yes, but they don't belong to the same world, and it seems rather cheeky of Freddie. I mean, I wonder if he told Mum he had tea with Sir Neville Franklin's daughter?'

'It probably wouldn't embarrass your brother Freddie.

Meeting all sorts of people, he would cope with such an encounter quite naturally. Besides, for all we know, they may have kept in touch since the accident. Wasn't it Miss Cynthia's horse that caused the accident?'

'Yes, and Freddie had concussion, and Aunt Lucy nursed him. Albert told me Miss Cynthia came every afternoon to sit with Freddie because all the family were busy in the hay-field.'

'So they are not strangers?'

'No.'

'Did you receive another letter from your cousin, Albert?'

'Yes, three pages. Why can he write such interesting letters when nothing much happens at Russets, and I can't think of anything to fill the page when there is so much happening to me?'

'Letter writing is a gift, and he obviously enjoys it. Besides, he is fond of you, and this would be his first opportunity to express his feelings.'

'Did you know he was clever at composition?'

'No, because we don't have composition in the Infants. That comes later, in a higher standard.'

Carrie nodded. 'He's going to be disappointed with my letters.'

'I shouldn't let it worry you, dear. I'm sure he won't be too critical. He seems to have grown into a very understanding person.'

'He's nice.' Carrie was shy of compliments. The working class do not indulge in fancy talk, and nice was an easy word. It could be applied to almost anything – the weather – aniseed balls – a new pair of boots – or a sweetheart!

'Cawie play,' demanded a small boy, growing impatient with all the chatter.

'Say please,' coaxed the young nursemaid in a vain

attempt to teach her charge the rudiments of good manners. He smiled beguilingly, and Carrie capitulated.

'That smile will break a few hearts one of these days,' said Teacher. 'What have you been doing all day? Has he been a good boy?'

'Good as gold,' Carrie answered, without a second's hesitation. Any minor misdemeanour, such as stamping on the windmill, could be explained as mischief, and mischief was a small boy's prerogative.

Steaming down the Suez Canal, nursemaids and children rushed excitedly from port to starboard, for there was so much to see.

'Camel!' shrieked Jimmy, clutching Carrie's hand.

'A train! A train!' came an answering shout from the bows.

Is this how it looked when Jesus was a boy? Carrie wondered, with white-robed Arabs and a caravan of camels in a cloud of dust, silhouetted against the sunset. The little train chugged busily on its single track. Ancient and modern transportation were of equal interest to the children who followed the drum from West to East. The scene made an unforgettable impression, and Carrie would remember it for the rest of her days. All too soon they had disappeared, the train and the caravan of camels.

'Where are we now?' Carrie asked Teacher.

'Look it up on the map,' came the prompt reply. Once a teacher, always a teacher!

'The Red Sea?'

Teacher nodded.

'But it's not red?'

'Some historians would have us believe it was so named because of the blood that was shed when the forces of Pharoah's army were drowned as they followed the Israelites. These shores won't have changed very much in

2,000 years. It all belongs to history – Biblical history if you remember what you were taught.'

'I do. Scripture was one of my favourite lessons, and I've brought the Bible I won at Sunday School for good attendance.'

'Good girl.'

'Will there be any more letters at Aden?'

'Probably. Then no more till we dock at Bombay.'

Carrie was studying the map again. 'The Indian Ocean looks very big.'

'It's vast, but I'm told it's the best part of the voyage.'

'It's funny, but it's difficult to remember Tidworth. It seems we have been on this ship for ages. It's like another world.'

'It *is* another world, bridging the old and the new chapters of our lives. You are not sorry you came?'

'No, I'm glad, and I've almost forgotten I was so sick and miserable. Shall you go ashore at Aden?'

'No, I will stay aboard and keep you and Jimmy company.'

'Thank you. Do you wish you had brought Philip?'

Teacher shook her head. 'He's the wrong age, dear. Not any of these children are more than 3 or 4, and they will be coming back to school when they are 8, or even earlier. The climate of India is not suitable for British-born children, unless they spend all the year in one of the hill stations, where they would hardly ever see their fathers, and may as well be living in England.' She was still missing her son unbearably, but Dick was pleased that he hadn't to share her. It fed his vanity and his ego to have her so subservient. He liked to stand in a tin tub and have her pour cold water over his head, when he came back to the cabin, sweating profusely after drilling his company. He flaunted his nakedness deliberately when she could not hide her repulsion. His sexual

398

appetite was insatiable. Even now, after more than four years of marriage, he was still experimenting with new ways to excite the senses and satisfy the demands of his strong, lusty body. It was, and always would be, a kind of torture, and there was no escape. She did not mention her husband to Carrie, and they seldom met because their duties kept them apart.

Bill Jenkins would watch the girl and the little boy from a distance, but he, too, had no excuse to be seen on the deck reserved for officers and their families. Bound by the ethics of Army discipline, and fearful of the consequences should he ignore those letters from Tidworth, the Captain's batman faced the future in gloomy anticipation.

Teacher was right about the Indian Ocean being the best part of the voyage. They seemed to be sailing over an endless sea of calm waters, sparkling under a tropical sun. Porpoises played, and flying fishes darted like dragonflies flaunting translucent wings. Canopies covered sections of the hot deck. Nursemaids and children revelled in the luxury of ice-cream and fruit juice, but mothers still drank hot tea as the temperature soared. Nobody enquired what the men were drinking, and the women and children were so accustomed to the barking of orders, the stamp of marching feet, and the bugles, they hardly noticed.

Jimmy languished in the heat of the day, and tossed restlessly on his bunk at night. It was difficult to keep him amused, even with the novelty of flying fish and schools of porpoises at play. He would sprawl on Carrie's starched apron, damp with sweat, his eyes screwed against the sunlight that filtered through the worn canvas.

'Jimmy want,' he demanded peevishly.

'What does Jimmy want?' was a question he was too young to answer. Perhaps it was the wind or the rain, for he revelled in both. Perhaps it was a vague remembrance of firelight and nursery tea. His vocabulary was still too limited to explain. Boys were often more backward than girls in this respect, but made up for it by being the first to walk, the well-travelled nurse told Carrie.

Disembarking at Bombay, followed by the long train journey to Peshawar, was a nightmare of confusion and discomfort – of strange smells and the babble of strange tongues in the sweltering heat and dust. Was it for this they had travelled all those thousands of miles?

She was worried. Jimmy was fretful and feverish.

'It's just the heat,' his mother insisted, for she did not wish to alarm her husband or the young nursemaid.

But Carrie knew better. He was sickening for something. Not for nothing was she reared in a crowded slum. Little children behaved in exactly the same way when they were sick, whether they were surrounded by comfort and luxury, or dire poverty.

'I will get the doctor to look at him as soon as we are settled,' her mistress promised. 'It will be cooler in Peshawar. We are travelling north all the time,' she added confidently.

Carrie would remember only vague impressions of that first day in their new environment. It seemed they had exchanged one parade ground for another, and the ugly barracks had been transplanted. But for the heat and the dust, they could have been back at Tidworth. The Captain's bungalow was blessed with a little shade. A native boy watered the green lawn, and someone had coaxed a few English flowers to grow in the dusty soil. Shutters were closed against the sun all day. Rush matting covered the floors. The light bamboo furniture had changed hands a number of times, and the native servants had served other sahibs and memsahibs. Their bare feet padded noiselessly over the floors. They smiled and bowed, and agreed to everything with deceptive

400

subservience. They had their quarters beyond the compound, and their own kind of hierarchy, as undisputed as their English counterparts. The servant who served the meals did not cook the food. The servant who swept the floors did not polish the silver. The servant who presided over the laundry did not concern himself with the garden. Only the head houseboy spoke and understood a few familiar phrases and translated for the rest of the household with much pride. Only the Sahib raised his voice. Only the Sahib was foolish enough to work in the heat of the day. A native servant could always find a shady corner to enjoy an afternoon siesta.

'Lazy bastards!' muttered Bill Jenkins enviously, sweating over his chores. He had no status now, no authority. It was humiliating to be ignored with such polite indifference.

The Captain and his wife had been conscientiously studying Hindustani on the outward voyage. They could converse on food, drink, wages and cleanliness, the latter an obsession with the English memsahib.

Carrie listened in wonder to the exchange of stilted conversation, but made no attempt to emulate her betters, for she was still struggling with the refinements of English grammar! From the start she made her requests known by sign language, and by repeating every word with careful enunciation as though the servants were not only deaf but stupid! Why hadn't they been taught to speak the King's English? She wondered if the Tower of Babel had been responsible for all this confusion of strange tongues. How much simpler it would have been if everyone in the world spoke English.

Too much had happened since Carrie had left her village. In a sense, the girl had spread her wings before her mind was ready to grasp the essentials of the ever-changing adult world. In her anxiety for the little boy who had been her constant companion since she left Richmond Row, she was burdened with a responsibility too heavy for her years. Nobody, least of all her Mistress, would want to blame such a young, inexperienced nursemaid for what had happened.

But how and where had her small charge picked up the germ? It took the doctor only a few minutes to examine his fretful little patient and to conclude his diagnosis. Jimmy was suffering from the early stages of typhoid.

Chapter Fourteen

'Baba sick. Baba die?' the servants whispered.

The doctor called twice a day; no stranger to tropical diseases, he was fully aware of the seriousness. To prevent spreading the infection, however, he isolated the child's mother and the nursemaid from the rest of the household, to share the nursing. The mother took the biggest share, releasing Carrie from the sick room whenever the girl's head nodded on her starched apron.

Then Carrie slept exhausted in the day nursery, each passing day merging into night, and night into day as she was roused to take her turn. Sponging the small, fevered body, tears would wet her cheeks, for her heart ached for the sick child. She could not bear to leave him, and he cried pitifully when she was sent away. It was 'Cawie' he wanted, not his mother. For all his mother's loving care and attention could not compensate for that familiar little person who had shared his world from the beginning. His hot little hand would tug at her starched cap impatiently. They were young together, and wholly dependent on the adults who surrounded them. So they clung together, the sick child and the girl who was still a child.

Closer than his mother, Carrie gave all of herself, pouring out her love because his desperate need of her could not be denied. The mother could not neglect her husband, and the husband, for all his anxiety, could not neglect his duties as an officer. So the parents were torn between love and duty, while Carrie spent herself in love. She had no fear of infection, and it did not occur to her that her own healthy body could be the next victim. In her devotion to the child, she hardly noticed what she ate, but went obediently to the small bamboo table on the verandah when she was summoned. So she ate what was provided without interest or enjoyment.

'You must keep up your strength, Carrie, for Jimmy's sake,' her mistress reminded her.

'Yes, Ma'am,' she answered dutifully. But it was not food that would give her the strength for the weeks ahead. She would survive, as her own mother had survived. The working class had a sturdiness and a stamina that battled against adversity. It was inborn. Generations of men and women had bred children in their own pattern and only a small minority had been defeated by the circumstances of their birth, once they had survived all the hazards of early childhood.

Carrie had no need to be reminded to keep up her strength for the child's sake. She was indispensable now, and they all knew it. Ruby Simmons had not foreseen such dangers for her only daughter when she left the village, yet it was doubtful whether the girl would have heeded her mother's advice once she had spread her wings. Carrie had passed beyond the stage when she cried for her mother. She would always be homesick. It was one of the penalties of being uprooted from the village. But now she was faced with a different kind of sickness, so much worse than anything she had known in Richmond Row.

Three weeks the doctor had told the Mistress, and every week would see a fresh stage and a new

404

development. They knew all the symptoms, and they were prepared, but even so, the danger was there. He was such a little boy, too small to fight for his life.

'But I can fight,' Carrie told herself. She was not afraid. Every waking moment was promised to Jimmy. Neither her mind nor her heart could contain anything else. The household revolved about them, and the native servants crept noiselessly about their duties. Men marched and drilled, cursed and sweated, on the parade ground. The bugler still summoned them to Reveille and Lights Out had to be obeyed. Nothing had really changed, only the heat and the dust – and the Captain's son too sick to follow the drum. Teacher was not allowed to visit. Bill Jenkins was told to keep away. It was a strange little world they shared, the mother, the nursemaid and the sick child.

The doctor came and went, but had no substance, only a strong smell of antiseptic. Was he old or young? Dark or fair? Carrie could not remember. It was not important. They knew exactly what to do now they had been told, at each stage of the disease. So when the rash appeared on the child's chest and stomach, and his bowels were loose during the second week, they were prepared. The sturdy little body was shrinking now, the cheeks hollowed, the bright eyes dulled with pain. So quickly had the germ spread its deadly tentacles they could hardly recognise the child who had revelled in the raging seas and the roaring winds at the early part of the voyage. Comforting promises to the little boy that he would soon be better could only be repeated again and again. What else could they say?

By the end of the second week, he was so weak the doctor feared he could not survive the third week with its risk of complications. If pneumonia developed, then he would die. It was as simple as that. Now both were exhausted, the mother and the nursemaid, but still the girl was the stronger, battling against those threatening complications with every passing day – till the danger was past.

It was like a miracle when the fever subsided, the emaciated little body felt cool to her touch – and he screwed up his eyes to ask, surprisingly, for his red engine!

With the immediate danger past, Carrie was told they would be taking Jimmy to Simla as soon as he was strong enough to make the train journey. Teacher would be coming with them. There were smiles on the faces of the servants now, and the boy watering the lawn played tricks with the hose to make Jimmy laugh. On the shaded verandah, the little boy, still weak and peevish, played listlessly with his toys, and would not allow Carrie out of his sight. Almost every day a new toy would be delivered at the Captain's bungalow, many of them handmade by the men in his Company, for the little boy was a great favourite. Surprisingly, no other child contracted the disease, but they still kept Jimmy and Carrie apart from the other families. He tired quickly, and fell asleep on Carrie's lap. She would sit there, rocking gently in the old rocking chair, listening to the familiar sounds of barrack life.

Spoiling was no longer frowned upon by the Captain. In fact, he actually encouraged it now. Nothing was denied to the small beloved son he had so nearly lost. If the sturdy little boy seemed to have slipped back into baby ways, he had to be indulged, not scolded.

The Captain's manner had noticeably changed towards the young nursemaid. For the first time since she joined the household, she felt his warm approval, and when he shook hands and thanked her for her care and devotion to her small charge, she blushed with pleasure.

'But I love him, Sir,' she answered him, with such

406

simple honesty, he was shamed by the tardiness he had shown towards a young village girl his wife had recognised as a potential treasure. There would be no more criticism, and he had apologised to his wife.

'You were right, darling.' The Captain seldom admitted he was at fault.

But one morning, as Carrie rocked the sleeping child on the verandah, she overheard a conversation between her mistress and the doctor that sent her heart racing, and she listened with bated breath.

'I am not entirely convinced, Mrs Saunders, that a few weeks' convalescence at a hill station is the right treatment for this particular child who has only just escaped pneumonia,' the doctor was saying. 'Some children should never be reared in this climate. They belong to the northern hemisphere,' he insisted gravely.

'You mean – we should not have brought him to India? That we may have to send him back?' Her Mistress's voice was choked, but then they walked away and Carrie had to wait till the evening to know what had been decided. When she saw the sadness on the faces of both parents, she knew that a painful decision had been reached. They came into the night nursery hand-in-hand, and stood there, gazing down at the sleeping child. With only one child, it must have been a heart-rending decision, and the mother was crying as she left the room. It was the Captain who explained, quietly, 'Our plans have been changed again, Carrie. You will not be going to Simla. My wife and I have decided to send Jimmy back to England. I am sure my mother will be overjoyed to have her grandson back. It will be like old times for her to have the child in the house. The nurseries will be made ready, and you will be back where you belong, among your own people. We only have to wait for confirmation from my parents, and your passages will be booked. Your friend, Mrs Martin, is going to miss you, but there it is. She has married a soldier and this is her life.'

'Yes, Sir,' Carrie agreed. She, too, had seen herself married to a soldier when Jimmy went away to school, and spending the rest of her life with the regiment. Now that everything was changed, she knew only a wonderful sense of relief, as though she had escaped from a world in which she had not rightly belonged. Because she could not bear to part from the little boy she had grown to love, she had convinced herself that her future destiny lay beyond the shores of England. It hadn't taken long to realise, however, that she was no adventurer, but a home-loving creature, for the novelty of travel had quickly faded.

'As soon as we get the sailing date from the P. & O. you can notify your mother,' the Captain was saying. 'No doubt she will be glad to have you back,' he added with a tight smile that hid his own acute disappointment.

'Mum will be ever so pleased, Sir, but I'm sorry for you and the mistress.'

'They do say it's an ill wind that blows nobody any good, don't they, Carrie?'

'Do they, Sir?' What did he mean?

'They say you are taking Jimmy back to England, Carrie. Is it true, or is it just a rumour?' Teacher asked anxiously the following day.

'It's true!' the girl could not hide her delight in the unexpected change of plans, and she hugged her friend exuberantly.

'Dick says there will be war in Europe before the end of the year. It seems risky to be going back now. Surely it was not necessary to make such a drastic decision, Carrie? They have not even tried Simla.' It was a bitter disappointment. A few weeks in that renowned hill station was something every Army family would enjoy.

408

'I don't understand.' She was shaking her head dubiously.

'The doctor has frightened them, I believe. It was after he had given Jimmy a thorough examination that he advised them to send him home. A spot on the lung, he said. Is that serious?'

'It could be. It means he will need a lot of care, especially in the Winter. But then his grandfather is a doctor, and he couldn't have a more devoted nursemaid. They are right, Carrie. Parents do know what is best for their children. But it's sad this had to happen. He was such a sturdy little fellow.'

They were watching him sprawled listlessly on the verandah, pushing his soldiers around without a spark of interest.

'Does he know he is going back home?' Teacher asked quietly.

'Not yet.'

'He won't mind if he has you, dear. He will soon forget all this.'

Carrie sighed. 'I wish you were coming.'

'So do I.'

'Philip will be surprised to see me back without you.'

'Yes. But at least I shall get more news, shan't I? He doesn't tell me very much, but then he's only a little boy. You will write?'

'Every week, I promise.'

'Thank you, dear.'

They smiled at each other with a complete understanding that was rare between a woman and a young girl.

'I shall be seasick again, shan't I?' Carrie shivered.

'I expect so, since you are such a poor sailor.'

'Who will look after Jimmy?'

'Don't worry. You will be travelling first class in the

409

care of the purser, and a nursery stewardess will be available to take Jimmy to his meals with the other children and to keep an eye on him during those few days you are indisposed. Besides, Mrs Saunders will make it her business to get in touch with other mothers travelling home with young children as soon as she has the sailing date. Some will be taking their ayahs back to England, and from what I have seen since we arrived here, they are devoted to their young charges. It's a matter of opinion, of course. Captain and Mrs Saunders don't altogether trust native servants, do they?'

Carrie shook her head. 'After what happened you can hardly blame them. Somebody was careless.'

'They need supervision, and their standards are not very high.'

'I can't make any sense out of them. Why don't they learn to speak English?'

'Isn't that just like one of the superior race. I'm ashamed of you, Carrie. These native servants understand far more than you give them credit for. They are not stupid. Anyway, I'm studying Hindustani. I haven't enough to do here, and my mind would soon get rusty in this climate.' She was thinking of the schoolmaster, and a son who would be a Grammar School pupil when they met again. Five years was an eternity, but it need not be wasted. She smiled at the girl, determined not to spoil her happiness. 'I've been thinking, Carrie, you will have a lot of fun at Russets this Summer. That's just the sort of place for Jimmy to grow strong again, and your cousin Albert is going to be so delighted to have his sweetheart back so soon!' she teased.

'Yes.'

Carrie was not at all sure how she would feel about meeting Bertie after receiving such affectionate letters.

'I must ask Mum to let him know we shall soon be on the way back. The Captain said I could send a cable.'

'You're glad to be going home, aren't you, dear?' Carrie nodded tremulously. 'I never did feel that Army life was right for you. Go back to the village. That's where you belong.'

'But so do you.'

'I know. But it's too late for me, Carrie. I married Dick, and had to choose between my husband and my son. Please God you will never be called upon to make the same choice. Mrs Saunders has all my sympathy, not the Captain. The men have the best of both worlds, but they don't often acknowledge it.'

Her eyes were smarting with tears. This girl was too young to realise the half of what a woman had to suffer for the sake of a man. 'Whither thou goest I will go' was probably more applicable to Army wives than any others. Yet they would have these long, anxious periods of waiting for news when the battalion marched North to defend the frontiers. It could happen at any time. The regiment had not travelled thousands of miles to beat the bloody dust from the parade ground at Peshawar – as Sergeant Martin had reminded them!

'Carrie play with Jimmy,' a peevish little voice interrupted.

'Did you hear that, Teacher? Jimmy said a *whole sentence*!' Carrie exclaimed excitedly. She gave him a hug, and scooped him into her starched apron.

411

Chapter Fifteen

When the working-class parishioners spoke of 'Parson's wife' in the village, they were still referring to Eleanor Wellington, not the new mistress at The Parsonage who lacked the personality and influence of her predecessor and was too much under the thumb of her self-important husband. They were not very popular with the upper class either, and church attendance had noticeably declined in the past few months.

That first Sunday would always be remembered by observant members of the congregation, and few could hide their smiles of pleasure and satisfaction in the incident. 'Parson's Wife', bowing and smiling to all the familiar faces, marched down the side aisle, holding her young grandson by the hand. He was home for the holidays, and home was now a cottage on the Big Estate and great fun, because of Charles and a pony called Snowball. With all the aplomb of one accustomed to take charge of every situation, 'Parson's Wife' took possession of the Parsonage Pew, sat down, and arranged the small boy in the Eton suit on a high hassock. There was nothing in her manner to suggest she had handed over the reins or that her status was in any way diminished by the change of circumstances. This pew was sacred to the Wellingtons.

Three little girls had been hushed by their nanny, and later by grim-faced governesses. When they could be trusted to behave in a ladylike fashion, they sat demurely, side by side, and smiled engagingly at their proud Papa. Only Marion forgot the rigid code of All Saints and waved her hand to Papa when he had climbed the steps to the pulpit. Time and again she was threatened with expulsion, but Parson always defended her, for he could see no harm in such a childish gesture. It was Eleanor who objected.

They were still kneeling on their hassocks – the little boy peering anxiously through his fingers, awaiting the signal from a rather formidable grandmother – when a discreet cough announced the arrival of a second parson's wife, determined to claim her rightful place. Nothing happened. Her face flushed with annoyance. She hesitated, caught the nod of approval from the new parson in the doorway of the vestry, and slid, rather clumsily into the corner. There was no room to kneel, and no hassock. After a long tense moment of waiting, her adversary rose from her knees, nodded graciously to the young woman, and bid her grandson pass a hassock. The head choirboy, digging his companion in the ribs, hissed maliciously, 'That'll teach 'er!' – and followed his angelic brood to the choir stalls. 'Parson's Wife' looked straight ahead, but she felt the new parson's displeasure in every tingling nerve, and gloried in the battle of wits about to be fought for possession of that particular pew. The young woman had scrambled hurriedly to her feet, still flushed with annoyance.

'You are being uncharitable, my dear. They are doing their best,' Parson Wellington reminded his spouse from his spiritual abode, never far from his beloved All Saints. She knew he was there, but his gentle ghost would not disturb her. 'Dearly beloved brethren,' intoned the

413

new parson piously. The fond grandmother pointed a finger at the open page of the old prayer book that had once belonged to the boy's mother. She smiled encouragement, but his thoughts were wandering. She had promised him a riding crop if he behaved well in church in the holidays, and he had already discovered she had been much stricter with his mother and her sisters. The nice, old-fashioned housekeeper had told him not to worry, for grandparents always spoilt their grandchildren.

Eleanor Wellington had no need for a prayer book. She knew every word, and her thoughts were also wandering. God moved in a mysterious way, His wonders to perform. The small boy in the Eton suit was living proof of His goodness. Five years was a long time. He would forget his parents and his sisters in far away Congo, and when they met again, they would meet as strangers. This was the penalty her daughter Marion must pay for marrying a missionary. Her duty was plain. She could not keep her sons, even if she kept her daughters. The heartache of a long separation from her first-born had to be endured. He would grow up completely independent of his parents' influence, a product of the upper-class system of formal education. It seemed that little boys were inclined to be lazy, for this beloved child was waiting for the hymn to be found. She shook her head, but she was smiling as she turned the pages. Her strong, resonant voice rose exultantly from The Parsonage Pew.

And the schoolmaster exchanged a meaningful glance with young Philip, who had begged his grandfather to be allowed to attend All Saints instead of Chapel – yet further proof that a grandparent was so much more amenable than a parent!

*   *   *

414

No two young people from the village could have been more surprised to meet in a London tea-shop than Cynthia Franklin and Freddie Simmons. The young solicitor showed no embarrassment, however, for he had acquired an easy informality in dealing with clients of a working-class origin, and saw no reason why a different approach should be necessary with the upper class. So he joined Sir Neville Franklin's daughter over a pot of tea and a plate of buns, and thoroughly enjoyed her company.

They both were living on a shoe-string, so to speak, for a nurse's pay was meagre, and Cynthia had refused to accept a penny from her irate parent. In her neat uniform, she was hardly recognisable as the same girl he last had seen at Russets. She was pale, and she had lost a lot of weight, but her tired eyes shone with such obvious pleasure, he had no hesitation in joining her, shook her gloved hand, and sat down. Did young ladies of the upper class always wear white cotton gloves when drinking afternoon tea?

'This is quite fantastic, Mr Simmons' she exclaimed, with a nervous little giggle. 'It's an unexpected pleasure, Miss Franklin,' he corrected, gravely.

'How do you like your tea? – weak? strong? milk? sugar?' She hadn't forgotten her drawing-room manners.

'Strong, please, with a dash of milk and two lumps of sugar.'

'Do you drink a lot of tea?'

'It's my favourite beverage.'

'Mine, too, but I like it neat. That is to say, without milk or sugar, and with a slice of lemon.' Freddie pulled a face. 'It's delicious. You should try it some time.'

'No thanks. I like it this way. I was brought up on strong tea. I don't quite know how Mother managed it, for the working class were drinking tea – and are *still* drinking

415

tea – brewed from the cheapest brand on the market, that is mostly dust. Perhaps she was entitled to a packet of tea as part of her wages at The Three Nuns. I never enquired. But I do know she brought home all the pies and pasties left over from the previous day, and also the tail end of a joint of meat and a jug of stock for soup and stews. Compared to our neighbours, we fed like fighting cocks. Bless her heart!'

'What did your mother do at The Three Nuns?'

'She was the charwoman.'

'I see.'

'No, you don't. You haven't the vaguest idea.' he contradicted her.

'I seem to remember hearing that once before, Mr Simmons, in very different circumstances,' she reminded him, with icy calm. 'A charwoman does the scrubbing, does she not? And a nursing probationer also scrubs, Mr Simmons. Would you like proof?' She peeled off the white cotton gloves, and turned over her hands on the table. They were chapped and roughened by hard work and scalding hot soda water. The nails were split.

Freddie had the grace to blush. 'I do apologise, Miss Franklin,' he said quietly. 'But why is a trainee nurse expected to scrub floors?'

'Not *floors*, Mr Simmons, but practically everything else you could mention has to be scrubbed.'

'Why must you do it?'

'In the first instance to escape from that ghastly ordeal of the London Season and the marriage market. Now I can't stop. I feel useful for the first time in my life. It's the Hospital for Women, and so far I've not actually done any nursing. We have to attend lectures and pass a preliminary examination before we are allowed on the wards, apart from making beds and the unmentionables!' She blushed, and he realised she was still a very raw

416

recruit to the nursing profession. 'The patients are darlings. I love them all!' she hastened to add. 'But of course there is no time to get to know them personally. We are kept so busy. The Sisters are tyrants. Its "Yes, Sister", "No, Sister", "I'm sorry, Sister", from morn till night!' She giggled again, and helped herself to another bun. 'I'm always hungry. The food is sparse and badly cooked, but the patients are fed on the same sort of diet, so why should we complain?' She sighed. 'Do you know what I miss more than anything?'

'What?'

'Freedom to walk out of the door, without asking for permission. I've been spoiled, of course, haven't I?'

'You can't be blamed for that. When we are young, we accept the environment in which we were born and bred. I was born in Richmond Row. You were born at Marston Park. According to our parents, the gulf that divides us is too wide to bridge. How do you feel about that?'

'We have bridged it to-day simply by sitting here and sharing a pot of tea and a plate of buns, haven't we, *Freddie!*'

'I see what you mean, *Cynthia,*' he chuckled. 'But it takes courage for a girl in your class of society.'

'Why? I should have thought it was even more difficult to break away from an environment like Richmond Row.'

'Not if you believe so passionately that all men are equal in the eyes of God.'

'So you do believe there is a God who rules our destinies?'

'*Profoundly.*'

Her mouth trembled on a wry smile. 'Up to six months ago, I had always believed it was Papa!'

Freddie shouted with laughter. A middle-aged

spinster at an adjoining table sniffed disapprovingly. 'Lovers,' she whispered to her companion. 'You can always tell.'

'Yet you had the audacity to defy your father?'

'Only because I had the support of Cecily. She encouraged me.'

'Cecily?'

'Cecily Wellington.'

'Parson's daughter?'

She nodded. 'But how does she come into it? I mean, I didn't know Miss Cecily hob-nobbed with the aristocracy?'

'Cecily hob-nobs with anyone. The Wellingtons are well-bred, every bit as good as the Franklins. I do admire the way Cecily's mother has adjusted to a cottage on the estate after being mistress of The Parsonage for years. That's where I met Cecily and we talked about nursing. She told me she was only waiting to see her mother settled in the cottage with her new housekeeper, and her little dog, then she had made up her mind to offer her services for training at this particular hospital. She is such a deliberate person and so forceful. I discovered I was as eager as she to get started. It was so refreshing to find someone like Cecily to take the initiative. We have always been so protected and so cosseted at Marson Park. I suppose if you have a mother like Eleanor Wellington some of her forceful personality must rub off on you?'

He smiled disarmingly. She still thought he was the nicest person she had ever met.

'Miss Cecily *is* forceful, isn't she? But one can't help liking her. I love the way she drives around in that trap, all loaded up with cans of soup and baskets of delicacies for the sick and the aged. Nothing stops her. I've seen her battling along in the wind and the rain, hanging on to

418

the reins with one hand and Parson's umbrella with the other!'

'Have you really? How terrifically funny!'

'Not any more, of course. I hear the new parson's wife has taken over all her obligations in the village.'

'Yes, that was actually the main reason why she decided to train as a nurse in a London hospital. To get away from the village. We are not in the same stage of training, of course. Cecily would be about ten years my senior, and has attended classes for first aid and home-nursing, so we don't see a lot of each other, but I do have to thank her for the introduction. I should never have had the courage to ask for an interview with Matron on my own initiative. Matron is a very formidable person. We pro's are absolutely terrified of meeting her. I am not expecting to pass my preliminary. You see, I am not at all clever, and we have not been encouraged to study, not since Cecily's sister Marion was our governess. Several of the girls have been to boarding school, and they seem to have the ability to concentrate. It's all rather difficult.'

'Don't look so worried. I am quite sure you will pass. Surely a sense of dedication counts for something?'

She shook her head. 'Nobody has yet enquired whether I have that sense. The importance of a useful pair of hands and the strict observance of all the rules and regulations is constantly emphasised. With Cecily so far removed, I do get a little discouraged.' She sighed and glanced at the cheap watch pinned to her print dress. 'I must fly! It's a crime to be late. You will excuse me?'

'Certainly.' He stood up and their eyes met across the table with something more than the pleasure of a chance meeting.

'Do you come here often?' she asked, breathlessly.

'Almost every day, about this time. I'll look out for you.'

'But I can't promise any particular day.'

'I shall be here.'

'And you don't think I have been very stupid?'

'I think you have been very brave.'

'Thank you.'

He took her hand very gently, frowning at the penalty she had to pay for her escape from Marston Park. 'If it's encouragement you need, you will find it here,' he told her, with that disarming smile.

'You are very kind.'

'*Au revoir*, Cynthia.'

'*Au revoir*, Freddie.' She walked away, but she did not look back, so he sat down to finish the last bun and discovered he was trembling.

On the way back to his furnished rooms, he purchased a tin of ointment from the chemist, and slipped it into his trouser pocket. He would touch it whenever he pulled out a handful of coins, and remember those poor hands. His feelings were confused, and he was a little afraid of getting involved. The only girl who had ever threatened his determination to remain a bachelor was Aunt Lucy's Emma, a little waif with gypsy blood, and a come-hither look in her black eyes. He blushed at the memory. This was something completely different. He felt protective, yet it still held an element of danger, and the example of his two married brothers, Albert and Jack, had made him wary. For years they had been struggling against the tide of poverty and depression, yet still begetting children. Both men had aged and lost their youth in the grim stuggle for survival. Freddie had no illusions. He was also a product of Richmond Row. But he did have the sense to stay single!

The next three days saw Freddie Simmons hurrying in the direction of the tea-shop, a little before 4 o'clock. He would confiscate a small table, place his hat carefully on a

420

vacant chair, and sit down. By ordering a cup of tea, he was entitled to sit there for as long as he pleased, but he was a busy man with appointments in the evening, after working hours, to suit his clients, so he had to keep an eye on the clock. He opened a small book of verse that he carried in his pocket rather self-consciously, because he did not wish to be thought effeminate. In his younger days, he had struggled over the difficult task of putting his thoughts and aspirations into verse, but was surprised and disappointed to discover creative writing had to be dragged out of his systematic mind. Unconsciously searching for the appropriate words to explain his own feelings in this unexpected encounter with Cynthia Franklin, he found himself glancing repeatedly at the swing doors. For the whole of the half-hour he had permitted himself to wait, customers came and went out, but the young nurse was not among them. For three successive days he pushed a penny tip under the saucer, picked up his hat, and walked out, reminding himself that she had not promised, and that she did not enjoy his own freedom to come and go as she pleased.

He had found London a fascinating place, and often walked miles on Sunday in the empty streets of the City to get the feel of an earlier century in Fleet Street and Lombard Street, the narrow alleyways and the old taverns and coffee houses, all claiming to be the favourite *rendezvous* of the celebrated Doctor Samuel Johnson, Inigo Jones or Charles Dickens. To feel so unreasonably disappointed because of a girl he had met for a brief half-hour, apart from that afternoon in Aunt Lucy's parlour, was quite ridiculous, he told himself as he walked back to his furnished rooms with hunched shoulders and a scowl on his lean, ascetic face.

''Ere, watch out where you're putting your big feet,' an irate voice demanded as he passed a cheap-jack stall in the crowded street market. Lifting his head to apologise, he stared at a familiar face.

'Lennie O'Brien!'

'Well, if it's not old Freddie!'

The two young men , whose early life had been limited to Richmond Row, greeted each other like brothers, and, in a sense, they *were* brothers, both deserving commendation for achieving a boyhood ambition. They were laughing as they gripped hands, then Lennie bent down to rescue a set of carvers – guaranteed finest Sheffield steel – that Freddie had missed by inches. They studied each other with renewed interest, the young solicitor, in his shiny conventional dark suit and bowler hat, and the street trader, in his check shirt, corduroys, knotted scarf and cap. The urchin grin had not changed since the days he had collected half-pennies from the little girls who did not care to have his grubby hands exploring under their drawers. Lennie O'Brien was born cunning and quick-witted. He would never starve. It had taken Freddie Simmons ten years of laborious, concentrated study to reach the goal he had set himself when he left the village school. It had taken Lennie O'Brien a matter of weeks after his initial apprenticeship in the market, to rent a stall and buy up the entire stock of the previous owner at a fixed price, to be paid off in monthly instalments. Unfortunately, the poor devil would never live long enought to collect the half of it. Freddie and Lennie had things in common, however. They both were products of the independent working class, and they both were living on a shoe-string.

Lennie's sharp eyes were darting about the crowded street. He could usually spot a potential customer, and his hapless victim would be sold some useless article before she had realised she had opened her purse. Freddie stood back to watch with fascinated amusement while two

422

well-dressed matrons with broad, mid-American accents were each persuaded to part with several English pounds for a pair of Toby jugs worth no more than a few shillings.

'Gee, Honey, just wait till I show them to Merman! Real, genu-*ine* Elizabethan Toby jugs!' shrilled one satisfied matron as Lennie wrapped their purchases in rather grubby brown paper. He hadn't stopped talking for a second. They had listened enthralled, their double chins quivering with breathless excitement. They had planned a six-month tour of Europe, the two retired couples, as a reward for forty years' hard slogging at their respective employment. (Unfortunately, they had left it too late, and would not get beyond the shores of England, for this was the Summer of 1914.)

'How do you do it, Lennie? It amazes me,' Freddie acknowledged, when the customers were swallowed in the crowd.

Lennie shrugged his thin shoulders. 'It's easy, mate. All you need is the gift of the gab and a bit of Irish blarney!'

'You're incorrigible!'

'If that means what I think it means, you're probably right. Say, Freddie, do me a favour, will you?'

'Gladly.'

'Keep an eye on the stall while I pop across to the caf for a cup of tea. I'll be back in five minutes.'

Freddie shrank from such an appalling responsibility.

'I'll fetch the tea. You stay here,' he said.

'I'll have a pie while you're about it,' Lennie called after him. Since he did not offer to refund the sixpence, Freddie decided not to make a habit of it.

Pushing through the swing doors of the tea-shop on the fourth day, with the dogged persistence that would never admit defeat, Freddie's heart missed a beat. She was there! He snatched off his hat and hurried towards her, all his doubts forgotten in this moment of reunion.

'Good afternoon, Freddie.'

'Good afternoon, Cynthia.'

If their greeting was formal, it belied the happiness in their hearts and the warmth of their welcoming smiles. For Freddie it was a sudden revelation, but for Cynthia it was the culmination of a cherished dream. He took her roughened hand gently and remembered the ointment.

'What's this?' she asked, as he pushed it across the table.

'Ointment for your hands. The chemist said he could recommend it.'

Her eyes flooded with tears. 'But how kind, how very kind,' she stammered.

'It's nothing.'

'Oh, but it *is*. You have no idea what it means to have someone notice.'

'Then you will use it?'

She nodded, tremulously.

The grey-haired waitress who had served Freddie with a cup of tea and found a penny tip under the saucer for the past three days interrupted breezily. 'So there you are, Miss! This young gentleman wasn't 'arf disappointed when you didn't show up.'

Freddie blushed. 'Now you're giving me away.'

'Not out of spite, Sir. I were sorry to see you looking so fed up. I been working 'ere for a good many years, and you can always tell when a young gentleman is disappointed. Now a young lady will manage to 'ide it. Never mind, Sir. All's well that ends well. Is it a pot of tea and a plate of buns to-day, Sir?'

'Yes, please.'

'What a fantastic memory. Fancy remembering us, with all the customers you have served this week.'

424

Cynthia was much impressed.

'It comes with long practice, Miss,' the waitress admitted modestly, and scribbled in the little order book. 'It makes my day to see a couple of young sweet'earts getting to know each other at one of my tables,' she confided to the other grey-haired waitress, nodding in their direction. 'Speaks ever so posh, the young lady. Upper class. Funny, ain't it, Maud? It don't seem to matter 'ow a person is dressed, as soon as she opens 'er mouth you can tell where she belongs. Wonder what she's doing in that uniform? I reckon she's run away from 'ome.'

'Go on with you, Glad. You read too many of them trash novelettes,' Maud retorted, and marched away with her loaded tray.

'Has it been a hard week?' Freddie enquired, sympathetically, as Cynthia poured the tea.

'It hasn't been any easier, but perhaps I am getting used to it. Then, of course, I had met you,' she added, simply, as she handed him the tea.

'Did it mean so much to you then, to meet me again? I thought perhaps it was just seeing a familiar face from the village that was such a pleasant suprise.'

'One particular face from the village,' she corrected quietly. It was her turn to blush, but she had waited so long, and time was short. She could not bear it if she lost him again. 'I love you, Freddie. I have loved you since that day in the Park when I thought Jason had killed you.' Her voice was so low he had to lean forward to catch the full implication of such an extraordinary confession. It was so *un*ladylike, so out of character, or so he assumed. He could see a little pulse beating in her temple, and her candid eyes were ringed by dark shadows. 'Please don't look so startled, darling. I have to tell you exactly what happened that day. Then if I've shocked you, I shall

425

understand if you don't want to see me again. You see, when I had sent my groom to get help at the farm, I had to wait some time because your cousins were busy in the hay-field, some distance from the house. So I held you in my arms till I heard them coming, then I put you down.'

That candid gaze never faltered.

'Go on,' he prompted, gently.

'They carried you away on a hurdle, and I followed. Your aunt was wonderful. She knew exactly what to do. Your cousins laid you on the couch in the parlour, and went back to the hay while she telephoned the doctor. She told me, as though it were the most natural thing in the world, that my father had the telephone installed at Russets as soon as he was informed the baby was a boy. She didn't need to explain to me that he would not have bothered if the baby was a girl. Poor Papa. Four daughters must have been a shattering experience. He adores Charles. We all adore him.'

Freddie sipped the hot tea and waited for further disturbing revelations from his companion with an anxious frown.

'I offered to sit with you for two hours every afternoon, while they finished the hay-making – and I willed you to stay unconscious for three days!'

'Why?' he challenged her.

'Because I wanted to touch you.'

He shivered involuntarily.

'Only your bare chest under your nightshirt,' she assured him. Their low voices held an intimacy for which Freddie had been totally unprepared. The candid confession, for all its potential threat to his independence, was touchingly innocent. Perhaps she was not yet aware that a man's loins had no defence against a woman's temptation. In that hospital for women, she would have no opportunity to get acquainted with the

426

male organs. But surely, as her training advanced, she must be prepared to recognise every part of the human anatomy, male and female? It was a solemn thought. Pampered and protected from birth by the ethics of her class of society, she would have no conception of the shocks that awaited a young trainee. His little sister, Carrie, would be so much more capable of coping with life's problems in her new environment, thousands of miles from home. But he would not spoil her enthusiasm for the work, or take her confession too seriously.

'Is that all you have to confess?' he teased her, gently.

'Isn't it enough? You are not shocked?'

He shook his head. 'I'm flattered. Thank you for telling me,' was all he said.

Swallowing her disappointment, Cynthia smiled bravely, glanced at her watch, and exclaimed, 'I must fly! How quickly the time has passed. Please excuse me.' She was pulling on her gloves, and when he stood up to take her hand, she avoided his intimate glance.

'Thank you for the tea. Goodbye, Freddie.' Her voice was choked with tears.

'Goodbye, Cynthia. You will find me here any afternoon you can get away.'

She nodded mutely. She had her pride. She would not come back. It had been a mistake to open her heart, a foolish impulse. She was shamed by her own candidness. It was not a virtue. What had she expected his reaction would be? He was so controlled, so kind and considerate, but not in the least in love with her. It was pity she had mistaken for love, and now she had frightened him away. He would find another tea-shop, and who could blame him? If only she could confide in Cecily? But she was such a strange woman, and she was a little afraid of her since that afternoon in Regent's Park – the only time they had spent their off-duty hours together since they started their training. To be suddenly petted and caressed intimately had surprised and disgusted her. This was something she had never encountered in her sheltered life. As sisters they had not been demonstrative, and Beatrice was too much like Mama to be considered cuddlesome. So she had pushed Cecily away, and hurried back to the hospital.

Yet Freddie could make every nerve in her body tingle with a sensual pleasure by merely holding her hand. It was so humiliating to discover that pleasure was not mutual. Poor Freddie! She would write and apologise if she had his address. She sighed. She had never felt more alone or more miserable. Then why stay here? Nobody would miss her if she left. In a matter of minutes she could change into civilian clothes, pack her valise, and take a cab to the station. To admit defeat would please Papa. He expected it. Then why did she hesitate? The decision was a difficult one to make.

For the first time in her life she must make up her mind without any help, support or encouragement. The only alternative to a nursing career was the London Season, and the marriage market from which she had fled. She *had* to make up her mind, now, today. She had upset Cecily and frightened Freddie. What next? How could she trust herself to make a friend of a stranger, even one of the young probationers, when two people from her own village had found her so unpredictable? The work was hard, but it was strangely satisfying.

Hurrying back along the crowded pavements, she was caught up in the medley of men and women with a purpose in life, and no time to waste. They were workers from a class of society she had always considered inferior, and only recently recognised as individuals. She liked what she saw of the working class at the hospital. Patients and staff had shamed her with their good humour and

428

sturdy independence. Of course they did not know or care that she was the daughter of Sir Neville Franklin – or did they? Perhaps Cecily had spoken of The Parsonage and Marston Park to her contemporaries. Perhaps her voice and behaviour had betrayed her secret.

It took all her limited courage and determination to report for duty that evening. The future seemed bleak. Sister was in a filthy mood, and the patients fretful with the heat. It was mid Summer, but the windows were closed against the noise of the traffic. The ward was stifling, and stank of disinfectant. There would be cocoa for supper and porridge for breakfast.

'What's the matter, duckie? She been bullying you again?' old Mother Harris whispered when she pushed a bedpan under her scraggy bottom. Here was an old woman dying of cancer and still as chirpy as a cricket, still concerned for her fellow creatures. Suddenly Cynthia saw the funny side of a situation that had seemed sheer drudgery. She smiled, and the smile transformed her young, sensitive face.

'Just a touch of indigestion,' she lied.

'Then 'elp yourself to a peppermint, my duckie. She ain't looking this way,' Mother Harris invited.

The peppermints were sticky, in a paper bag. She took one and managed to conceal her distaste. She would get rid of it in the rubbish bin in the kitchen. Fortunately it was against the rules for nurses to eat or drink anything in the wards, and this rule was strictly enforced.

'You got to remember, duckie, she ain't always been a Sister. Once upon a time she were a young pro, like you,' the old woman reminded her.

Cynthia giggled. 'My imagination doesn't stretch that far, but thank you for reminding me.' She squeezed the old woman's hand and hurried away.

WAR DECLARED! ENGLAND AT WAR WITH GERMANY! LATE
SPECIAL! READ ALL ABOUT IT!

The newsboys were enjoying their hour of notoriety.
Their papers were selling like hot cakes. The whole of
London seemed to halt with shock, then the momentary
silence was broken in a way that was completely foreign to
the majority of British citizens. Strangers stopped to chat
on the pavements, passengers on buses scrambled to buy
copies of the 'Late Special', shop assistants crowded into
the streets, office clerks and typists hung out of windows.
The traffic slowed to a halt to avoid the rush of excited
pedestrians who seemed determined to get themselves
killed.

'What will War mean to *me*?' Every woman was asking
herself anxiously, for she saw no farther than her own
husband, her own sons, her own brothers – her
sweetheart, or her lover. War was a personal calamity not
a national or international suicide. It would have to be
explained in tears and torment that it was a man's
patriotic duty to get involved, but only a few would
understand – and Cynthia Franklin was not among the
few.

She had been too busy to read a newspaper since she
started her training, and the rumours circulating all
Summer had not reached the wards. Her mind was not yet
capable of grasping the awful significance of war with
Germany. That would come later. She was tired to the
point of exhaustion, for she had been on her feet all day.
Yet who could sleep in such a clamour of excitement?
Instinctively she thought of Freddie. She *had* to find him.
And there was only *one* place in the whole of London
where he might possibly still be drinking tea. Her
weariness was forgotten as she hurried towards the
tea-shop. Once again she did not stop to consider whether
such an impulse would be welcomed or rejected. She had

no pride in this crucial moment of history – only a sense of urgency that could not be denied.

Her wide eyes were searching the crowded room as she rushed through the swing doors, and her pale face quivered when they found him. He was waiting! He knew she would come! He was standing, unsmiling, at the table, and he took her roughened hands and held them. She had forgotten the white cotton gloves, she had forgotten everything but the urge to see him. They sat down, one on either side of the narrow table, still holding hands, but they did not speak. Their eyes spoke for them, with an eloquence no voice could imitate. His hands were cold on this hot Summer evening, and he looked like a man who had not slept. Was he always so thin? Had she forgotten that lovely sheen on his dark hair, the generous mouth and determined chin? It seemed that she was seeing him for the first time. She could feel his trembling in her own trembling, his caring in her own caring. They were no longer divided by pride or misunderstanding, by class or incompatibility.

The grey-haired waitress smiled and waited. It would be a shame to interrupt. She knew the tea-shop would soon be a *rendezvous* for men in uniform and their sweethearts. This war in Europe would change all their lives. So she served all her other customers, cleared and wiped the tables, then she asked quietly, 'The usual, Sir?'

The glance they turned on her was so warm and friendly, she felt herself to be of some importance in their young lives on this momentous day 4th August, 1914.

'Yes, *please*!' they chorused, and laughed. It was strange to hear themselves speak after such a long silence. But the spell was not broken. This hour was theirs, to be remembered in the long and lonely years that lay ahead. It could never be taken away, this lovely hour. Surrounded, they would still be lonely for each other;

431

separated by events beyond their control, they both would crave for moments of peace and solitude in which to find the loved one in spirit. But those moments would not coincide. When Cynthia was quiet, Freddie would be fighting, killing, deafened by shell-fire, in a terrifying holocaust. Nobody could foresee the horror of such a cruel war, least of all the young who would rush in their thousands to recruiting stations all over the country in a frenzy of patriotic fervour. Boys of 17 from all classes of society would forget their youth, their dreams and aspirations, in a vision of glorified manhood and heroism. Their elders would argue and condemn and deplore to no avail. They would not listen. The could not wait to get into uniform. The Hun was a universal enemy, to be destroyed as quickly as possible. Only the women wept, but for Cynthia Franklin the time for weeping was postponed till the morrow, Freddie hadn't the heart to tell her he was joining the queue at the nearest Army Recruitment Centre after he had left the tea-shop.

To-day, for the first time, she turned to wave and smile before she disappeared through the swing doors. Freddie sat down, pale, but determined, to wonder why it had to take a war to bring them together in this sweet understanding, only to separate, to go their separate ways? They had no choice. Tomorrow he must tell her. He was not alone in postponing the telling till after he had signed on. Thousands of men from all walks of life would be doing the same. It would be here, in this public place, that he would tell her. It would be here, where they had known this lovely hour of awakening to truth and love that he must shatter her hopes of a lasting relationship. It was cowardly to shirk the private confession in his rooms, or in some secluded corner of the park. In the bustling atmosphere of a busy tea-shop there would be many such anguished partings in the near future. Cynthia would not make a scene. He would be spared any angry protests and the noisy weeping so many men would have to endure. She would not embarrass him. He knew, or he thought he knew what her immediate reaction would be. Those wide eyes would flood with tears, and her mouth would tremble. That cultured voice would plead, quietly, 'Don't go, *please*, darling. I couldn't bear it.'

How could he answer her? How could he be certain of her reaction when they had had so little time to get to know each other? Hadn't she already demonstrated she could act impulsively on more than one occasion? 'I love you, Freddie,' she had told him, with the simple candidness of a child. She was so immature, so vulnerable. Yet she was not a weak character, for she had shown much courage and determination in leaving the environment in which she had known security and social prestige. Was he being too optimistic? he asked himself. Would she accept this cruel separation without some attempt to change his mind? But his mind had been disciplined since early youth. It was not swayed by emotion. He saw everything clearly and objectively, and had already decided, in *theory*, the precise nature of the priorities to be observed after his enlistment. He must notify his clients, write to his parents, close the office and report for duty, in that order. It had seemed so clear-cut, so uncomplicated until an hour ago, when he looked up to see that slim, uniformed figure hurrying towards him, and he knew that nothing was simple or settled. Personal obligations and responsibilities had suddenly invaded his methodical mind, and he was involved in a situation he had neither intended nor desired. What had happened to rock the foundations of his disciplined way of life?

He sighed and helped himself to a bun. He was still hungry. They had forgotten the buns. That nice, motherly waitress had poured the tea today. But he would have to pay for the buns because he had ordered them. It was strange to think that he hadn't to worry about his shiny suit after today, or the shoes that were stuffed with newspaper because the soles were so thin. London pavements had a disastrous effect on footwear, he had discovered.

From tomorrow, he supposed all his clothes and equipment would be provided by the Government. So there would be no need to explain to Cynthia that he had signed on. It would be obvious. He shivered. Dear God! what did it mean, to be a soldier in the ranks? Khaki uniforms were rarely seen in the village, and then only for short periods before a regiment was drafted overseas. He remembered that Christmas Eve when young Joe O'Brien had been caught poaching, and had to serve 30 days' prison sentence because he had no money to pay the fine. It broke his mother's heart when he joined the Army and was posted to India. He never came back to Richmond Row, not her Joe.

Thinking of the O'Briens, he decided to say goodbye to Lennie in the street market. Trade was still brisk, and everyone seemed to be going about their business in the normal way.

'Volunteer? – not bloody likely! They can come and fetch me if they want me!' said Lennie decidedly, wiping his sweating face with a grubby cloth.

The two elderly waitresses had an eye on the door as they served their customers the following evening. They were brisk and cheerful, in an atmosphere of mixed emotions, but they had been fully aware of the young recruit for the past half-hour, and he had refused a cup of tea. In his ill-fitting uniform of khaki serge, he was sweating profusely on this warm Summer evening. They felt very sorry for the young recruit as he waited for the girl.

434

When she stepped out of the swing doors, he sprang to attention and stood there, a stiff, solitary figure.

'Oh my gawd! She's going to faint!' gasped Gladys, clattering the tin tray on the table. But the girl recovered quickly, braced her slim shoulders, and walked purposefully towards that stiff, solitary figure.

'Good evening, Freddie.' There was no warmth in the greeting, and her dark eyes were blazing.

'Good evening, Cynthia.' His hands were gripping the edge of the table, and his confidence was shaken by her frowning disapproval. Now that he had demonstrated his profound belief that a man's first duty in such a crisis was to serve his king and country, he was momentarily incapable of sustaining such an heroic attitude. He felt rather foolish.

She sat down and motioned him to be seated with an imperious gesture. 'How *could* you? It was a cowardly trick to play on me. Did you suppose I would stop you?' she demanded, all the proud arrogance of her class erupting in this crucial moment.

He shook his head, surprised and saddened by that hateful class barrier they had sworn to demolish. Her voice was pitched so low only the customers at the adjoining table caught the gist of the girl's angry tirade, and they thought she was being very foolish, since it could be their last meeting for a long time.

But the two elderly waitresses were not so easily deceived by the girl's attitude. Their observations of human behaviour had the shrewd understanding of long experience.

'She's putting a brave face on it, ain't she, Maud? Reckon she's breaking 'er poor little 'eart underneath all that bluff,' muttered Gladys.

Maud nodded, for once in total agreement with the sentimental Glad. 'It's class what counts, Glad. There

435

won't be no tears, not in public, and she won't raise 'er voice to 'im, but blessed if she ain't ticking 'im orf good and proper, the poor sod. Any minute now she'll up and walk out. You'll see!'

'What did I tell you, Glad? There she goes!' hissed Maud a few minutes later.

Freddie Simmons was no longer a conspicuous young recruit, but surrounded by a noisy, jostling crowd of recruits on Paddington Station. A bulging kit-bag contained the equipment with which he had been issued, and a rifle was flung over his shoulder. He had been swallowed up in the mighty machine set in motion by the politicians of Whitehall, stripped of his individuality as well as his clothes, poked and prodded by an Army doctor who examined his testicles with a careful scrutiny and ignored his flat chest.

'Get a move on! We ain't got all day!' roared the sergeant to a long line of trembling, naked recruits, all wondering what had happened to their independence.

The rifle was just a cumbersome article to carry around, not an instrument of war, to be used for killing the enemy. Freddie Simmons was a man of peace. He valued human life and liberty, and to destroy it would be as foreign to his nature as cruelty to a child or an animal.

It was bedlam here, in this noisy, jostling crowd, far removed from his quiet little office in a back street of Soho. He could see the strained faces of men, peering anxiously at the women clasped in their arms, and young boys, fresh from school, with weeping girls hanging round their necks. He was searching desperately for one particular face in that sea of faces, with little hope of finding it. Even if she had forgiven him, she hadn't his address.

Fresh batches of new recruits were leaving for

436

Salisbury Plain at regular intervals. Trains had been commandeered. Civilian passengers were kept waiting for hours. He had mentioned Salisbury Plain, but Cynthia had been so angry. She was not listening. He let her go. She had no right to lecture him. But now he was wishing he had followed her and apologised. Then she would be here. Somebody had to apologise.

A group of very young officers, fresh from Sandhurst, stood together, self-consciously, at the end of the platform; conspicuous in their smart new uniforms, they watched the sergeants mustering the men with mixed feelings. The hissing engine of the waiting train seemed impatient to be off, and when the shrill blast of a whistle penetrated the ears of the clinging couples, they shivered and broke away. Some of the women were distraught, sobbing now, but all the men, pale and tense, were anxious to get the ordeal over.

'Break it up! Break it up now!' There was no sympathy in the harsh voices of the sergeants, only irritation. The hundreds of raw recruits had little or no conception what the future held, but they recognised authority in the bellowing sergeants, and climbed into the train, crowding the doors and windows. Somebody raised a cheer, and it was echoed from the tight throats of every man and boy packing into the train like sardines in a score of tins. The cheering was intended to boost their morale, and it certainly made an impression on the weeping women and girls, who dabbed at their wet eyes and smiled bravely. Babies were lifted up to be kissed. The group of young officers stepped smartly into their reserved carriage. Mothers and sweethearts had been warned to stay away. They had said their farewells in private, and their presence could only have embarrassed and jeopardised their determination to assume the role for which they had been trained.

The doors were slamming when a girl's voice was heard calling urgently, 'Freddie! Freddie Simmons!' A young nurse was pushing her way through the crowd of women, and they let her pass because she was young and one of them, and had a right to be there.

Freddie had been standing quietly in the background, now he was fighting for a place at the door where the window was pushed down.

'That you she's 'ollering for?' a hefty ex-dustman demanded.

'Yes.'

'Let 'im through, you selfish bastards!' The hefty one shoved and pushed, and suddenly Freddie found himself hanging out of the window, yelling frantically, 'Cynthia! Cynthia! Hurry! For God's sake, hurry!'

'Good old Fred! She's made it, mate!' They shouted and cheered, and slapped him on the back as the two hands met and clung together. The train shuddered and moved slowly on its way.

'I'm sorry, darling!' Cynthia gasped breathlessly. 'Am I forgiven?'

'It was my fault,' Freddie insisted, gallantly.

'It was not your fault. I was absolutely beastly!' She was running now, as all the women and girls who had fought for a place were running, clutching at the hands in a last desperate attempt to prolong the moment of parting.

'I'll write,' he promised.

'I'll write,' echoed the others.

'I'll write.'

'I'll write.'

The iron wheels clattered.

'Goodbye, my darling. I love you!' Cynthia was shouting, for all the world to hear.

'Goodbye,' Freddie was too choked to say more and darling was a foreign word in his vocabulary. He would call her 'My Dearest Girl' in that first letter, and she would search in vain for other endearments, quite unable to grasp the simple fact that a product of the working class had to dig deep for such endearments, and they were not yet available.

There were no tears in those bright, searching eyes when she dropped his hand and stood back to wave. He was very proud of her then, and would tell her so in that first letter. In the sea of faces left behind on the platform, he saw only that one face, pale but resolute, smiling bravely.

When the platform slid away he sighed, and knew a moment of such awful desolation, he could have wept.

'She's a classy bit o' goods, that gal of yours,' said the ex-dustman, approvingly.

And Freddie Simmons was comforted.

439

Chapter Sixteen

Doctor's wife opened her arms in welcome to her little grandson when the young nursemaid stepped on to the platform at Fairfields that warm evening in August. But he clung round Carrie's neck, and hid his face in her shoulder.

'He doesn't remember me, but it's been such a short time since he went away.' She was disappointed and vexed, for she had visualised instant recognition and a warm hug. But this puny little boy, whimpering like a baby, was not the same child, she quickly realised.

'He's been very ill, Ma'am, and he's seen so many new faces in the past few months, he doesn't feel safe, and little children like to feel safe, don't they, Ma'am?' Carrie explained carefully.

Dulcie Saunders sighed. 'Oh well, let us hope he will soon settle down. Did he make any fuss when he said goodbye to his parents at Bombay?'

'No, he didn't, Ma'am, but I don't think he understood what was happening, and only the mistress came to see us off. The Captain had been called away with his battalion to some fresh disturbance on the frontier the week before we left. Mrs Martin came along for company on the long train journey back to Peshawar.'

'Who is Mrs Martin?'

'The wife of one of the sergeants in the Captain's regiment.'

'I am surprised at my daughter-in-law associating with the ranks. What has happened to the strict protocol that has always been practised in the British Army stationed in India?'

'Mrs Martin is a local person, Ma'am, and they were friends at Tidworth.'

'I see.' Carrie's new mistress obviously disapproved of such familiarity, and the girl could foresee a troubled period in this house that must be their home for several years. 'Was my daughter-in-law very distressed?' Doctor's wife was asking.

'Yes, Ma'am. It was a big decision for a mother to make.'

'But a wise one under the circumstances. Doctor fully approves. There is no country like England, and no healthier place than Fairfields, in my opinion. My own three boys were healthy enough. The normal childish ailments, of course, but nothing serious. A pity my son didn't take my advice and leave James here with me, then all this disturbance could have been avoided. Now we have a delicate child on our hands, and he is behaving like a baby.'

Carrie made no answer. She had forgotten the Captain's mother refused to call her grandson Jimmy. They were walking down the platform of the quiet country station, so far removed from the fierce war waging on the other side of the Channel, but soon to be made aware of it as was everyone throughout the country, as men and boys enlisted for service. The porter followed with the luggage on a trolley, and when they were seated in the trap, he stacked it neatly under the seat, received a small tip from the doctor's wife, touched his cap, and trundled away This was his last day as a porter. He had volunteered for the Merchant Navy, and was joining his ship in Liverpool on the morrow. A boyhood dream was coming true, thanks to Kaiser Bill! He was going to see the world, but he would soon discover he had left behind a peaceful backwater for a hazardous voyage that would end in tragedy.

The little boy lifted his head from Carrie's shoulder, surprised at the new kind of transport, but he was too tired and too confused by all the changes to bother to talk. That would come later, when he found himself in a clean, comfortable cot in a new nursery with his beloved Carrie kissing him goodnight. Then he would say, with sleepy approval, 'Nice.' And Carrie would agree. 'Very nice, my pet. You are a very lucky little boy to have such a kind Grandma.'

The old-fashioned elderly maid had carried up supper for two, but Jimmy had pushed his own supper away, fretfully. Carrie had long since decided there was only one sensible thing to do with a tired and grubby child – a quick wash and into bed. But her new mistress would not be satisfied with such a procedure, and would lose no time in establishing her authority in the nursery since she saw no reason to change her original opinion of a young village girl who should never have been engaged in the first place. Yet Carrie had travelled back to England without a chaperone, with a sick child, and with the full approval of the Captain and his wife. They trusted her implicitly now, since she had proved her value in an unforeseen emergency. But they were not here. They were thousands of miles away. It was Carrie's turn to sigh, and she busied herself with unpacking and finding a place for everything. The nursery suite had been cleaned and redecorated; the door of the toy cupboard stood invitingly open, but Jimmy turned his head away. He had

Teddy cuddled in his arms, and the red engine on the cot. It was enough for tonight.

The elderly servants resented the new order and all the extra work entailed. They had been accustomed to a quiet, regulated household for some years, and Cook voiced her displeasure in no uncertain terms when she received back the untouched supper dishes.

'What did I tell you? That chit of a girl 'as been spoiling the child. We are going to get a lot of waste, and I'm the one to answer to Madam. What can you expect from a girl what's growed up in Richmond Row.'

Parsons sniffed disapprovingly. 'Expecting me to carry up the luggage. Blinking cheek!'

'Well, she were carrying Master James,' the simple-minded maid pointed out, reasonably.

'Mind your own business and get on with your work!' snapped Parsons, who had been offered an increase in her wages of a paltry one pound a month for the extra work.

'You will wish to visit your family, Carrie, and your mother will be expecting you, so you may have the day free,' her new mistress decided the following morning.

'But Jimmy – James – ought to get used to you, Ma'am, and everything is strange. I can wait till next week. Mum will understand.'

Dulcie Saunders bristled impatiently. 'My grandson is not likely to get used to me, as you say, while you are here to pamper him, and I am not accustomed to being contradicted.'

'I'm sorry, Ma'am, but he's such a little boy, and he's been so ill, I thought . . .'

'That will do, Carrie.'

'Yes, Ma'am.'

'While we are on the subject of free time, you are entitled to one free half day every week, but it will not

443

always be the same day. It will depend on my own commitments. Is that understood?'

'Yes, Ma'am.'

'Very well. When you have tidied up here and hung out the washing – Parsons will show you which clothes lines to use – you may go. Leave James with me on the way down. The pram has been well polished, but in future, of course, this will be one of your duties.'

Carrie bit her lip and made no answer. She dare not, for fear of saying too much. She had to hold her tongue or be dismissed with a week's notice, and this would break her heart for she loved Jimmy like she would her own child and he loved her and would need her for a very long time. She wondered if her new mistress was being deliberately disagreeable in order to have a good reason to get rid of her and engage one of the posh nannies from London. She was such a snob.

Jimmy had been pushing his red engine around the floor, and had taken no part in the discussion after being reminded by Carrie to say 'Good morning nicely to Grandma'. He had obeyed automatically because it was Carrie who asked, but she knew how contrary he could be since his illness, and she carried him downstairs dreading the moment when she must leave. His screams of rage could be heard all over the house as he fought to be free of his grandmother's restraining arms.

'Go! Get out of his sight!' she panted, and Carrie fled, choked with tears, hating this impatient, autocratic woman who would rule their lives.

As soon as the door had closed on the young nursemaid, Dulcie Saunders smacked her grandson's bottom with a hard hand. She felt him stiffen with shock. He was holding his breath, and she was frightened. Dennis had frightened his young nursemaid at the same age with these naughty tantrums, and she knew how to

444

deal with it. Hurrying upstairs, she turned on the cold tap
and planted him firmly in the bath. The second shock was
too much for a little boy who had been so cosseted.
Gasping and whimpering, he slumped in the ice cold
water and she scooped him on to her lap, snatched off his
clothes, and wrapped him in a warm towel.

'There, there, my darling. It's all over and Grandma is
sorry she had to be cross.' She spoke soothingly and
cuddled him in her arms, but he stared at her, wide-eyed,
distrusting her sudden changes of mood. He would
remember for a very long time. But he would accept the
drastic changes in their way of life as he had accepted all
the other changes, because he had Carrie, and she would
explain, carefully, when she came back, that he was a big
boy now, and mustn't make a fuss or upset Grandma.

The long day passed. He was quiet and docile, and his
grandmother was pleased with his behaviour. After all,
she told herself, she had reared three sons who adored
her. A firm hand, a little spoiling, and a nursemaid who
recognised her authority!

Doctor was a little shy of his small grandson, and was
waiting with his usual patience to make contact. He had
been told about the scene in the morning when he came in
for a late lunch, and the child was having his afternoon
nap in the night nursery. Dulcie was very agitated, but she
was seldom calm these days. The menopause had started
late and not yet finished. Poor Dulcie. She was one of
those unfortunate women who suffered a long period of
discomfort, of hot flushes, and irritability and
unaccountable dislikes. She had taken an instant dislike
to the young nursemaid, probably because she was
jealous of the girl. However, he had listened to the tirade,
then suggested, quietly. 'It could have been convulsions.'

'It was not convulsions. It was sheer naughtiness. I
blame the girl. She has been allowed far too much

445

responsibility. If I had my way, I would give her notice and engage a properly trained nannie, but I suppose that would upset Felicity.'

'I wouldn't advise it, dear, not in his present state of health, and she is so obviously devoted to the child.'

'I have to contend with the servants. You don't seem to realise that I now have to cope with Cook complaining of wasted food, and Parsons sulky because of all the extra work. Now I am informed by this little upstart of a nursemaid that James will not drink milk. Since his illness he will drink only water. Did ever you hear such nonsense? No wonder he is so puny.'

'Did our boys drink milk when they were little?'

'They drank nothing but milk up to the time they went to prep school.'

'Then it's probably a question of patience and persuasion. Even a little bribery would be justified in such a good cause, eh, my dear?' he suggested, with a hint of mischief. He wanted a peaceful household, not a disturbed one, and it was so unlike Dulcie to bother him with domestic matters.

When she got up abruptly and walked out of the room, he thought he had seen tears in her eyes, but couldn't be sure. Neither could he make up his mind whether to follow her and apologise for not treating the matter more seriously. He sighed, pushed back his chair, and went back to the surgery. Then he saw her from the window, taking the dog for a walk. She must have instructed Parsons to keep an eye on James.

'Oh, *Mum!*' Carrie sobbed as her mother's arms closed round her. 'I don't know how I'm going to put up with it, honest I don't.'

'Why, luv, what's happened? I thought you was so 'appy to be back 'ome?'

'Not with HER.'

446

'Doctor's wife?'

'Yes. She started on me right away, Mum, as soon as we got off the train because Jimmy wouldn't go to her, but he didn't seem to remember her, Mum, and he was tired after all the travelling. I couldn't believe it when she said I had to take the day off on our first day back, but she wouldn't listen when I explained that everything was strange, and he was such a little boy, and he's been so ill. She said she was not used to being contradicted. It was awful, Mum. I heard him screaming, but I daren't go back. What shall I do, Mum?' What shall I do?'

'We'll 'ave to talk about it, luv, but it looks as if you'll 'ave to put up with 'er, for you can't just walk out and leave that child, not when 'e needs you and depends on you.'

'I don't want to leave him. I love him, and I promised the mistress I would stay and look after him for the next five years; then he goes to boarding school. But I'm sure his grandmother wants to get rid of me.'

'It's too soon to say, luv. You only got back yesterday. It's a bad start, but I'm sure things will settle down in a day or two.'

'No, they won't. And I'm not going to get any help from the other servants neither, for they've shown their feelings already. It will make extra work with the nurseries on the top floor and they're not young. They don't want their regular routine upset, I suppose. Cook ticked me off this morning when I went through the kitchen to hang out the washing. She said I had to use the side door and go through the conservatory.'

'But you've stayed there for holidays with the Captain and his wife. I thought you got on well with the other servants?'

'So I did, but it's different now they know it's permanent, not just a holiday.'

447

'What does Doctor have to say about it?'

'Nothing. He's either too busy or he won't interfere.'

Ruby untied the nursemaid's bonnet and kissed the wet cheeks. 'Cheer up, luv. It's not like you to be so down 'earted. It's good to 'ave you back. We've missed you, Dad and me, and your Dad 'asn't been too well lately.'

'What's wrong?'

'Always tired, and sort of breathless. Mind you, 'e don't complain, but I get worried.'

'Now I'm worrying you. I'm sorry, Mum.' Carrie's arms were warm about Ruby's neck. Her little girl had grown up in the past few months. A daughter was a great comfort.

'I'll put the kettle on. You'll be glad of a cup of tea,' she said. 'I've got the day off, too. I told Miss Victoria my daughter was coming 'ome from foreign parts and I 'ad to be 'ere to welcome 'er. She wasn't too pleased. They're a fussy pair of old maids, them two sisters. I shouldn't be sorry to give up that job, but we need the money. Beggars can't be choosers. I did wonder if you would bring the little boy with you?'

'I shan't be bringing him home, Mum. His grandmother doesn't wish him to associate with the common folk in Richmond Row.'

'Did she say that?'

'Not in so many words, but her meaning was plain enough.'

'It don't surprise me, Carrie. Doctor's wife 'as always been a snob, and always will be. Don't let it bother you. Life's too short, and I know somebody what's going to be pleased to see you.'

'Who?'

'Your cousin.'

'Bertie?'

448

'Yes. I think you should see 'im this evening, luv, for 'e may not be 'ere next week.'

'Where's he going?'

'Volunteered for the Merchant Navy.'

'Bertie in the *Navy*? But he's a farmer!'

'That's what your Aunt Lucy says, but he's made up his mind. Harry and Tom will have to manage without him. And that's not all the news, my luv. Freddie 'as already enlisted. We 'ad a card from Salisbury Plain. It's an Army training camp. Can't imagine our Freddie in the Army.'

'Neither can I.'

'And Jack says 'e's only waiting to get 'op-picking over and the shop back to normal, and 'e's joining up.'

'What's happened to everyone? Have they all gone mad?'

'Seems like it, but it's not only working class. The upper class 'as gone mad, so they say. Young boys enlisting straight from college and public schools, and some not even 17. Their poor mothers. It's a shame. Your Aunt Lucy's thankful that Charles is too young to get mixed up in the war. If anything 'appened to that boy, she would break 'er 'eart.'

'Is Charles away with the Franklin family as usual at this time of year?'

'No. Sir Neville was expecting war to be declared. 'e said if they went to France they might not get back. Charles is 'elping on the farm for the Summer 'oliday, and that don't please 'is lordship.'

'Good for Charles. I'm glad somebody stands up to him.'

'There's going to be a fine old bust up one of these days. It wouldn't surprise me if Charles defied 'is father when 'e comes of age, and went back to Russets for good. 'e loves 'is mother, and 'e's got a will of 'is own.'

449

'How about Albert, our Albert? Don't tell me he has enlisted?'

'No, that wife of 'is 'as the last word on everything, and she threatens to leave 'im if 'e joins up. Our Albert is proper 'en-pecked.'

'Well, somebody has to stay at home to grow the crops and feed the cattle. That makes sense.'

'That's what all the farmers are saying.'

'Has hop-picking started?'

'Next week. It would take more than a war to stop the 'opping!' Ruby chuckled.

'Elsie will be taking her tribe of children to Monks Farm as usual, then? What does she think about Jack enlisting?'

'She doesn't know. Jack tells 'is Mum what's on 'is mind, but don't always tell 'is wife.'

'It's like that, is it?'

'Yes, it's like that.'

They were drinking their tea at the kitchen table. The back door was open, but the 'fresh air' was polluted by the unpleasant odours of the neighbours' privies and rubbish heaps. Nothing had changed in Richmond Row.

By the late morning, Carrie was feeling more like her old self, for she had her mother's happy nature and optimistic outlook on life, an attitude that would serve her well in the troubled years ahead. While Ruby prepared the dinner, she went to call on her brother Jack at the grocery, and was pleased to be recognised by so many people as she walked down the High Street, till she reminded herself it was only a few months she had been away, though it seemed like years, so much had happened. The baker's boy whistled shrilly as she went past the shop, but she tossed her head. He was much too young and uncouth to be worthy of the notice of a much-travelled young woman. Glancing at The Three

450

Nuns, she remembered the time when she was rushed down the alley at 7 o'clock for Mum to start on the scrubbing. It was hard work, but Mum was always cheerful. Mum was a charwoman, and she, Carrie, had accepted the fact without question as little children always accept their environment and their parents. To follow Mum around with her bucket of hot soda water and scrubbing brush, nursing her ragdoll, to kneel on the floor cutting out pictures from old magazines with a blunt pair of scissors, to suck sticky peppermints and to be petted by the customers, this was a way of life completely natural and satisfying until she was 4, when she suddenly felt the need for something more. Standing on the seat in the saloon bar, watching the children running past to school, she knew it was school that she wanted. Poor Mum! She gave her no peace till Freddie offered to see the Infants' teacher.

That was a start of a new way of life. She was a big girl, completely absorbed in the mysteries of 'reading, writing, and 'rithmetic', sand trays and slates. Teacher was the most important person in her new world. Teacher? She signed, remembering the sadness of parting as the ship moved slowly away from the dock at Bombay. Next to Mum and Jimmy, Teacher was still the most important person in her life. They would always be friends, for they had shared so many new experiences, some happy, some sad, and she had promised to see a lot of Philip, and to write long letters with all the news of the village. Five years seemed an eternity to wait to see her beloved Teacher again.

'Mornin' Carrie' 'Mornin' Carrie.' Two postmen were greeting her now as they pushed their bikes up the High Street on their way back to the post office, after the early morning delivery. She smiled and waved. In her neat nursemaid's uniform, she walked with a proud little swagger, very much aware of all the admiring glances.

Jack came out from behind the counter to give her a hug. She could smell cheese on his white apron. It would seem strange not to see Jack in the grocery, and stranger still to see him in khaki uniform. She enquired after Elsie and the children, and promised to call on her next free half day.

'You'll have a good long walk, for they'll be down at Monks Farm, picking hops,' he reminded her.

'Then I'll wait till they get back. Elsie might expect me to help with the picking, and I'm a bit fussy about my hands. It's such a horrible stain.'

'You always were a fussy little beggar, and not only hands!' he teased her affectionately.

'Mum tells me you're enlisting as soon as they've finished picking, in about six weeks from now?' They had lowered their voices because of the customers.

'That's right, and I'll be away to camp at Sandwich.'

'We are going to miss you, Jack, but I expect you will soon be back behind the counter. Everyone seems to think it will all be over before Christmas.'

'Not everyone. It's a matter of opinion. Some of our older, upper-class customers seem to think it will be a long war. I was discussing it with the churchwardens on Sunday, and they all agree the Huns will want a lot of beating. We had quite a long confab in the porch after the service. I've never known them to be so affable and friendly.'

'I had forgotten you were a sidesman, Jack.'

'Had you? You've travelled a good long way, little sister, since we last met, but I'm glad you're back for Mum's sake. With two of her boys off to the war, and Dad pretty seedy, she'll be glad to have you around.'

'What's the matter with Dad? Is it serious?'

'It could mean an operation, any time. He's seen

452

Doctor, but Mum doesn't know so don't tell her. Time enough to start worrying when Dad has to give up work.'

'But she's worried already, Jack, and it's not fair. Mum has always been the one to shoulder all the burdens and responsibility.'

'I know she has, but Dad won't hear of it.'

'But what's wrong? Did Doctor tell him why he had to have an operation?'

'Yes – cancer.'

'*Cancer?* Oh, *no!*'

'Shush, Carrie. Don't cry. The customers are staring.'

'Sorry.' Carrie rubbed her eyes with the back of her hand and sniffed miserably. 'It's all happening at once – the war, you and Freddie enlisting, now Dad seriously ill. Was it necessary for Doctor to be so blunt?'

'Dad insisted, and Doctor always knows when a patient has the courage to face up to the truth.'

'I suppose you're right.'

'Look, Carrie, I have to serve Mrs King. She's getting impatient. I'll call in home this evening. So long for now.'

'So long,' she echoed, and walked out of the shop, saddened by the thought of a time when Dad would no longer be there and home no longer in Richmond Row. It` was railway property, and only railway gangers had a right to a cottage. What would happen to Mum? Where would she live? Was it too soon to start asking these questions? I shall speak to Doctor when I get back this evening, she decided. I have to know what to expect. I believe he would tell Mum the truth. If he seems to be too blunt with his working-class patients, he knows they can stand up to almost anything. The majority of his upper-class patients had to be handled more gently, and cushioned from shock. But the war would change all that. There would be no class distinction when a telegram was despatched from the War Office or the Admiralty. Just

453

the shattering statement. 'We beg to inform you . . .' Husbands, sons, brothers, sweethearts.

Carrie shivered. It was suddenly a terrible reality. It could be Jack or Freddie or Bertie?

She walked back to Richmond Row deep in thought, and choked with tears.

'Does your Aunt Lucy know you are back?' Ruby asked, as they sat chatting over an early tea.

'Yes, I wrote to her from Port Said to say I was on my way, and I posted a note to Bertie yesterday, telling him I should be seeing him this evening.'

'A nice lad, Albert. The best of the bunch, I reckon, and he's very fond of you, Carrie. I wouldn't be surprised if he wanted to get engaged so as to make sure of you before he went off to the war.'

'I don't want to get engaged. I'm too young to be tied up with an engagement.'

'Me and your Aunt Lucy was married at your age, luv.'

'Yes, I know, but it's different with me. I've promised the Mistress to stay with Jimmy till he goes to boarding school, and even if I was free, I wouldn't get engaged to Bertie. He seems more like a brother.'

'Then you'd better tell 'im straight, luv, for I know for a fact 'e don't think of you as a sister.'

'I know that,' Carrie sighed. 'I keep thinking about my little Jimmy. I can't get him off my mind, not after what happened this morning.'

'T'ain't no use getting worried and fretting over that child, for when all' said and done, you ain't got no authority, Carrie, and you'll just be asking for trouble if you don't pipe down. Take my advice – be polite and don't answer back, for Doctor's wife won't stand for it, not from a girl your age. A week's notice, my girl, and you'll find yourself without a job, so you'd best mind your manners. You've got to remember she's never been the

454

same not since Mister Dennis went away so sudden like. They say she 'ardly goes outside the 'ouse, only to take the dog for a run across the field. She don't 'ave no visitors, and she used to be such a sociable lady once upon a time, but not any more.'

'Did the police ever discover who murdered Betty Mason? Is it still a mystery?'

'Not really. Servants talk, and it do look suspicious, don't it, for Mister Dennis never come back. It's a big load of trouble for a mother to bear, and she so proud of them three boys. Can't 'elp feeling sorry for the poor soul.'

Carrie made no answer, for she had no pity to spare for her new mistress. It was not a happy house, but they had to live there for a very long time. It was a sad, disappointing homecoming, she was thinking, and she started on the long walk to Russets with mixed feelings, remembering the long affectionate letters she had received from Bertie at every post. The quiet country lanes held the stillness of late Summer, and the flowers were fading. No birds sang. She trudged along disconsolately, a brooding heaviness like a weight on her heart. But she hadn't expected to see Bertie leaning on the gate, smiling a welcome, and she was suddenly shy of this young cousin she had known all her life. He was tanned by the sun, and his hair was bleached. He was tall and lean, and very good looking.

'Hullo,' he said.

'Hullo,' she echoed. He was unlatching the gate, but she shook her head. She had always climbed over the gate. Why should it be any different to-day?

'You look very pretty in that bonnet, Carrie. It's the first time I've seen you in uniform,' he said.

'Do I?' She was blushing, and Bertie was her cousin. How silly to feel so embarrassed! She walked towards the gate with a little swagger, pretending a casualness that her

455

thumping heart belied, and stood there, waiting. He took her face in his hands and kissed her. His hands were rough on her cheeks, but the kiss was gentle, and his blue eyes tender with understanding of her shyness. She was so young and vulnerable. Her lips were still the lips of a child, but her body had matured since last they met, and her little pointed breasts filled the tight bodice of the print dress. She had lost a lot of weight, but the new Carrie was very attractive.

'Coming over, then?' he invited. She took his hand and swung her legs over the gate. He kept her hand, and they raced down the long, dusty track towards the farm, laughing merrily. It was so long since she had laughed, so long since she had felt so light-hearted and carefree. The big kitchen was empty and cool.

'Where is everyone?' asked Carrie, breathlessly, snatching off her bonnet.

'In the fields, busy with the harvest.'

'Is Charles here?'

'Not to-day. His father came to collect him, but he'll be back tonight. Sir Neville doesn't get all his own way, not with Charles.' Bertie had taken her bonnet to hang on one of the hooks behind the kitchen door. Now his admiring glance travelled over her curly head and flushed cheeks, while her bright eyes darted about the familiar room.

She sighed enviously. 'You don't realise how lucky you are, Bertie. You just take it all for granted. I've always loved this house, as far back as I can remember.'

'That's not very far, little cousin!' he teased. 'I'll get you a glass of lemonade.' He disappeared into the spacious larder with the stone floor.

He hasn't changed, she thought, but I've changed because I have travelled thousands of miles and had so many new experiences.

He came back with two brimming glasses. The

456

lemonade was ice-cold, with a sharp tang that was more refreshing than sweetness. The shyness still hung between them. It was a tangible thing that prevented the easy familiarity they had always known before.

'Are you hungry?' he asked, solicitously. She nodded. 'There's gingerbread or fruit cake?'

'Gingerbread, please.'

He took a plate from the cupboard and went back to the larder. Then he asked, politely, 'Won't you sit down?' But before she could take a chair, he suddenly cupped her small waist with his hands and sat her on the table. He stood very close to her now, his hands pressed hard on the table to stop their trembling.

'Carrie, sweetheart, I am going away, as soon as we've finished with the harvest. I may not see you again for quite some time. I want you to know I love you very much,' he told her, gently. 'There won't ever be anyone else, only you.'

'Oh, Bertie!' she wailed. 'I feel awful! I'm ever so fond of you, but . . .'

'You don't love me?'

She shook her head.

He grinned boyishly. 'I'll wait. Young ladies have been known to change their minds! Come, eat up your cake and we'll find the rest of the family.'

When she had been kissed and hugged, she sat on the bank to watch the family working as a team in the harvest field. Bertie had joined them, but his eyes strayed frequently to the girl in the grey dress. He did not need a photograph to take away, for Carrie's image would be imprinted on his heart. Being in love with his young cousin had taken his mind off Charles, and he was no longer jealous of the boy who had stolen his mother's affections. She deserved to be happy. When Charles was around, she glowed with pride and joy, for not one of her

457

three fair sons could hold a candle to his dark beauty or his vivid personality. Charles was his father's son, and now the boy had grown to his exact likeness, it was easy to understand the fascination of the man, and his mother's 'fall from grace' only a year after his father's death had to be seen in the light of that fascination. Yet, surprisingly, she hadn't become the squire's mistress. Perhaps another child had satisfied her strong maternity, though she had longed for a daughter to complete the family – a girl like Carrie.

The twin sisters, Lucy and Ruby, would have been very like Carrie at the same age, but circumstances had placed them in such widely different environments. Aunt Ruby was his mother's twin, but she had no envy of her sister who was mistress of Russets. To spend her married life in Richmond Row, and most of it as a charwoman, would have embittered most women, but not Aunt Ruby. Looking at the girl, Bertie knew for certain now that Carrie had inherited not only her mother's looks, but her character.

Walking hand in hand across the field to join the rest of the family, he had asked her about her job, and was surprised to hear of the difficulties she had already encountered at the doctor's house, and her determination to put up with anything rather than forsake the delicate little boy entrusted to her care.

'Jimmy's grandmother wants to get rid of me, but I'm staying,' she told him.

'That's the spirit!' He had squeezed her hand approvingly. Sitting on the bank, watching the family at work, Carrie seemed far removed from that troubled little world to which she must return by 9 o'clock. In the big farm kitchen, when they sat down to supper, the smell of earth and the heat of the sun seemed to linger in the clothes of the family who had worked all day in the harvest field. Lucy's sun bonnet was hanging behind the door with Carrie's bonnet. Her fair skin would scorch exposed to the sun. Emma's dark complexion had weathered sun, wind and rain, and with gypsy blood in her veins, she still had the urge to run wild on moonlit nights. At hay-making and harvest, outdoors all day, Emma was happy. To be confined to the house was the biggest punishment, yet there were so many days in the Winter when the valley was buried under a thick blanket of snow, or swept by torrential rain, when humans and animals alike were kept indoors. Then the barns and sheds would echo to the clang of hammers and axes, and the hum of saws, for the men were never idle. Emma's black eyes still flirted with Harry's, and Tom was still the quiet one, conceding to his quarrelsome elder brother.

But now it was the youngest brother who had taken the initiative. By volunteering to serve in the Merchant Navy for the duration of the war, Bertie had isolated himself from the rest of the family. Not since the death of Bert, on just such an evening in late Summer, had Lucy felt such a rift in their unity.

'Bloody young fool!' Harry had blustered, and Tom had suggested mildly that a farmer's first loyalty was to the land. Lucy had wept and pleaded, but Albert had made up his mind. War talk was banned from the supper table that evening, however.

'I want to hear about Carrie's travels. That's much more interesting,' her aunt insisted, as she carved the joints of home-cured pork and ham. Emma poured the tea. It was Albert who had helped to lay the table, and when he had fetched a fresh pat of butter and a jug of cream from the dairy, he sliced the crusty loaf and poured vinegar over the beetroot. Nothing had changed over the past few months, Carrie was thinking. It had always been the youngest who lent a hand in the kitchen, while Harry and Tom sat waiting to be served.

'I'll walk back with you, Carrie,' he decided after they had finished the apple pie.

'Are you courting?' teased Emma.

'I wish we were, but Carrie has turned me down!' Albert told her.

'Too bad,' Harry shrugged, and Emma refilled his mug with home-brewed cider. He had no taste for blondes, and his little cousin had no sex-appeal, not for him! Emma knew how to attract a man. He would take her tonight, when the rest of the family were abed, and they would lie together under the spreading branches of a beech tree in the wood. In the Winter they made love in the barn. They had no use for beds!

With the contrariness of her sex, Carrie was disappointed when Bertie did no more then peck her cheek when he left her at the side gate of the doctor's house that led directly to the surgery. Having rejected him as a suitor, she still expected to be kissed with a lingering sadness to which she could attach the strings of a broken heart!

'So long, little cousin. I'll write as soon as I get a chance to put pen to paper, but don't expect anything much in the way of news, because all letters will be censored. It may only be a postcard,' he told her, cheerfully. Then he walked away without a backward glance, leaving her feeling miserably neglected.

Doctor had seen the last of his patients, but he was prolonging the time to lock the surgery and the dispensary, reluctant to return to the private part of the house and a wife who was behaving so irrationally. This state of menopause was a baffling affliction for which few doctors could find a remedy. Some women escaped with nothing more serious than hot flushes and erratic menstruation, while others, like Dulcie, seemed to suffer

460

a kind of mental breakdown. He blamed Dennis for his mother's sad condition. Such a terrible shock, combined with months of constant anxiety, could not have come at a worse time than the early stages of the menopause. If only she would confide in him? It was a sad state of affairs when a doctor's own wife was the only one of his patients *not* to confide in him. Now it was too late to restore the happy marital relationship they once had known. The boys had claimed her when they were young, and when they no longer needed her, she was lost and lonely. An occasional telephone call from Roger, a rare letter from Lesley, and nothing from Dennis. No wonder she grieved and longed to put back the clock to the days when she was the central figure in their small world.

He was surprised to see Carrie when he opened the door. 'Good evening, Carrie. What can I do for you?' he asked, kindly.

'Good evening, Doctor. Can I speak to you for a minute? It's about Dad.'

'Sit down,' he invited, and took a seat behind the desk. This was one of those interviews that a doctor dreads but cannot escape. 'What is it you want to know?' he prompted.

'My brother Jack has told me Dad has cancer, and may have to have an operation. Is it very serious, Doctor? I mean, he's not going to die, is he?'

'It *is* serious, Carrie, but with modern surgery and with one of the finest cancer specialists in the country, there is every hope of a full recovery. I am making arrangements to have him admitted to a London hospital.'

'London. But Mum won't be able to see him, will she?'

'There is always at least one visiting period every week, usually on Sunday afternoon, but most hospitals

461

now allow visitors on Wednesday as well as Sunday.'

'How much would it cost, Doctor – the train fare to London?'

'A matter of only a few shillings.'

Carrie shook her head. 'Mum can barely make ends meet now, and she's a good manager.'

'Don't look so worried, child. We will surmount that obstacle when the time comes.'

'Yes, Doctor,' Carrie agreed, with the implicit trust of all his working-class patients.

'Your father will have to give up work, of course. I understand he is a ganger on the railway?'

'Yes, Doctor.'

'About the last job he should be doing with that weak chest.'

'Yes, Doctor.' Carrie still hesitated so he asked kindly, 'Is there something else that's bothering you, child?' He was expecting to be told about the scene with his little grandson this morning, but he was mistaken.

'It's just, well, I do think Mum ought to be told now. It would be a much bigger shock if Dad suddenly told her he had to have an operation in a London hospital.'

'You may be right, Carrie. It was only that your father particularly mentioned it. Yes, she should be told. I will speak to him.'

'Thank you, Doctor.'

'Goodnight, Carrie.'

'Goodnight, Doctor.'

After the door had closed, he sat for some time thinking about this eternal problem of whether or not the patient and the patient's nearest relative should be told the truth in the case of a serious illness that could prove fatal. He had discovered in the years of dedicated practice that he usually knew by instinct and acted accordingly, but no doctor is infallible, and he had been mistaken in this respect. Generally speaking, he found the women less prone to shock and able to cope with emergencies. And Carrie should know whether her mother could cope. Children of the working class always knew because they were closer to their parents, and shared every eventuality. The upper class, in their so-called privileged society, lost contact with their children in the nursery, and were deprived of their company through long years of boarding school and university, at the end of which they were almost strangers – as he was a stranger to his own sons. Dulcie had insisted on supervising her nursery, but thereafter clung to the illusion that the boys still regarded her as the most important person in their lives, long after they had transferred their affections to masters and friends of their own age. Poor Dulcie! It was pathetic when a mother failed to realise the umbilical cord should be severed before a male child has reached the age of puberty.

When the last hop-pickers special had steamed out of the country station, *en route* to Cannon Street, and the last of the gypsy caravans departed for their Winter quarters, the shop-keepers and the publicans breathed a sigh of relief, and set about clearing up their premises, sadly neglected during the busy season. Six weeks was a long time, too long they all agreed, yet it was good for trade and the inconvenience had to be endured.

Jack Simmons had the additional job of training two young girls straight from school, as well as removing all the wire netting barricades and putting everything back in its rightful place. These girls had been recommended by the school master as being his two brightest pupils, but were frowned upon by Grocer, who considered female assistants most unsuitable unless for the job of cashier. However, the War was now demanding drastic changes in every walk of life, in every town and every village throughout the land, for the men were flocking to recruitment centres. Within a few months, only boys under 16 and men over 60 would be left to carry on the work on the home-front.

Jack had quarrelled with his wife, Elsie, who had threatened to put all the children in a Home, and take a job in a munitions factory, where, it was rumoured, high wages could be earned, and transport provided to collect the workers from outlying districts.

'Don't talk so daft, woman!' Jack had exploded, testily, for it was not a question of wanting to leave his family, but a matter of principle and patriotism, and Jack was credited with both.

'And what are we supposed to live on, while you're gallivanting off to France, may I ask, Mr Simmons?' Elsie demanded, with righteous indignation.

'I shall get an allowance for you and the children, though it won't amount to as much as my present wage. I'm sorry about that.'

'*You're* sorry? A fat lot of help that will be when it comes to keeping your children fed and clothed.'

'I'll tell you what I'll do. I'll ask if you can help at our place. Those two girls won't have the time to put up the orders for delivery as well as serve at the counter, and the boss will have his hands full keeping an eye on them.'

'And what am I supposed to do with the kids?'

'You would have to take them with you, but keep them out of the shop.'

'No, I couldn't do that. It just wouldn't work.'

Jack's forehead was creased in a worried frown, and Elsie began to relent.

'I suppose I could help out at The Parsonage. They always seem to be in trouble there, for they can't keep their servants. Daily women always take their youngest children with them unless they can be left with a grandmother.'

'I'm sure Mum would oblige, only she has to keep her own job now Dad has given up work.'

'Your Mum has got enough on her plate without being bothered with our problems. What with your Dad in hospital, and having to leave Richmond Row. Only a month's notice. It's a shame, after all these years to be turned out because your Dad had to give up his job on the railway. We could offer Mum a home with us, couldn't we, Jack, while your Dad's in hospital and you're away? I should be glad of her company.'

'You wouldn't mind, Elsie? Could you make room?' She nodded.

'Thanks,' he said, gratefully. Elsie's bark was worse than her bite, as the saying goes, and it would be one worry less to know that Mum had a roof over her head. The furniture from Richmond Row could be stored in their big shed.

'Well, it's a poor lookout if we can't offer a home to your Mum, temporary like, till your Dad gets back. She's been good to us.'

'I don't think Dad will be coming back.'

'Don't talk that way, Jack. It's not like you to look on the dark side. Haven't you always said while there's life there's hope?'

'That's true, and Dad won't give up, not till he's drawing his last breath.'

'What makes you think he's not going to get over it?'

'I spoke to Doctor yesterday. He said it was just a question of time. It could be a few months or just a few weeks.'

'Why didn't you tell me last night?'

'I was too worried about us, about you and me and the children. You do understand, Elsie? I've got to go. It's my duty.'

465

'I know. I'm sorry I was so ratty. I'll manage. Don't fret yourself.' She pecked his cheek. They were not a demonstrative couple, and both would have been embarrassed by any emotional display of their affection. Actually, this enforced parting would prove to be a turning point in their relationship, for it had been rather strained for some time. Perhaps they had seen too much of each other, for Jack was a man who came straight home from work, and never called in at The Three Nuns for a drink, or had any hobbies beside the garden and the carpentry. He was a good husband and father, and if he sometimes wished Elsie had been satisfied with a small family, he was proud of his children. The time would pass. He would soon be back, and they would settle down again to the old routine, he told himself, confidently.

So Elsie went off to The Parsonage and offered her services as a daily house-parlourmaid, for this was the work for which she had been trained. Since the present servant had already given notice, in order to join the ranks of factory workers, Elsie was well received and no objections were raised about bringing the children. Dinner would be provided, together with a cup of tea morning and afternoon. No Sunday work, and she would be finished by 4 o'clock. Twelve and sixpence a week was a fair wage, and Elsie was pleased to get it settled.

In the cottage in Richmond Row, Ruby spent her evenings turning out drawers and cupboards in preparation to move out at the end of the month. It was lonely, and she missed her man intolerably, for they had never been separated for a single night since their marriage. Doctor was providing the money for the weekly train journey to London every Sunday.

'This is just between ourselves, Carrie,' he insisted, as he handed it over in an envelope every Saturday when he made his regular visit to the nursery before evening

466

surgery, to play with his little grandson. Granpa had become a firm favourite. It was a happy relationship between the two, and heart-warming to a man who had seen so little of his own sons in their early years.

'Mother!' gasped young Philip Martin, his eyes wide with shock and surprise. He was just home from school, and had the puppy on a leash for its afternoon walk before tea. He had got as far as the gate when the station cab drew alongside and his mother stepped out. His face had blanched, and he stood there, staring, as though he had seen a ghost, till she spoke his name, then he flew into her arms. She was hugging him passionately while the driver was dragging out two tin boxes and a bulging portmanteau.

'Anybody about, Missus, to 'elp with this 'ere lot?' he demanded truculently, for he was an elderly man and it was not his job to drive the cab. He was porter and odd-job man at the Station Hotel, and the proprietor's son, who usually drove the cab, had already enlisted.

Martha disengaged herself to say quietly, 'Philip, dear, will you ask Bob and Alf if they will please come and carry the luggage into the house – and don't forget the please!'

He snatched up the puppy and ran off, shouting across the yard, 'Mother's back! Mother's back!' The wheelwright, the two workmen and the apprentice all busy in the workshop, dropped their tools and came to meet him. 'She's back, Grandad! Mother's back!' The boy's voice was choked with tears. He was laughing and crying. They had never seen him in such a state, for he was normally a quiet, controlled child. But it was all too much to grasp in the space of a few minutes. His mother had said goodbye only a few months ago. She had sailed away to India with his father and the regiment for *five years*. Now she was actually standing on the pavement; he had seen

467

her. It was like a miracle. If he had Aladdin's lamp and been allowed only one wish, he would have asked for her return, but it happened without the lamp. He had been taken to see the pantomime last Christmas, and was entranced by the magic, for he was just the right age to be impressed by such a performance.

Now his Grandad was hurrying across the yard, followed by the two men and the apprentice. 'Why, Martha, my lass. What are you doing here? What's happened and where's Dick?' he asked her, and she answered him quietly and unemotionally.

'Dick is dead.'

'How? When?'

'He was killed in an ambush on the frontier. He was in charge of a small contingent from the company, sent out to reconnoitre. Only one survived.' She was so calm, they stared at her in amazement, but she had shed all her tears on the long journey home, and now she felt nothing but a sense of relief. 'So I've come back, Father. Do you mind?' She kissed his cheek and he patted her shoulder in gruff sympathy.

'Mind? Where else would you go, lass? This is your home, and you're more than welcome. I can't say more than that.'

'Thank you, Father.'

She greeted the men and the lad, who touched their forelocks respectfully to the master's daughter, and waited to be instructed.

'Take it upstairs. Put it in the front bedroom,' he barked.

The men took up one of the trunks and the lad staggered away with the portmanteau.

'What does my daughter owe you?' he asked the driver, taking out a little leather bag. Since he saw no reason to add a tip, he counted out the exact fare and put the bag away. So he got no more than a grunt from the old chap who climbed into the cab and slammed the door.

Philip was standing quietly in the shelter of his mother's arm. He was turning over the extraordinary information she had just disclosed in his young mind. The hateful father was dead. He was never coming back. He sighed and cuddled up closer to the one he loved best in all the world. There was understanding in the fleeting smile that passed between them, and mother and son followed the men across the yard and into the house, hardly daring to believe they were together again.

The elderly housekeeper was grudging in her welcome, however, for she could see an end to her reign as mistress. To have the master's daughter back, giving her orders and fussing over the dust, shaking the mats, and changing the bed linen, as women do, was not the sort of prospect she had anticipated when Martha went away. But she need not have worried, for Martha had no intention of interfering, only to offer her services tactfully, so when she had been upstairs, washed her hands, and tidied her hair, she asked the old woman whether she could lay the table for tea.

'Aye, I don't mind,' came the grudging answer, and mother and son once again exchanged that fleeting smile of complete understanding. Then Philip was sent off for a short walk with the puppy.

'Can I go as far as the School House and tell Mr Robinson you're back?' he asked, eagerly.

'If you like,' his mother agreed. She watched him running back across the yard. Even in the few short months they had been parted, he had grown. She could hear the men hammering in the workshop and the lad whistling shrilly as he passed the open window. It was good to be back.

Philip was sent to the doctor's house after tea with a

469

note for Carrie, and she too was shocked and surprised by the extraordinary sequence of events that had brought her friend back to the village so soon after her own return with Jimmy. It appeared she had reached Bombay just in time to board the first passenger ship to travel in convoy from Port Said because of the danger of enemy submarines. It was strange to return to a country at war, and she wondered about her own involvement and how she could earn a living once again, for herself and her son.

There was no question of taking up her old post at the school, for it would not be fair to disrupt the Infants with yet another change, and the present teacher was quite satisfactory, according to Andrew.

As she unpacked the trunks and put everything away, Philip sat on the bed watching her, remembering the time he had slept with his mother before that horrid man came back and banished him to the tiny bedroom. It was past his bedtime but he had begged to stay up to see everything unpacked, for then he would feel quite sure that his mother was here to stay and would not be going away again. It was the most surprising and the most wonderful event in his short life. Mr Robinson thought so too.

'That's wonderful news, Philip,' he said, his grave face flushed with pleasure.

'I expect Mother will be coming to call on you, Sir,' he told the schoolmaster. But the days passed and she did not come. He was disappointed and restless, for it was only a short distance. Was she waiting for a formal invitation? They had parted such good friends, and he had assumed she would be anxious to hear how Philip was progressing with his studies.

By the end of the week he could wait no longer, and he decided to call at the wheelwright's. It was Saturday afternoon, and the place seemed deserted, for work finished at midday. Then he heard the voices and laughter

470

of women and children from the back of the house and went to investigate. Philip was pushing a little boy on a swing under the apple tree. Martha and the young nursemaid were struggling, helpless with laughter, to dislodge a root of yellow flowers. Apparently it was a kind of weed, for it was growing in some profusion in the badly neglected garden. He stood watching, but felt he was an intruder, suddenly self-conscious and reluctant to interrupt such a happy occasion. Martha was digging at the roots with a spade, and the girl tugging manfully at a mass of foliage. Her nursemaid's bonnet was hung on a branch of the apple tree, and they both had rolled up their sleeves. Walking slowly across the patch of rough grass that had once been a lawn, Robinson coughed and Martha looked up. She would know that nervous little cough anywhere. Caught unawares, a hot blush swept over her neck and face. She could no more control the blush than Andrew could control the cough. It was shyness that had kept her away all the week. In a sense he was still her superior, and she regarded him with the deepest respect. It was Philip who saved the situation, as children do.

'It's Mr Robinson!' he called out eagerly, and ran to meet him, dragging the small boy. Now it was easy and natural to greet the mother. She was pulling off her gardening gloves and he removed his hat. They shook hands and Martha was smiling tremulously.

'How are you, Martha?' he asked, and she answered, as a child might have answered when addressed by the schoolmaster.

'Quite well, thank you Sir.'

He understood her shyness and reluctance to appear familiar in front of the girl and the children. He must be patient and wait till they were alone together, then he would kiss her. So he turned to the girl who was pert and

471

pretty, and had no shyness of her superiors. She was still giggling.

'You would never believe that roots could burrow so deep in the soil, would you?' she asked, with simple directness.

He shrugged. 'Why do they have to come out? Is it a weed?'

'Not exactly, but it grows like a weed and it smothers all the rest.'

'What is it called?'

'Golden rod.'

'I've never heard of it, but then I'm not a gardener. I would recognise a rose, or a carnation, or a violet because those were flowers I bought for my mother at the florists.'

'Yes.'

'But you don't need to be a gardener to tackle such a job. I could help if you would find me a tool of some kind?'

Carrie shook her head. 'You would mess up that nice clean jacket.'

'It will wash. It's linen. Anyway, I will take it off.' He did so, and stood there, feeling rather naked in his shirtsleeves.

'There's a fork in the shed. I'll fetch it, Sir,' Philip volunteered, eager to see the schoolmaster in such an unusual role.

'Thank you, Philip. Wait! Take my jacket. Perhaps there's a peg handy?'

Philip frowned. 'Where shall I put it, Mother?'

'I'll take it into the house,' she said, and hung it over her arm. She followed him down the garden. The jacket was warm on her bare arm from the heat of his body, and it smelled faintly of tobacco. Since when had Andrew been smoking? She draped the jacket over a chair in the parlour and stood there, smoothing the collar with a hand that trembled. She must not allow herself the pleasure of

472

Andrew's company, for it would start the tongues wagging. She was Dick's widow, and she must conduct herself accordingly. She sighed, remembering they had parted in anger the morning he went away because she was humiliated by the way he took her, in the kitchen, bending over the table. He was fully dressed, sweating and brutal.

'Go away! You take me like a dog with a bitch!' She wept. And he went away, for ever. She was shivering with the memory. It would be a long time before another man could touch her. Her husband had made the act of intercourse a dirty and degrading experience.

When she went back to the garden, she found Andrew already digging furiously with the tool that Philip had brought from the shed, and already sweating. Unused to manual work of any kind, he quickly tired, and was breathing heavily, yet he had to make a good show with such an observant audience. Philip was standing there, watching, holding the small boy by the hand.

'I'se Jimmy Saunders. I been sick. I'se better,' the child had informed the schoolmaster. And Carrie had exclaimed proudly, 'Clever boy! Would you believe he was hardly saying a word a few weeks ago?'

They all smiled indulgently, and he felt very important. He couldn't bear to be ignored. 'Swing me!' he commanded Philip.

'Please,' Carrie prompted, automatically, but he closed his mouth.

'Come on then,' said the boy, and they went back to the swing.

Martha took up the spade and began to dig at another root, so Carrie joined her, leaving Robinson to work on alone.

'We shall have to go soon,' the girl was saying.

'I wish you could stay to tea,' Martha answered.

473

'So do I, but Mrs Saunders doesn't know we are here. She would have a fit. She thinks we are taking a walk. I'm not supposed to do any visiting, only on my free half day.'

'Won't Jimmy tell her now he's talking?'

'I don't know, but I'm going to risk it, for I want to see you. It's so wonderful to have you back.'

'It's wonderful to be back.'

'Shall you teach the Infants again?'

'No.'

'What then?'

'I don't yet know, but it shouldn't be too difficult to find a job with so many men away enlisting.'

'Would you serve in a shop?'

'Anything to earn an honest penny!'

'They need an assistant at the bakery. There's a notice on the window.'

'Then I'll walk along after tea and offer my services.'

Robinson leaned on his fork, wiping his sweating face with a clean white handkerchief, and regarded the uprooted plant with much satisfaction.

'You've done it!' Carrie exclaimed excitedly.

'I think you have done enough. It's hard work,' said Martha, quietly, for she couldn't bear to see him working and sweating like a navvy. 'And it's time for tea. You will stay to tea, Mr Robinson?'

'Thank you.' He had hoped to be invited. There would be no embarrassment with the boy as go-between, and when the wheelwright came home, he would be airing his views on the conduct of the War. It was the main topic of conversation in the village these days.

So they wandered back to the house, put the tools away, and washed their hands at the kitchen sink. Then Carrie tied on her bonnet, straightened her face, bade Jimmy kiss Martha goodbye, and went away reluctantly, back to that troubled house in the High Street.

474

The elderly housekeeper was spending her free half-day at the School House. The two housekeepers had become very friendly in the past few months, and enjoyed a good gossip over their tea. They would exchange views on their respective employers, and grumble about the obligation to carry their shopping home. With no near relatives to worry about, and no man at the Front, such trifling inconveniences would be regarded as a personal attack on their rights as regular customers. The wheelwright's house had been swept clean of all the accumulated dust and muddle. The rugs and mats had been beaten on the clothes line, the furniture polished, the curtains washed, and the rooms aired. Martha had taken the sensible view and worked hard, not demanding any assistance, but the elderly servant felt obliged to lend a hand, however grudgingly, for she knew the reins had been taken out of her hands, and she was no longer mistress. It had been a busy week, and a strain on Martha's tact and patience.

'I'll lay the table, Mother,' Philip was saying, as Andrew slipped on his jacket.

'Father said not to wait tea, for he may be late back. It's a long trek out to Barton Manor, and uphill all the way back, so he will have to push his bicycle,' Martha told Andrew. So they sat down to tea – the man, the woman and the child – and it seemed to the man and the child that they belonged together, and it was right and proper. But the woman felt guilty, and much disturbed by Andrew's steady gaze.

As soon as they had finished tea she left them to wash up, put on her hat and gloves, and walked along to the bakery. The baker and his wife were delighted to engage such a useful, intelligent woman. An ex-teacher would have no difficulty in adding up the pennies and halfpennies! White overalls would be provided, and cups of tea morning and afternoon, with a choice of buns. An hour for dinner, and finish work at 6 with Wednesday afternoons off. One pound a week was a fair wage, and both parties were pleased to get it settled so amicably. But when Martha suggested 15s. for their board and lodging, her father shook his head.

'Not a penny piece, my lass. I can well afford to keep you both. Put a bit aside in the savings bank. You will need it later when the boy goes to Grammar School.'

They both assumed he would pass the entrance examination, and the schoolmaster had assured them they would not be disappointed.

Three months had passed and Tom was still in the London hospital.

'You can take your husband home next week, Mrs Simmons,' the consultant informed her kindly.

'We haven't got a home, Doctor,' Ruby answered, and explained the circumstances. He looked at her with compassion. She was brave and cheerful, like most of the wives of his working-class patients. The upper class went into nursing homes or were cared for at home, so he had no contact with them, but he admired women like Mrs Simmons, who travelled up from Kent every Sunday to spend two hours with her husband and was first in the queue of visitors waiting to be admitted on the stroke of 2 o'clock. The word 'cancer' was never mentioned among the patients, and close relatives hid their anxiety in a forced cheerfulness that was a strain on both parties.

'Then we will keep him here. He understands the position, so he won't complain, will he?' the consultant was saying.

'Tom never complains, Doctor.'

'So I've noticed. I wish we had a few more like him, but you can't change human nature. For some of our patients

476

it's the ultimate disaster. The stronger the man, the more he will rebel against it. Bitterness and despair will make him a bad patient.'

''ow long will it be, Doctor?'

'Difficult to say, but with one lung collapsed and the other functioning only partly, it could be any time.'

'Tom's so terriby thin, Doctor. 'e ain't never been a big man, but 'e do seem to 'ave shrunk away to nothing in these past few weeks.'

'Yes, I'm afraid it's all part of the pattern. It's a wasting disease. I'm sorry.'

Ruby sighed. She had sat by Tom's bedside for two hours and felt completely drained. When he wanted to pass water, a young nurse had put a screen round the bed and she was so shocked and horrified by a glimpse of his wasted legs, it had taken all her determination not to break down in front of him. Time enough to have a good cry on the train, if she was lucky enough to find an empty carriage. It was the only bit of privacy she enjoyed these days, for she slept with Elsie, and she wouldn't upset her grand-children with her tears. She tried to concentrate on what the doctor was saying, but she felt quite stupid with heartache and anxiety. He was asking if she were on the telephone, and she shook her head.

'Then we will get in touch with the police and they will notify you quickly when we see any change in your husband's condition.'

'Thank you, Doctor. And thank you for all you've done for Tom, and the nurses too. Tom tells me they've been wonderfully kind. I'm ever so grateful, Doctor.'

'You've been very brave.' He stood up, laid a kindly hand on her shoulder and shook hands. She was a pretty little woman, he thought, and must have been quite a beauty in her younger days. Now the gentian blue eyes were ringed by dark shadows, and her cheeks were pallid.

477

It was the women who were suffering now on the home front, in this ghastly War. One wing of the hospital was given up to patients with multiple injuries, sent direct from the field hospitals, on the Western Front. The ambulances arrived in convoys, and some of the casualties were so young they were little more than schoolboys.

Although she had been travelling to London every Sunday for three months, it was still a hazardous experience for Ruby. In all kinds of weather, she had more than a mile to walk to the station, carrying a bag with two clean nightshirts, a dozen handkerchiefs that had once belonged to Parson, half-a-dozen eggs from Monks Farm delivered by Albert every Saturday afternoon as regular as clockwork, a tin of boiled sweets and a few grapes from the Conservatory at The Grove. The small packet of sandwiches would be eaten in the station buffet at Charing Cross, where she could buy a cup of tea for 2d, keeping an eye on the clock. Boarding the right bus was still a hazard, and even when the conductor had assured her it was right, she still had to ask the passenger sitting beside her. Sunday was a day to be endured. The War was something outside her own private little world, too big and impersonal to be of any significance unless and until her two sons were casualties. She tried not to think of that awful possibility, but several mothers in the village had already lost sons. Jack did not write direct to her, and she didn't expect it. Elsie shared her letters with her mother-in-law.

Freddie's letters she treasured, and read aloud to Tom. He had been recommended for promotion from the ranks, and was sent back to take a special course of training. They were proud of Freddie, but equally proud of Jack when he was promoted to corporal.

The burden of Tom's long illness lay heavy on Ruby's

478

shoulders. To be parted after so many years seemed quite unbearable, yet she had to bear it for Tom's sake. Work was the answer to a troubled heart, and she kept busy all the week, but she found no pleasure in it these days. The Misses Langtry were kind, and it was good of Miss Victoria to cut a few of her precious grapes to take to Tom, but they were so fussy, and expected the same service and attention from tradesmen and servants as in pre-War days. Ruby would have given notice, had she been certain of another situation. They would like to have her back at The Three Nuns, but it would embarrass Carrie to see her Mum scrubbing the steps of the pub – the doctor's house was just across the road. In some ways they had been the happiest years. Being a charwoman was no disgrace. It was her children who had persuaded her to apply for the job at The Parsonage after the old Cook had died of a heart attack. She had done her best, but it was not good enough for Parson's wife whose standards were too high. When Parson died, it was a good excuse to give notice, and almost immediately she had been engaged as a daily cook-housekeeper by the Misses Langtry. Since she had left The Three Nuns, her work had provided a living but no enjoyment. She had missed all the good-humoured banter from the customers and the friendliness of the publican and his wife, a working-class couple with no swank. For a time she had been pleased and proud of her new status, but not any more. She was still a servant in cap and apron, still answering dutifully 'Yes, Miss. No, Miss.' She still entered and left the house by the back door – and still used the gardener's privy.

Freddie was due for a short leave of 48 hours on completion of the course, and he had written to Cynthia to arrange a meeting at their old *rendezvous*. She had contrived to get leave for the same period, since she had been saving up her free days for just such an occasion. When she stepped out of the swing doors that afternoon, wearing civilian dress and carrying a valise, Freddie sprang to attention, took the bag, and kissed her cheek.

'Have you left the hospital?' he asked, quietly.

She shook her head. 'I'm on leave.'

'Good.'

'You look simply splendid, darling, in that new uniform.'

'Do I? I feel a bit conspicuous.'

'Why should you?'

He shrugged. 'The wrong class, I suppose?'

'Don't be ridiculous! This war will abolish class.'

'Never!'

When she had pulled off her gloves, he took her hand and examined it carefully. 'Still scrubbing?'

'I told you a probationer was nothing more than a glorified charwoman.'

'How much longer?'

'Another three months.'

'Good afternoon, Sir. Good afternoon, Madam,' their favourite waitress interrupted. 'It's nice to see you back, and both looking so well. What can I get you, the usual?'

'You *can't* have remembered after all these months?' Cynthia giggled.

'Pot of tea and a plate of buns.'

'Amazing!' said Freddie.

'I don't remember every Tom, Dick and 'arry, Sir, only the specials.'

'Thank you.' They smiled at her and she went away wondering about the relationship, for there was no engagement ring on the girl's finger. When she had poured the tea, Cynthia asked quietly, 'Will you marry me, Freddie?'

He put the cup down, blushed and stammered, 'My dear girl, what a question!'

'Unorthodox, perhaps, and highly improper, but if I waited for you to pop the question, my love, I could wait for ever!'

He grinned and teased her. 'This is so sudden.'

'I'm serious, Freddie.'

'I'm sorry. It's just not possible.'

'Why? Give me one valid reason why it's impossible?'

'I have no money, no home, no prospects – and I'm still working class, remember, in spite of the uniform.'

'That's four reasons, but not one convinces me. If you said, I don't love you, that would be different.'

'It would not be true. I do love you.'

'Ah,' she breathed, ecstatically, her eyes soft as velvet. 'At last! I have waited so long, my darling.'

He took her hands, his face grave, his own eyes misted with tears. 'There is so little time, dear,' he whispered.

'Forty-eight hours. We won't waste a minute. We are not the only couple to get married and have a honeymoon in forty-eight hours. Everybody's doing it, Freddie. It's an epidemic.'

'Your father will never forgive you.'

'He might be quite relieved to get rid of one daughter so easily.'

'And your mother?'

'She will shed a few tears and blame Papa, but she will soon forget. Poor Mama! She lives in her own private little world, and dare not put a foot outside for fear of becoming involved in something.'

'When will you tell them?'

'After we are safely married. I shall send a telegram. And you, darling? Will your parents object?'

'Mother will disapprove most strongly.'

'Why?'

481

'Because you belong to the upper class. She has always believed profoundly in that hymn we were taught at the village school.'

'What hymn?' They were whispering together, still holding hands, the tea forgotten. He quoted:

> The rich man in his castle,
> The poor man at his gate,
> God made them high or lowly,
> And ordered their estate.

Cynthia giggled. 'But how priceless! And your father?'

'He died the first week I was at Sandhurst, but it was expected. He had been ill for a long time.'

'I'm sorry, darling, and I'm sorry that your mother will disapprove, but I can't alter the fact of being born and bred at Marston Park. It's all in the lap of the gods.'

He smiled whimsically. 'I shall write a letter. A telegram would give her a nasty shock. She would immediately decide my brother Jack had been killed, and would be afraid to open it. At least I can spare her that. I wish there was time to see her, but I can promise her a day of my next leave. We will go together, dear, you and I.'

'Yes,' she agreed, because she had got her way with him. She hadn't really expected him to acquiesce, for there was a stubborn streak in his character that had shown itself on more than one occasion since they had first met. She was convinced, however, that love would provide all the answers to all the problems that would have to be faced – that love was the only antidote to this ridiculous barrier of class distinction. She was wrong, of course, and time would prove it was not strong enough to fight the principles and prejudices of the working class. She would find her future mother-in-law a formidable adversary. They were worlds apart, and Freddie's wife might never bridge the barrier that divided them. Even now, before they were man and wife, she would discover

482

that Freddie had his own kind of pride, from his own roots, and that she must compromise.

'It's going to be great fun, darling. We can afford to spoil ourselves. Two lovely days and nights in a West End hotel, wallowing in the lap of luxury!' She was trembling with anticipation.

'What do we use for money?' he asked, quietly.

'I've got ten pounds – Beatrice sent it for my birthday.'

'You didn't tell me you had a birthday.'

'You didn't ask. Anyway, what does it matter about birthdays? I mean, we can catch up on all those details later. So you will let me spend the ten pounds, won't you, darling?'

'Not on our honeymoon. Certainly not!'

'But why? Now you are being contrary,' she pouted.

'I don't like posh hotels, and we are *not* spending your money.'

'You are mean. It would be such fun, and we do deserve it.'

He shook his head. 'Sorry.' His mouth was stubborn.

She sighed. 'Where do we sleep and eat?'

'We sleep at my lodgings in Soho, and we eat when we are hungry, wherever we happen to be. It's for you to decide where you want to go.'

'*Thank you*, Mr Simmons!' She was annoyed, but he had to make a firm stand about money. He had his Army pay. They would manage.

'Cheer up, old girl,' he coaxed. It was a funny sort of endearment, but she would get used to it and he would get used to the 'darlings' she sprinkled so liberally over the conversation.

But when the brief ceremony was over, and Freddie had bought a drink for the two witnesses in the nearest pub, they had a meal at Lyons and walked back to Soho, arm in arm, and Freddie introduced his wife to Lennie O'Brien in the street market.

'Pleased to meet you, Miss,' said Lennie, spitting on his grubby hand and wiping it down his trousers. 'You're a bloody dark 'Orse, young Freddie. Where you been 'iding this good-looking filly? She's a bit of orlright, chum – a bit of orlright,' he nodded, knowingly. She had class, good breeding. It was written all over her, and Freddie looked as proud as a peacock in that ruddy officer's uniform. But he wasn't giving anything away. Not Freddie Simmons. He would have to wait some time to discover a boy from Richmond Row had married the daughter of Sir Neville Franklin.

'What a funny man,' Cynthia giggled, as they walked away. 'A friend of yours, darling?'

'A neighbour,' he said, shortly, and they both laughed.

But Cynthia was shocked and surprised at the shabby furnished rooms he rented in a back street, and the slatternly landlady in curlers and carpet slippers. Cynthia was the one to be embarrassed, not Freddie. He was perfectly at ease in such surroundings.

'This is my wife.' He introduced her proudly.

'Blimey! You ain't wasted much time, ducks. Didn't even know you were engaged.'

'We weren't, we aren't. I mean, there was no time for an engagement,' he explained, and she chuckled.

'Well, the best of luck to the pair of you, and may all yer troubles be little 'uns.'

'Thank you, Millie.'

She pecked their cheeks. Her breath was sour. Cynthia shuddered involuntarily.

'We shan't be wanting any supper. We had a meal at Lyons,' he told his landlady.

'What about the cocoa?'

'Yes, please, Cocoa as usual. I'll come down and fetch it.'

'Thanks, duckie. Save me poor old feet. Never 'ad a more considerate lodger. I'm going ter miss 'im when 'e leaves for good,' she told Cynthia.

'But I'm not leaving for good. I'm coming back. Don't you dare let these rooms, Millie, while I'm away. I'll settle up with you before I go. We shall need this place later, and the office is convenient for most of my clients. The War won't last for ever, Millie!'

They wished her goodnight and climbed the narrow stairs. A strong smell of garlic drifted down from the upper floor.

'Italians,' Freddie explained, briefly.

His own two rooms were crowded with furniture and nothing matched. The big double bed, wardrobe, chest of drawers and washstand with one chair filled the small bedroom. They skidded on the mats that covered the worn patches of linoleum in the sitting-room, and Freddie muttered irritably, 'I wish she wouldn't polish under the mats.'

'Well, at least it proves she lifts the mats. What's that great ugly plant, darling, blocking up the window?'

'Aspidistra.'

'What's it doing there?'

'It's traditional. A sort of relic of Victorian days.'

'Do we have to live with it?'

'For the moment, dear. It would upset Millie if we asked for its removal right away.'

Cynthia shivered. It was unbelievably shabby and depressing. She had not known such places existed. It had been so long, this eventful day, and she wanted to cry.

But when Freddie had pulled the curtains and put a match to the gas fire, the room looked quite cosy. He smiled and held out his arms, and she went into them.

Then it no longer mattered. Nothing mattered, only that they were in love, and they were man and wife.

'Happy?' he whispered.

She nodded, tremulously, her arms warm about his neck. It was the first time he had held her in his arms, the first time they had been alone together since they came to London. She remembered the day of the accident in the park, when she had cradled his head on her breast, and lifted his light, unconscious body to lie across her own body while she waited for his cousins to bring a hurdle from Russets. She remembered her body had trembled, as it was trembling now, and that she had known she loved him, even then. But they were worlds apart, and only the War had brought them together again. A man in uniform on leave from the Western Front, with the horrors of modern warfare, and the screams of the dying still tormenting his memory. Such a man had no resistance against the determination of a woman in love. And Freddie Simmons was no exception.

Their hats lay together on the red plush cloth. The gas fire hissed and flickered. The street was quiet now, the prostitutes on their way to Piccadilly.

'Where's the bathroom, darling?' Cynthia asked, innocently, some time later.

'No bathroom. Sorry,' he grinned, quite unabashed by the inconvenience. 'There's a jug of water and a basin in the bedroom.'

'Give me ten minutes, darling.' She cupped his face in her hands, touched his mouth with her wet lips, and slipped out of his arms.

It seemed a long ten minutes, squatting on the mat, gazing into the flickering fire, his thin hands clenched between his knees. So much can pass through the mind in ten minutes, and he was no longer sure of anything, but filled with doubt of his own adequacy. His sensitive face

486

was pale, and every nerve in his body quivered with the anguish of a nightmare from which there was no escape. He was no hero. He was afraid, terribly afraid. The three months at Sandhurst and the officer's uniform had done nothing for his morale, and he was easily persuaded by his own lack of enthusiasm, that his superior officer had been mistaken in recommending him for promotion. Leaders were made of sterner stuff, he told himself. An officer must set an example to his men. He must have the courage of his convictions, the ability to act quickly and decisively, and a sense of responsibility for the men under his command. He had found the system superficial and his shyness a handicap. The working-class tag was still attached to his person, and his knowledge was limited and confined to one particular sphere. Self-taught in his lone struggle for a hold on the ladder of achievement, he had never permitted himself the time to associate socially with his fellows, and they found him poor company. He shivered and remembered the girl waiting in the next room – the girl he had married.

So he turned off the fire and the light, and walked slowly out of the room.

'May I come in?' he asked, hesitantly in the doorway of the bedroom. She looked very young and childish in the big bed, with her wide eyes and flushed cheeks, and they stared at each other for a long moment, unsmiling, uncertain, for their own separate lives, so different in every respect, had not prepared them for this moment of intimacy. The still were strangers.

'Hello, darling,' she whispered.

'Hello,' he said.

The girl in the bed, in her dainty chiffon nightgown, had a delicacy and refinement that was unrelated to the small crowded room in which she found herself on her wedding night. The gaslight was harsh, and the shabbiness intensified. A solitary candle and a box of matches had been provided by the landlady as a precaution against lodgers who invariably found themselves in the dark without a coin for the meter. Freddie lit the candle and turned off the gas.

'That's better,' he said.

'Much better, darling,' she agreed. She knew now that he was embarrassed, and that, in this one respect, they were similar since both had been reared on the old-fashioned ideas of modesty. Their shyness was natural and mutual. She lay back on her pillow and closed her eyes, a secret little smile playing about her mouth. She could hear him moving about, the coat hangers rattling in the wardrobe, the water splashing in the basin, then tipped into the slop bucket, a drawer pulled out, and a faint smell of clean linen – his pyjamas? The darling! He was so sweet. She adored him. Now she knew for certain he had not slept with any other woman, and they both were virgins.

In the kind darkness they lay together, tense with shyness and apprehension, their hands clasped tightly. They were waiting, and the waiting was intolerable. They had come too suddenly upon this intimacy from their separate worlds that were so far apart, and their courtship had been confined to those brief periods in the tea-shop, the language of love spoken only with their eyes. Now their eyes stared into the darkness, and had no part in this strange ritual that must be performed to consummate their marriage. The man must take the initiative or forfeit his manhood on their wedding night. That was a fundamental truth they both recognised.

So the girl waited. She had still to discover there are no set rules to the mating of a man and a woman in love, and that instinct, not experience, would decide. When the waiting became too intolerable to bear, she touched

488

his cheek with a tentative hand and found it wet.

'Darling, what have I done to you?' she whispered, contritely.

'It's not you. I'm sorry.' His voice was choked. 'It's Hell over there, and I have to go back. I'm a coward.'

Now she was all maternal, cradling his tense body in her arms, soothing and comforting, like a mother with a hurt child.

'My poor darling. I didn't know. I didn't understand. You should have told me.'

He was shuddering convulsively, and her arms tightened about his lean young body.

'I love you. I love you.' She pressed his head to her breast.

Gradually the nightmare faded, and he relaxed in the warmth and comfort of her cradling arms. He could feel her heart fluttering, and his dry lips found the damp little hollow betwen her breasts. It was the most delicious sensation he had ever known, and he gave himself up to it, utterly and completely, drifting into a blissful unconsciousness. His relaxed body was heavy now, and her arms were cramped, but she made no move to disturb him.

Time stood still. This man in her arms was no longer a stranger. She felt she had always known him. They had found each other in his silent tears and in her own awareness of his desperate need of comfort and reassurance.

He woke to the warmth of her body, his mouth suckling her breast, his hand on her flat, trembling stomach.

Part V

Chapter Seventeen

By the end of 1916, it seemed there had never been a time without the War that had changed the pattern of all their lives. Few families in the village had escaped, and all classes of society had suffered. Jack Simmons' name had been added to the list of casualties pinned on the wall in the church porch, and prayers for the dead, the wounded, and the prisoners of war saw many a sad wife and mother in tears on Sunday. The three religious denominations, in which parson, priest, and minister had always maintained a strict conformity, had a tendency to merge in sympathetic charity, for all shared the common cause.

Among the severely wounded officers slowly recuperating in the Military Hospital at Marston Park, Lieutenant Simmons was in no way conspicuous, for many had lost a limb and were dragging themselves around on crutches. There had been a time, however, when the multiple injuries would have defeated a less determined character, and his chances of recovery had been slim. Freddie had only a vague recollection of the shell that exploded in the trench as he reached its sheltering haven, dragging the wounded sergeant he had rescued from the mangled bodies of his comrades. And sergeant Wilson, for whom he had risked his life, was dead. In the long, disturbed nights, when pain and discomfort kept him awake, Freddie would wonder why his own life had been spared. It made no sense when Wilson had left four young children fatherless. Corporal Gibson, an only adored son, had died screaming for his widowed mother, and Sergeant Major Blunt, that sturdy indestructible disciplinarian who had survived Spion Kop in early 1900, three years of Pathan skirmishes on the Khyber Pass, and two years of terrible slaughter on the Western Front, had been killed by a small fragment of shrapnel. When the stretcher bearers picked him out of the mud, his wide staring eyes still held a look of shocked surprise and disgust at such an unheroic end to a distinguished career. Nothing made sense. It was all a terrible mistake, and all that splendid loyalty and patriotism had been wasted. On this one particular issue they all agreed, but on the trifling question of whether or not to contribute a small donation towards a wedding present for Sister Gregory, there was some disagreement. Sister Gregory was neither pretty nor popular. Even so, she could not be blamed for the collection, and would probably be extremely embarrassed when she discovered her secret had leaked out, as secrets were apt to leak in the closely-knit community of a hospital.

It was neither beauty nor charm that had claimed the heart and hand of Doctor Warrington, the most confirmed bachelor on the hospital register, but admiration for the skill and the dedication to her profession that matched his own. Both would continue to serve that profession, and the only change in their respective situations would be the accommodation. The old nursery wing had been allocated for their use for the duration of the War, and since nobody could foresee the end, their temporary home would have the settled

494

atmosphere of permanence. Sister Gregory was 35, Doctor Warrington was 53.

It was Freddie who volunteered to collect the donations, and Freddie who told the few reluctant subscribers exactly what he thought of their attitude. The Army had only contributed its inevitable quota of disciplined endurance to a man already disciplined by years of hard necessity. The discerning dark eyes in that lean, ascetic face, had been temporarily blinded by the blast, but now they were clouded only by the memory of that last horrific incident, and the maimed and mangled bodies of the men he had led to their death. This was another nightmare, replacing the old dread of being incapable of leadership. He had proved himself not only capable but courageous, but in doing so, had lost his youth and his leg. Neither could be restored, and the consequences could only be endured because of Cynthia. And Cynthia loved him.

Her letters had kept him sane during those long, agonising weeks in the Field Hospital before he was removed to Marston Park, and she had been his first visitor. Slim and neat in her nurse's uniform, she walked down the ward with the determined air of one accustomed to disciplined behaviour, only her set lips and tired eyes revealing the strain of that first meeting. She saw only the one beloved face on the piled pillows. The rest were blurred images that would swim into focus later.

In his weakness, his eyes flooded with tears, and he was tense with the effort to appear normal and natural. But he was proud of her dignity and restraint. Her breeding, combined with the strict hospital training, kept a tight rein on her emotions. There had been several distressing scenes in the ward with young wives and elderly mothers at breaking point on arrival, and the wounded men

495

having to comfort when they themselves had expected to be comforted.

'Hello, darling.' She was smiling now, and she took his limp hand in a warm clasp and kissed his grey lips. He returned the smile tremulously, but he was too choked with tears to speak. Here again he was fortunate and grateful, because of her understanding and sympathy. Seriously ill patients could not be expected to communicate properly. It was enough for the moment just to have her sitting there beside the bed, holding his hand, smiling bravely, not worrying him with questions. He sighed, and gave himself into her kind keeping, as on their wedding night. It would be a long, long time before he felt the urge to be master of his fate and captain of his soul again. In resigning all responsibility, he was reduced to a state of passive acceptance, wholly in contradiction to his former independent self. If Cynthia was expecting co-operation in her plans for the future, she was doomed to disappointment, for he was just not capable of assembling his thoughts coherently. The will to survive had taken all his strength of purpose, and with almost constant pain in one or several parts of his maimed body, he was exhausted. Nothing was normal any more, and the only reality was the girl he had married sitting so quietly at the bedside. To look beyond this moment into a future they must eventually share was too vague and too far removed even to contemplate. His tired mind dismissed it, and he lay in a kind of trance, staring at her pale, mobile face.

After a while, she turned her head and looked about the ward. 'Once upon a time this was our dining-room,' she said. He nodded and she went on, 'Papa sends his regards. I see quite a lot of him these days, since he took over that job in Whitehall. We lunch in the canteen on our free day, then we go to see a newsreel and a comedy at the

496

cinema in the Strand. I've got quite used to seeing Papa as part of the wartime scene, but it seemed strange at first. Now I give him full credit for sticking to that desk in Whitehall. It's just a dull, routine, secretarial job, and he took over from a civil servant. By the way, darling, he wants to meet you.'

'No.'

'Not yet. Later. Don't worry. Have you seen your mother?'

'No.'

'Would you like to see her?'

'Yes.'

'Then I will write to her.'

She would not speak again for a full ten minutes, timing herself by the new little gold watch on her wrist – a present from Papa on her 21st birthday. It was a test of emotional constraint, for there was so much to say, and so much she would like to know about that period in the Field Hospital. She had yet to discover he would never talk about it, and that she must accept the fact he was changed, mentally and physically, and that her own strength and vitality would probably torment his weakness. Before the ten minutes had expired he had closed his eyes and his shallow breathing told her he was asleep. While he slept, her eyes travelled round the ward. All the patients were young, even younger than Freddie. A nurse was holding a feeding cup to the lips of a boy with his eyes swathed in bandages. Was he blinded? How terrible! She was choked with tears, but she must not cry.

Soothed by her quiet presence and the clasp of her warm hand, Freddie slept for nearly an hour. Nobody disturbed them, and the nurse went about her duties with the dedicated love and efficiency Cynthia could recognise. She had deliberated in the past few months on whether or not to ask for a transfer to this military hospital, but now that she had seen Freddie, she had decided not to ask. It would be embarrassing, and it would worry Freddie. Besides, they were short-staffed at her own hospital, for several nurses, including Cecily Wellington, had volunteered for the Medical Corps in 1915.

She had lost touch with Cecily since she had married Freddie, but it was rather a relief. Cecily's friendship had been too possessive, too demanding. They had quarrelled over Freddie. Cecily had very decided views on class distinction.

'You cannot get away from the fact that young man is working class, born and bred in Richmond Row, and you cannot make a silk purse from a sow's ear,' she had asserted scornfully.

'What a beastly thing to say! I call it sheer hypocrisy for Parson's daughter to hold such views!' Cynthia had retorted.

No friendship could survive such a blatant attack on her own established views on that controversial subject, for she had long since accepted Freddie's simple philosophy that all men are equal in the sight of God.

Sitting there, surrounded by the devastating evidence of every woman's firm conviction that war was a terrible mistake, Cynthia Simmons was not only saddened, but determined to make her marriage something more than just a temporary escape from the burden and brutality of war. She had married Freddie 'for better, for worse, for richer, for poorer, in sickness and in health, till Death us do part.' She knew instinctively now that Freddie's chance of a complete recovery was slim, and that she must be prepared to carry the burden of their future on her own shoulders, and that it would take all her resourcefulness and patience. There was so much to reject in those happy plans she had made for post-War. They both had to adjust

498

to an entirely new concept, a new chapter. Some time, but not yet. Long weeks and months of separation and suffering had still to be endured. An artificial leg was the ultimate test of endurance, then a long convalescence at the seaside. Each stage would separate them. A few hours each week was the most they could expect to be together, and always in the public eye, never, or hardly ever alone. *But he was alive!* She must be grateful that he had been spared, when so many had died. She sighed and stretched her cramped limbs, but Freddie did not stir.

'Poor darling. My poor darling.' Her lips framed the words and her heart ached with compassion and tenderness. This man who had been restored to her was not the man who went away, she had to get to know him all over again. All those wasted years of striving and struggling, to what purpose? But was it wasted? Is any endeavour wasted?

On her second visit, she was allowed to push Freddie in a wheeled chair, and she walked away from the house towards the lake. It was a warm afternoon in June. The still waters shimmered beneath a cloudless sky, and the silence was broken only by the distant rattle of a hay-wagon. It was inconceivable that the War was still raging across the Channel, and that men were being killed and cruelly wounded even as they enjoyed the luxury of this peaceful place. The lake was symbolic of Cynthia's world, and Freddie found its beauty and grandeur rather overwhelming. The pond in the field behind Richmond Row was more to his taste. It was homely and familiar, with pleasant memories of fishing for tadpoles on just such an afternoon as this. With a sherbet bag for refreshment, and a jam-jar filled with the slimy green water, he would sit for hours, alone, but never lonely. There was a difference.

When he was 13 there had been no more time for

catching tadpoles, and he lost his taste for sherbet in the adult world of work and worry. 'Life was real. Life was earnest,' according to his mentors at the village school, and one put away childish things, almost overnight it seemed. Fishing for tadpoles had been the only pastime he had actually enjoyed as a boy. Climbing trees, kicking a ball around, smashing a peg-top and sliding on icy puddles had been Jack's idea of fun. Now Jack was dead. The thought saddened him, and he opened his eyes to look at Cynthia, who was sitting on the grass hugging her knees, staring at the lake. She turned her head to look at him and asked quietly, 'Had a nice little nap, darling?'

'I wasn't asleep,' he said, but he did not explain about the pond or the tadpoles because she wouldn't understand. You couldn't expect her to understand when she had been brought up here. This was *her* familiar environment – the vast estate, the mansion, the lake. Yet she had sacrificed it for his sake when she became his wife. He felt very humbled by such a sacrifice.

'I'm sorry,' he said, contritely.

'For what?' she asked, smiling at his troubled frown.

'For taking you away from all this.'

'But you didn't. I left of my own accord.'

'Did you?'

'You know I did.'

'I had forgotten. I've forgotten so much.'

'It doesn't matter. Don't worry about it.' She kissed him gently. He was her child now, and she was his mother.

Two figures appeared from behind the trees and came towards them across the grass. A young VAD nurse was escorting a plump little woman in a white blouse and a trailing black skirt. A faded straw hat, adorned with an artificial rose, perched on her piled hair at a precarious angle. Her face was flushed with exertion, and she carried a bulky parcel.

500

'I've brought you another visitor, Sir,' said the girl, importantly.

'Hullo, Mum.' Freddie greeted his mother shyly. He had not seen her since his marriage.

'Hullo, luv.' She dropped the parcel on the grass and cuddled him in a warm embrace, then stood back to study him more closely. 'There now, you don't look too bad, luv, not as bad as I was expecting after all you've been through.' She had no eyes for anyone but Freddie. The girl had walked away, and Cynthia was standing quietly, waiting to be introduced.

Ruby was shocked and saddened. She thought Freddie looked terrible, but it wouldn't do to break down, not in front of *her*.

'This is my wife, Cynthia,' he told her, and she turned to look at Sir Neville Franklin's daughter with hostile eyes. She hadn't expected to meet her today, or to see her in uniform.

'How do you do, Mrs Simmons.' Her new daughter-in-law was waiting to shake hands. It was an unfamiliar gesture. Working class didn't shake hands as a general rule.

'Pleased ter meet you, Miss.' She was surprised to find the hand so big and firm, and so roughened by hard work it matched her own. She liked what she saw, but she wasn't prepared to capitulate without having her say.

'Won't you sit down, Mrs Simmons,' Cynthia asked graciously, as though to a guest in her own drawing-room.

Ruby flopped on the grass. She was breathing heavily, and she fanned her face with her skirt. Damp strands of hair curled on her neck.

'Makes you sweat, this weather, don't it?' she said.

'It does indeed,' Cynthia agreed, dropping down beside her. 'Wouldn't you be cooler without your hat?' she suggested, tentatively, for she knew she was in disgrace and that so much was at stake at their first meeting.

When she had taken the pins from her hat, Ruby set it down carefully on the grass. It was her best hat, and she was wearing her best blouse and skirt because her son was an officer, and she was very proud of Freddie.

'I envy you your beautiful hair, Mrs Simmons.' Her new daughter-in-law was being very charming, but Ruby was wary of charm. She liked plain speaking, and her blue eyes were still hostile.

Freddie stirred restlessly in his wheeled chair. Mum would speak her mind. Better to get it over. He still had to meet his father-in-law, but Cynthia had already paved the way. Two years had passed since their marriage. His promised leave had been cancelled twice. It was just the fortunes, or the misfortunes, of War. Mum was having her say, and Cynthia was crying.

'You could 'ave knocked me down with a feather, Miss, when I got Freddie's letter afore 'e went orf to that training camp,' Ruby declared, categorically, as though it had happened only last week. 'Whatever would 'is Dad 'ave said, I asked meself, only Dad wasn't there, so 'e never knew. Freddie knowed what we thought about class, for we've argued about it often enough. Class is class, and working-class folk don't 'old with getting familiar with the upper class. It's all wrong, Miss, and when I 'eard you 'ad married our Freddie, it were a nasty shock. I could 'ave wrote and told you, only I'm such a poor scholar. So I waited till I could see you. There now, I've got it orf me chest, and I'm sorry to make you cry, but I 'ave ter speak me mind. After all, a mother 'as a right to speak 'er mind, especially when 'er children get ideas above their station, like our Freddie. Seems like 'e don't belong to us no more.'

'That's not true, Mum. I shall always belong,' Freddie

502

reminded her quietly.

'He *will*. Oh, he *will*! I shall see to it, I promise you. *Please* will you try to understand? I love Freddie, and he loves me. Isn't that the most important factor to be considered?' Cynthia pleaded, tearfully.

'Well, I dunno. I never thought to see one of me own children making so free with the upper class. We've got 'igh principles, Miss, we working class, what 'as been 'anded down from father to son, and mother to daughter, and it takes a bit of getting used to.' Ruby sighed gustily. She was not a woman to bear a grudge, yet she had made no attempt to get in touch with her new daughter-in-law since her marriage. 'She's not a bit stuck up. She's nice. I believe I could get quite fond of her, and it would please Freddie,' she was thinking. She looked from one to the other and patted Cynthia's workworn hand. 'Well, it's like I said, Miss. You've got ter give me time ter think it over, for it don't come easy to change what you've been brought up ter believe since you was little, but don't you worry. I guess I'll get round to it.'

'Thank you, Mrs Simmons. Thank you very much.' Cynthia dabbed at her wet eyes. She liked Freddie's mother, but she must tread carefully, for this new relationship was unlike any other and would need all her tact.

'If you will excuse me, I will take a little walk. I am sure you have family matters you would like to discuss,' she said.

They watched her walk away.

'She's got lovely manners, Freddie,' Ruby admitted, a little grudgingly.

'She's a lovely person, Mum,' he told her, decidedly.

'Everyone sends their love. I got presents 'ere.' Ruby was unwrapping the bulky parcel. Now that her daughter-in-law had taken herself off for a walk, she had

503

Freddie all to herself. A mother always feels a certain jealousy over her sons' wives, and this particular young woman had not waited to be properly engaged but just got married on the sly. It weren't decent! Not that Albert's Eva was any better. Hadn't she made sure of a second husband afore the first was cold in his grave?

'The cake's from Martha Martin – 'er that was Martha Carter afore she married Dick Martin,' she explained. 'She's back 'ome with 'er Dad, and she works at the bakery. That's 'ow she wangled a cake. It's a rare treat, luv, a nice fruit cake with all this rationing.'

'But of course I remember her, Mum. It was a sad day for the Infants when she married Dick Martin. He got killed on the North West Frontier, didn't he? Carrie told me in one of her letters.'

'That's right and good riddance to bad rubbish, for 'e treated 'is poor Mum and 'is wife somethink shocking. She's ever so friendly with our Carrie since they went orf to Tidworth together, and then out to India. A good friend she's been to our girl. But she will 'ave told you in 'er letters all about it. Carrie do write a good letter, bless 'er, when she's away from 'ome. Now I don't get no letters with you and Carrie both back. Now this 'ere's a present from The Three Nuns. They made a collection in the pub, and they all sent their best wishes. You're quite an 'ero in the village now, luv. Everybody's that proud of you.'

Freddie was embarrassed. He only did what had to be done on the spur of the moment, and would probably do the same again if he had no time to consider it. Hadn't he been in a blue funk while they waited for action? He was no hero, and he couldn't understand all the fuss.

'Please thank them for the cigarettes. I don't smoke, but you needn't tell them. They can be handed round the ward. Some of the chaps get a lot of comfort from a cigarette, but I don't feel the need to smoke, probably

504

because it hasn't become a habit. Couldn't afford it.'

'You always 'ad a strong will, luv. You take after me for that, you and Carrie. Now, 'ave a look at the rest of the presents afore she comes back.'

'Why? Don't you want my wife to see how highly I'm respected in the village?' he teased.

'She knows. Everybody knows, but she don't *belong* to the village Freddie.'

'She does now because she's married to me.'

Ruby shook her head and changed the subject again. 'A nice bunch of grapes, luv, from Miss Lavinia and Miss Victoria, with their regards, and peaches from your late boss. Whenever I run into 'im in the 'igh Street 'e always enquires after you. A real gentleman. Albert sent a dozen new laid eggs, and 'opes you'll soon be better. Anybody would think you was just a bit poorly, but Albert never did 'ave much imagination!' Ruby was glad to see the boyish grin on the grave young face. Her visit was doing him a lot of good. 'Now this 'ere book was delivered to Doctor's place and Carrie brought it along. It's a book of poetry from the schoolmaster and 'e's wrote inside. Shall I read it to you?'

'Yes, please, Mum.'

Ruby took a deep breath. She had been very impressed by the autograph. 'For Lieutenant Frederick Simmons. A small appreciation of a gallant officer from a sincere admirer. Andrew Robinson. Isn't that nice, luv?'

'Very nice,' Freddie agreed quietly, overwhelmed by so much kindness. The weak tears that so often pricked his eyes had to be blinked away, but not before Ruby had seen them. She went on talking. It wouldn't do for Freddie to know how badly she wanted to cry. She had to be cheerful. Seeing her son so weak and helpless reminded her too vividly of all the hours she had sat beside Tom in the hospital. Not one of her children had realised what it meant to watch him slowly die.

'Carrie sends 'er love. She'll be along to see you on 'er next free day,' she told Freddie. 'Trouble is, she don't never seem to know whether she can get away, not till the last minute. Doctor's wife seems proper daft these days, and leads them servants a fine old dance. Carrie seems proper scared of 'er now she's taken to wandering about the 'ouse at night. Doctor won't 'ave no doors locked neither. She's quite 'armless, so 'e says, and I suppose a doctor ought to know. Mind jew, that son of 'ers murdered that nice young school teacher. She ain't never got over it, and it's preyed on 'er mind all this time.'

'Can't you persuade Carrie to get another job?'

'She won't leave that little boy, not till 'e goes to school.'

'Any news of our cousin Albert?'

'Not for twelve months or more. Your Aunt Lucy were notified when 'is ship was torpedoed, but no details, only that Able Seaman Albert Blunt were missing, believed drownded. Carrie broke 'er poor little 'eart. They been sweet'earts since she were 14, but I didn't think it were serious. You know Carrie, she's got a pretty good opinion of 'erself, and it's my belief she were sorry she turned 'im down. Now it's too late. Silly girl. Lucy's Albert was the best of the bunch, in my opinion. It do seem strange, but we twin sisters 'as the same sort of trouble, what with both losing our 'usbands, and our youngest sons.'

'But *you* didn't blot your copy-book, Mum! My esteemed father-in-law seems to be behaving himself since that affair. Cynthia thinks he was really fond of Aunt Lucy, but to have a mistress on his own estate would have been too embarrassing.'

'Isn't that typical of upper class? 'oo does 'e think 'e is? – God Almighty?' scoffed Ruby, indignantly.

Cynthia left mother and son together for a full hour,

506

and went to call on Freddie's Aunt Lucy at Russets, but they all were busy in the hay-field and had no time to entertain a visitor, other than to suggest she help herself to lemonade from the big pitcher under the tree.

She sat in the shade and was reminded of that other hay-making day when she fell in love with Freddie. Here, on the farm, life went on, and the work had to be done seven days a week in due season. Nature did not wait for the War to end. But this would be Harry's last hay-making. He would soon be joining the Army, and his regiment drafted overseas. This goodly heritage would be lost for ever. No premonition of death troubled his young mind, however, on this perfect Summer day, and his strong, healthy body revelled in the hard work.

Harry had been accosted by a neighbouring farmer who had lost two sons on the Western Front. They had met one market day at the Rose and Crown, and the encounter had left no doubt in his mind of his duty.

'Tell your mother to apply for a couple of strong girls if you want to do your bit, Harry – unless you are waiting to be conscripted.' This had rankled. It made him feel very uncomfortable, and shamed by the truth. The girls had duly arrived, and lost no time in getting acquainted with the two good-looking young men. They were sensible girls, with an eye to the future. Good-looking young men would be scarce when the War was over, and a surplus of women would find themselves old maids before they were 30. But the over-confident Mavis had to reckon with Emma, and Emma had no intention of standing by while *her* Harry succumbed to the dubious charms of a strapping girl in breeches and gumboots. All is fair in love and war, and Harry was enjoying his new role. The two girls had nothing in common. While Mavis was ready and willing to be tumbled in the hay, Emma had still to be caught, and was as cunning as a little fox. Over the years

507

the excitement of the unexpected had not paled for the two lovers had no specific location for their love-making. On a warm Summer night it could be on the bare earth or the long grass. In the Winter, when Harry's alert senses caught the creak of the stairs as Emma crept down from her attic bedroom, his loins would tremble in anticipation. He would find her crouching in the shepherd's hut or the hideout in the wood the brothers had built for themselves as children. They knew every inch of their land and every wild creature that shared their nocturnal pleasures.

But Cynthia know nothing of this as she watched the group about the wagon. She was thinking of Freddie, and comparing him with his cousins. Her poor darling. She knew there must be hundreds of other War casualties as grievously wounded as Freddie, but her woman's mind baulked at the thought of mass disablement. It was her own husband who claimed all her love and compassion, since she had no brothers to be involved in the War, and her father was past the age to volunteer for military service. She was tired, and the first meeting with her mother-in-law had been a nervous strain. The future was bleak, and unpredictable. The doctor had told her it would be all of twelve months, possibly longer, before her husband could cope with an artificial limb since his other injuries would be a deterrent. Mentally and physically he was a very sick man, and her heart ached with a desperate longing for a glimpse of the man she had known and loved before the War in those few brief periods when they could be together. She could not reach him or communicate. He was a stranger again. But his mother had been rewarded by a fleeting smile, and he seemed to be listening quite attentively to her views on class. Yet he must have heard it all before. They were very close, mother and son, and the bond between them was a

508

tangible obstacle. She felt shut out, and annoyed that a mother had prior claim over a wife – or did she? It was one of those debatable questions that depended on the nature of the individual, and her own environment had been no preparation for this first encounter with her mother-in-law. They were worlds apart, and for all her determination she could not visualise a time when they could meet as equals. In theory it was simple, but the reality had been disappointing. She was jealous of that indomitable little woman with her high principles, and sturdy independence, and felt only resentment that she had to share Freddie with his mother on her own free day.

Papa had been quite disgruntled over their mid-morning coffee in a tea-shop in the Strand, for he had expected to have her company for the rest of the day. He had seen her on to the train at Victoria, however, and surprised her with a suggestion that might be useful later.

Sitting in the shade of the tree, her thoughts drifted back to that suggestion, and she was undecided whether or not to mention it to Freddie. It might worry him at this crucial stage of recovery, but it was kind of Papa to suggest it.

'There may be an opening for that husband of yours in the not too distant future, my dear,' he had told her, as they waited for the train to leave. 'My bailiff will be retiring next year, and going to live with a married daughter in Canada. His cottage then becomes vacant and it's quite adequate for a couple. Think about it. It's an idea.'

'It's a wonderful idea! Thank you, Papa.' She had kissed him affectionately as the train moved away, and he lifted his hat in salute.

But it was too far removed from the present, and the future still looked bleak because there was nobody to share the problems, or the burden of responsibility. She

509

looked at her watch, waved to the hay-makers, and walked slowly back to the lake.

'I should have sat with her for a few minutes. That was mean of me,' Lucy was thinking, as she wiped her sweating face on her petticoat.

Young Philip Martin had passed the entrance examination to the Grammar School, and was catching the 7.45 a.m. train to Tonbridge six days a week. He would peck his mother's cheek and hurry away, after a hasty breakfast. No amount of scolding or coaxing would get him out of bed until it was absolutely necessary. He timed everything with a precision that irritated Martha. So many minutes to wash and dress, so many minutes to gobble the boiled egg and two slices of bread and butter his mother insisted on, and so many minutes to run the mile to the station. He hadn't yet missed the train, and could boast that the porter would have a door open in readiness as he raced, breathless, to the up platform.

Philip had grown tall, and had to wear spectacles – a sad handicap for a boy, and a target for ridicule. He was a quiet, sensitive child, old for his years, since he had no close friends of his own age. The academic influence of his godfather in those formative years had set the pattern, and Philip had been an apt pupil. They shared an interest in nature – in birds, trees and flowers – and took long walks together on Sunday afternoons at all seasons of the year, coming back to tea with healthy appetites. No more lonely Sundays for the schoolmaster, and he walked across the yard and into the wheelwright's house as naturally as he once walked across the field with Parson. The scholarly Andrew Robinson and young Philip Martin were creatures of habit and convention. They liked to feel a sense of security and comfort, and the War had not yet deprived them of this privilege. One could say

510

they were almost indifferent to the tragedies that surrounded them, yet both would feel compassion for an injured bird, and take infinite pains to mend a broken wing. The village had suffered acutely. Fatherless children wept over their copybooks and the Grammar School had lost a number of ex-pupils, boys who had visualised war as a big adventure, and a patriotic duty and had died in vain, sadly disillusioned. Philip had not known these boys personally, only as very superior prefects, and he joined in the appropriate hymns and prayers with no sense of loss.

As for his godfather, that worthy man was too concerned with the problems of his own little world to get involved in a war for which he felt only the distaste of a confirmed pacifist. Two of his most experienced and reliable teachers had been tempted by the generous wages to be earned in a munitions factory, and he was obliged to teach two standards personally. The Infants were once again without a teacher, and herded into the Standard One classroom, already overcrowded. The last pupil-teacher had left to join the VAD. Time and again the harassed schoolmaster wished he could call on Martha Martin to step into the breach, but she seemed to be avoiding him, and they were never alone together, even on Sunday, for Philip was always there. The years were passing. Martha was middle-aged, and Andrew in his early 50s. Their love had not blossomed as expected, and their friendship had become stale and uneventful as they settled down to the familiar pattern of their separate lives.

But Martha was not happy. It was a most unsatisfactory affair. She was very fond of Andrew, but she had her pride. Surely he hadn't forgotten that unguarded moment when she had revealed her love while still married to Dick? But she had been widowed for two

511

years. She could not understand his strange reticence, and could only assume he was reluctant to change his way of life. A confirmed bachelor, that short period of intensified emotion with Parson's sick daughter had left no lasting mark, and he no longer placed flowers on her grave.

Philip had long been aware of an estrangement between two of the people he loved best, for he was close to both, and had an affinity with his mother that was not uncommon in the only son. His grandfather had enjoyed the same close affinity with his own mother.

'Why don't you marry Mr Robinson, Mother?'

They were getting ready for bed one Sunday evening, and the question shocked and surprised her. She was blushing and confused. It was so unexpected.

'He likes you very much,' the boy persisted.

'Perhaps I'm waiting to be asked, dear,' she said, with deceptive lightness.

But the boy was not deceived. 'It would be nice to live with my godfather in the School House. I should have much less than a mile to run to the station, shouldn't I?'

'Philip, you're incorrigible!' Martha scolded. 'Give me a kiss and run along. It's past your bedtime.'

'Yes, Mother.' He sighed. It was so simple. If Mother was only waiting to be asked, why didn't his godfather ask her? Grown-ups were supposed to be sensible, but they often contradicted their teaching and made a mountain out of a molehill.

They met in the butcher's shop one Summer evening when both had finished work. Shopping was a hazardous business these days, with the rationing, and they joined the queue of customers in a desultory manner, waiting their turn to be served with whatever the butcher had to offer from his meagre supply. They were tired after a busy day on their respective jobs, and the heatwave was

512

exhausting. The school holidays were several weeks away, and the customers in the bakery had been difficult to please. They chatted politely about the War and the weather, the two main topics of conversation in the village. Then it was Martha's turn. It was a choice between stewing beef and a half shoulder of mutton as usual, and whichever she decided on would be unpopular with one or the other. Her father was tired of mutton and Philip was tired of stews.

'Who would be a housewife these days?' she sighed.

'Who would be a butcher!' came the prompt retort from behind the counter. Tempers were short in the shops.

'I'm sorry. I hadn't thought of your side of the rationing. It must be difficult to please your customers?' said Martha, contritely.

'Difficult? It's impossible! Nothing from overseas, and the best of the meat from the home market lands on the tables of the hotels and restaurants whose clients can afford to pay the high prices demanded. It's not fair. We village butchers just get what's left. No more Argentine beef or New Zealand lamb, not till this bloody War is over! Begging your pardon.' He grinned at the customers who nodded sympathetically.

'I'll take the stewing beef, thank you, and make another casserole. We've plenty of root vegetables in the garden, and it's quite tasty with an onion and a sprinkling of herbs.'

Andrew was wishing his housekeeper would take a few lessons from Martha. Her stews were thin and tasteless, her pastry heavy, and potatoes boiled in their jackets never tasted the same. As for the cold mutton. He enjoyed it on Sunday with Martha's home-made chutney. Wartime rations could be improved upon with a little trouble and imagination.

513

The smile they exchanged over the butcher's angry tirade did not pass unnoticed. It was no secret that the schoolmaster was invited to Sunday lunch at the wheelwright's. That he was the boy's godfather and had coached him privately after school for that entrance examination to the Grammar School was common knowledge too, for nothing was sacred in a village. School children and postmen spread the gossip through the parish.

Andrew was quickly served with a pound of stewing steak. He was not yet accustomed to doing his own shopping, and found it extremely embarrassing. But his housekeeper was complaining of her 'varicose veins' and threatening to give notice. 'The devil you know is better than the one you don't know,' so they said.

'It's your turn for suet this week, Mr Robinson,' the butcher was reminding him.

'Suet?' Andrew looked blank for a moment. For suet puddings, of course. He shuddered involuntarily. They were served with black treacle these days, since Golden Syrup was unobtainable at the grocery.

'Excuse me, Mr Robinson. I would be very glad to buy it from you if you can spare it. Philip will not complain about the stew if it contains dumplings,' Martha had got as far as the door and waited. Now she was blushing because of her boldness, and Mrs Browning was frowning. Her Bobby was also fond of dumplings in his stew.

'Half a pound of suet is worth its weight in gold!' Martha giggled, as the small packet was handed over.

'Your turn next week, Mrs Browning,' the butcher reminded her cheerfully.

Andrew followed Martha out of the shop, and they lingered on the pavement, both reluctant to part.

'Are you in a hurry, Martha?' he asked, quietly.

514

'No.'

'Then shall we take a seat for a few minutes? It's such a very pleasant evening.' He pointed to the circular seat under the plane tree, usually occupied by the old men in the daytime, but now they would be enjoying a half-pint of ale in their favourite pub. The seat overlooked the village pond, where a number of small boys were paddling their feet in the slimy water. The swans were resting on the grass, their heads tucked in their wings. It was a peaceful scene, far removed from the Western Front. A cart piled with swedes climbed the hill from one of the farms in the valley.

'Give us a turnip, Mister!' begged an urchin from Richmond Row who had no opportunity to differentiate between the two. A swede landed heavily on the grass and the boy claimed it, fighting off the rest. Taking a clasp knife from the pocket of his torn breeches, he peeled it carefully, cut off a chunk, speared it on the knife. and chewed it with relish. He was always hungry, and the raw swede would give him a nasty pain in his empty belly. We all learn by our mistakes.

'Give us a bite, can't yer?' the others begged. 'Greedy guts!' they jeered. But he took no notice.

From their seat under the tree the schoolmaster commented drily, 'Little savages, aren't they?'

'Why do you say that?' Martha asked, defensively.

'Well, aren't they? Look at the way that boy feeds himself with a raw turnip, and what is he doing with that dangerous looking knife?'

'Have you never seen a labourer eating his bread and cheese that way?'

'No.'

'Stan's father was a ganger on the railway. He died of a heart attack a short time ago. The clasp knife would be Stan's most treasured possession now. Being the eldest

515

son in a family of six, he would naturally claim it when his father died – and it's *not* a turnip, it's a swede!'

'Where do you gather all your information?'

'In the bakery. Customers like a little gossip, especially during the War, with so much sadness and anxiety.'

'I didn't know that boy had recently lost his father? And I didn't know his name was Stan. The boys are called by their surnames, and there are so many names to remember. I'm not very clever at remembering their names. What's his surname?'

'Higgins.'

'I seem to recall he was sent to me for caning not so long ago. It could have been about the time he lost his father? In which case his bad behaviour was excusable and should not have been reported.'

'Do you enjoy caning the boys?'

'No. I dislike it intensely.'

'Then why do you do it? I'm sorry. Now I'm being presumptuous.'

'Not at all. You have grown up in the village, Martha, and you are much closer to these working-class families. I should value your opinion on punishment for boys. The girls are kept in after school, as you know, to copy lines, fifty lines for a small offence, and a hundred lines for a big offence.'

'Do you ever check on the nature of the offence?'

'No, I take the teacher's word, and the children, on the whole, are very honest about their misdemeanours. Don't you agree?'

'Yes, but I have always considered corporal punishment to be a mistake. I never used the ruler for rapping knuckles in the Infants. A naughty or a disobedient child stood in a corner for about twenty minutes. It was punishment enough, for even the naughtiest child feels ashamed to be so conspicuous.'

516

'Nobody has ever managed the Infants so successfully.'

'Thank you.'

'If you have any personal opinion on this question of punishment for boys, I wish you would share it with me?'

Her slight hesitation was natural, a result of the respect that was due to him. After all these years, Martha was still a little in awe of the grave schoolmaster. Brief glimpses into his scholarly mind, and a mutual liking, could hardly be called intimacy. His reticence had always been a barrier to friendship, and Martha's pride was a hindrance not an asset in such a relationship. They both relied on Philip as a go-between.

'I'm waiting, Martha,' Andrew reminded her quietly.

'You could punish the boys by giving them certain chores to do during school hours when they would be seen. You see, Andrew, boys are never expected to lift a finger in a working-class home. It's always the girls who mind the babies, wash the dishes, sweep the floors and fill the coal buckets. I think a boy would be so shamed and embarrassed to be given a broom or a bucket, he would be more careful in his behaviour. The cane is not really a deterrent, Andrew. These boys are used to being thrashed by fathers who take off their belts and believe me, that hurts! I had no brothers, but I would often hear the neighbours' children yelling.'

'It seems an odd sort of punishment, but I'm willing to try, for to tell you the truth, I actually shrink from corporal punishment, and I'm sure the boys are aware of it. So you think a naughty boy could be given a broom to sweep the classrooms, or a bucket to fill with coke for the stoves? But that's only a Winter chore. What else do you suggest?'

'The inkwells have to be washed, and that's another chore always left to the girls.'

'Is it? I didn't know.'

517

There is so much he doesn't know about these children, Martha was thinking. He was respected, but not loved, and he was a very lonely man. Perhaps all schoolmasters were lonely in their isolated position of authority. She had no means of comparison, for she had known only one. He had asked for her opinion and she had given it, but whether or not he put her suggestion into practice was another matter. She turned her head to find he was looking at her with such compelling directness, a hot flush swept over her face.

'My dear, I need you. Will you marry me?' It was a cry from the heart of a lonely man. It was a question she had been waiting for and almost given up hope of hearing. It did not occur to her that her young son had actually intervened, or that he was capable of deciding what was a logical solution.

'Yes, Andrew,' she whispered, her voice choked with emotion.

He sighed and smiled. His rare smile lit his face with a lovely radiance, and she took his hand and returned the smile.

The boys beside the pond were watching. 'Old Robbie's gone all soppy over Mrs Martin,' muttered Stan knowingly, and wiped the precious clasp knife on his breeches. Then he clutched his stomach and wailed. 'I got a nawful pain in me belly!'

'Serves yer right! Greedy guts!' they jeered.

'Oh dear, he's going to be sick,' said Martha, sympathetically.

'Who?' Andrew had not noticed.

'Young Stan Higgins.'

'I should appreciate it, my dear, if you could give me your whole attention,' said Andrew, in exasperation.

'I'm sorry, dear.' Martha was suitably contrite. It was no surprise to discover her future husband could be

518

quickly disturbed by petty annoyances. She loved him dearly, and respect was a vital ingredient of that love.

'I didn't pay you for the suet,' she said, irrelevantly, a few minutes later.

He shook his head, but now his eyes twinkled. 'If ever a child was rightly named, it's you! The ever-practical Martha!' he teased.

'But it was Mary whom Jesus loved.'

'So the Gospel writers would have us believe. Personally, my sympathies have ever been for Martha. Does that please you?'

She nodded tremulously.

'Several of the parables take a lot of understanding, don't they, Martha? The Prodigal Son, for instance. Again, it's the son who stayed at home who has my sympathy. And the workers who were hired in the early morning and worked all day and received the same pay as those who had started in the afternoon. Surely a most unsatisfactory arrangement?'

Martha agreed. 'I have always been puzzled by the parable of the talents. The master who went away after giving his three stewards money. Two of the stewards were given more, and invested it sensibly. The third steward must have been disappointed at receiving less, so didn't bother but simply handed it back to his master on his return. Why should the master give it to the first steward who had made a good profit on his investment? "*To him that hath, more shall be added,*" Jesus is supposed to have said. Can you make sense of that, Andrew, for I can't?'

'The only parable that makes sense to me is the Good Samaritan. Even a child can understand its meaning. It's so plain.'

'Even to this day a kind and sympathetic person in an emergency is called a Good Samaritan,' Martha

519

reflected. 'Have you got a favourite disciple, Andrew?'

'Yes, my namesake. He seemed such a sensible fellow, but always in the background with that flamboyant brother in the limelight.'

'Yes, Peter was a dominant personality. Paul is my favourite follower. He was so human and honest, so brave in the face of misfortune. Why was John the favourite disciple, I wonder?'

'For the same reason that Judas was the black sheep, I suppose. It's typical of our own day and age. In a large family you will usually find a favourite and a black sheep, so I'm told. In a sense, they set the pattern for nearly two thousand years. But what a strange discussion, my dear, on this auspicious occasion. How did we arrive at such an unlikely topic?'

'You started it by saying I was rightly named Martha.'

'So I did. Well, let's get back to more personal matters, shall we?'

She nodded.

'How will you like living in the School House?'

'Very much – if you allow me to take over the Infants again! *Please*, Andrew, just for the duration of the War. It would make me very happy.'

'Very well. That's settled. I will see Parson about the banns right away. There is no reason to wait. We have waited too long already, my dear.'

'But I couldn't be married in church, Andrew. I have been brought up a Methodist.'

He frowned and stroked his beard. 'And I have been brought up Church of England. This is quite a vital question, Martha. It seems I must compromise, but I shall feel like a fish out of water. It's so very different, isn't it? The Methodists have a reputation for heartiness, and I am not a hearty person. I like my religion quiet and reverent.'

520

'It is rather hearty, but most sincere.'

'Oh well, I suppose I shall get used to it. Could we sit in a back pew, I should hate to be stared at for my ignorance.'

'We shall be stared at anyway, Andrew dear, but you mustn't take offence. It will be just a natural curiosity, and kindly meant. The village schoolmaster is quite an important person, and our marriage will be something of an event.'

'Do we have to endure a crowded Chapel on our wedding day – or can it be arranged discreetly?'

'Only by disappointing a lot of people, and it would be a pity to deprive them of some excitement. Everyone needs a little pleasure to lighten these dark days. I'm rather worried about leaving Father. He is going to miss me. It's not easy to find the right sort of person as a resident housekeeper. A widow might be glad of such a post, someone homely and sensible, and a good cook.'

'Where can you find such a person?'

'I don't know, but I shall make enquiries in the bakery. At the same time I can find a replacement for myself in the shop. That shouldn't be too difficult. A bright girl leaving school next month would suit. Do you know any bright girls, Andrew?'

He frowned thoughtfully. 'There's the Channing girl – Dora Channing. A bit too bright for my liking.'

'You mean precocious?'

'Yes.'

'That mightn't be a disadvantage in a shop. I remember Dora in the Infants. I often had to stand her in the corner for naughtiness, but she bore me no grudge. It would please her mother, Andrew.'

'Dora is an only child, and Mrs Channing obviously has ideas above her station, as they say in the village. Yes, I shall recommend her.'

521

The church clock chimed 7, and Martha stood up hurriedly.

'You must excuse me, dear. Father will be waiting for his supper.'

'Do I ask his permission to marry his daughter?'

She blushed. 'It would please him.'

'Come along then. Let us go together and break the news.' He took her arm and smiled down at her radiant face.

'I've got some good news for you this week, Mum.' Carrie announced on her free half day. She found her mother mixing pastry for a plum pie in her daughter-in-law's kitchen. It still seemed strange to find her in Elsie's kitchen, but she had no other home. Since Elsie had taken over Jack's job in the grocery, the chores were shared by the two women. The War had changed all their lives.

Ruby lifted her face to be kissed, and was pleased to see Carrie looking happy again. Things hadn't been going too well for her daughter for some time.

'That's a nice change, luv, I must say, to hear some good news.'

'Teacher is going to marry Mr Robinson – and that's not all. I've heard from Bertie. A card from Constantinople. Would you believe it?'

'Where's Constantinople?'

'Turkey.'

'What's he doing in Turkey?'

'He's a prisoner of war. Listen, I'll read it to you.' Her voice quavered with excitement as she read:-

'Dear little cousin, I bet you thought you had seen the last of me! Thanks to the Red Cross we are now allowed to send these postcards. You can write to me, Carrie, though I can't guarantee delivery. Apart from an empty belly, a shaved head and a few battle scars, I'm okay. Wait for me sweetheart. Love to all, Bertie.'

Oh, *Mum*! I'm so happy!' she sobbed.

'It's a miracle, luv. My, won't 'is Mum be pleased. That is, if she's got one of them cards? You'd better take a walk down to Russets this afternoon, and make sure she's 'eard the good news.'

Carrie nodded, tremulously. 'I *do* love him, Mum. I wasn't sure, but when I thought I'd lost him then I knew for certain.'

'They do say absence makes the 'eart grow fonder. Seems like it in your case, don't it, luv? It was different with me, for I never 'ad no doubts, not with your Dad, and your Aunt Lucy was the same way with your Uncle Bert. Just made for each other, as you might say. Mind jew, we wasn't taking no chances, for we wasn't the only fish in the sea. So we both got ourselves in the family way afore we was married.' Ruby chuckled at the memory, but her daughter gasped.

'Mum!'

'Thought you knew. You only 'ad to work out the date of our wedding day and our Albert's birth day, and there 'twas, plain as plain.'

'I never thought of it, and the boys never mentioned it.'

'They wouldn't luv, not their precious little sister. You was idolised.'

Carrie agreed. 'It's good news about Teacher too, isn't it?'

'When did she tell you?'

'I saw her in the Bakery yesterday. She always keeps a couple of sugar buns for our tea. She hides them under the counter. It will seem strange when we visit her in the School House after she's married. She said she was looking for a resident housekeeper for her father.'

'Now there's a job for me,' said Ruby, surprisingly. 'I'm proper fed up with them two old maids at The Grove. And between you and me, Carrie luv, I'd like a bit of peace. We don't get along so badly, Elsie and me, but there's nothing like your own kitchen, and your own bed. I've been sharing me bed ever since I come to live 'ere, and there's no peace, not with Elsie's children, for she's allowed them to get out of 'and since she took over Jack's job at the Grocery. She's tired, poor girl, at the end of the day, and she can't be bothered, and she don't like it if I interfere.'

'I'm sorry, Mum. I didn't know it was so difficult for you. Why didn't you tell me?'

'You've got enough troubles of your own at Doctor's place.' Ruby was shaping a scrap of pastry into a little man for her youngest grandchild who spent the day with his mother in the shop. With currant eyes and currant buttons, the little pastry man would be much enjoyed.

'I remember you always made one for me when I was little,' Carrie reflected. 'Mum?'

'Yes, luv?'

'Would you really like that job?'

'If you think I would suit Mr Carter?'

'Suit? He'd be jolly lucky to get you.'

'I wouldn't want 'im to think I was looking for another 'usband, Carrie, because there won't ever be another man to take the place of your Dad. That I do know.'

'Don't you worry. I'll explain to Teacher. Shall I see her right away before she starts to make enquiries?'

'If you like. Then we'll 'ave a nice cup of tea when you get back.'

'Isn't it exciting, Mum? Everything's happening at once!' Carrie hugged her mother exuberantly, and hurried away.

'I wonder if I'm making a mistake?' Ruby asked herself. 'They do say old Carter's a bit of a bully. But I reckon I can stick up for meself.'

'Wait for me sweetheart' – 'Wait for me, sweetheart'.

Carrie's heart was singing as she hurried along to the bakery. Mum was right. It *was* a miracle. Perhaps if she had known she still had to wait nearly another two years to see Bertie safely home, and that he would not receive even one of her long, loving letters, Carrie would have been feeling less happy. But it was love that would keep hope alive, together with an occasional postcard from Constantinople. The prisoners of war would receive their first parcels from the Red Cross the following Christmas, and Carrie would contribute her share to the fund that was raised by Parson Wellington's widow who had been working tirelessly for this good cause since the outbreak of War. It had given her a fresh purpose, and a sense of usefulness she had sadly missed in this new chapter of her life. But she would have Cecily back when the War was over. Her daughter had seen enough of suffering humanity and would be thankful to settle down quietly with her mother.

Nobody could foresee the end. For the thousands of women who had lost husbands or sons it was a bitter experience. For those whose husbands and sons had been spared, the agony of waiting would continue, and the fear of opening the door to the telegraph boy was a haunting possibility.

As Ruby sat waiting for the plum pie to bake on that particular day, she was remembering her own three sons – Freddie, a gaunt, hollow-eyed cripple, Jack killed, and Albert conscripted with the latest batch of Army recruits. Farming was no longer a reserved occupation, for girls had been trained as replacements, and German prisoners were being drafted to the farms. There was no escape, even for those who had been graded as Class Three in the early days of the War. 'The cream of British manhood has been skimmed' one national daily newspaper announced dramatically, two years after that fateful day in August, 1914.

But Ruby was concerned only for her own 'boys', and she was sorry for Albert, who had cried like a child when he came to say goodbye. Freddie and Jack had volunteered, but Albert had to be fetched. That was the difference. You couldn't change human nature, and her eldest son had no sense of duty or loyalty, only a grudging acceptance of this compulsory enlistment. Ruby was no fool. Eva had ruined her son. She was a bitch, and it was no secret that she would waste no time in taking a lover while her husband was away on active service. The German prisoners of war were young, some hardly more than boys. It would make a nice change.

Now Ruby's thoughts had switched to Freddie's wife, Cynthia. She was feeling a little guilty that she hadn't been kinder at their first meeting in the Park. Compared to Eva and Elsie, this daughter-in-law certainly had style. She loved Freddie and would always love him and care for him. Could a mother ask more than that? She had said so in a recent letter that began, surprisingly, 'Dear Mother – may I call you Mother?' Ruby was touched. All her firmly rooted prejudices seemed to be in doubt. Was she being fair to this young woman?

'May I call you Mother?' Tears pricked her eyes. She would show the letter to Carrie and they would talk it over. What did Bertie mean by 'battle scars'? Would he be disfigured? It was Elsie who brought home horrifying tales of torpedoed ships, and men being picked out of the sea with terrible burns. It was a cruel war. She wondered if Elsie would be annoyed over her decision to change her job and her abode. Elsie's temper was short these days, and she would probably accuse her mother-in-law of leaving her in the lurch.

Ruby sighed. It was difficult to please everyone, and she was tired of trying to keep the peace among Elsie's quarrelsome brood. Of course there would be snags in

526

her new job, and it wouldn't take her long to discover them. But she would manage. She hadn't been beaten yet. She had her working-class pride, and she knew her worth.

ler hair, less painful than beginning to thin out
hang, but a casual glance at the hair would have
revealed that the winding glass panel and she occasio
gazed.

Chapter Eighteen

'Congratulations, Sir.' They shook hands gravely, for young Philip Martin was a serious boy, and regarded his godfather, soon to become his stepfather, with due respect. They were inspecting the School House and his mother had been asked to make suggestions for improvements. It was a typical bachelor establishment, but Martha would make no sweeping changes because she was not a woman who cared for frills, fripperies, and Victorian bric-a-brac. Her tastes were simple and Spartan. She would make new curtains and cushion covers on the old treadle machine she had brought from home and garden flowers would replace the dusty artificial roses the ex-housekeeper had favoured. The dingy brasses and windows would shine again, and the gloomy house would become a bright, welcoming home for her husband and son.

A week's holiday had been arranged for early August, before the start of the hop-picking season. The honeymoon would be spent at the School House, cleaning and polishing. The sewing machine would rattle every afternoon. Martha would enjoy the novelty of being mistress of the School House, with the increased respect of the children.

When the new term started in late September, she would take up her old post as Teacher in the Infants' classroom. The village welcomed the usual invasion of hop-pickers from London's East End, and Martha would be busy in the bakery, training her young assistant fresh from school. They could expect a stampede of late customers every evening from the farms and cottages when picking had finished for the day. It was customary for the shops to remain open till 8 o'clock, for trade was brisk, and no customers were to be despised.

During this second year of the War, it would enliven the heavy atmosphere of sorrow and suspense; the Londoners were cheerful souls, in spite of their own heartache, for all had suffered the loss of husband, son or brother.

The wedding was a very happy occasion, with the Chapel bursting at the seams, and friends and neighbours contributed refreshments for the wedding breakfast in the adjoining hall. Andrew was secretly dismayed at the heartiness, and so nervous he found himself stammering and tongue-tied. Fortunately, no speech was expected, and no toast proposed, since only tea was served. Martha enjoyed every minute, but when they were back at the School House with Philip, she began to dread the ordeal of the first night in that big double bed in the main bedroom. The two years that had passed since she lost Dick had still not eliminated the memory of his lustful domination. He had used her body as an instrument for his own satisfaction. Without love or tenderness, the act of intercourse had become nothing more than a degrading sexual performance. Would she ever forget?

She kept Philip with them that evening, long after his usual bedtime, and all three were busy in the garden till dusk. Philip cut the small lawn with a blunt pair of shears, and Andrew dug holes for the rose bushes they had

529

received as a wedding present from her father's employees. Neither Andrew nor Philip were keen gardeners, and they handled tools clumsily. Martha was the practical one. It would be Martha who would put a new washer on a dripping tap and clear a blocked drain. Such chores as filling lamps with paraffin, scuttles with coal, and chopping firewood, would automatically be left to her, for neither her husband or her son would give a thought to such menial tasks.

They lingered over supper in the parlour, and she thought of Ruby cooking supper and sitting down to her first meal with her new employer. She hoped her father would recognise his new housekeeper's status, and that they could be friends, not master and servant.

When Philip had kissed her goodnight and his bedroom door had closed, it was after 10 o'clock, and Martha could no longer postpone her own retirement. The original box-room had been converted into a bathroom. This was a luxury they had not enjoyed at her father's house. Andrew had slipped away quietly into his little study. She supposed he would follow her to bed when he was ready. He would not change his bachelor habits overnight, she reminded herself. She hardly knew what to expect from her second husband.

It was nearly midnight when she heard his heavy step on the stairs. She had been dozing, but now she was fully awake, tense with distaste for that physical act that would seal their marriage vows. She wondered if Andrew had delayed coming to bed because he, too, was reluctant. That heavy step on the stairs could hardly be called eager. It could have no particular significance, this late hour, and it was just his usual time to retire to bed. There was so much she had still to discover about her second husband's habits and personality, for the early relationship of master and teacher had been one of respect and affection, but not close enough for intimacy. In the past two years there had been ample opportunity to court her, but he had not done so. Their friendship had not developed into something deeper, and seemed to depend on Philip for its survival. Yet, all this time he had been needing her, or so he insisted. She loved and respected him, but she could not pretend that her love was reciprocated. 'I need you' was not the same to a woman as 'I love you'. These were the magic words the heart listened for in a marriage proposal. No two men could be so unlike in every respect than the two men she had married; an extrovert and an introvert, an uncouth soldier, and an intellectual schoolmaster, a dominant dictator and an undemanding gentleman.

She had left the bedroom door ajar, and she could hear him cleaning his teeth with a thoroughness that brought a smile to her tight lips. It did not surprise her, for it was typical of Andrew. He was a thorough person, and he had taught her son to be thorough. 'Whatsoever thy hand findeth to do, then do it with all thy might', was one of several maxims he used to illustrate his principles. 'If at first you don't succeed, then try again', was another. A disobedient child in his own Sixth Standard would be kept in from play to copy out one or other of these proverbs. This particular punishment was unpopular with the boys. Two strokes of the cane was quickly over.

Now she could hear the water running into the wash basin, and the familiar splashing sound that men and boys usually made when they cupped their hands to wash their faces. Then silence, for several minutes. Was he undressing in the bathroom? Was he washing his 'private parts'? Now her face was burning. Dick had never stopped to wash. He was too impatient. Andrew would not come to her unclean. He was so fastidious. Yet his body was still a mystery to be revealed. There was no

531

other way to establish a lasting relationship between a man and a woman. It was foolish to have overlooked this fact until tonight. What did she really know of Andrew as a lover? Beneath that grave façade was there a passionate man, a stranger, with strange ways of satisfying desire? She shuddered at the memory of Dick's sadistic experiments. He was seldom satisfied until he had her in tears, pleading for mercy. Her sheltered girlhood, innocent of the facts of life, had not prepared her for the overwhelming emotions that took control of her virgin body that Summer afternoon, with the young Dick Martin. It was quickly over, and there had been no ugliness or nakedness. Then he was gone, and the Dick Martin who returned some years later was a stranger, a man of rough speech and uncouth manners, a man who shocked her with the violence of his passion. Her modesty had amused him. For a wife to find nakedness embarrassing was a lewd joke he shared with his pals in the Sergeants' Mess. She still found nakedness embarrassing, probably because it had been forced on her too often. Only a child's body is beautiful, she reflected now, as she lay waiting in nervous anticipation, for her second husband. She remembered the happy hours of bathing her own child's perfect little body, but now they were both embarrassed by nakedness, and Philip would lock his bedroom door before he stripped off his clothes.

A clean calico nightgown covered her trembling body. Why couldn't she have been content with her widowhood and her son? They had been happy enough in her father's house. Now it was too late.

She glanced at the tall, bearded figure in the doorway. His clean striped pyjamas were faded, after years of washing, and his thinning hair lay damp on his high forehead. The fleeting smile was reassuring, however. The gaslight flickered and faded.

When he climbed into bed, he smelled of soap and toothpaste, and seemed surprisingly calm and cool. As he slipped an arm about her shoulders, he kissed her burning brow and told her, with gentle consideration, 'You must be tired, Martha. It has been an exciting day. Just relax. There is no hurry. I am not an impatient man. I can wait.'

She sighed and tucked her head into his comforting shoulder. 'Thank you, Andrew,' she breathed gratefully – and slept like a child till morning.

Another hop-picking season was over. The evenings were drawing in, and Ruby lit a fire in the parlour after tea. She began to dread the long dark evenings, when she would be sharing the parlour with her employer. According to his daughter, Mr Carter would be reading the works of Charles Dickens and Sir Walter Scott, for that was his usual relaxation after supper on Winter evenings.

Martha had been a great help in advising the new housekeeper on her father's routine, his food, and his habits, for he was a very conservative man, and these further changes in the household most unwelcome.

'Why can't Ruby Simmons sit in the kitchen?' he had demanded, truculently.

'Because she is Carrie's mother, and Carrie is a dear friend. It would not be seemly,' Martha explained patiently.

His gusty sigh was not very encouraging, and he would not be a very cheerful companion for poor Ruby.

'What does she do? Does she read? I don't want her fidgeting around,' he grumbled.

'I expect she will knit and do her mending and that sort of thing. She has probably never had time for reading. Like most working-class mothers, her education was neglected, so there would be no enjoyment in reading.

533

I'm sorry, Father, but I just don't see how Ruby can be banished to the kitchen.'

'Then see she understands that I don't wish to be disturbed by her chattering.' He always had the last word, so it didn't surprise Martha.

Ruby had quite enjoyed the novelty of gardening during the light evenings, and she went to bed early and was an early riser like the majority of country-bred women. Martha had done her best to smooth the way, so that Ruby should feel at home in her new surroundings, but Ruby was not feeling at home. She was missing her family, for now she was seeing Elsie and the grandchildren only on Sunday afternoons, and Carrie spent part of her free evening at the School House. It was too quiet, deadly dull, in fact, but she would get used to it, Ruby reminded herself.

The early years in Richmond Row had been the happiest years with her husband and children depending on her for everything. Now her world was small, and confined to one elderly man, of uncertain temper, who seldom spoke, and ate what she provided without comment. She had to admit, however, that she was enjoying a good night's sleep in her own bed. Yes, she would get used to it, for really there was no alternative, and you could not pick and choose. To serve behind the counter at the grocery would have suited her fine, but it was only right and reasonable for Elsie to get the job after Jack was killed, fighting for his King and Country. Apart from the fact Elsie was quick at figures, and adding up the customers' bills would have floored her mother-in-law.

So Ruby upbraided herself for feeling sad and discontented, when she should have been counting her blessings, for she still had her health and strength, and a roof over her head, and her remaining children to worry about. She hadn't seen Freddie and his wife since they

534

met at Marston Park, but Cynthia had written to suggest a brief visit on her next free day, on Tuesday of next week. She would call in on her way back to the station in the early evening, and there was no need to reply. There was only one place where they could talk privately. Why should she be ashamed of her kitchen? The range shone with black lead and elbow grease. Copper pans gleamed on the wall. Willow-pattern china adorned the Welsh dresser, and one of Martha's home-made mats brightened the hearth. The table was scrubbed white. She always felt a sense of belonging in a kitchen because she had never been invited or expected to sit in any other room when her work was finished. All her happiest memories were of kitchens.

So she awaited her visitor in the twilight hour, between tea and supper, and looked about the room with satisfaction. A lamp was homely. Mr Carter disliked gas, and they still went to bed by candlelight. The men were working late in the workshop, and she had taken them a pot of tea and a plate of hot buttered scones on her own initiative.

'You're spoiling those men,' Mr Carter had grumbled. He was a difficult man to pleae.

The tall figure in nurse's uniform greeted her warmly.

'Good evening, Mother,' she said, and kissed her cheek.

'Good evening, luv,' Ruby responded. 'My, but you're wet. I never knowed it was raining.'

'It's nothing. Just a drizzle.'

'And you've walked all the way?'

'Shanks's pony is the only means of transport these days in the country. It's different in London.'

Ruby was hanging the damp coat over the back of a kitchen chair, not too near the fire because of the danger of shrinkage.

'How are you getting on? Are you happy here?' her daughter-in-law was asking, as she took off her hat and shook out her short shining hair.

'It's not so bad, luv. I'm getting used to it. Sit you down in that wicker chair and I'll brew the tea.'

'But there's only one comfortable chair. Where will you sit?'

'Don't worry about me. There's a kitchen chair. That wicker chair was provided for the last housekeeper what used to sit in the kitchen in the evening. I been told to sit in the parlour.'

'Why? This is such a pleasant room. Why can't you sit where you please?'

'They seem to think I should be insulted because Mr Carter's daughter is a friend of my daughter, Carrie.'

'And would you be insulted?'

'Not me, luv. I'm working class and I feel at 'ome in the kitchen. What would you do? I don't want to cause no trouble.'

'I should sit in the kitchen, and tell them to mind their own business.'

They laughed companionably and drank the strong, sweet tea. There was a time when Cynthia would drink only weak tea with a slice of lemon, but that was a long time ago. Everyone drank strong, sweet tea these days. It was the national beverage in wartime. It soothed shattered nerves and sad hearts.

'Tell me about Freddie. Tell me the truth, luv.' Ruby handed the plate of hot buttered scones to her visitor, and asked, plaintively, 'Will our Freddie always be a cripple for the rest of his days?'

'NO!'

Ruby was quite startled at the vehement reply to her question, and the change in the girl's attitude. The dark eyes were brilliant with unshed tears, and the wide generous mouth was trembling. 'We must be brave and hopeful, and we must be strong for Freddie's sake – you and I, Mother. It's going to take a long, long time, possibly as long as two years, to mend his broken body and spirit. The healing process cannot be hurried, so we have to be patient. My poor darling.' She spread her hands in a gesture of resignation.

'You make me feel badly, luv,' Ruby confessed. 'I wasn't expecting you to be like this. I should 'ave given you the benefit of the doubt, as they say. I thought the upper class was soft, and they couldn't face up to real trouble, not like us working class. But you've got pluck. I can see that now, and I'm sorry I misjudged you, luv.'

'It's all right. It's not your fault, I was equally to blame. It was a natural misunderstanding. I should have made the effort to get to know you better in the early days of our marriage. So much time has been wasted. I am the one who should feel guilty. Supposing Freddie had been killed? We might never have known each other, you and I. Now I feel I have always known you. It's good to be sitting here, in this pleasant kitchen, drinking tea, sharing our troubles. There is nobody else who is so understanding. My father has been kind and sympathetic, which is more than I deserve, but my mother lives in her own private little world. My younger sisters are just biding their time till the War is over, when they have been promised the London Season, and an opportunity to find husbands. I call it the Marriage Market, and I was lucky to escape. My elder sister, Beatrice, was persuaded into marriage with a man old enough to be her father, who wanted a son and heir to inherit his estate. Unfortunately for him and my poor sister, the first-born, a son, was delicate, and lived only a few months. My sister has since given birth to three girls in such quick succession, and the family doctor has advised no more children. Beatrice is not strong, and all this child-bearing has been too much for her. The privileges of her class do not alter the fact that she still has to carry a child for nine months, and all have been difficult births. I wish we hadn't to be separated by hundreds of miles. They have a London house, but they don't use it. My brother-in-law is nervous of zeppelins, and I can't ask for time off to visit them. Besides, I wouldn't leave Freddie. He comes first.'

'What 'appens when Freddie leaves Marston Park?'

'He will spend some time at Roehampton, being fitted with an artificial leg, and getting accustomed to the feel of it. When he is sufficiently confident to walk without a stick, then we shall see the miracle. A new man will emerge – a new husband, a new son we may hardly recognise. Then we shall have to adjust to a new way of life. I have not yet mentioned to Freddie that my father has offered us the bailiff's cottage on the estate if Freddie will take over the job when the bailiff retires. We think he could manage it quite well, if he used the old mare and the governess-cart. I am not pushing him into it, Mother, and there is plenty of time to make up his mind when he has finished at Roehampton. There would be no scope for another solicitor in the village, but Freddie may want to start another practice in Tunbridge Wells. We must wait and see.'

'I think it's very kind of your father, luv, and I 'ope Freddie accepts the offer.'

'Papa is not as bad as he's painted, actually. You'd be surprised. He is really quite generous. One could almost call him a reformed character since Charles was born, and we have your sister to thank for that. Were you very shocked?'

'I was ashamed of 'er. We all was ashamed. Couldn't understand it, not after Bert. Another farmer, or some chap in 'er own class wouldn't 'ave been so bad. Bur *Sir*

538

Neville? That didn't make no sense, for Lucy were proud, and so respected, and she only ever loved Bert, that I do know. Why couldn't Sir Neville 'ave laid some other woman? Why did it 'ave to be our Lucy?'

'I believe he saw her as the perfect mother for his son. She was obviously strong and healthy, she was attractive, and she already had three fine sons. It was selfish, but then he has always been selfish, and so incensed with his four daughters. Poor Papa.'

'They tell me 'e's the spitting image of Sir Neville. I never seed 'im, but Carrie 'as seen quite a lot of 'im.'

'And she likes him?'

'She loves him.'

'Everyone loves Charles. I think he combines the best qualities of both parents, but he is very strong-willed, and will certainly please himself when he comes of age. His loyalties are divided at present, but he never misses an opportunity to visit his mother. She adores him. One only has to see them together to realise it's a very close relationship. His earliest years, the most impressionable years, were spent at Russets, so that environment is too deeply rooted to be ignored. Whatever he decides when he comes of age, somebody has to suffer. I don't envy Charles, yet he seems quite capable of separating those two distinct environments, and it doesn't appear to worry him unduly. He spent a week in London last month, and stayed at Brown's Hotel. It was Father's treat because they've not had their usual holiday in France since the Summer of 1913. I managed to get a couple of hours off duty on his last evening, and had dinner with them. Charles had been enjoying himself enormously seeing the sights. But the main attraction, it seems, was the Music Hall and Marie Lloyd. He had seen the same show every evening for a whole week, and was carrying round an autographed photograph of his favourite.'

'I'm glad 'e enjoyed 'isself in London. I were scared stiff that time I 'ad ter visit my Tom in the 'orspital. Went up every Sunday I did. Never been so scared in all me life!'

'I wish I had known you then. I would have met you.'

'Would you, luv? I should 'ave been ever so pleased to see you, and when I'd seen Tom, we could 'ave 'ad a nice cup of tea together in one of them Lyons tea places. They make a poor cup of tea in that tea-room at Victoria Station.'

'What a shame. Never mind. You and I *will* have tea at Lyons one of these days, when Freddie gets to Roehampton.'

'Thank you, luv. That gives me somethink to look forward to, for I do like a bit of life. It's what I missed when I left The Three Nuns. That were a big mistake, but the family was worrying me to better meself, so I took on the cook's job at The Parsonage, and from there I went to The Grove and now I'm 'ere, so I never went back to charring,' she sighed, nostalgically, for the good old days.

'I know about charring. Freddie was horrified when he saw my hands that first time we met in London, just before the War. He went to the chemist on the way back to his lodgings and bought some ointment. I was so touched I wanted to cry. I'm rather proud of them, actually.' She spread them out for Ruby's inspection.

'It's the soda water what does it, luv, and the 'ard soap. Soft green soap is what you need. I've always used it for washing our 'air, Carrie's and mine. She uses shampoo now, but I swear by that soft green soap.'

'No wonder. Your hair is beautiful. Tell me about Carrie. Is she going to marry her cousin after the War?

'Seems like it. She were proper flummoxed when she 'ad that card from Bertie. "Wait for me, sweet'eart" that's what 'e said, bless 'is 'eart.'

'How sweet.'

540

'I 'ope she won't 'ave ter wait too long, for Doctor's wife is getting 'er down, she's that peculiar.'

'Must she stay there?'

'She won't leave that little boy. Carrie dotes on that child. Mind jew, she might 'ave ter change 'er mind if things get any worse.'

'You mean it could be dangerous?'

Ruby nodded. 'She took a dislike to our Carrie right from the start. A village girl wasn't good enough to be nursemaid to 'er grandson. She thought 'er daughter-in-law should 'ave engaged one of them posh nurses from London. Doctor's wife 'as always been a snob. Not like Doctor. Treats all 'is patients alike, and don't neglect the working class. That I do know, for 'e were good to my Tom.'

'So he should be. A dedicated doctor should make no distinction between rich and poor unless he chooses to practise in Harley Street when he is classified as an upper-class specialist.'

'They do say Doctor don't always get paid, but that's taking a liberty.'

Her mother-in-law was very definite in her views, Cynthia was thinking, but she was already feeling a genuine fondness for Freddie's mother. The barrier was down. There was no more pretence or embarrassment.

'I must go. I shall miss my train,' she said, reluctantly.

'You'll come again, won't you, luv?' Ruby was holding up the coat. It felt warm and dry.

'I should love to. Thank you for the welcome and the tea. Goodbye, Mother – and don't let them bully you into sitting in the parlour.' she whispered, confidentially, on the doorstep.

For young Jimmy Saunders, nursery tea was the high spot of the day. They always called in at the bakery on the way

541

back from the afternoon walk to collect the sugar buns. Actually, it wasn't a walk, for he rode his tricycle. Sometimes – not more than once a week because Carrie paid for these luxuries from her own small wage – she also bought a cottage loaf, and they ate all the crusty bits for tea.

On the day they bought the cottage loaf, they called in at the grocery to see Elsie, who passed a quarter of butter over the counter when the grocer was looking the other way. She also allowed him to choose a biscuit from the tin they kept for the customers' children since biscuits were also strictly rationed. Once upon a time, before the War, there were no less than a dozen tins with glass tops, all arranged at a convenient level below the counter. Jimmy knew all about rationing. Once upon a time they had honey for tea, and strawberry jam on Sunday. Now they had jam made with rhubarb or marrow, and flavoured with ginger.

'I don't like ginger,' Jimmy told Cook, decidedly, for he was a very forthright little boy, and Carrie encouraged it.

'Little boys should eat what is put in front of them, and it so happens that your Grandma likes ginger,' Cook retorted.

There was no golden syrup for the suet pudding, only black treacle. Nobody could explain who was eating all the honey and strawberry jam and golden syrup. There was so much that went unexplained these days, with Carrie on tenterhooks, threatened with dismissal, Grandma muttering to herself as she prowled about the house; and the servants bad tempered and sulky. Because of the rationing, Cook spread the nursery bread with margarine, and kept the butter for the drawing-room, but it was still called bread and butter.

'I wasn't born yesterday,' scoffed Carrie. What did she mean by that? Jimmy wondered.

'Is it the War that makes everybody so cross?' he wanted to know.

'Not in this house, my love. It's your grandma. But she's not well, so we have to make allowances.'

'What's a 'lowance?'

'It's – it's trying not to mind when somebody is being awkward.'

'Grandma makes me say grace when I have my tea in the drawing-room on your half day, and she makes me 'peat the Lord's Prayer after I've said my Gentle Jesus when I go to bed.'

'*Re*peat,' Carrie corrected automatically. 'And Gentle Jesus is quite enough prayer for a little boy.'

'Grandma says it's time I went to church on Sunday. She says I am growing up to be a proper little heathen.'

'That's not true!' Carrie exploded.

'What's a heathen?' he asked innocently, and she giggled.

'Jimmy Saunders, you'll be the death of *me*!'

They had no secrets from each other, and he always told her everything that had happened on her free half day – with a little prompting, of course.

'What else did your Grandma say?'

'She said I must have a governess 'cause I'm a big boy now.'

'A *governess*?' Carrie nearly choked, she was so angry. 'She can't *do* that, Jimmy. Your Mummy said I was to look after you till you were 7, and then you would go to prep school.'

'That's right.'

'But don't you *see*, if your Grandma engages a governess, I have to leave.'

'Why?'

'Because you can't have both, and your Grandma wants to get rid of me.'

543

'Don't cry. I shall tell Grandma I don't want a governess. I think I would like to be 7 quite soon, then I can have a real bicycle like Philip.'

'Eat up your bread and butter, there's a good boy,' sniffed Carrie, miserably.

'It's so dry. It makes me cough. Could I have a little sugar on it, *please* Carrie, could I?'

'You see that sugar in the basin? It has to last all the week. You have my share. You mustn't be greedy.'

He grinned disarmingly, and held up his plate. Her heart melted with love for this child. How much longer could it last, this happy relationship between a nursemaid and her charge? she asked herself, as she sprinkled sugar on the bread and margarine. It was unfortunate that his Grandma chose to call on the nursery on the very day they had the crusty cottage loaf on the table, and the small pot of butter. The bread and margarine from the kitchen had already been scooped off the plate into a paper bag to feed the swans on the pond the following day. With a pleasant sense of anticipation Carrie was slicing off the crusts, and Jimmy waiting to spread the butter. What followed may never have happened but for that cottage loaf. On such small incidents the course of our lives can be decided.

The door opened so silently they were not aware of her till she spoke, her voice sharp with irritation.

'Where did you get that loaf?'

Carrie stared, wide-eyed. 'at the bakery, Ma'am.' It was snatched out of her hand, and Jimmy wailed.

'No, Grandma! It's ours. Carrie bought it with her own money.'

Ignoring the child, she demanded, 'What have you done with the bread and butter from the kitchen? Answer me, girl!'

'It's here, in the bag. It was stale, Ma'am.'

'Of course it's stale. Haven't I given orders to Cook?

544

And what do you intend to do with *this*?' Her eyes were blazing, her hands trembled, as she lifted the paper bag.

'It's for the swans, Grandma,' said Jimmy, appealingly.

'So you feed the swans, and children are dying of hunger!' She emptied the bag on to the plate and commanded, 'Get on with your tea, James.'

'No, I won't! I want a new crust.'

His ears were boxed so soundly he yelled with the pain and dived for Carrie's comforting breast. 'You hurt!' he sobbed accusingly.

'Disobedient children always get hurt.'

'It's not fair to punish him, Ma'am. It was my fault.' Carrie was hugging him protectively. Then her face blanched, and she pushed him away. Dulcie Saunders had picked up the bread knife. The child's screams echoed through the house. Servants rushed from the kitchen. The doctor had not moved so quickly in years.

'What is it, child? What's happened?' He caught up the small figure on the stairs.

'It's Grandma. She's got a knife. She's going to kill Carrie.'

'I'll take him, Sir.' Cook had stepped forward from the little group in the hall, and opened her arms.

Leaping up the stairs, the doctor's heart was pounding, but he spoke quietly, authoritatively, in the doorway. 'Dulcie, put down that knife.'

She was standing over the terrified girl, her body tense with hatred and jealousy. Suddenly, she sagged, the knife dropped to the floor. He caught the limp figure in his arms, carried her to his dressing-room, and laid her on the bed. She was deathly pale. It was not unexpected, this collapse, but he hadn't been prepared for the knife. He stood there, looking down at her with a tenderness he had not known for a very long time. She had lost a lot of weight. There were deep hollows in her neck. As far back as he could remember, Dulcie had never fainted or shown any sign of weakness. She deplored weakness in others. It was the main reason why that unhappy affair with Dennis and the young school teacher had affected her so deeply. She had never been the same since he went away. But she had expected too much of Dennis, knowing he was weak and unstable. If only she had confided in her husband, or sought his advice, she might have been spared so much of the heartache. All classes of society were included among his many patients, and to every one he gave individual attention, for no two cases were alike.

He sat on the edge of the bed, and took her thin wrist in his sensitive fingers. Her pulse was weak. He reached for his night bag and took out the stethoscope. Unbuttoning her dress and camisole, he felt a strange shyness and reluctance. It was so long since he had touched her so intimately, so long since they had shared the marriage bed. But he hadn't forgotten they once had been lovers. He remembered how it all started with a punt on the river, and a girl in a white muslin dress, a pretty hat, and a frilly parasol. In his immaculate white flannels, college blazer, and boater, they made a charming couple. When he tired of punting, he would pull into the bank, under a drooping willow. Dulcie would close the parasol, and they would remove their hats. With his head pillowed in her lap, he would close his eyes and envisage her slender body naked and unadorned, for a medical student was no stranger to the female anatomy. If she noticed his trembling loins, she made no comment. She probably thought he was feeling a little chilly after the exertions with the punting.

Dulcie was so blissfully innocent of sex in those early days, and he would not frighten her. But that same breast had pillowed her three sons, and she had given all her love and devotion to her children. She was all maternal, and he hadn't known that motherhood could deprive him of a loving wife so soon, and so completely.

He heard the girl running downstairs. She had been badly frightened, but she was young, and she would soon recover from the shock in the kitchen. Somebody would make a fresh pot of tea. It was still the best antidote to shock. The house without Dulcie would be strangely peaceful, for they all had suffered from the tension of not knowing what she would do next. Yet he still postponed the moment when he must pick up the phone and call Steve. They had been students together at medical school all those years ago, and kept in touch. Steve Bates had specialised in mental illness, and his private clinic at Tunbridge Wells was as far removed from an institution as could be imagined. There were no bars on the windows, and no doors were locked. Supported by a large staff, Steve Bates was as firmly established in his chosen environment as his life-long friend, the village doctor. At the age of 44, Steve had snatched the prettiest nurse at Barts from under the noses of several admirers, and married the girl. Cathy was 20, and she adored him. He had always kept in touch with Barts. As Consultant Lecturer, his services were invaluable. Steve was a big, broad-shouldered, gentle giant. Cathy was petite.

It was very quiet in the house now, with the girl and the child in the kitchen with the servants. The village grape-vine would soon be buzzing. He shrank from the pitying glances and kind condolences as he went on his way. How would Dulcie react to her new environment? With an injection to calm her nerves, and her own husband driving the car, it should be managed without any further disturbance. But one could never be sure. Mental illness was always a hazard, and patients unpredictable.

'I'm sorry, my dear,' he told her, chokingly – and picked up the phone.

Jimmy was comfortably seated on Cook's lap, eating a hot buttered scone when Carrie burst into the kitchen.

'Come and sit down, girl,' said Cook, kindly. 'You look as though you've seen a ghost. Make a fresh pot of tea, Martha.'

'It was no ghost,' Carrie shuddered.

Parsons pushed forward a chair and asked, 'What's happening upstairs?'

'Doctor's with her in the dressing-room. She fainted.'

'So it's come to a head at last. I've been expecting it. Poor Madam.' She sighed sympathetically. But Martha was enjoying every sensational minute. She could hardly wait to slip in next door to tell the full story to Emmie, the young housemaid engaged to be married to one of the postmen. It would spread through the village like a prairie fire.

'They'll 'ave ter take 'er away, won't they? I mean, it's not safe for any one of us, is it?' she contended.

'Get on with that tea. Nobody asked for your opinion,' said Cook, scathingly.

'Grandma doesn't like Carrie,' Jimmy explained.

'Your Grandma is a very sick lady, my duckie,' Cook hadn't called him her duckie for a very long time.

'We have to make 'lowances, don't we?' he reminded her.

Martha giggled. Carrie managed a wan smile and sipped the hot sweet tea gratefully. It was so comforting to be sitting there, in the company of the other servants. She often felt they resented her, and they grumbled about extra work, yet she carried up all the nursery meals, and was careful not to offend Cook too often. Cook was easily offended.

548

'Why did Madam turn on you? Did you say something to upset her?' Parsons wanted to know.

And Carrie remembered the cottage loaf, and flushed guiltily. But the phone was ringing in the hall, and it was Parsons' job to answer it. When she came back, she had forgotten the question.

'That was your sister-in-law, Elsie. She asked me to give you a message. She said to warn you to keep Jimmy away from other children. Several children have been whooping in the shop lately.'

'That was kind of her to phone. I wouldn't want him to catch it, but he doesn't play with the village children, only Philip Martin, and he's at Grammar School. Philip had measles, chicken-pox and whooping cough when they were living at Tidworth.'

'Martha Carter that was has done quite well for herself marrying the schoolmaster, but she had a poor deal with her first husband. Them Martins are an uncouth lot,' Parsons reflected.

'Did you know Madam was thinking of engaging a governess for Jimmy?' Carrie looked from one to the other, but they shook their heads.

'That means you would get the sack, and that wouldn't suit you know who,' said Cook, meaningly.

'Don't want a governess. Want Carrie,' Jimmy asserted, and they all laughed.

'Well, you won't hear nothing more about that, so you don't have to worry. Help yourself,' Parsons invited, pushing a couple of buttered scones across the table. She was not usually so agreeable, and the cottage loaf still threatened. Any minute now Jimmy could mention it, quite innocently. They could still eat their crusty loaf and sugar buns for supper. Suddenly they were startled by Doctor's quiet voice in the doorway.

'Sorry to disturb you. Parsons, would you pack a bag

549

for Madam, please. She is taking a little holiday for a few weeks. You will know what to pack. I leave it to you.'

'Yes, Doctor. I'll come right away.' Parsons followed him up the stairs.

'Poor man,' Cook sighed. 'I reckon he could do with a holiday, but not that sort.'

'Doctor don't never take a holiday, do 'e, Cook.' Martha had settled herself on a kitchen chair.

'There's no call for you to be sitting around doing nought. Get them potatoes peeled what I left in the scullery,' Cook reminded her tartly.

Carrie also got up, thinking to take Jimmy back to the nursery, but he had dropped off to sleep on Cook's ample bosom. So they talked quietly till Parsons came back.

'Poor Madam. She went off so peaceful. No trouble at all.' She sniffed miserably.

Now they settled down to a house without a mistress, but it ran smoothly, and Doctor did not interfere. Old-established servants could be trusted to do their work properly.

'How is Madam?' Parsons would ask kindly, when he returned from his regular Sunday visit to Tunbridge Wells. It was no secret now that the 'holiday' was being spent in a clinic. Doctor never went empty-handed. Hot-house flowers and grapes were delivered to The surgery every Saturday from Marston Park and the Grove. Farmers' wives sent eggs and the tradesmen little gifts of rationed food to tempt her appetite. Doctor had aged ten years since that afternoon when he found Dulcie threatening the girl with a knife. His shoulders were stooped, his hair was white, for he blamed himself for her nervous breakdown. Constantly busy and engrossed in his practice and his patients, he had neglected his own wife. But it was never too late to make amends.

When the War was over, he would take her to visit

550

Dennis, since Dennis could not visit them. He dare not set foot in the country, or he would be arrested for the murder of the young school teacher. The case had never been closed and Scotland Yard had long memories.

Steve was optimistic. 'Leave Dulcie with us for six months. Then it's up to you, old chap,' he told his friend. 'Give her your time. Give her back her self-importance. Dulcie is a proud woman, too proud to beg for love and understanding. Why not retire? Hand over the practice to a younger man and enjoy a few years together. You've done enough.'

'I'll think about it,' the village doctor promised.' Steve was right. The time had come to hand over the reins. The future belonged to Dulcie.

Ruby was appalled at her daughter's narrow escape. 'You've got to get somethink settled afore she comes back 'ome, Carrie, luv. I won't 'ave you taking no more risks with that poor soul what's not accountable. You must talk to Doctor. Ask 'im to get in touch with 'is daughter-in-law. It's time she was told what's been 'appening 'ere. Too much responsibility for a young girl. Let 'er come back and look after 'er own child!'

'But what should I *do*?' wailed Carrie.

'There's a War on and there's plenty of work. You could earn good money in one of them factories where they make the shells for the guns.'

Carrie shuddered.

'Tain't no use you being squeamish, my girl. Somebody 'as to do it. Them Germans 'as to be taught a lesson, once and for all. Two years already, and we was told the War would be over by Christmas, 1914. And 'ere we are with our third Christmas on the way, and not 'ardly enough fruit to make a decent pudding, and I been saving it up all Summer. The poor little kiddies won't get much in their stockings this year, I'm thinking. No oranges, no nuts, no dates or figs, and none of them lovely boxes of preserved fruits your Dad was partial to, so Elsie tells me. It won't seem like Christmas without them lovely brazils, will it, Carrie?'

'We can always roast chestnuts, can't we, Mum? And there's a good crop of apples this year. We shall have to make do. Cook's made a few pounds of jam with the blackberries we picked in October, and the Bramley apples Mrs White allowed us to pick up in the grass in her orchard. Only she's keeping it for Christmas. Cook's like an old miser now, hoarding everything for Christmas. I wonder if Bertie will get that nice big parcel Auntie Lucy posted in September? The Red Cross are doing their best, and it's not their fault if parcels and letters go astray. I wonder if those socks I knitted for Bertie will be big enough? I can't remember if his feet are big or small. I can't even remember the colour of his eyes.'

'Blue. All them boys 'as got blue eyes. Fair as lilies, like your Auntie Lucy, and mine as dark as gypsies like their Dad. Good thing you took after me, Carrie luv. Now don't forget what I've been telling you about getting somethink settled. You been looking proper poorly lately, and no wonder with that poor soul not accountable. Your Dad would be turning over in 's grave if 'e knew you was in danger. Worshipped you, 'e did.'

'And you, too, Mum,' Carrie reminded her.

''ose looking after Jimmy today?'

'His grandpa. I said I would be back for tea. I left them cleaning out the rabbit.'

Teacher was helping the youngest of her Infants' Class into their coats and tying on bonnets. It had been a bright frosty day, and they had played outside for a brief quarter of an hour, morning and afternoon. Teacher called it 'letting off steam'. The worst weather of the Winter had

552

to be endured after Christmas in the Weald. Then all the children brought their dinner of bread and margarine or bread and lard with a sprinkling of sugar. They were given hot cocoa at midday. Wet boots would be steaming round the coke stoves. Mufflers and woolly gloves hung on the guards to dry. Some of the boots were stuffed with old newspapers, the soles were so thin, and fathers who had cobbled the boots before the war were fighting and dying for King and Country, the children were constantly reminded.

The Infants could hear the older children singing 'Land of Hope and Glory'. Soon they would be dismissed, and big sisters would collect the little ones like cackling hens collecting their chicks.

Teacher always stayed to see her Infants safely on their way, but once outside the school gate, she was no longer responsible for them. When the last of the shouting and squealing had died away, she went back to tidy the classroom, then she bustled along to the School House to put on the kettle. Martha Robinson was a happy woman these days. With a husband past the age for conscription, a son too young to get involved, and a father settled comfortably with a good housekeeper, she was counting her blessings.

The man who had made all her dreams come true would be tidying his desk while the kettle boiled. They enjoyed this quiet cup of tea together in the warm kitchen. Dear Andrew! His gentleness and understanding had gradually conquered her physical revulsion. To stiffen her body was involuntary. Relaxation was a state she had never known with her first husband, but Andrew was patient. He was not a passionate or a demanding man, and sexual intercourse had none of the urgency she had experienced with Dick.

It surprised and delighted her to discover he invariably

553

fell asleep with his head on her breast, and the warmth of her plump little body did not tease his loins with desire. When they made love, it was a shared experience with mutual enjoyment and a total lack of embarrassment. Everything was shared between these two who had waited so long to be united in marriage. Their marriage had not changed the happy relationship between Andrew and Philip. The boy's respect for the schoolmaster was a link between them. The family was complete – stepfather, mother and child – and the harmony in the School House was reflected in the classrooms. It was Martha who decided the small issues, and Andrew the important ones, such as whether or not they could afford to buy the two second-hand bicycles advertised in the local press. They could and they did.

But it was Martha who decided, on the first Sunday after their marriage, they would in future accompany Andrew to church. Father must make his way to Chapel as always. In a sense, this *was* an important issue, for Philip was persuaded to join the choir and the Scouts. Martha became a useful member of the Mothers' Union, and Andrew, who had always avoided publicity, was actually seen to be taking the collection in company with Sir Neville from Marston Park! But Martha missed the heartiness of the Chapel services, and the friendly atmosphere. Parson shook hands only with his upper-class parishioners, while the Minister had shaken everyone by the hand. That was only one of the many differences to be observed and accepted.

It was no surprise when Carrie walked into church one Sunday morning, leading Jimmy by the hand and joined them in the pew, for she had consulted Doctor on the matter, and also on the more urgent question of getting in touch with his daughter-in-law.

'I have already done so, Carrie. I sent a cablegram to

554

Peshawar, so we should soon hear she is on the way. It may take a little time to book a passage, and the hazards of such a long voyage cannot be overlooked, but she will come. In the meantime, try not to worry too much about the future. We all have to compromise,' he told her kindly.

When the second telegram was delivered to Russets, in the Summer of 1917, it was Emma who snatched it from the boy at the kitchen door, and ran, gasping and sobbing, to the hay-field. Lucy stood waiting beside the loaded wagon, the dusty sweetness of the hay in her nostrils, seeds in her hair. She could see the girl running and stumbling, the envelope flapping in her hand. In the faded print frock she looked like a child – she *was* a child. In so many ways Emma was still the same skinny little orphan the carter had dumped in the yard at the age of 13. It was Harry who had seen her first, and Harry who had mocked as she struggled to drag her box towards the house. He had pushed her away and carried it easily, showing off his strength.

Lucy could see it all so clearly, as though it had happened only yesterday – the spark that was kindled between her eldest son and the servant girl. It was a hostile attraction, primitive and demanding. Like two healthy young animals, they had scented each other, and were blatantly aware of the scent of that first moment.

Tom was on top of the wagon. Her second son had been spared. In his quiet way, he had ignored the taunting tongues that his elder brother had found so disquieting on market days. Tom had his father's dedication to the land, and his loyalties were not divided. He had neither volunteered nor been conscripted, and he worked hard all the hours of daylight, and loved his mother devotedly. She had been reminded of Bert when she looked up and saw him standing there on top of the wagon, and now her

555

heart ached with memories of happier days, when the boys were young. First her husband, and then Harry had stood atop the wagon at hay-making and harvest, in just such an attitude. Bert had fallen to his death on their own land. Now Harry had fallen in a foreign land, and Albert, her youngest, was a prisoner of war.

She had no need to read the contents of the envelope Emma pushed into her outstretched hand, but it was a formality every mother in the village had to endure if her sons had reached the age of 17. 'We regret to inform you . . .'

The sun scorched her eyelids and dried the tears on her lashes. Tom leapt from the wagon and folded her in his arms.

The land girls stared, and Mavis whispered, 'Is it Harry, Mrs Blunt?'

'Course it's Harry, you soppy bitch!' Emma screeched hysterically, tearing her hair. Nobody took any notice. Nobody cared, only Harry – and Harry was dead. She turned and ran away, without a backward glance, sobbing noisily. Lucy lifted her tear-stained face to call after her, but Tom advised quietly, 'Let her alone, Mum. She'll come back when she's ready.'

But she didn't come back. Some hours later, with the shadows falling across the stubbled field, they called and searched every nook and cranny, but she was not there. Lucy's choked cry, calling 'Emma! Emma!' from the edge of the wood, echoed across the Valley.

Ruby had hurried off to Russets to comfort her twin sister, leaving a cold supper in the parlour for the wheelwright. One of the land girls had delivered the sad news earlier in the day, and her heart ached as she went about her chores. Carrie had called in with the little boy in the afternoon, and they had sent him outdoors to pedal his tricycle in the cluttered yard. It wasn't much

556

fun, but it was better than listening to their crying in the kitchen.

Jimmy was getting a little tired of all the crying. He could not remember a time when they were greeted by smiling faces on their afternoon walks. Only the children were happy as they tumbled out of the school gate.

'Can I come to school when I'm 5?' he asked Teacher, because he knew already he was not going to like boarding school if he couldn't take Carrie.

'Why not leave him with me for an hour, Carrie, while you have a cup of tea with your mother?' she suggested. She hadn't answered his question, but it was a splendid idea, and Carrie agreed. Now that Grandma was away on a nice long holiday, they were enjoying a kind of freedom and independence they had never known before. No questions were asked about their afternoon walks, so they hadn't to feel guilty telling these little white lies. Jimmy had outgrown most of his toys, even the tricycle, and the strange little world of the village school was a fascinating place. Teacher sat him down on a tiny chair with a slate and a slate pencil, with the Infants staring with solemn faces at the well-dressed little boy from the upper class. He was segregated from the other children, not because they were working class, but because of something called 'germs' that was catching, and Carrie was fussy about his health.

The first time he was invited to stay for an hour, he was regarded with suspicion by the rows of Infants sitting at their desks. It was not fair! He would be Teacher's pet. But she gave him no more than a smile and a nod from time to time, and he sat there quietly, absorbing the happy atmosphere in his first classroom, waiting to be collected, a little anxiously, for it was the first time he had been parted from Carrie – her free half-day didn't count, because it had been explained – and she was still the most

557

important person in his small world. Carrie told him everything – well, almost. She hadn't told him why they were crying again, but she would do so later, over nursery tea. Somebody had died. When the butcher's married son had been killed fighting for King and Country, he had left a widow and four young children. All the customers had cried in sympathy when they stood in his shop and were told about the son who was his mother's pride and joy, being her first-born. The worst part, for those who are left, is not having a funeral, and no grave where the widow and orphans could lay their flowers. 'It helps to soften the blow,' Carrie explained carefully. Jimmy was puzzled by this explanation, but he was busy buttering a nice new crust at the time, so let it pass.

It seemed that Elsie at the grocery, who was Carrie's sister-in-law, was one of the many widows in the village, and her children were orphans.

'Should I be a n'orphan if my Daddy was killed fighting for King and Country?' he had asked Carrie, one Saturday afternoon, when Elsie had pushed the small packet of butter across the counter hidden in a pound of apples.

'Yes, you would,' she answered, clutching his hand more lightly.

'Then I should be like Philip, shouldn't I?' He wanted to be like Philip, but he didn't want Daddy to be killed.

'Philip isn't an orphan now. He has a stepfather. His mother married the schoolmaster. Have you forgotten?' she reminded him.

Yes, he had forgotten, because the only time he saw them together was in church on Sunday morning, and the schoolmaster was not a person to take kindly to a small boy who dropped his penny on the floor. 'Take him out before the sermon,' Teacher had whispered. What was a sermon? He didn't want to miss it if it was something important. But Carrie took his hand and they crept out of a side door, followed by the Sunday School children. Grandpa was waiting in his car outside the church gates to take them for a drive. He had to visit a patient at Marston Park, and they would wait outside, but it was one of those exciting events that seemed to be happening all the time now Grandma was taking a nice long holiday.

Grandpa had exchanged the horse and trap for a car, and was allowed to have petrol even in wartime because he was a doctor. The Sunday School children stared enviously as Jimmy climbed into the front seat.

When they had turned into the Park gates and could see the Big House in the distance, Grandpa told him quietly, 'Mummy is coming home soon.'

'And Daddy?' he asked eagerly.

'No, only Mummy.'

'Has Daddy been killed fighting for King and Country?'

'Good heavens, no! Whatever gave you that idea, child?'

'Lots of soldier daddies have been killed fighting for King and Country.'

'That's true,' Grandpa agreed.

'When will Daddy come home?'

'He has another two years to serve in India.'

'Where's India?'

'You don't remember it?'

Jimmy shook his head.

'He was very ill, Doctor. I think he *has* forgotten everything that happened before the typhoid fever.'

'That is not uncommon, Carrie.' He had braked the car, and turned to smile at her. 'But for you, Carrie, he would not be here?'

'Where should I be, Grandpa?' Jimmy interrupted.

'In heaven, with all those daddies!' He patted the

child's head, bade him be good, gave him a boiled sweet to suck – for he always carried a few in his pocket – and walked away with his black bag.

Their worlds were so wide apart, they seldom met, but when they did, it was as though they had never been parted, these twin sisters, Ruby and Lucy.

The big farm kitchen was a homely place, and the smell of freshly baked bread still lingered. Emma had polished the stove and scrubbed the floor early that morning. Now she was gone, and Harry was gone.

Lucy had been sitting in the old rocking chair since they stopped searching for Emma. Rocking back and forth, with closed eyes, she wished she had a small child to cuddle on her lap, for there is no greater comfort to a stricken mother who has lost a child who once suckled her breast. Now that breast ached with the memory. How proud they had been of their first-born son. She was nothing but a girl when Harry was born. Now, today, it seemed but yesterday to her aching heart. The years had slipped away so quickly.

She had left Tom and the land girls to finish loading the wagon, cart the hay, milk the cows. There was so much to be done on a farm, seven days a week, but it was her life, and she wouldn't exchange it for any other. She had never had a holiday. Like her twin sister, Ruby, she would be utterly bored and miserable with time on her hands. Only the upper class had holidays. 'What you never have, you never miss,' she conceded sensibly.

Still a pretty woman, Lucy Blunt had changed very little from the young widow Sir Neville Franklin had seduced on that Michaelmas Day. Her body still smelled of sweat, and hay-seeds sprinkled her hair. A vigorous brushing later in the day would send them flying to the bedroom floor, to be swept up by Emma. But not any

560

more. How would they manage without her? Time and again the girl had disappeared. The call of her gypsy forbears had been too strong to resist. She came back when she was hungry, and her mistress did not scold. Nobody could have been kinder than Lucy. Tom and Albert had treated her like a sister. She was one of the family, sharing their table, not segregated, as were most farm servants. But it was Harry she wanted, and Harry had treated her roughly right from the start, and he would never marry her, even if he had survived this terrible War. His mother was to blame for Harry's reluctance to marry, and Tom had also decided to stay single. Albert was in love with Carrie, but it was unlucky for cousins to marry.

Her own 'fall from grace' had shocked her three sons so deeply, the old close relationship had never been restored. She had lost their respect, and respect was a precious quality between parents and children. A rough tongue was licking her clasped hands, and she looked down to see Harry's dog, Gyp, gazing up at her with limpid eyes. Lucy patted his shaggy head, but was too choked to speak. She felt drained and limp with exhaustion, but it was not sleep she wanted, and she would sit all night in the old rocking chair, with Gyp for company.

Tom had made tea. He had stepped into Harry's shoes when his elder brother went away with quiet, unassuming diffidence, always asking her advice and her opinion.

When a shadow darkened the doorway, she looked up to see a replica of herself, a plump little figure in a print dress, with flushed cheeks and wet eyes.

'Oh, Luce, me duckie, I come as soon as I could get away.' She panted breathlessly, and folded her twin in her arms. 'We always 'as to copy one another, don't we, luv, since we was youngsters?' she sobbed. 'I lost my Jack, now you've lost your 'arry. My Freddie was wounded bad, and your Albert is wounded, only you won't know 'ow bad it is till you get 'im back 'ome. It's a cruel, wicked War, ain't it Luce?'

Lucy nodded mutely. She had shed all her own tears, and now she could comfort Ruby.

'Poor Rube, you're so hot, and you must be tired after that long walk from the village. Sit you down and I'll make a fresh pot of tea.' She pushed Gyp's head off her lap and stood up, squaring her shoulders.

'That's your chair, Luce,' Ruby protested, but she was glad to sit. Taking a clean handkerchief from the pocket of the faded print dress, she dabbed her eyes and blew her nose. 'This 'ere 'an'chief 'as been around a few years, Luce,' she reflected. 'Our Jack gave it me one Christmas when 'e were just a little nipper, and I 'ad one every Christmas till 'e started work at the grocery, then I 'ad a bottle of lavender water every year since. Our Jack was a proper old stick-in-the-mud, bless 'im. No imagination. Always knew what to expect from Jack. Look at the way 'e courted Elsie. That poor girl was proper flummoxed 'e were so long popping the question. Made up 'is mind 'e wasn't getting married till 'e were earning enough to keep a wife and start a family. A nice little 'ome they 'ad, Luce, and Jack were so proud of 'is children. It do seem strange to me, 'ow a chap as steady and reliable as our Jack could chuck it all away when 'e see that picture of Kitchener stuck up on the notice board outside the village 'all. YOUR COUNTRY NEEDS YOU – and that pointing finger. That means me, Mum, and I'll 'ave to go, said Jack. Don't be a fool, lad. You wait till they send for you. It's not fair to Elsie. I told 'im straight, but 'e could be stubborn. All our children 'ad this stubborn streak, and when they set their mind to somethink, they won't budge. Mind jew, Luce, our Jack wasn't the only one what took that pointing finger so serious. There was Barney Lindridge and Dickie

562

Long, all three married men with families, but it didn't stop 'em from enlisting. They was at school together. Now all their wives is widows and their children orphans. It don't make sense, do it, luv?'

'Not to us women, Rube.' Lucy stood waiting for the kettle to boil. The big brown teapot was warming on the hob, and she reached for the tea-caddy on the mantelpiece. 'This caddy was a present from Harry, from the Michaelmas Fair. Let me see, that would be 1901 – the year the old Queen died. The boys always brought me a gift, so did Emma.'

''ow's she taken it, Luce? She were fond of Harry.'

'Badly. She's gone.'

'Gone? – you mean, for good?'

'Tom says she'll come back when she's hungry, but she won't, not this time. I know how she felt about Harry. Heaven knows where she has gone, but we shan't see her back at Russets.' Lucy sighed and brewed the tea. 'We shall have to manage without her until I can get another young girl from the Orphanage. But I was fond of Emma, for all her wildness, and it takes time and patience to train a girl to our ways. They are sent out into the world at 13. It's too young. Emma was quick and adaptable, but I couldn't rely on her. Likely as not she would be away to the woods when I left her in the dairy. But look at this range, Rube. You can see your face in it. And the floor scrubbed every day. Those orphans certainly know how to work. I'm wondering how we shall manage after the War when the land girls leave us. Even when Albert gets back from that prisoner-of-war camp, we don't know what condition he's in, do we? His health could be ruined, or he could be crippled like your Freddie. A few battle scars. That's all he has told us, and it could mean anything. We have to wait and see.'

Ruby sipped the hot tea thoughtfully, and made no answer.

563

'What's on your mind, Rube?' her twin asked quietly, as she perched on a kitchen chair.

'It's our Carrie. I been worried to death about it. But now I see it could all work out for the best.'

'What could work out?'

'Carrie 'as to leave that little boy. Doctor 'as sent for 'is mother, on account that 'e can't be responsible for the child now 'is wife is incapable, poor soul. Mind jew, Doctor's daughter-in-law won't be back for some time. It could be three or four months. Carrie says the ship will 'ave to come the long way round because of submarines. She showed me on the map.'

'Round the Cape?'

Ruby nodded. 'I was never any good at jography. It's like this, Luce. Carrie ain't got no 'ome now, and I can't 'ave 'er at the wheelwright's place. I'm only an 'ousekeeper, and Mr Carter ain't an easy man to get along with. And Carrie 'as ter work, don't she? Now, if she come to work for you, Luce, she could live in, and there won't be no problem. She'd be a real 'elp in the dairy, and I've taught 'er to cook. What jew say, Luce?'

Lucy smiled. 'I should love to have her. You know I have always envied you. We should have been so happy, Bert and I, if we had been blessed with a daughter to complete the family, but it was not to be. But now I shall look forward to having Carrie as a daughter-in-law, one of these days. By the time Albert gets back, she should be ready to settle down as a farmer's wife. When one door closes, another opens, so they say. I feel quite hopeful again. You won't mind if Carrie marries her cousin? Isn't it supposed to be unlucky?'

'That's an old wives' tale, I reckon. What do it matter if they love one another?'

'And they do.'

The twin sisters were satisfied.

564

Six months have passed, and the time had come for Carrie to leave the little boy she loved as her own child. Very gradually she had been separating their close relationship into two distinct identities, but it was a painful process for both.

First she had taken just one free day in the week, then a weekend, and left him to the care of Parsons. While he adapted himself to the new order, she was trying to adjust to her own new chapter at Russets. Carrie had assumed she was indispensable to Jimmy, and Jimmy was happy in his own small world, for Grandma was still on holiday, and the doctor's household revolved around a lively small boy they all adored.

'Mummy is coming home,' had been repeated so many times, but Jimmy was still not prepared to meet the stranger who stepped off the train, early in the New Year. Meeting the train was fun, because his special friend, Philip, would arrive on the same train as his mother, and it was Philip he greeted first – a tall, neat figure in his school uniform, who stepped off the train with all the assurance of a seasoned traveller, as indeed he was. Jimmy dropped Carrie's hand and ran to meet him, shouting excitedly.

'Hullo,' Philip mumbled irritably, embarrassed to be singled out for so much attention. The little group on the platform looked amused at the small boy dragging his hero to meet them. Philip touched his cap politely and bade them 'Good afternoon'. His mother nodded approvingly. Carrie said 'Hello'. Doctor shook hands and introduced the strange lady as James's mother. Then why wasn't the silly little kid greeting her in the proper way?

'How do you do, Philip? You don't remember me, do you?'

There was something vaguely familiar in that cultured voice. He frowned and shook his head, waiting for the usual inane remark about his rapid growth. But she didn't say it. She smiled kindly, shook his hand, and hoped he was well.

'Say how do you do to your Mother, James,' Doctor reminded his grandson a little testily. Jimmy complied obediently.

'Have you got a kiss for Mummy?' Felicity Saunders asked with pathetic self-control. She had envisaged a welcome with a small boy racing down the platform, flinging himself into her arms. But the small boy had rushed past, and she dropped her outstretched arms and stared after him as he hurled himself on the boy Philip. Memories of the barracks at Tidworth came flooding back, and her first encounter with the boy. She had been cycling too fast, as usual, and knocked him down. Then she had taken him home to apologise to his mother, and they had formed a friendship that defied all the Army protocol between the ranks and their officers. She was here today to welcome her back. They had kissed affectionately, and Carrie had also been kissed. But her small son brushed her cheek absentmindedly. She must be patient. It was a long time they had been parted.

'Excuse me.' Philip was moving away, dropping the small clinging hand.

'Where are you going?' Jimmy demanded.

'Home,' Philip mumbled.

'Philip has his bicycle, dear,' his mother explained.

They watched him walk away, staggering under the weight of a heavy satchel. Then Jimmy slipped his hand in Carrie's, watching the aged porter lifting the pile of luggage on to his truck.

'Can I ride in the front of your car, Grandpa?' he asked.

'*May* I?' Carrie prompted automatically.

He grinned, and echoed, '*May* I?' Carrie had been very fussy lately. 'When Mummy comes home, she will expect to hear you speaking correctly, like a little gentleman,' she had insisted.

'I don't want to be a gentleman. I want to be a *man* – and when I'm a man, I shall marry you!' he added, importantly. Now why had Carrie cried when he had expected her to be pleased with such a proposal? He asked Cook and Cook shook her head. 'Carrie can't wait for you to grow up, Master James.'

'Why can't she?'

'Because when you are a man, Carrie will be quite old – and Carrie is *working class*,' she concluded, as though it settled everything.

As they turned to follow the porter to the doctor's car, their attention was caught by a solitary figure, stepping carefully on to the platform at the far end of the train. He had no luggage, and his dirty, ragged clothes hung loosely on his weak, emaciated body. His head was cropped, his face scarred, and his sunken eyes stared blankly at the departing train.

'Bertie,' whispered Carrie, in a choked voice. She dropped Jimmy's hand and walked slowly down the platform. The little group watched silently, saw the girl hesitate, but only for a second, then the man was enfolded in her arms, and she was sobbing with relief, and joy, and love.

The small boy was puzzled, but surprisingly obedient. The stranger, who was his mother, and the woman he called Teacher took his hands and led him away.

'Is that Carrie's Daddy?' he asked, as he climbed into the car.

'No, it's a poor wounded soldier, home from the War, and Carrie will look after him,' Grandpa explained.

'Then he will soon be better,' said Jimmy, decidedly.

THE END